Buzz for *Keeper of Sorrows*

'A deeply original book. Centering women in this surreal high fantasy, Rachel Fikes creates an incredibly unique magic system that sets the stage for a mystery filled with political manoeuvring, transformations and so much more.'
Sunyi Dean, author of *The Book Eaters*

'A gorgeously dark and seductive fantasy debut, buzzing with mystery and sweetened by mellifluous prose. Fikes deftly balances familial love against grief while the deaths, disappearances, and dual timelines escalate toward a riveting conclusion.'
Essa Hansen, author of *The Graven Trilogy*

'Rachel Fikes has crafted a beautifully original fantasy full of sumptuous language and breath-hitching mystery. In *Keeper of Sorrows*, there are horrors around every corner, yet this gothic high fantasy is told through the lens of two protagonists who manage to find beauty in bees, humanity's last hope in an ecologically devastated world robbed of wind. Fikes tells a story that feels like a descent into madness, where nothing is ever as it appears, perfect for readers who want to feel their skin crawl while being immersed in a narrative full of heart. It's impossible to ignore the passion seeping through its pages.'
Gabriela Romero Lacruz, author of *The Sun and the Void*

RACHEL FIKES

KEEPER OF SORROWS

This is a **FLAME TREE PRESS** book

Text copyright © 2024 Rachel Fikes

FLAME TREE PRESS
6 Melbray Mews, London, SW6 3NS, UK
flametreepress.com

US sales, distribution and warehouse:
Simon & Schuster
simonandschuster.biz

UK distribution and warehouse:
Hachette UK Distribution
hukdcustomerservice@hachette.co.uk

Publisher's Note: This is a work of fiction. Names, characters, places, and
incidents are a product of the author's imagination. Locales and public names
are sometimes used for atmospheric purposes. Any resemblance to actual
people, living or dead, or to businesses, companies, events, institutions, or
locales is completely coincidental.

Thanks to the Flame Tree Press team.

The cover is created by Flame Tree Studio with elements
courtesy of Shutterstock.com and Inara Prusakova, Vitalii Hulai,
Vladimir Mulder, wichai bopatay.
The font families used are Avenir and Bembo.
The map and chapter ornaments are created by Gabriela Romero Lacruz.

Flame Tree Press is an imprint of Flame Tree Publishing Ltd
flametreepublishing.com

A copy of the CIP data for this book is available from the British Library
and the Library of Congress.

PB ISBN: 978-1-78758-914-8
HB ISBN: 978-1-78758-915-5
ebook ISBN: 978-1-78758-916-2

Printed and bound in Great Britain by Clays Ltd, Elcograf S.p.A.

RACHEL FIKES

KEEPER OF SORROWS

FLAME TREE PRESS
London & New York

For Naomi, a true force of nature whose existence alone has kept my world from razing.

SISTERLY BONDS

Because of bees' unusual genetics in which males arise from unfertilized eggs containing one set of chromosomes and females from fertilized eggs with twice the chromosomes, sisters are more closely related to each other (seventy-five percent shared genetic code) than mother to daughter (fifty percent), and thus predisposed to higher degrees of altruism. In layman's terms? Sisters are innately programmed to selflessly serve one another.

The Haplodiploidy Hypothesis

CHAPTER ONE

Stone

She blew through the portcullis like a tempest. A thundercloud of charged chiffon. Her presence alone jostled the red ivy, snaking the citadel, thrumming the spire beneath my claws. My shoulders crackled, my wings flared, and I awoke. But after how long? A day, a year, or twenty? Memories were a heap of stained glass, shattered and shapeless without time's brace. Waves of inky hair spilled over her shoulders, and her jaw squared with purpose, with conviction. No bystander dared crossing her path. She was striking, undeniably, but it was her surety of movement – heels clacking, long, crimson train frothing over cobbles like rapids of blood – that rendered me weak. The doors slammed open with a resounding thud, bathing her in amber. She cocked her head, eyes blazing right through me, then strode into the foyer, leaving me in darkness. Once again, all alone. I shuddered and twisted, trying to silence the murmurs prickling my skin. I would later learn this was sentience, and more, that she was the Keeper, and I, the gargoyle. Yet, she was the one made of stone.

CHAPTER TWO

The Razing

Sweat stung Naokah's eyes. She dashed it away, gloves scraping her cheeks. Every muscle ached, the fumes clouding the ship deck near suffocating, but she kept heaving the line. The Midworlders packed along the lug ropes couldn't afford a second of weakness inside the Razing. The vast chasm spanning the equator spitting up walls of steam and smoke took mercy on no one.

Ash geysered the vessel, the stench of burned corpses bloating the air. Though Naokah's fellow Mids chanted a steady cadence, inching *The Andreia* closer to the beacons – mere glints beyond the Razing – they failed to drown out the shrieking under the hull.

She cringed. *Soon.* They'd escape this cursed region soon.

Naokah peered up at the blackened sails. Legions of gulls flew in tight formations behind the canvas, generating wing-power to help propel the dame o' war forward. For three days and three nights the flocks had strained alongside the humans, fighting the smoldering columns and the roiling sea. Desperately trying to ignore the haunting keening of whatever lurked beneath. But with exhaustion marrow-deep, and no reprieve from the boiling heat, how much longer would they last?

A thunk, by Naokah's boot. She didn't have to look. Her patri, pulling in front of her, flinched. Another bird down. Out of the many tow ropes, he picked the one under the mainmast as it had the best view of the blue-footed gulls. Naokah chose the spot behind him. A decision she regretted since entering the Razing. Before the price of wing-power spiked, they'd relied on flocks to pollinate their crops. Since the wind vanished from the world, birds weren't just a means of survival. They were kin. Now, as gull after gull plummeted to its death, the old farmer shrank further, and with him, Naokah. A daughter could only watch her patri suffer for so long before breaking.

A whistle pierced the haze, and a hulking man materialized on the forecastle. The comandante. "Half a league out," he shouted. "But stay sharp. Last stretch is a real beast—"

The ship pitched. Tow lines staggered. *The Andreia* juddered like she'd run aground. Metal grated. Something clawed the stern, the portside. A crith? Nightmares from her childhood of soul-slurping demons flooded her thoughts. Naokah steadied Patri, chills needling her spine.

"Hold strong!" the comandante bellowed at the Mids, then waved wildly at the outer crew.

A series of hisses as fuses lit. Shadows tentacled the topsail. The gulls flew faster and faster, a fray of beating wings, of squawking. Thunder ignited, a screech. More cannons fired, rattling Naokah's teeth. A loud plop, a moan. The ship bobbed as the monster released the mast. Clouds rifted; a globe of light emerged. The beacon. They were almost there—

"Heave!" The comandante's eyes bulged.

Naokah yanked, blisters popping on her palms.

"Heave!"

Guttural cries arose from the starboard side. More cannons. She shut her eyes. This couldn't be it. She had to reach the Isle of Bees, had to see her big sister. Had to apologize, to beg forgiveness—

An agonizing wail, a retreat. The air fizzled, lightened. Smoke cleared. Sobs of relief rained the deck, and the tow ropes slackened. She opened her eyes, sank to her knees. A calm sheet of cobalt stretched into the horizon as they finally emerged from the Razing. Patri twisted around, eyes wet. Naokah leapt up and crushed him in a hug, inhaling greedily. The pipe smoke from his tunic never smelled so sweet.

They'd made it.

★   ★   ★

Abelha, the Isle of Bees, was a tongue of smudged black circled by cliffs that made a jagged maw against the bruised sky. After clearing the Razing and a few days of recovery, the gulls were back at it, thrusting the dame o' war forward. At this rate, they'd port by sunset.

Progress, yet bittersweet.

No longer in the throes of the chasm, Naokah had nothing but dread, thicker than gristle, to chew on. She envied the other passengers their simple fears, sidestepping the severed limb of the beast that tried to capsize them. A tentacle big as a tree trunk, pocked in squid eyes and lamprey teeth, oozed black over the deck. When the Scorned Son stole the wind from the Divine Daughter, spawning the Razing, anything in its path was decimated. Animals melted into blobs of bones, scales, and ash that, over time, cooked back together and morphed into new, composite beasts with misaligned joints, jaws and teeth on bellies, fins all over. Scary, yes. But Naokah's destination, brimming with bees and a jaded sister whose sting was just as lethal, was scarier.

"Lenita will be eager to see you," Patri said, a little too reassuringly. "Bet she doesn't even wait for us to dock before she dives into the sea."

"Eager to see *you*. She hasn't written me since she left."

"You don't think the Keepership had anything to do with that?" His ochre eyes glinted.

It had everything to do with it, but not in the way he meant. Even if Lenita were busy, she'd have carved out time to write. But that was before their fight. When the Council of Croi Croga chose Lenita over Naokah to apply for the coveted position of Keeper, they'd also driven a wedge between the two. The sisters had beaten out over a hundred applicants for the top two positions, and that, in itself, was a triumph. But she would've rather been last. Being a runner-up was merely a bitter reminder that, when pitted against her big sister, she was always second best.

"I...." She choked on her shame. "I was cruel, Patri. Said things I never should've said."

"Lenita doesn't hold grudges." He squeezed her shoulder. "It's you who must forgive yourself."

Her throat knotted and, though she wanted to believe him, to lean in and accept his comfort, she wasn't worthy. He only saw the good in her, but if he'd overheard her that day? Even he would undoubtedly agree – some words were too vile, too despicable, to deserve absolution, and not all broken bonds were meant to heal.

Two men in suits that sheened like crow feathers approached the mainmast. Stray gusts from the gulls ruffled their long hair. Father and son, likely, with the same flinty eyes, aquiline nose, and the smooth complexion of those not forced to drudge beneath the harsh, Midworld sun. Raptor flock tycoons. Smug as they were beautiful. And rich. Their nation monopolized wing-power and had repossessed Patri's starling flocks when he failed to pay. Since Raptoria was the northernmost country in Vindstöld, they'd boarded the dame o' war long before Naokah and Patri. But she'd yet to see them. Like the other affluent Poler nations, they didn't have to work for passage. While the crew and Mids battled the Razing's fumes and choked on ash, the Raptors had sheltered inside their private cabin, safe and spineless.

Patri followed her glare and stiffened. "Those money-grubbing—"

Naokah shushed him and grabbed his shaking hand, tugging him towards the railing. "We knew they'd be here," she whispered. "The Keeper requested that all first runners-up attend Lenita's ceremony."

"Doesn't mean I have to like it," he growled and ran a hand over his slick scalp. "We're here at the edge of the razing world, thanks to them."

He wasn't wrong. Yet, "If they hadn't raised their rates, we wouldn't have been forced to move to bee pollinating, and Lenita wouldn't have made history." No Midworlder had ever won the Keepership, but no Mid was as tenacious as Naokah's big sister. With Lenita getting sworn in as the new Keeper tonight, Croi Croga would never be without pollinators again. The farms, and thus the people, would endure. Whoever ruled the bees, ruled the world.

He cocked a brow. "How'd you get so wise?"

"I listen to my patri."

A ghost of a smile flickered across his weary face, and she nudged him playfully, grateful his anger had receded. As they neared the cliffs ringing the isle, a large shadow crawled through the fjord. The comandante blew a shrill whistle. *The Andreia* jolted, slowing to a moaning halt as the gulls spiraled from behind the sails and thundered to the deck, awaiting their next command.

The dame o' war stopped within a rock throw of the shadow – a monstrous, bee-armored barge needing to pass. *The Andreia* wasn't small by any means, but the vessel from Abelha was a giant of giants and, beside her, the dame o' war was a sardine. The barge shook the ship as it passed, veiling them in darkness, its sides buzzing with thousands of hives. Every hair barbed, Naokah didn't dare move until it faded into the trailing fog. The gulls squawked, returning to the sails and pushing the ship into the fjord. Shadows slipped over the deck, and the air condensed.

A feather floated down, and Patri caught it, tracing the pearlescent threads. He cleared his throat and fidgeted, ashamed of being wistful, as though nostalgia were a luxury reserved for all but him. "Still miss my flocks."

"Wish we could afford them," she said, and meant it. The fight with Lenita might've never happened.

He planted a kiss on her temple, then averted his gaze. A failed attempt at hiding his sentiment. His eyes had gone soft as clay.

A hiss drew her attention up. Atop the narrow cliffs pranced a young girl. No more than thirteen. Skin white as skimmed cream. She danced close to the edge. Precariously close. One wrong step and she'd plunge to her death. Dress puffing around her, she stopped short. Her dark eyes, too big for her face, found Naokah. She hissed again. Goosebumps pricked Naokah's neck, and she jerked around. Patri stared forward, still sulking, and the crew carried on. No one acknowledged the girl. When Naokah risked a glimpse back, she was gone.

The change in pressure stayed, however. Naokah's ears popped as Abelha leered over them. The sun's departure bled down the spiked walls forting the isle. Dusk clung to the shoreline, and fog concealed the water. She frowned. The Council of Croi Croga described the Isle of Bees as 'The Paragon of Paradise', an oasis frocked in flowers and honey and dreams. All luxuries to Mids, having spent their lives coughing up dust and ash, sweltering in barren regions pillaged by the Razing. But *this* monstrosity with jagged edges and thorny overgrowth? A far cry from that colorful depiction. Perhaps the encroaching darkness and dread of facing Lenita soured Abelha's air.

Perhaps not.

When the ship veered into port, something sticky, laden with dark, nauseating power, weaved over Naokah's skin. Tati would have called it witchcraft, but Matri, averse to tall tales, would've vehemently disagreed. Her aunt had traveled the world many times over and if anyone ever encountered the preternatural, it would've been her. Yet Naokah, prone to self-preservation and whatever might confirm her bias towards safety, sided with her mother. Still, she couldn't help but feel she'd just been flung into a great, malevolent web. Where was the plotting spider?

The comandante whistled, the gulls swooped to the railing, and *The Andreia* groaned to a stop. A few seconds passed before an orange orb glowed on the dock. A torch. Its dingy flames silhouetted the grim sentry holding it.

"Doesn't look very welcoming," Patri whispered.

Something wasn't right. Where was Lenita?

"There will be no ceremony tonight," the sentry barked.

Gasps and gripes rumbled from the ship. Naokah exchanged a bewildered look with Patri.

"Ridiculous," the comandante said. "We're right on time. Why has she moved it?"

"Forgive me. I misspoke." The sentry cleared his throat. "There will be no ceremony at all."

"What?" the comandante yelled over the rising din.

"Lenita Hansen is gone."

CHAPTER THREE

Once Upon a Time

The moaning susurrus from the forest always came first. Followed by, to the untrained ear, droplets chiming leaves. But this wasn't inclement weather. For the timpani of dark clouds, the chords of damp soil, the rich timbre charging the air before that very first drop – all key players in storm's symphony – were missing. No. These were scrim. Legions of writhing, bite-sized shadows (if bees had wraiths, these were them) mounting full-scale assaults every new moon. I tensed, bracing for the attack.

"This is why you exist," said the eldest gargoyle from the western tower, once.

Once when? Could've been days or weeks or years ago. For the life of me, I couldn't remember. Time wasn't linear here, atop the crimson spires of the citadel, nor was my cognizance. The more I unfurled into existence, the more I seemed to wither. A paradox, really. Like autumn's kiss of the maple tree, yet I'd been pruned of its haunting beauty. This grotesque I inhabited, a winged bull with tusks, wasn't just hideous, but petrifying. The first time the scrim attacked, and I attempted to defend myself, my claws wouldn't budge. I struggled and fought, begging my stone joints to move, but they refused. The gargoyle wasn't my body but a tomb and, like the course of all maple leaves, I dreaded the inevitable – when would I fall?

Though a legion of gargoyles guarded the curtain walls and her many towers, their carved animal rears saluting the fortress, I couldn't have felt more alone. Why was I the only one facing inward? Shadows peeled off midnight's heavy cloak, flitting closer, and the droning amplified. My kin remained stalwart, gaped mouths and serrated teeth poised for battle. Did their bladders not threaten to burst too? I had one, once upon a time. Echoes of pressure still clanked there, old pipes suffering from disuse.

Once upon a time. How I loathed that phrase. Vague, trite, unhelpfully hopeful, just like my mind. Whatever I'd been, I was no more. Without flesh, I was residual static. The zap from a charged rug, an incessant eye twitch, the tingling of blood flow in a sleepy limb. I prickled with yearning, with an aching loss for what I couldn't remember. If I didn't hurry and discover who I was, what my purpose entailed, I feared I'd be trapped inside this stone prison forever.

The screaming shadows pelted my shoulders, my wings, colder than sleet. Although my bullish, stone body wouldn't move, my consciousness, if I focused hard enough, could. I shut my eyes and shepherded the millions of effervescing motes that comprised my soul – my glimmer, I called it – pulling them into a tight, throbbing star and imploded. I leapt out, catching the beasts, wisps of snarling char, one by one. Me, or whatever was left of me, wasn't unlike the scrim – amorphous and empty, but for our tangible bloodthirst. If it were a full moon and a human glimpsed at the towers, they'd confuse me for lucent, drifting fog. Though, in a world robbed of wind, fog didn't drift, only clung. Nor did it kill.

Tonight, I moved like a cat snatching birds. My phantom hands clenched around their squirming bodies. At first, they fought back. Cursing me. Howling to release them. I embraced their fury. It paired with mine like the sweetest port wine, but when they cried, my heart, a clock without hands, shattered.

The eldest refused to answer any of my questions. They just repeated, over and over: "This is why you exist." Maybe they were broken too.

What kept me awake most nights wasn't the many deaths by my claws, my jaws, but the question, cold, domineering, that no matter how hard I tried, would not subside. Who was the villain? The scrim or my kin? We murdered inherently, like birds flying, bees buzzing, flowers blooming, but had anyone ever dared to ask why?

CHAPTER FOUR

A Fate Far Worse

The sentry's words robbed Naokah of air. Her knees shook as Patri lit her torch. Lenita was gone? Missing or…dead? Her vision blurred as more torches ignited, their flames prowling the haze and creaking floorboards.

"All right, folks, clear a path." The red-faced comandante pushed through the throng.

The sentry trailed, close as a shadow.

"Our new mate has an important announcement to make." The comandante waved impatiently at the guard, who trundled forward, eyes shielded by his visor.

"The Keeper would like to apologize for the current… extenuating circumstance. The Keeper-select, Miss Lenita Hansen, has been missing for nearly a month." A razing month? They never sent word. Murmurs seethed through the congregation, and Patri tensed. She placed a hand on his fist. "A thorough inquest was conducted, but we were unable to find her."

"A thorough inquest?" Naokah pressed, voice shrilling. Abelha, not a massive isle by any means, was home to a citadel, an apiary, and a farm, all operated by the Keeper's staff. There were no villages, no other inhabitants, save for the wildlife in the woods and lakes. The oppressive power from before returned, pressing against her temples and scuttling up her throat. She forced back bile. Unless they were hiding something. "This is supposed to be the safest place in the world—" barring the bees,

"—fortified and warded so that only a fool would try to trespass. And you're telling us she just vanished? What happened to her?"

The sentry heaved a sigh, as if Naokah's question about her missing sister was such an inconvenience to *him*. "We don't know. She disappeared from her quarters one evening. We searched the woods, every cave and lake, every hill and dale, and not a trace. We fear the worst, yet there are more pressing matters to attend to."

Midese expletives tore from Patri's mouth. Naokah tried to quiet him, but he grew louder, angrier. He pleaded to the Divine Daughter and cursed the Scorned Son, tripping over words, spittle flying, confusing his missing daughter with Matri, Naokah's mother, whom they'd left home for she was too fragile to travel. Mental afflictions had stolen her will to speak.

Murmurs swarmed. The air grew hot, heavy with moisture, amplifying the sea's stink and plucking at Naokah's bearing. If Lenita were here, she'd know how to calm him.

"This may help." A green skirt swished over the floorboards, and a pretty Poler woman uncorked a bottle and offered it to Patri. He stopped mid-curse, seized it, then chugged it like water.

Naokah stiffened. "What'd you give him?" Polers weren't known for hospitality. The few she'd had the misfortune of running into treated Mids like trifling nuisances, bird shit to be wiped off their fancy shoes.

The woman shifted, and big, emerald eyes met hers. "Only marc," she said, but after noting Naokah's expression, added, "wine's wilder, more reckless cousin."

"Oh. Grand. Thank you...er...?"

"Brielle of Vintera."

Was that how Polers introduced themselves? Should she? She blinked away the sting behind her eyes. "Thanks, Brielle. I'm Naokah of—"

"Croi Croga," Brielle said with a kind smile. "Yes, I know. Your sister is...has...." She paused, lips twitching.

A mere hour ago, Naokah's greatest fear, even over death-by-bee-swarm, was failing to earn Lenita's forgiveness. It never crossed her mind there might not be a sister to reject her plea for grace. Still, with her sister missing, probably hurt or trapped or in danger, all she could do was think about herself, her lack of closure. Lenita didn't deserve her fate. Naokah did.

Patri hissed in Midese, "What's more pressing than my daughter's life?"

The sentry twisted around, hat wobbling. "What did he—"

"My patri wants to know what could possibly be more important than my sister's life?" Naokah's voice shook as the man fumbled his chin strap. "The Keeper sent invitations a fortnight ago, but my sister was already missing. You lied and sent them anyway. Why?"

"The Keeper-select's disappearance is a regrettable, unprecedented event. But the sitting Keeper must find a replacement as soon as possible. And since Miss Hansen had already defeated everyone in her class—"

"You needed their runners-up for a second Praxis," said a voice like ripping velvet. A lithe man with a curtain of hair blacker than midnight stepped forward, flames alighting his high cheekbones. The younger Raptor from before.

"Precisely," said the guard, eyes still hidden beneath his tilted visor. "Runners-up are invited to stay and contend for Keeper."

Someone scoffed. A few people grunted. Everyone stirred, including the gulls. Feathers rustled and squawks echoed off the railing. They'd been tricked into sailing here, at world's end, and the current Keeper was so craven, she'd sent this poor fool in her stead to deal with the aftermath. Sweat streamed down his neck, and he wavered as if he might keel over any moment.

"Invited to stay and contend for whatever happened to the former victor?" The Raptor folded his arms over his plumed blouse and smirked. "Who could resist such an enticing offer?"

The thing was, even if Abelha wasn't the haven it had been reputed to be, even if someone could get lost or stolen or die while vying for Keeper, which of the seven agrarian nations of Vindstöld would turn down this opportunity? None. Not with the chance of controlling the world market for the next fifty-odd years. Without the wind, a mighty pollinator in itself, the Razing's fumes had wiped out all the prolific pollinators save two, the birds and the bees. Birds, already innate pollinators, had also been trained to fly in huge murmurations to mimic the wind's touch. Although they ensured the fruition of many trees, flowers, and cereal crops, their reach only went so far. Bees were more efficient and direct, their span of influence far greater. Even Raptoria, which catered their flocks to the richest, couldn't deny – only a couple nations needed wing-power, but almost everyone relied on Abelha to survive.

So, why the deception?

"What about our families?" asked Brielle, eyes caressing Patri. Naokah swelled. If she hadn't already warmed up to her, she did now. "Should we choose to stay?"

"Will be coming with me." The comandante sneered at the sentry. "Apparently, the rest of us aren't welcome here. Isle of Nathair is thirteen leagues northwest. My gulls are weary but should get us to port by morning."

"And if we choose to stay," Patri said in Poli, the international tongue, loosing every taut word like an arrow, "storm the citadel and find my daughter—"

"You'd be marching to your own funeral," said the sentry, finally lifting his chin. Face grave, carved by shadows, he could've been a gargoyle. A chill combed Naokah's clammy skin. "The Keeper's been…agitated since the Keeper-select went missing, so her bees are on edge too. Any intruders won't be intruders for long."

Patri jerked to Naokah, flames reflecting off his bald head. "You aren't staying here."

"But Patri—"

"The Scorned Son would sooner crawl from the depths of his afterscape before I let you stay here. We've lost too much already. Tati, Matri, and now your sister—"

"You heard him," she said in Midese. "They've declared Lenita good as dead. If I leave, who will look for her then? No one. I don't have a choice, Patri. I must stay."

"I can't let you. If you don't come with me, I'll—" he choked, "—I'll have two daughters to bury instead of one."

Something was undeniably off here, poisoning the sparkly illusion the Council had spoon-fed her and every other Crogan since they could crawl, but that didn't mean her sister was dead. Only in trouble. "I'm a woman grown, Patri," she said, throat thick. "I don't need your permission. Croi Croga needs Lenita, and Lenita needs me."

"If you stay, you could die." Tears spilled down Patri's leathery cheeks.

She clenched her jaw, damming her emotions in. Now wasn't the time. She had to stay strong, for him. "If I leave, I'll suffer a fate far worse than death. Only a coward would abandon her sister."

CHAPTER FIVE

Thicker Than Ashlar

Unable to derive anything aside from grunts and glares from my gargoyle kin, I opted for answers elsewhere. Though I had no recollection of time, how long I'd been trapped here, how long I'd even been aware of being trapped here, something unnerving condensed my phantom bowels into water. Something dark and cold and preternatural marched our way, stinking of unchecked power and fury, perhaps even tied to the scrim. But was it coming for me or the citadel? I suppose it didn't matter. Our imminent demise wasn't mutually exclusive. I may've had an empty hive for a mind, yet if one little egg survived, it had hatched to tell me this: ignorance was a dungeon, and only uncovering my identity would set me free.

When I concentrated hard enough, my glimmer could slice through the ashlar like softened butter, past the maze of halls buzzing with hives, and focus on Her. The Keeper, the key to my past. Not that I had any concrete proof. After all, my awareness keened and blurred around her at the same time. She was the eye of my hurricane, my refuge, and only once I reached her could I embrace any semblance of calm. Even with no audience, save me, this evening she sat at her vanity with perfect posture, her long, glossy braid skimming the floor. Latticed with sculpted flowers and bees, her mirror glowed beneath the sconces, reflecting her glare. Unlike most humans, anger twisting their features ugly, seething suited her like lightning in a storm, dazzlingly dangerous.

Her door slammed open, thumping the wall of red roses. Loose petals whispered to the floor. A thin, uniformed woman with sharp features marched in. Captain of the guards. Had I known her in a former life or was she simply there when I awoke?

"Another dead end," she said, breathless.

The Keeper picked at her nails, not bothering to look up. "Never took you to be easily defeated, Avice."

"Tried everything." The captain's gaze dropped to the glass floor. "They refuse to speak."

Torture? The room went cold. If the citadel was conducting vile business, was I not also vile for guarding them?

"Then move to the next." The Keeper rose, silk nightgown clinging to her curves. Like everything she wore and most of the citadel's décor, the ivy and metal fixtures, the ornate carvings and my tower, it radiated red. The deep red of good wine, of unbridled fury, of pooled blood. She sashayed to the window, petals swirling around her slippers. From the tilt of her hips, the flounce of her braid, she knew the captain was watching. Did she know I was too? "Should I assign the task to someone better suited?"

The captain flinched like she'd been slapped, then followed. Her carmine trousers, piped in bronze, swished with each urgent step. She squeezed the Keeper's shoulder. "I'll handle it."

I squirmed and lost focus, nearly getting sucked back into my stone jail. How dare this creature touch the Keeper? But she didn't take offense. If anything, she leaned in like a cat getting scratched above the tail. Red flared, blurring the edges of my vision. This wasn't the first time they'd touched. I sucked in measured breaths, attempting to tamp down my nonsense. They'd just mentioned they were interrogating someone. Had alluded to torture, that there'd be more, and this was what I'd chosen to prioritize? Irrational, unfounded jealousy. Could I have been more selfish? Whatever I was, I deserved my lot.

"I need a drink." The Keeper passed a goblet to the captain, who bowed, about-faced, then strode off. "Pour one for yourself, too."

Avice halted as if to argue but thought better and continued to the wrought-iron shelf where the Keeper's collection of spirits glinted like dark gems. She grabbed a sapphire bottle, light flashing off her hand. I squinted. From her ring, a six-sided emerald with gold filigree. Distinctive, winking with keen familiarity. But from where and when?

Rum sluiced the air. No, not rum. Fermented cloudcane. A fruit fluffier, sweeter than spun sugar, with the bite of spicy peppers. My mouth watered. I'd tasted this before. I'd *loved* this before. Curse my damaged mind.

The Keeper accepted her goblet, but instead of drinking, stared out her windows: an impressive row of arches spanning the wall. With the new moon just elapsed, outside was murky as my memory, yet she surveyed the isle like she could see every mossy pebble, every flower petal. What was she thinking? Perhaps I could find out who they were interrogating, or a clue to my identity? I homed in, moving past her black locks, past the bone—

Resistance rumbled, nudging me back. I tried again. A flash. White crackled, blinding, severing my hold. Clawing me from her chambers, through the walls, back to my haunt. Crickets chirred, and I shivered. Strange. My glimmer could pierce the citadel but not her skull? What was thicker than ashlar?

CHAPTER SIX

It Wasn't Bravery

Patri's eyes blazed as Naokah slung her bag over her shoulder. If she stayed another second, she'd burst into tears. She pecked him on the cheek and turned to go, but he pulled her into a back-cracking hug.

"Stay keen, and don't trust anyone," he whispered, "no matter how kind they seem."

She nodded, nose brushing his collar. Pipe smoke and sharp, cloying fumes from the marc wafted from him. Her throat ached. The depth of her hasty decision finally sinking in. Before, her plan was to beg and grovel if she must, to earn Lenita's forgiveness, attend her ceremony like a supportive sister, then sail home with a clear conscience. But now? The future of her family and nation rested on none other than a fraud's shoulders. What would her countryfolk think should they ever discover Naokah's humiliating secret?

She blinked. Croi Croga, half a year back, unfurled, the afternoon air ripe with tilled earth and spun sugar. Lenita effervesced with glee beside her. She'd just won the bid for Keepership. Over Naokah. While they walked through the rows, cloudcane stalks shielding them from the morning sun, Lenita babbled about her plans. How she'd be the first Mid to become Keeper, that Croi Croga would never suffer again. All beautiful goals, righteous goals. But Naokah's hands balled.

"Nao?" Lenita nudged her. "You hear anything I said?"

She forced a smile. "Sure. I'm...happy for you." She was, truly. But also jealous.

Lenita stopped short, kicking dust up around them, and gave her *the* look. "I'd hoped you'd be. Or at the very least, relieved."

"Relieved?"

"Yes. You and I both know you only competed because you wanted to beat me."

How did she always see right through her? Naokah cocked her chin. "And?"

"Suppose I should be honored." Lenita shrugged. "You find me such a rival, you competed for a position that would've placed you smack dab on an isle swarming with your greatest fear."

Shame burned Naokah's cheeks. She couldn't deny it. The only thing that scared her more than bees was the Razing, and everyone was terrified of the chasm that could suck you in, then spit out a deranged mutant. But being afraid of fuzzy little bugs that kept their world alive? Irrational and foolish, and Naokah hated Lenita for calling her out on it. Hated her for being so good at *everything*.

When they were young, Naokah would stay up all night studying for an exam, be it math or Midese or animal husbandry, and barely pass. Lenita, having never opened the course book, would earn top marks. Naokah would practice her cloudcane flute meticulously between chores and homework, tired fingers moving repeatedly over tricky notes, and win second chair. Only for her sister, whose flute collected dust between rehearsals, to win first. And it wasn't merely academics. Lenita was beautiful and bubbly, sashaying through life with a natural ease, attracting people like bees to a flower. Everyone wanted to be her friend, to court her, and she was never without numerous invitations to dances or festivals every weekend. Naokah tried. She really did. But without her sister's allure, her peers didn't even know her name. She spent her formative years as 'Lenita's little sister' and was very much alone. Even after, when she was grown, working the farm alongside her sister, her family preferred Lenita. Especially Tati. Naokah was fated to be Lenita's shadow, and that's how it would always be.

"Crith got your tongue?" Lenita teased.

No. Fury did. Commandeered it, really. Years of envy and frustration pelted her big sister. Each word more potent, vicious than the last. When she finished, her head was a throbbing haze. She couldn't remember exactly what she said, but a glimpse up, and tears glittered Lenita's cheeks. It must've been bad. Her sister rarely cried.

"Lenita. I'm so sorry—"

Too late. Her sister sprinted away.

Naokah sighed, returning to the present. Guilt weighed heavy in her chest. Despite her many shortcomings, she'd always prided herself in hiding her jealousy, her compulsions, the temper she'd inherited from Patri. Not that day. She had to make amends. That fight couldn't be their last exchange.

She hugged Patri a little tighter. "Don't worry. I'll find her."

"I'll be worrying aplenty." He stepped back, still holding her hands. "I've no doubt you'll find her. You're stubborn like me. But Nao, something ain't right here. Feel it deep in my gut. Be careful not to lose yourself along the way."

He'd felt it too. Ever since they'd cleared the fjord and Naokah hallucinated the girl – dreading this trip, she hadn't slept a full night in a fortnight – unease had been creeping in. Entering this foreign domain was like sinking into a murky waterhole while something hid beneath. She kissed Patri's palm, the calluses scraping her lips, and joined the line of runners-up before she lost her nerve.

Lanterns bobbed along the gangway; their flames, teardrops of red-orange, pulsed the haze. Though the crowd had thinned, the mist falling liberally now, each breath was dense, as if trying to breathe under water. A heavy thunk behind her. She started, then relaxed as a brass handle winked beneath the flames. A trunk. A large one, at that.

"Forget the bees." Brielle swiped a clump of matted curls from her brow. "It's the humidity that'll kill ya."

Naokah offered a faint smile, recalling Patri's warning. Just because the Poler was friendly didn't make her a friend.

"Suppose you're used to it?" The blonde pulled her hair into a fluffy bun, eyes hungrily taking in Naokah's threadbare attire.

A Poler envying a Mid? The night kept growing stranger and stranger. "The heat, yes, but dry heat." Naokah peeled her tunic from her chest. "Even scamall can't wick away sweat fast enough here."

"Scamall," Brielle repeated, stepping closer and gingerly touching Naokah's sleeve. "Made from your cloudcane silk, yes?"

She could only nod. The Poler's scent, citrus and peppery vanilla, made her mouth water.

"Maybe I shouldn't complain." Brielle pointed her chin at the front of the line, where the young Raptor argued with the comandante. "Hope Kjell brought more than velvets."

Of course they were friends. Their nations were allies. Was Brielle feigning camaraderie so she could make fun of Naokah and her simple Midworld ways later with her real friends? Naokah rubbed a palm over her shorn scalp. Polers held that Mids shaved their heads because they were dirty, covered in lice. Conveniently ignoring the truth: Midworld nations straddled the equator and were more devastated by the Razing than the northern and southern Poler countries. A Mid wouldn't survive a day's worth of labor with a full head of hair – heat stroke would seize them by noon.

"Something wrong?"

"Oh, no." Naokah smoothed her frown. "Just agreeing with you. Surprised he hasn't fainted yet. Such a thick suit."

"Nah." Brielle grinned. "He's cold-blooded."

Kjell's voice rose, cutting through the mist. "What? They're too small to harm any bees. Come on. The bees are bigger than them!"

"No hummers." The comandante held out his hand.

"What are they arguing about?" Naokah leaned around the railing.

Kjell huffed, tugged out an earring, and dropped it into the staunch man's palm. Humming prisms flocked around the comandante, who took out his own hoop, replaced it with the dangle, and smirked.

"Had to relinquish his fancy portable fans." Brielle giggled at Naokah's meshed brows. "Just wait. You'll soon see."

The line progressed slowly, or maybe it just felt slow because Naokah was anxious to see what the Poler surrendered. That, and she'd offered to help Brielle with her coffin-sized trunk. A mistake. Even with the Poler pushing, Naokah's shoulders ached, and sweat bloomed down her back. She was out of breath when they reached the comandante. The earring he confiscated was a gold trumpet flower. Its center glittered red, and colorful birds, no larger than pebbles, with long beaks flitted about, sipping at the ruby fluid.

"Fairy hummingbirds," she said, though the one Tati had brought back from the far east hadn't been so small. It was years ago, but Naokah could still feel its warm feathers, its teeny heart beating rapidly in her palm. Tati's big amethyst eyes like Matri's, which only Lenita inherited, had twinkled so bright. A pure, happier time before her aunt sailed away and never returned.

"Naokah? You ready?" Brielle asked.

She glimpsed at the dame o' war one last time, the distant torches fading into the fog like dying fireflies, but couldn't find Patri. She rolled her shoulders, filled her lungs with heavy air, and disembarked, hoping this decision, be it brave or dumb, wasn't her last.

CHAPTER SEVEN

Nothing

Avice proved too difficult to tail. Whoever she was interrogating/
torturing wasn't on the isle. Every morning before the sun crested
the mountain terraces, she'd conceal herself in a homely Midworld
cloak and take the south gate, where a hooded figure in a paddleboat
awaited her. I tried to reach out my glimmer, but whatever warded
the isle, protecting the bees from outside predators, also trapped me
inside. After a week of this nonsense, the invisible ward nipping me
like a pack of feral hounds, I deduced: if I wanted answers, I'd have
to go to the source myself.

A superb, if not obvious notion in theory, but in practice? It was
almost impossible to maintain a cohesive train of thought without
being seduced. The way the Keeper gazed at her bees, running her
long, tawny fingers down the hives, singing, filled me with longing.
How might it feel if she regarded me the same way?

A gentle hand traced my cheekbones, and a warm breath tingled
my lips. I trembled, skin prickling. Yes, skin. Not stone. An echo
from my past. A lover's touch. Could it be the Keeper? I struggled to
hold on. Soft kisses traveled beneath my jaw, along the racing pulse
in my neck, down to my nipp—

The glimpse wriggled, fading. I swam after it, trying to pull it back,
but it slipped from my grasp and sank. A black pearl in a current. I
ground my teeth. My mind was an ocean riddled with dark trenches
holding even darker secrets, and the tide was a tease. Only dredging up

broken shells of incomplete memories. Patience wasn't my virtue, so I gathered the wilted tendrils of my glimmer and pursued the Keeper.

I'd begun piecing together the malign aura marching our way, twisting with such ancient power that, had I an actual belly full of food, it would've emptied it. It came in waves. Growing the loudest, most excruciating, the night of the attacks, but then fading to tiptoes the next day. Since the scrim were akin to bee wraiths, it couldn't be them. Maybe their proximity to the citadel, their millions of flitting bodies, served as some sort of celestial navigation, beacons to whatever was trapped on the isle. I tried not to think about what might happen should that eldritch presence finally break free. The Keeper would have a solution, hopefully.

She walked through the hedge maze, yards of red chiffon trailing. Her eyes, typically bright with purpose, were adrift. Avice followed a hedge length behind, her pale skin reflecting the gauzy light. Her hair, slicked back in a tight bun, flashed copper between the shadows of towering foliage. Aside from her early morning excursions, she never let the Keeper out of her sight. The citadel had a full staff, but like the Keeper, I paid them little notice. They bored me. Yet the Keeper regarded the captain like the corridors brimming with bee colonies. Full of respect, devotion. Avice's blue gaze mirrored the Keeper's, but with facets of fierce, unequivocal protection. The only reason I didn't hate her. She'd have given her life to defend the Keeper.

I would have too.

Had I been the Keeper's devout servant? A friend? A lover? Why else would I forget everything but for my violent need to guard her, understand her? Even fantasize about her touch?

The Keeper reached the maze's south side. Rolling knolls of foxgloves flanked her, and fat bees buzzed around the colorful cones. When she approached, their shimmering wings changed direction, and they swarmed to her – the most striking flower of all. The captain stood at the hedge's gate, still as ashlar. I didn't blame her. Thousands of bees collected on the Keeper's long train. So thick, one couldn't tell it was even red. She spoke to the creatures like they were her best friends. She turned her palms over, and they spread to the stiff ruffles over her shoulders, down her slender arms.

At any moment, should one sting, others might've followed suit, killing her quickly. The captain thought the same, evident by her posture. All hard edges, angled with defense. Our mutual anxiety was for naught, however. As a song poured from the Keeper's rosy lips, humming joined in. A chorus to her melody. She craned her neck to the side, smiling. Her cheek sparkled from the string of rubies vining up her ear. Her induction videira, passed down from one Keeper to the next. She was in her element, surrounded by family. Her worries scattered like dandelions gone to seed.

"Your happiness warms me," I said amongst the hedge leaves, forgetting my place.

She jolted up, smile gone. Bees peeled off like a snake shedding skin. I panicked, lost my grounding, and was wrenched back to my stone form.

"Avice."

The sentry rushed forward, sharp features sharper. "Yes, Madam Keeper?"

"Did you hear that?"

Avice shook her head. "No. What?"

The Keeper spun to the citadel. Her eyes flew to the spires, to me. I gulped, throat clicking. Her eyes narrowed, fury scoring my stone curves. "Nothing."

Not only could she hear me, but she could've ripped me from my tower and chucked me into the sea. I'd naïvely left 'foe' out of my former equation. Yet if she hated me, then she also knew me. Hope sparked, burning off any dread. She could help me untangle my past. I'd just have to give her a reason to want to.

CHAPTER EIGHT

Rivalry

Naokah had never felt so small. She could've been an ant peering up at the steep slopes of the isle, the imposing walls blocking out the sky. There were no stars, no sparkles of promise – the clouds above were thick as the fog at her waist. Vines clawed at her trousers, and the mist had gone from whimpering to weeping. It seemed all of Abelha had conspired to stop Naokah in her tracks, but Abelha didn't have a sister to find.

"Even the rain is hot here." Brielle kicked the brambles, skirt flapping. "Feel like we're plodding through soup." The Poler slipped beneath a slab of fog.

Naokah was drenched and miserable, but the corner of her mouth crept up as she reached down. A muddy, nonetheless dainty hand latched on, and she hoisted the disheveled, curse-spewing Brielle up.

"You were saying?" she asked, unable to suppress a grin.

"The Divine Daughter let her wind-thieving brother off too easy, exiling him," Brielle spat, brushing muck from her lips. "The wretch should've been chained to this very isle, where he could forever slog through his own filth."

Naokah didn't disagree. Wind, if it truly was anything like what the pollinating flocks conjured, would've been close to divinity. Fatigue gnawed at her calves as they trudged up the scarp, and her tunic and trousers stuck to her like a gross second skin. She'd been a cloudcane farmer since she could hardly walk, but no amount of digging, planting, or picking could've prepared her for this trek. Croi Croga was flat. From the looks of the runners-up above and below, hunched over, crawling through the sheets of rain, she wasn't the only one taken aback.

Still, they pressed on. Despite the fact that the Keeper-select had gone missing and Abelha was clearly dangerous, there was too much at stake to turn back. Not a single nation of the seven had declined the Keeper's invitation to compete. A spark of anticipation burned deep within. A whisper of a thrill. The same fluttering ache she felt when she'd competed against her perfect sister. How might it feel to be sworn in as Keeper? To have something of her very own? To have people bow instead of pity her for being Lenita's shadow? A cramp shot through her calf, and she bent to massage it. That's what she got for trying to steal her sister's dream.

The Poler stopped beside her, panting.

"Could be worse," Naokah said. "At least we aren't carrying that coffin of a trunk you brought too."

Brielle snorted. "Thank the Divine Daughter for that."

"Probably best to thank *them* instead." Naokah gestured at the port, now a couple hundred feet below, where sentries struggled with a cart loaded with luggage. The least they could do. With the citadel's complete lack of decency, it was no wonder Lenita went missing.

With Abelha secluded and heavily guarded, one could only visit if they were expressly invited by the Keeper herself. Most citizens of Vindstöld would never know what lay beyond these spiky walls. But that didn't mean there wasn't conjecture. The Council spoke of clement weather, of tropical fruits and vegetables and exotic flowers. Of a kind, genteel staff who treated both bees and humans alike with the utmost care and respect. *Hah*. Not the case so far. What else had they been wrong about?

As the slope leveled out and they neared the outer gate, the rain tapered off, but the fog stayed. A low, collective hum rumbled Naokah's bones, and the hedges flanking the entrance rattled. Beasts with long snouts, erect ears, and tusks – the latter of which particularly caught her attention – surrounded them. Her mouth went dry, and she froze. So did Brielle.

"Guardhogs," said one of the runners-up as he approached. He ran a hand over the animal's coarse hair as if it were a pet, not a feral creature eyeing her up like dinner. "They're friendly, as long as you aren't attempting to smuggle something on or off the isle." Doubt terraced Naokah's brow, and he smiled. "I'm Clisten of Svinja, if that helps?"

"It does," she managed with a fat tongue. Rain dripped through her cropped hair, into her eyes and down her back. "So, this…beast is one of yours?"

He nodded, tucking one of his many long braids behind his ear, and waved her through the gate. Svinja was a southeastern Poler nation known for its prolific swine operation. As they were absurdly wealthy like all Polers, Naokah had assumed its citizens' manners would match their precious resource. But Clisten wasn't so swinely. He had an affable, open face with bronzed skin and strong shoulders that spoke of a life outdoors. Quite the contrast to the fine-boned Kjell, whose sharp, ivory cheeks pressed his lips into a permanent pout.

Clusters of coned flowers, dark purple in the gloaming, leaned into Naokah's path. Enchanted, she moved to stroke a dripping petal, but Brielle grabbed her hand.

"Don't touch."

"Why?"

"They are the bees' greatest allies, but are no friends of humans," she said. "Poisonous. You don't have foxgloves in Croi Croga?"

"Just cloudcane. Anything that doesn't produce fruit is weeded. Need the farmland."

"That's sad." Brielle slid her a pitying look.

Lack of flowers wasn't the saddest thing in the Midworld, but she shrugged it off.

Hills of foxgloves and other strange, barbed flowers oozing viscous fluids spilled shadows over the path, and fog, having stalked them from the port, snaked their knees. Despite the rainfall, the night was hot, thick with scents of foliage and decay, but still. Unnaturally still, save for their boots crunching over gravel and that deep, resonating hum from earlier. Every step was like wading through a sinkhole and, the closer they got to the inner gate, the more Naokah's stomach clenched. The guards, rigid in their carmine uniforms, stared her and Brielle down before allowing them through the portcullis. Yet, even after they passed beneath the vine-strangled arches, Naokah's skin crawled. Someone or something was watching her.

With a web of flying buttresses, spiny turrets, and glaring windows, the citadel sprawled over the envoys like a beast loosed from the Razing. Blanketed in silence, the group of seven shuffled to the entrance, a scaling, stained-glass beehive, fogged up from the rain. The hum deepened to a resounding growl, vibrating the stone beneath Naokah's feet. Spiking her pulse. The apiary was close. Behind the courtyard, perhaps. But from this angle, cloaked in shadows, she couldn't actually see it. No fear clawed deeper than that of the unknown.

The doors flung open, and the staff lined up on each side, stiff as statues. They wore the same, blood-red uniform as the sentries and the same wary gaze. One of them had to know what happened to Lenita. Maybe more. Maybe helped vanish her too. Naokah fought the impulse to stop right then and there and beg for answers. If only it were that easy. But no. She had to play their game first.

The door slammed shut, startling a few runners-up and painting the foyer in damask shadows. The air was heavy, laden with candle wax and flowers, a failed attempt at masking some sour, underlying stench – hopefully mildew, but this place had all the charm of a crypt, so she assumed worse.

"Follow them," said a raspy, disembodied voice.

Naokah squinted at the staff, their faces now obscured by dust motes, as a cortège of white-gloved hands pointed at a tall figure leaning against a pillar beyond the foyer.

No one moved or even breathed until a draft swept through the huddled group, raising the hair on Naokah's arms. Candles flared above, revealing a daunting, fan-vaulted space hundreds of feet high and dozens of chandeliers hanging from faded frescoes. For an isle that was supposed to be a cornucopia of wealth, where its inhabitants wanted for nothing, it reeked of gloom. What had she and Lenita gotten themselves into?

"I'm Samara, head savvy and curator, for I know most everything worth knowing here at the citadel." The androgynous staff member traced a foxglove carved into the pillar. "And, due to the extenuating circumstance—" that phrase again, as if Lenita's disappearance could be reduced to canceled dinner plans, "—you seven are no longer runners-up, but official envoys vying for the most coveted job in Vindstöld. A job that will ensure your nations want for nothing for the next fifty years, or for however long you're lucky enough to carry this burdened blessing. It is earned through diligence and perseverance, through duty and selflessness. All of which don't stop after you're sworn in but expand a thousandfold." Their gaze, hard as cobalt, rolled over each envoy and stopped on Naokah.

Her knees jittered, but she stood her ground. Feigned confidence was better than no confidence. At least, that's what Lenita would've said. The savvy finally looked away and continued to speak, but their words dulled to a murmur as buzzing increased behind them.

The iron chandeliers clinked, their flames skittering over the envoys, and Naokah's chest hollowed. No wonder she hadn't spotted the apiary outside. Corridor after corridor forked from the great room. Each long and serpentine and, like the barge they'd passed today, wriggled with millions of pulsating shadows. The bees were housed *inside*. The citadel and apiary were one and the same. The room grew hot, the frescoes a whirl of blurred colors—

Cold hands vised her waist. "Steady," pressed a husky voice. Kjell's dark eyes assessed her, amused, as she regained her balance. "Forgive her," he told the savvy. "Mids don't get out much." He placed a hand on the small of her back, seemingly to offer more help, but his placement was too low, and she twisted from his grasp.

"We were just talking of room assign—"

"No need to repeat yourself, Samara. I was listening. She's in the room beside me." Brielle winked at the savvy and tugged Naokah after the group. "We share a lavatory. Isn't that grand?"

Naokah forced a nod, too overwhelmed to speak.

The mezzanine's railing, a lacy assemblage of crimson metal and glass, glittered as they walked beneath. When they entered a corridor, Naokah quickly switched sides, opting for the wall that held only doors, no bees. Brielle lifted a brow, but she ignored her, trying to keep her eyes ahead, trained on Kjell's swishing hair. It was too dark to notice before, but now, under the torches, the tips looked like they'd been dipped into a sunset. Someone had too much time on his hands.

Naokah's shoes squeaked, dropping her attention to the floor. They walked on glass that sealed a meandering stream. Fish with metallic scales and feathery fins zipped through bioluminescent algae. The citadel was trying too hard to appear welcoming.

Naokah spent years studying late at night, compiling tomes of research to improve cloudcane yields. A vain hope to impress the Council of Croi Croga so they'd choose her over Lenita. This dark, creepy place that stank of decay was a far cry from what she'd pictured. She never thought she'd miss their shack, but she also never dreamed she'd be imprisoned in an apiary. How was she to sleep, to eat or even function with no reprieve from looming danger?

"I apologize for the abbreviated tour." Samara turned, walking backwards. "The welcome ball will be upon us soon, and I'm sure you're eager to change into some clean clothes."

A ball, tonight? Lenita's disappearance really meant so little?

"Samara," a woman called from the far side of the corridor. "She's coming."

Samara scowled. They flung open the nearest patina door and waved everyone in. "Hurry up."

After Naokah brought up the end and filed into the stuffy room with the others, Samara snicked the door shut. With no torches nor candles, the envoys crowded around her were silhouettes, the dark walls pushing in like a cave.

"Is that her?" Naokah asked.

Samara nodded absently. The sharp click of heels ricocheted outside the door, matching Naokah's pulse, hot in her neck. As the Keeper approached, the adjacent hives crescendoed, then softened as her steps faded.

"Why can't we meet her?" asked a rough voice, Kjell.

Samara opened the door, and Naokah almost ran them over. They threw her an odd look, then turned to Kjell after closing the door.

"The Keeper isn't...well these days. Your presence would only cause her undue stress—"

"*Her* undue stress?" Naokah scoffed. "My sister went missing on *her* watch and instead of doing the honorable thing and meeting the ship, she sent a guard. And now, even still—" her voice bladed, "—she's too big of a coward to face us? Keeper or not, how dare she?" A cool hand wrapped around Naokah's. Brielle tried to soothe her, but flames coursed through her veins. "Lenita deserves justice. Respect. Honor. Not to be written off as an *extenuating circumstance* while everyone drinks and dances and acts like she never razing existed." If the others stared, she couldn't tell. Didn't care. Tears stung her eyes, and her ears whirred.

Her mind shifted to Croi Croga, years prior to the dreaded fight. When sisterhood had been easier. On that final day, before the Raptors seized their flocks, she and Lenita ran together, zigzagging between rows, tilled soil hot beneath their feet. Starlings soared above, and her big sister swung her, going faster and faster while singing, 'This is how the wind dances.' So simple yet magical – Lenita's eyes gleaming in the fading light; Naokah squealing as the air kissed her cheeks; specks of pollen glittering around them.

After, they lay on the soft dirt, heads touching as the starlings' orange bellies floated above like paper lanterns. She'd asked her sister if the Scorned Son would ever return the wind, so that the world might heal. *No*, Lenita had said, a drifting shadow clinging to her face a fraction too long. *You know how it is with sibling rivalry. It never ends.*

"Please." Samara motioned to the throbbing wall, and Naokah took a wobbly step back. "You have every right to be furious. I am too. Lenita deserved...deserves better. But I advise you all to keep your emotions in check. Humblebees don't take too kindly to being disturbed."

Naokah nodded, wiping her eyes. Her temper had always been a liability but would undoubtedly get her killed here. *Stay keen*, Patri had warned. That's how she'd find Lenita. Not brute force. Brielle rubbed her back and, as her breathing slowed, so did the swell of the hives she'd riled.

"This isn't so much a citadel with an apiary," Samara continued calmly, "as it is an apiary fortified by a citadel. Abelha is home to all sorts of bees, from orchid to carrion, but our breadwinners we like to keep close." They held out their hand and a fluffy bee crawled over their thumb. "Humblebees, a cross between honey and bumble, are who you'll be rooming with. They are tenacious, resilient and, for the most part, inherited the mild temperament of their origin species. However, no fiery exchanges unless you'd like an expedited trip to your afterscape. Unlike honeybees, humblebees can sting for infinity. On that note, steer clear of the west wing too. The Keeper's wrath will make an angry swarm feel like a sneeze if you trespass into her quarters."

Sting for infinity? The night couldn't get worse.

The wall opposite, hosting patina doors with scrolling rose vines, was a collection of murals. Women with seductive eyes held lovers in passionate embraces.

"Exquisite, aren't they?" Brielle whispered, warm breath tingling Naokah's ear. She placed her hand on a mural's nipple and circled it.

How might it feel to touch Brielle like that? She blushed, tamping down her desire. She was here for Lenita, not an affair. Besides, what would the beautiful Poler want with her?

"So you've noticed another shiny facet." Samara smiled, nodding at the back of the group where Brielle and Naokah stood. "Every Keeper since Abelha's rise to power has contributed something special to the citadel during their time. The stained glass, ubiquitous you'll come to find in the daylight, was a gift from our very first, the aquatic floor from seventy-seven, and those murals you're admiring now? Painted by our reigning Keeper Gabriella França Costa. If you're so inclined—" they laced their fingers, "—now's as good a time as any to think about what you'd contribute if you're worthy enough to win."

"A harem," said one of the Polers, earning snorts from his pals and eye rolls from everyone else.

A shadow crossed the savvy's face and, when it receded, took their warmth with it. "All right, that's enough for now." They pointed at the sequence of patina doors. "See you in the great hall at the twentieth hour. No stragglers." Shoulders rigid, they strode briskly through the group.

"What about the rest of the tour?" the jester asked. His hair, a waterfall of raven black, glowed jade beneath the turrets. Dazarin, she'd heard someone call him, of Zerşil.

The savvy didn't slow.

"At least tell me where the fitness arena is?" Dazarin called after them, cracking his knuckles.

Without stopping, Samara said, "Check next to your harem."

Startled giggles echoed as the savvy dissolved into the shadows.

So much for getting a lay of the land. "Where did Samara say I was rooming?"

Brielle finally stopped caressing the mural, allowing Naokah to breathe. She nodded at the closest door. "Right beside me." She thudded it open and yanked Naokah inside.

The room was dark and musty from disuse, so Naokah's mood didn't improve. Brielle wasn't affected, though, and bounced about lighting sconce after sconce until the room was filled with hazy light. Naokah absently pushed on the mattress beneath the canopy of black sheers.

"Feathers?"

Brielle studied her, lips quirking, but didn't answer and leapt on the bed instead. "Find out for yourself." She patted the silk duvet.

It was a dark wine, almost black, blending in with the rest of the unsettling décor.

"Better get dressed," Naokah said, reluctantly dragging her eyes from the curve of Brielle's hips.

The room was larger than her home in Croi Croga, which wasn't saying much. Her father, mother, brother, and sister lived in a tiny, sun-stripped shanty, nestled in a valley between fields of cloudcane – just north of the Razing. There was no privacy, hardly any room to move, in fact, but it was home, and she already missed it. The sweet musk of soil beneath her nails, the stalks shielding her from the sun's glare, the sticky cloudcane nectar running down her chin. More than anything, she missed Lenita, swinging her between the rows.

Therein was the problem. Croi Croga wasn't home. Lenita was.

A surge of renewed purpose coursed through her as she eyed up the velvet drapes, the bronze windows, the mural of a woman, wild hair wreathed in flowers, butterflies hovering over her nipples. She stopped at her bag, a worn leather thing Tati had gifted her. It leaned against the floor-length mirror, the latter of which she wanted no part of making its acquaintance. The trip, days upon days of heaving, followed by the muddy trek to the citadel, had done a number on her even the hottest bath couldn't fix.

The bed squeaked as Brielle rolled off, shooting her a crestfallen look.

"What?" Naokah tugged open her bag to the scant pile of eclectic attire Tati had acquired on her many trips around the world. Not fancy in the least, but colorful, quirky as her aunt.

Brielle tapped a recess in the wall, and it hummed, sliding open. Naokah rose from her bag and followed her into their shared lavatory. The tub, shaped like a cell from a beehive, matched the sink. Both were coated in glossy black, but as moonlight seeped from the turret above, threads of crimson glittered across the marble. The floor matched the rest of the citadel. Glass, fish swimming beneath.

"Hmmmm." Brielle trailed her fingers along the sink's edge, making eyes with Naokah in the mirror. "We'll have to take turns."

She nodded at the adjacent door that led to a room almost identical to hers, save the colors. And the mural. The woman on her wall jutted out from beneath the lip of a waterfall. Long black hair streamed down her chest to the juncture of her hips.

The Keeper couldn't be faulted for honoring the female form. A gifted artist and bee whisperer, she was also the youngest envoy to ever win the Keepership. At only age fifteen, she'd sworn in. Naokah buried her envy and plodded after Brielle to her chambers, noting her sky-blue trunk leaning against the bed frame. The Poler tugged at the buckles, and it splayed open, silks of pink and purple, green and crystal-trimmed aquamarine billowing over its edges. A sword-nosed fish beneath the floor, enamored by the colors, tried to nibble at one of the shiny stones on the blue gown.

"What do you think?" Brielle picked up the violet gown, holding it up to her chin. Iridescent beads on its gauzy train clinked the floor.

"It's lovely," Naokah said. It would've looked better puddled around Brielle's ankles, but she kept that to herself. She wasn't sure if the Poler liked her or was just toying with her, nor did she have any business flirting. Lenita was missing. That's all that mattered right now.

Brielle's face lit up. "What will you wear?"

"Whatever has the fewest holes," she joked.

The chartreuse curtains by the canopy shimmered beneath the sconces. Even they had more elegance than the bundle she'd brought. Pity eddied in Brielle's mossy eyes but then settled like sediment in calm water, thankfully. Naokah would rather be punched than pitied.

"The ball's in an hour." Brielle shoved Naokah back into the lavatory, handing her a fluffy towel and slippers. "Since you don't have much hair to wash, you go first." She winked, then shut the bedroom door behind her, leaving Naokah alone in the cave.

Brielle wasn't being snotty about her cropped hair. Just logical, straightforward. Still, she rubbed her hands over her scalp. Not a single Keeper had ever boasted the clipped cut of a Crogan, or any other Mid for that matter. Not one. Lenita would've been the first. Could that be why someone took her? They couldn't stand the thought of a dirty Mid controlling the world? Was one of the Polers Lenita competed against responsible? But they'd already been sent home the night she vanished. That didn't mean they didn't have supporters within these walls. She sighed. She didn't even know where to start.

Naokah tossed the towel and slippers by the sink, then turned the faucet to the hottest setting, filling the room with steam. Maybe Brielle feigned kindness because she didn't see her as competition. Naokah had told Patri there was no choice but to vie for the Keepership to find Lenita. It wasn't a lie. Finding Lenita was top priority. Yet now, something she was ashamed of, something she'd attempted to sequester as it had ultimately caused the rift with her sister, floated to the surface of the water as she scrubbed off the trip's grime – rivalry.

CHAPTER NINE

Circling Vultures

A few days before the new moon, the air condensed with unrest as we awaited the next attack. The sun hid behind dark clouds, and fog thick as slate patrolled the hedge maze. The Keeper packed her pipe for the third time before noon, lit it, and took a deep drag as she stood beside her wall of windows. Smoke the hue of blackberry jam unfurled from her stummel, a carved cluster of foxgloves rimmed in gold. Avice didn't approve, much to my amusement, nose squinched as if she'd stumbled upon a corpse instead of sweet, velvety euphoria in smoke form. But I didn't mind. Smoking calmed the Keeper and, with the encroaching marching, me.

When Avice made some flimsy excuse and left – she wasn't fooling anyone, likely the Keeper had lit up to get some space – I considered approaching her. Now was my chance. Yet every time I pressed those tiny motes together to form lips and attempted to speak, only fear creaked out. And creak, it did.

The Keeper furrowed that lovely, sun-kissed brow, and whipped her head around. But by then, I'd scattered and fogged up her window. Her shoulders dropped with a sigh, and she puffed her pipe. The citadel was constructed by the Divine Daughter's cohorts long ago, when there was still wind and, like all old structures, it too was prone to groan.

I cursed myself. She was here. Alone. With me. She could answer my questions, could save me from this miserable existence.

But I was a coward. Her searing glare from the garden had yet to heal, and that's when she'd been happy moments before. Now, her crimson gown bunched tightly around her back; her free arm cinched her torso. She was already on edge; would my voice not push her over? I attributed her foul mood to the group of seven envoys who'd arrived last night. The way they eyed her sparkly videira, I didn't blame her.

For once, my attention floated to the staff. Even the savvy was rigid, and that worried me. They always seemed calm. From what I'd gathered via the gardener and the chef during one of their not-so-secretive trysts in a hedge maze alcove, everyone was on high alert. These seven would stay over the next few months, vying for the Keeper's position. I didn't like it, and more, I was confused by it.

Impotent of any gumption, I forced my glimmer out her door and twisted through the Hall of Keepers. Row after row of large, oval portraits in filigreed frames showcased the Keepers' inaugurations and the day they passed on their ruby videira to their successor. All the former Keepers, upon stepping down, were old, frail, deep wrinkles trenching their skin. But this Keeper? My Keeper? Gabriella França Costa, endearingly called Bee by her closest mates? – Wait. How did I know that? I shrugged and chucked it into my ever-growing collection of questions without answers – Bee's big amber eyes were still bright and clear with youth, her copper face, smoother than silk. Only on the rare occasion when she smiled did tiny threads appear around her eyes. So why now?

She had coughed nonstop at dinner last night. Avice was concerned, but the Keeper claimed she'd choked on wine. If today were any indication, I'd put all my coin on her smoking habit. Yet, cloudcane pulp, unlike other forms of pipe tobacco, soothed the lungs. It was even prescribed to those suffering from breathing ailments. And that's all she smoked. So, something else then. Was she...could she be.... No! She was not dying. A woman tough as the Keeper would never bow to sickness.

I returned to my stoop, glaring at the group as they ambled into the stained-glass foyer. So why were these vultures circling? Surely, one of them was to blame for this cruel turn of events?

"Every half century or so, this repeats. Nothing to fret over. A new Keeper will rise, and the former will spend the rest of her days relaxing on one of the southern isles," the eldest gargoyle said, irritated. They were always irritated. They didn't care for my questions. Told me to stop wasting my energy. Better to preserve it for the upcoming attack.

I pitied them. How tedious their existence must've been, hunched over the neighboring spire, only awakening before each scrim attack. What kind of life was that? Their glimmer, milky and dull, drooped inside their feline-crow frame. Even it had curdled with time. Had they once been like me, desperately trying to escape, only to resign themselves to this lackluster life? I shivered. Was this my future too?

"Does your mind ever shut the raze up?" said a voice of rusty nails. Where had that—

"Here." The elephant-headed gargoyle with the seal body glowered.

"You can hear my thoughts?" I said, unnerved. I'd tried talking to this dour gent when I'd first awoken. I'd failed.

"Not all, thank the Divine Daughter. Just the loud, obnoxious ones."

I winced. "My apologies."

He grumbled something unintelligible. A flood of possibilities, of questions, swept my chagrin away. Had I found a confidant, a friend? Or at least someone who could—

"I'm not your mate," he spat. "Our stone bodies may've been sculpted and placed upon the citadel at the same time, but you're not the spirit who arrived after the great wars, after the typhoons and tidal waves and tempests. Nay. You arrived here much later, methinks. The Scorned Son had already relieved us of the wind's burden."

"Burden? But—"

"Your shock confirms you aren't an ancient one." He cocked his head, smug. "These days, every soul is reminiscent, placing the wind on a pedestal as though she were a martyr. But if you were from my time, lived through the atrocities caused by her, over her, you wouldn't call her a saint."

The wind, a villain? I couldn't process it. My mind was a mess, but this stone body remembered the wind's stolen kisses, her delicate caresses—

"Didn't say she was a villain. All make mistakes. Most are forgivable. But our kind, and more so, humans, tend to revere the gone, latching on to only their favorable memories. Yet even roses have thorns."

"What exactly...is our kind?"

The elephant-seal paused for a moment. "The spirit once inhabiting your vessel was a guardian of the citadel, like me, like the rest of us. But you? I've no clue what or who you are, other than you aren't my mate."

I began to ask if he remembered when his friend left, so that I might construct a timeline, but his glimmer, once bright as the midday sun, darkened to full night. And any more questions I asked, then pleaded, were answered with hollow silence.

I still didn't know what I was, only that I wasn't like them. Progress, if slight. I should've been pleased. But the confirmation that I was indeed different, that I wasn't supposed to be here, that I was an aberration or perhaps even a body thief, only caved me in more. So, I returned to my previous plan. One of these seven foreigners had clearly conspired to take the Keepership before she was ready. I would find them. I would stop them. I'd remove the source of her suffering. Then, surely she'd forgive my past trespasses, whatever they were – even roses had thorns, the elephant-seal would agree – and help restore my memory.

CHAPTER TEN

Off

A cloud hunched over the turret, darkening the lavatory. The only light gasped up from sconces beside the mirror. Unsettled, Naokah crawled out of the tub. Flames winked off scores of carved cones drooping from the wall fixtures. Recalling Brielle's warning about the actual foxgloves, Naokah reached across the sink to stroke the bronze flowers, when goosebumps scurried down her spine. She spun around, blinking rapidly to clear the steam. Naokah had once caught a neighbor boy spying on her and Lenita as they swam in what they'd thought was a secret waterhole. That same unease, eyes greedily combing over her damp skin, plucked at her nerves now. But the lavatory was empty. She shivered and wrapped herself in a towel. Lemon and lavender floated from the warm plush.

"Brielle?" She knocked on her door, which opened slightly. She peered through the crack, pale light spilling over her feet. "Lavatory's free."

No answer.

"Brielle?"

Flat silence.

Cinching her towel beneath her arms, she nudged the door aside. Steam trailed, slithering her ankles, dissolving in the dry air. The room was empty. Brielle's trunk had been rummaged through; gowns in rich jewel tones were strewn across the floor. Silver glinted beside an iridescent gown, a school of fish trying to nibble through the glass.

A loud chime, behind her. Naokah flinched, and the silver scattered. It was just the old grandfather clock in the corner, announcing thirty minutes past the hour. Brielle wouldn't have gotten ready and left without bathing first? Or saying goodbye?

A perch swam beneath her heel, eyeing her warily before darting to the mural. The wall looked different. Something was missing. She padded over to where the thick, chartreuse curtains had hung before. The paint was darker. The sun blazing through the turrets had leached color from the uncovered sections, only noticeable now that the drapes were gone. A shadow passed over the mural's face. Naokah jumped, dropping her towel.

"Scondra tai!" she shrieked in Midese. A filthy curse.

"Sorry." Brielle stood before her in a thigh-length slip. But she wasn't sorry. She smirked, eyes trailing Naokah's bare curves. "Suppose you could go like that." She shrugged. "Far better than anything else you've packed."

Without anything clever to spout back – she hated that – Naokah grabbed her towel, wrapped herself, and stomped off to her room, ignoring Brielle's giggle-punctuated apology.

Only when she stepped inside and slammed the door did she understand where the Poler had been. The simple ivory gown she'd planned on wearing tonight – well, gown was generous, Brielle's slip had more flourish – hung from her mirror. Attached at the waist with glittery new thread were the missing chartreuse curtains, ruffles cascading the floor. A train even the Keeper would've adored.

★   ★   ★

Naokah's hands trembled as she clipped on a chandelier earring. Brielle's, of course. *They bring out your eyes*, the Poler had said, pouting, when Naokah tried to refuse. She already felt like a fraud with her new train, even if it was made of curtains, but these earrings, their delicate gold wiring, their clusters of pearls and diamonds and yellow garnets that caught the torchlight, were so extravagant, they could've fed an entire Crogan village for a year.

If anything, she should've been wearing black. It matched her mood, the cold, sinking gravity she faced if she didn't find her sister. The guilt she'd carried the last few months was an illness. Festering, spreading, debilitating. Lenita's forgiveness was her only remedy. Without it, shame would consume her whole. That, and although her door was closed, she could feel the bees wriggling on the other side, their droning burrowing into her skin.

The floor pinged, by her slipper. One of the gems had come loose. She pulled up her hem and was reaching for the pearl when it rolled towards the wall. She stumbled after it, tripping over her skirts. It tinked a curtain by her headboard. As she snagged it, the black sheer shivered, revealing a tall glass pane. A door? She slid the drape aside, unlatched the iron lock, and pulled it open. Night, showcasing her own train of wispy fog, greeted her.

"Close that, quick. Before you let all the humidity in," Brielle said, emerging from the lavatory in a towel.

"What is it?"

"Someone wasn't paying attention to Samara's tour." The Poler's eyes twinkled as she prodded the golden hair hilled atop her head. "It's the veranda, wraps around the citadel."

"The whole citadel?"

"Yes."

"Suppose it goes by the great hall too?"

"Yes..." Brielle pursed her lips. "Why?"

Naokah smiled. A flame of hope warmed her insides. "Think I'll get some air."

★   ★   ★

Columns laced in red ivy lined the veranda, and large, patina sculptures of bees in various stages of a navigational dance wove between topiaries. It was warm and sticky, with fog up to their knees, but they were safe. At least compared to inside. Lanterns hung from above, their ethereal glow haloing Brielle. Naokah struggled to keep her gaze forward. The Poler was radiant in a swoony, backless gown that matched her emerald eyes. Tiers of chiffon trimmed in silk ribbon cascaded around her like a waterfall. Too bad she wore her mood like a clunky, ill-matched necklace. Her heels clicked impatiently over the wood, and she huffed every few seconds. Naokah bit back a grin.

"Why are we going this way?" Brielle whined.

"I told you. Fresh air."

"You find this fresh?"

Compared to the walls of wriggling hives? Absolutely. But she kept that to herself. Admitting she was terrified of bees would either inspire more pity from the Poler, or worse. Knowledge of her weakness would spread, and who knew what the other envoys might do to get ahead. "Fresher than those stuffy halls, yes. Smells better out here too."

"Fine." Brielle snorted. "But it's your fault when I show up looking like a poodle that lifted its leg too close to the Razing."

"Impossible." Naokah turned to her. A stray lock fell across the Poler's cheek, almost touching her wine-painted lips. "And you know it."

Their eyes locked for a few, wavering breaths. Fine freckles dusted Brielle's small nose. Naokah hadn't noticed them before, yet she'd also never stood this close.

The Poler jerked away. "Stop looking at me like that."

"Like what?" Heat rose up Naokah's neck. The attraction was one-sided, then.

Brielle forced a laugh. "Like I just rescued your favorite lamb from sacrifice."

"Oh." The tension corseting her midsection released. "You did, except I'm the lamb."

The blonde shot her a guilty look. The Polers would've had a riot with her gown had Brielle not embellished it. Naokah peeped back at the bee statues glinting in the misty haze. A forager could waggle her body, a few movements left and right, and lead her sisters to food – the closest to magic Naokah had ever seen. If only there was a dance that could lead her to Lenita. Or, at the very least, like the bees' halt signal, steer her clear of predators.

"Why'd you help me?" Naokah asked. The end of the veranda brightened, and her pulse quickened, chiming sharply at her temples. Big groups were nerve-racking alone, even without the certainty that a kidnapper was among them, and here, there could be many.

"Must I have a reason to be nice?"

"Most do." How many times had her big sister sweet-talked Naokah into helping bake cookies and, when the first batch was done, Lenita, having already eaten her fill, abandoned her with a bowl full of dough to bake for the rest of the family? Every single time.

"Well." Brielle stepped behind Naokah, picked up her train, and tugged it down in one swift movement. Its beaded fringe clinked the floor as it petaled around her. "I'm not most." She held out her arm, gold ruffles trimmed in lace and crystals flowing from her elbow.

Naokah raised a brow. "Don't I feel regal."

"Don't get too used to it." Brielle winked and pulled her inside the great hall.

The Polers were easy to pick out in their thick brocades, flashy velvet suits, and even flashier confidence. They buzzed around tables laden with cheese wheels, meat tiers, tropical fruit, and fine Zerşilian chocolates. The garb of the other two Midworlders matched their expressions: fatigued and threadbare. Guilt needled Naokah's waist below her newly fastened train. Would it not have been kinder to refuse Brielle's gift and stand in solidarity with her fellow Mids? They looked painfully out of place here.

Sconces flickered against stained-glass arches wrapping the perimeter, sending refracted jewel tones across the dance floor. Each window depicted scenes of Vindstöld's torrid creation. The Divine Daughter's sparkling seas, the lush, agrarian and pastoral nations, and her brother the Scorned Son, jealous of her perfect world, stealing the wind and spawning the Razing. The Divine Siblings battled for millennia, decimating much of what they'd created and, unable to retrieve the wind, the Divine Daughter ultimately banished the Scorned Son to his shadowy afterscape. Still, the Scorned Son may've been judged too harshly. Those who held him in the greatest contempt clearly hadn't spent millennia trapped in their big sister's shadow, eons of being compared to the perfect Divine Daughter, eons of getting smothered with unsolicited commisery and unhelpfully woeful looks. No wonder the Scorned Son had opted for hatred over pity. Naokah couldn't blame him. It was easier to swallow.

The presence from earlier, the shadowed watcher, found Naokah, stinging like a glass shard in her cheek. She turned. No one was there. She stiffened in Brielle's grasp.

"Stop fidgeting." Her lithe acquaintance leaned in. "You look nervous."

"I am."

"I know, but no need to let the others in on our little secret." A waiter with a tray of ruby flutes approached. Brielle grabbed two before Naokah could protest. "Drink."

She shouldn't. She had to focus. Someone in this hall knew what happened to Lenita. Now was the time to ask innocent questions while the staff got giddy on wine and melgo, a sweet, honied liquor Abelha was praised for. Spirits were the best lure for snagging guilt.

"Drink." Brielle nudged her as a trio of Polers approached, Kjell in the lead.

He wore a dark green tailcoat, peacock feathers glittering with sapphires crowning his collar. His hair was braided on each side and along the top, showcasing his sunset tips. He was stunning, save the cloak of contempt billowing around him with each stride.

"Rather elegant for a Crogan, no?" He smirked at Naokah's train.

"Rather rude, even for a Raptor, no?" Naokah said through a gritted smile. Brielle giggled. Why did she let him get under her skin?

"Excuse us." He wedged between them, broke their hold, and pulled Brielle off to talk by the refreshments, leaving Naokah alone.

The cold flute sweat in her hand. One drink wouldn't hurt. She took a sip, and it zinged her throat. Trying to ignore Kjell and Brielle's argument, faces red, arms waving, she turned to her competition. Did she need to interview the new envoys too? None of them were here when Lenita disappeared. Their formers had already been kicked off the isle. But, did they know their predecessors? Perhaps been privy to what they'd experienced while competing? Too many variables. She'd have to be thorough.

Any scrap of comfort left with Clisten, the tamest of the Polers, when he excused himself to the refreshment table. His tiered braids gleamed in the soft light.

Dazarin no longer seemed like the jester with the bad harem joke. With waves of glossy hair so black it neared blue, he towered over her like a sea god. Cerulean damask stretched across his broad shoulders, a series of gold straps buckled down his very bare, very tan torso holding the thick fabric in place, and long, silk-lined sleeves that split above his elbows showcased mythical creatures and thorny vines inked around his powerful arms. So vivid, so colorful, the renderings were breathtaking—

"See something you like?" purred a deep voice.

Naokah jerked up, and large, kohl-rimmed eyes met hers, twinkling. He'd caught her staring. "Yes," she said, failing to keep the heat from coursing up her neck. "Your skin ink is…well, I…I've never seen anything like it. It's quite striking."

"Thank you." Dark lashes fringed his cheeks with humility. "To be honest? Was quite painful too."

"Was it worth it?" The tentacled beast coiling around his bicep looked too much like the Razing's spawn that tried to capsize them.

A couple of floundering heartbeats passed before he said, "Often, the worthiest things are also the most painful."

Naokah swigged the rest of her drink. He leaned in, notes of chocolate and something roasted, nutty, teasing her. "Let me know if you'd like to inspect the rest of my ink. You know, to determine if it was worth it?" He brushed the top of his trousers where his muscles formed a sleek V and winked before strolling off.

Shuddering, she grabbed another flute from a passing waiter. Dazarin must have been toying with her, but that didn't prevent her body from responding. Lenita, far prettier, always won the crowd over. Naokah wasn't used to getting attention. Admittedly, she enjoyed it, and instantly felt guilty. Her sister was in trouble, and here she was flirting with Polers. The same craven group who hid in their cabins while the Mids fought the Razing. A double betrayal.

Naokah was nursing the bubbling wine, the tart berries soothing her fraying pulse, when a man in cream, hair even shorter than hers, approached. A Mid.

"Do Crogans dance?" He rocked back and forth in shoes that creased above the toes.

She chuckled. "Not well."

The string quartet on the dais changed to a lively Midworld folksong. Surprised, Naokah gave the musicians a double take. In sea-blue uniforms, each boasted long horsetails of hair, segmented every few inches by silver ribbons. Certainly not Mids. The bearded cellist winked at her prospective dancing partner as he offered her his hand.

"Figured we could teach these Polers a thing or two. You can dance the brimble, yes?"

Throat tight, Naokah accepted his hand. Lenita had taught her the fast, swinging number when she attended the harvest ball the first time. She could still feel the damp soil beneath her feet as her sister spent half the night teaching her the tricky steps. Naokah had had trouble loosening up, staring at her toes, but Lenita was patient. She'd been more of a mother than Matri ever was.

"You trying to swindle me?" the lean envoy asked, spinning her.

"What?"

"You said you weren't a good dancer. You're doing well."

"I've had assistance." She nodded at a waiter with a tray full of flutes. "And an impressive partner."

His russet cheeks flushed to port. Despite his haggard appearance, he moved with precision and skill, courteously draping her new train over his forearm. From Okse, she decided after he leaned in, notes of molasses grain feed and hay trailing.

"Didn't know Oksens had time to dance with all the livestock you raise," she teased.

"Cows aren't too bad dancers, as long as you feed them first."

"Funny." Her eyes met his, now a soft gray beneath the chandelier. "Same goes for Crogans."

He smiled and twirled her. "You look lovely tonight."

"It's the train."

"It's you."

"Why are you so kind?" She curtsied and stepped toward his hand as he turned her, his earthy cologne like a spritz of home. "Aren't we supposed to be rivals?"

"Not until tomorrow." He bowed, taking her hand, firmly but gently. "Besides, we Mids have to stick together. Should you win, I'm hoping for some love, as allies, of course."

"Allies, right." Now was her opening. "I'm Naokah, by the way."

"Laerte."

"So dignified," she said, relishing his blush, then caught a pointed stare from over his shoulder. Brielle, dancing with Kjell. Green chiffon winged around her, and annoyance flickered over her lips. She wasn't impressed. Either with her partner or Naokah's. Maybe both.

"A family name," he said, "but you can call me Leo. If it's easier."

"I'll call you Laerte. Monikers are for those who don't like their name. Or for Polers who can't pronounce them."

He nodded sheepishly, then twirled her. The stained glass blurred.

"The envoy before you, do you know how he was eliminated from the Praxis?" she asked, hoping her tone mirrored small talk.

His grip tightened. "Was the first to fall, in truth."

"Surprising," she said without thinking, "heard Oksens were stubborn as Crogans."

"True, but Felipe was from the Dead Forest. A tough life, that. One of isolation, poverty. Unlike Abelha, surrounded by all of this." He waved at the decadent displays of food and finery. "Can overwhelm someone rather quickly."

If he was first to go, he probably wasn't involved in Lenita's disappearance. Still....

"You were friends." It wasn't a question. His tone was soft but protective, like when she talked about her younger brother.

"*Are* friends. Losing didn't kill him." The music stopped, and Laerte whispered in Midese, "But maybe it should've."

She tensed. "Why?"

His eyes narrowed, skimming over her shoulder, falling on the head table.

"The Praxis happens every fifty years, when the old Keeper wishes to retire in peace. So, I'm not sure how the envoys usually return after losing. The state of their minds, that is."

"What do you mean?"

"The Felipe I knew, warmer than a shallow pond on a summer day, wasn't the same man who returned. He came back a shell of a human, eyes distant. He barely speaks. It's like this place sucked the life right out of him."

And he was first to leave. How would Lenita fare after being missing for over a month?

"Did he say anything about what happened?"

"Just that he was lucky enough to return at all. And...." He paused. Everyone had cleared after the song faded out, save them.

"And?" She squeezed his clammy hand.

"Not everything is as it seems. Something's...*off*. I felt it the moment I stepped foot here. A change in pressure, like right before a thunderstorm?"

"The air's so charged a spark would explode it all." Her stomach flipped. "I've felt it too." If she wasn't paranoid, then all of this – the sinister presence, the prickly tension, the mounting unease, was real. A certain uncertainty.

"Whoever prevails may inherit more than just an isle of bees and world supremacy—" the knot of Laerte's throat leapt to his chin, "—but a curse as well."

CHAPTER ELEVEN

Stinging Memories

I glared at the neighboring spires where the lion-peacock gargoyle and elephant-seal perched, their shadows growing long in the sweltering afternoon heat. How could they sleep so soundly? Ever since the seven foreigners arrived, that sick, foreboding sense had worsened, wriggling like maggots in my gut. It wasn't the marching, rising and falling with the moon cycle. That I'd come to expect, to ignore. No, this was something more. Why weren't my kin alarmed?

Set on winning the Keeper's favor and thus my freedom, I'd foregone sleeping, keeping a close eye on the envoys from dusk to dawn, but that was the extent of my usefulness. As of now, the power I used to crush the scrim didn't extend to anything…human. I blew out a candle in one of the envoy's chambers last night, gave him a good fright – me, a good laugh – but beyond that? My fingers were motes and slipped through skin. I had to work on it. Master it. Channel all my scattered energy.

A crow passed over the ward that covered the isle, cawing obnoxiously. A beam shot through a cloud and gleamed off the dome's translucent fibers. It may've protected the bees from predators but didn't prevent birds from mocking it. Bird shit, still sizzling from the ward's bite, plopped from the metallic sky and splattered the lion's nose. I snickered, but my kin didn't stir. Why weren't they pissed? Why didn't they ache with loneliness nor fight for better treatment?

Had time atrophied their will to live? Per the eldest, pondering was pointless. So instead, I homed in on the threat.

Although I could stretch my glimmer to great lengths, the citadel's walls were most receptive. The ashlar hummed beneath my myriad specks, tingling, sucking me in. The fortress was a living, breathing extension of me. Or rather, I of her. I stretched to the outer gardens, where the seven foreigners gathered. The first test, I'd learned from the savvy. Some of these envoys had spent the better part of their lives prepping, researching, and studying hive husbandry and theory, hoping to earn the bid from their nations to be here. Now, it was time to evaluate what they'd learned via the Praxis.

Sweat glistened on the cropped cuts of the three Mids, who still donned their thin, scamall tunics and trousers, holes eating through the knees and sleeves. The four Polers had braided their long hair and traded in their heavy brocade gowns, their tailored suits trimmed in flashy stones, for pastel blouses and loose pants. A prudent choice. The sky was overcast, but that didn't deter the sun. Heat shimmered in waves over the rolling fields of foxgloves.

The envoys lined up behind a grove of shaggy trees and spoke in clipped, somber tones. So far from my perch, I crept around a clump of hostas, their broad, teal leaves silvering beneath the filtered light, and strained to hear.

"Before we begin," said Samara, eyes keen, "I encourage all of you to slip on one of these." They held out their arms as if holding a pile of coats, but all I could see was their own carmine sleeves. Confused frowns rippled across the faces of the envoys. It wasn't just me, then. The savvy grinned and moved slightly. The invisible attire refracted like sunlight through a spiderweb. "Smoke cloaks. The stink deters bees from stinging...most of the time." They handed one to each envoy.

A Poler with a braid of long, inky hair curled his nose. "These positively reek." He held it away from his periwinkle blouse like a dead rat. "Will keep more than just the bees away."

Tense giggles bubbled among the group, but Samara remained grim.

"Wear it. Don't wear it." The savvy shrugged. "Doesn't matter to me. Like I said, the cloak *can* prevent the random sting. But with your attitude, Enzo, I wouldn't put it past the bees to swarm you. Little good it'll do then."

The other envoys quickly slipped on their smoke cloaks and, after rolling his eyes, the surly Poler pulled his on as well.

"Perfect. Let's begin." Samara smiled, though it didn't touch their eyes. "A Keeper must always listen to their hive. An angry queen means what?"

"An angry hive," said the envoys in unison.

"And an angry hive?" Samara pointed a stick at the grove. The light flickered from green to black where the colonies zizzed. Workers soared between tangled trunks and a knoll of magenta foxgloves. The staff had transported these seven hives outside earlier.

"A lethal swarm."

"Followed by certain death—" they twisted around, brass braid whipping, "—unless the healer finds you in time. Now, each of you will approach your respective hive and remove a wedge of comb. But only if the bees acquiesce. If they protest, do not approach. It's just not your day. You'll have to excel at another stage. I repeat, if the bees don't invite you, don't intrude. Understood?"

Murmurs and nods rippled through the seven. Fear drenched the air, bitter as bile. I was latent energy, no actual vessel, but—

Barbs pierced my cheeks, my palms. My past reclaimed me. I shrieked. Flailed. Desperately trying to fight the stings piercing every inch of my body. Venom curdled my blood, now pounding thick in my ears. I fought. Kicked. Tried to run away. But I was strapped down. I clawed the bindings. *Wake up!* I didn't want to relive *this*. My voice snagged, rendered useless like in all nightmares. Tears burned my eyes. *Wake up!* My tongue was swollen from the stings. Darkness shuttered my eyelids.

"Wake the raze up!" I cried, victorious. Finally. Teal leaves brushed my wings.

"What was that?" A twitchy envoy stepped back from the line.

Sweat trickled down my phantom nose, itching something fierce, but I didn't dare scratch. A squad of boots faced the hostas. They'd heard me.

Samara waved his question away. "Abelha has her...quirks. One of the joys of winning the Keepership. Carry on."

More mumbling from the envoys as they eyed the bush I hid under. Only one seemed unfazed. Her gaze on the hives, her shoulders were relaxed despite my outcry.

"What did you expect?" she asked. "The Keepership must be earned. If you're scared, best you head back now, so the worthy can assume the position faster."

With that bold tone? The envoy from Croi Croga. Lenita, I'd heard Samara call her. Though leaner, smaller than the rest, the other envoys feared her. And because they feared her, they hated her. I didn't hate the Crogan, but I was wary. For if she boasted this much confidence, she must've been undermining the Keeper and, therefore, had to be eliminated. But how? The buzzing drew nearer, swelling to an atonal chorus. The ground trembled, and I shrank to peer between silvered leaves.

"Felipe!" shrieked an envoy chasing after a figure draped in a writhing cloak. No, not a cloak. A swarm. "Help him!"

All the envoys fled but one. Lenita. She removed her smoke cloak, cropped hair winking with each meditated step. The savvy yelled to cover up, that the bees were riled, but she ignored them. She hummed a deep, throaty tune. A Midworld chant, I recognized. The buzz softened and, one by one, the bees extricated themselves from Felipe and moved to her, covering her. But differently. They were drawn to her like a vibrant foxglove, delicately landing, purring up her neck, her arms.

Angry red bumps covered the Mid's face, and he collapsed. A lot of good his smoke cloak did. My skin pricked, mirroring his pain, the pain from my past, and I dug my claws into the brambles, fighting to stay. The healer, Marguerite, rushed forward and fell to her knees. She took out a large syringe and jabbed his chest. Nothing. Another. Nothing. On the third, his shoulders heaved, and he gasped.

The bees had engulfed Lenita, except her tawny face, which now glowed with relief like the healer's. The other envoys, cowards, all of them, hid behind the grove, arguing in strangled tones. It was hard to hear them over the drone of hives, the mounting distance, but 'witch' and 'Crogan' razored from their huddle. They thought she was a Midworld enchantress. Lenita was either a hero, incredibly stupid, or just plain mad. Perhaps a potent cocktail of all three. But that also meant she was a threat to be taken care of. And, as the poltroons whispered and stung her with glares, I now knew I wasn't her only enemy. If I couldn't physically reach her, could I not manipulate the others to do it for me? An enemy of an enemy, as the saying went.

CHAPTER TWELVE

Smiling Pricks

Laerte's warning stuck to Naokah like a wet blanket, hampering her every step. A possible curse? Was Lenita's disappearance linked to the cloaked watcher? She shivered and sipped another flute. Flowers had evolved over time, displaying striking patterns, lavishing themselves in seductive scents, some going as far as drugging their nectar to enchant bees into visiting. Naokah's daydream of a lush Abelha had acted in the same, deceptive way. This wasn't the paradise she'd surrendered a decade of sleep to, had given up all her free time, scant that it was between farming and caring for Matri and her little brother, to study for. Most of all, this nightmare of an isle wasn't worth the fight she'd lost her sister over. And, though she tried to cling to that seething disappointment – fury was easier to manage than fear – she was shaken.

Because in the end, despite the ominous fog, the sinister presence and harrowing walls of bees, her sister never would've left willingly. Securing the Keepership could have sustained Croi Croga's cloudcane production for decades. Even if she'd felt like Naokah, who currently wanted nothing more than to catch the next ship home, Lenita's honor, loyalty, and dedication to duty would have kept her here. Her goodness had been her undoing, and *that* was heartbreaking.

"Shouldn't grimace," Brielle whispered. "Premature aging, love."

Naokah snorted, finishing her drink. She had a lot of worries at

KEEPER OF SORROWS • 59

the moment, but her looks weren't one of them. "Is the room hazy, or is that just me?"

Brielle surveyed the hall, green ruffles circling. "It's definitely you."

Naokah yawned into her hand, ignoring the Poler's wrinkling nose. Her many sleepless nights and drinks had caught up with her. Her eyes burned, and fatigue fuzzed her brain.

Brielle grabbed her arm, steering her towards the refreshment table. "Eat."

Food would only hasten her drowsiness, but she *was* hungry. She was stuffing peppered ham into her mouth when a striking staff member with brassy hair approached. Samara.

"Naokah," they said, face curious but kind, a contrast to the sharp lines of their plum suit, ivory lace flaring at their sleeves. "I wouldn't have pegged you for Lenita's little sister."

Naokah forced the meat down, eyes watering from the pepper. "Lenita was blessed with our matri's beauty, whereas I take after our patri." Big frame, brown eyes. Nothing against him. He was handsome in a rugged way. But Naokah would've preferred to look like their graceful matri.

"Lenita was...is...wonderful." A pained expression creased Samara's face, and their chin dropped. "I...we miss her. And I'm so very sorry for your loss."

"Kind of you to say." Naokah squeezed her glass to stop her trembling hand. Brielle had attempted to offer condolences back on the ship, but she'd shaken her off. She didn't want pity nor to admit Lenita's disappearance could be more, worse, final.

Though it was nice to have her missing sister acknowledged, did the savvy seem more than just sympathetic, perhaps guilty? Or were they merely uncomfortable like anyone discussing sorrow? Was it better to put her foot down and proclaim that her sister was alive and press for details? Her spiking pulse said yes. But now wasn't the place. Too many people were around for the savvy to speak freely. Besides, would it not be wiser to pretend that Naokah accepted the citadel's narrative, that Lenita was as good as dead?

Better to leave the guilty parties thinking they got away with their crime. They'd let their guard down. And one good lesson Naokah had learned from Matri before she lost her voice, was that one could attract more bees with cloudcane nectar than vinegar. She'd play docile and wait.

Samara, after realizing Naokah studied them, tucked away their vulnerability, features hardening, then grabbed an olive. "See you ladies in the morning. Be careful tonight." They walked away without another word.

"Hmmm." Brielle fussed with her pearl belt.

"You think they meant 'be careful' as in, not to overindulge?"

Brielle's eyes trailed the savvy until they vanished into the corridor. "No."

"Me neither." The great hall, though full of warm bodies, now felt drafty – eerie for a world stripped of wind. Naokah picked up a shortbread cookie. A pressed flower with round violet petals sprinkled with sugar crystals stared up at her.

"That's a pansy. And unlike foxglove, it's edible." Brielle grinned as Naokah debated trying it. The edge carving out her belly wasn't so much hunger as it was uneasiness, but her nerves won out anyway. Soft, buttery granules melted in her mouth. "Did you get a chance to look over the itinerary for tomorrow?" Brielle asked after Naokah had scarfed the rest of it down.

"Itinerary?"

"Yes, it should've been on your end table. Red parchment? Queen bee seal?"

"Didn't see it. But, suppose I didn't look too hard either, was a bit...preoccupied."

Brielle hmphed. "It's an early start. Fifth hour wake up, breakfast, followed by the savvy's orientation and breakdown of the Praxis and rules, and then we tour the citadel grounds. Maybe the whole isle if we have enough time."

"So much for sleeping in," Naokah joked, trying to chase away the dread coiling her chest. Upon learning the lay of the land and citadel, she'd planned to conduct most of her inquest at night, when everyone was asleep. But if every morning was just as early, that meant less time to pry and sleep. She'd need to narrow down a suspect list and fast if she were to solve Lenita's disappearance before getting tossed off the isle. Her older sister had outlasted all her competition, but Naokah wasn't Lenita. She'd start with the savvy. They seemed kind but mysterious and were hiding something. What better person to observe than the staff member in charge of the envoys' training? And with that wistful look, they either knew what happened or had knowledge that could point her in the direction of the person who did.

★　★　★

Cruel laughs came from the far side of the room, near the grand piano. Instinct told Naokah that people were laughing *at* someone rather than with. She passed small groups of staff members to find a redheaded Mid backed against the wall. Ludmila, who went by Mila. She'd met her on one of her shifts in steerage. Like that of any Mid, her gown was similar to Naokah's before Brielle had enhanced it. Off white, thin, frayed. A slip, essentially. Beneath her worn boots was a puddle of what looked like diluted blood. It had spread through the rump of her gown as though she'd started her cycle while sitting. No wonder she'd pushed up to the wall, eyes wild like a cornered animal. Someone, Kjell most likely, had poured wine on her seat.

Naokah rushed to her, pushing through the smiling pricks who were responsible for the laughter. Clisten, at least, had the good sense to look ashamed and put distance between the other two, but a smirk passed between Dazarin and Kjell, the ringleader. Polers were like dogs. One on its own was harmless. But put them together? Savage.

"Leave her," Kjell teased, eyes rippling with malice. "Red's an improvement."

She ignored him. "You all right?"

Mila nodded meekly, eyes averted. More laughing flamed behind them, feeding the fire already wild inside her. From a Mid nation, her tattered dress was likely the only thing close to presentable she had, and the Polers, willfully ignorant to the Midworld's plight, had ruined it. How was she supposed to get back to her chambers without the entire hall gawking at her?

"Take your friend and go. Leo too. Leave the Praxis for those who were bred to rule," Kjell said, the rouge along his cheekbones sharpening his sneer.

Naokah exhaled slowly. It took all her restraint not to spin around and clock him right in that makeup-glazed face. Instead, she settled for how Lenita would've handled it. "An animal only attacks when threatened."

He cocked his head. "What does that have to do with me?"

"Everything. You could be stupid or just plain cruel, and maybe that's also true. But more? What you've done has proven only one thing – you're scared." She stepped forward, and he backed up. "You know, after the last upset, a Crogan of all nations winning the Keepership? Means Mila, Laerte, me, we're your real threats, and you'll need more than infantile pranks to scare us off." Something had rattled loose inside of her. What was stronger motivation to compete than to save nations of starving people? To put the spoiled Polers in their place, once and for all? Initially, the Praxis was Naokah's cover to gain access to Abelha, so she could find her older sister. But couldn't she do both? Give it her all during the tests, down cacao at night, and search for Lenita?

Kjell cracked his knuckles. "We can do more than just pranks."

She dismissed him with a wave and spun back to Mila. Her shoulders were no longer slumped but squared, her chin erect. Naokah bit back an approving smile. Still, how to get her out without calling attention to the spreading red stain? She kicked her train out of the way, pacing, the beads clicking against the floor – then stopped abruptly and turned to Brielle.

"Sorry," she said, then yanked at her waist, pulling the new stitches loose with a few tugs.

Brielle's lips thinned at first, then she sighed, taking – after a few attempts with clumsy hands – the pearl-encrusted belt from her own waist, and helped Naokah attach the train to Mila.

"Should hold until you get to your chambers. Would you like us to escort you back?"

"No, but thanks. For everything." Mila bowed, then strode towards the exit, head high.

Laerte was right. The Mids had to stick together. That, and her newfound Poler friend who, for some reason, had adopted her. She didn't wholly trust her yet, didn't know her well enough, but how well does anyone ever know anyone?

"Call it a night too?" she asked Brielle, who was having significant issues walking in her long gown. She'd lost track of how many glasses Brielle'd downed, but Naokah herself had stopped after Samara's condolences and her friend's acknowledgement of the early schedule tomorrow.

"Already?" Brielle slurred, smile crooked. "But tonight is our last night of freedom. We must take—" hiccup, "—full advantage of it, you know, before they lock us away."

"You've certainly taken full advantage of the bar. Come." She didn't wait for Brielle to respond. She wasn't making any sense, and her drunk stupor was frightening. Who was the 'they' she referred to?

The great hall was still relatively packed, the staff in their carmine and bronze trim around the perimeter, peering sideways at the huddle of envoys. The tension was so thick between the two cliques, it was like plodding through a bog.

"Don't you find it odd the Keeper didn't come to her own welcome ball?" Clisten asked Dazarin as they pushed by. His gaze, dark with remorse, snagged on Naokah, then dropped when she grimaced. Likely, he hadn't been part of the nasty prank, but he hadn't intervened either.

"Likes bees more than humans." Dazarin shrugged. "Besides, we aren't deemed worthy until we pass into senior phase."

Naokah had wondered where the Keeper was all night. One would've thought she'd have wanted to spend as much time as possible with the replacements to ensure she chose the right successor. But this was a historic year. Never had the world witnessed the next Keeper vanishing. There was talk that something was off in the citadel. Most Keepers retired old and haggard after a lifetime of service, but the current, according to the paintings Naokah had seen in her study materials, looked to be no more than forty.

A loud thud, behind her, followed by gasps, shrieks. Naokah twisted around, pulling drunken Brielle with her. They pushed through the crowd to find an envoy with sunset-tipped braids lying on the floor, foam spewing from his mouth.

"Kjell!" A scream ripped from Brielle.

Naokah pulled her back. "The healer's already here."

"Everyone, please. Give him some air." A silver-haired woman in an ivory tunic knelt beside his seizing frame, took his pulse, then forced him to swallow an oily substance from a vial. He stilled for a few seconds, eyes rolling back, then vomited. Chunks and stomach juices pooled over the floor, souring the air. The healer sighed, rubbing Kjell's back with each heave. His face, now that some of the powder had rubbed off, took on an unnatural, waxy sheen.

Brielle cursed, muttering something beneath the chatter.

"What?" asked Naokah.

Her friend nodded at the vomit. "She gave him liquid charcoal. Helps eject contents of one's stomach. If administered fast enough. Which means—"

"Someone poisoned him."

CHAPTER THIRTEEN

Wicked Games

The Mid who'd been stung twenty-seven times survived. His body did, anyway. Felipe's mind buzzed off with the swarm that attacked him and never returned, so the Oksen was the first envoy to go. I was relieved. The bees took care of my job for me. One down, six more to go. How could I play them against one another?

Stealing into their chambers at night was the best option. The citadel was never not sinister, yet when the morning rays streamed through the stained-glass turrets, splashing her corridors in shades of blue, violet, green, the fortress seemed less predatory. Not welcoming by any means but akin to a crocodile in a ballgown, more disconcerting than scary. As the sun set, however, what looked like fresh blood spilled over the walls and oozed over the floor. All part of the first Keeper's grand plan, the savvy had explained to the envoys on their tour. The mosaics of glass were positioned to follow the sun's daily path, thus coaxing the worker bees to follow their favorite hues every dawn, funneling through the opened panes to the outer gardens. But when dusk fell, the industrious little creatures didn't see red, for it appeared black to them. They'd return to their hives and sleep. Which also explained why almost everything inside was coated in crimson-black or other muted shades. I would've surmised the same about the Keeper, as her entire wardrobe was a spectrum of blood, yet the bees still crawled all over her. Something beyond my detection drew them in and whatever it was drew me in too.

With how the envoys reacted to the swarm incident, I figured my wicked games would either rile them up enough to turn on one another or drive them mad. And to some degree, I was right. Envoys of Zerşil, Svinja, and Vintera – all Poler nations, coddling softened the spine, apparently – were easily spooked, and I consequently was easily amused. I blew out their sconces when they bathed, scratched their windows, shook their beds, made grotesque shapes from their curtains, and whispered dividing lies about their friends when they tried to sleep.

My absolute favorite? I crawled beneath the sheets of the Svinjan as he lay stiff, eyes wide, while his comforter hilled up over him. I growled, he screamed, then bounded out of bed to his lavatory and slammed the door, rattling the walls. I howled deep belly laughter, rolling about his mattress until I flopped into something warm, wet, that stank of terror. Poor fellow didn't make it to the facility fast enough. In truth, I deserved much worse than a urine bath. Deriving joy from their fear when I should've been ashamed? In my defense, I'd been stuck inside a gargoyle for Daughter knows how long, lonely, sad, teetering the edge of sanity, with little entertainment to be had. I would come to regret my misguided pranks much, much later, but for the time being, I felt good, accomplished. Soon, they'd all be gone, and the Keeper would release me from my stone prison.

I was wrong, of course.

Two envoys shocked me more than I managed to rile them. The first, Lenita of Croi Croga. The day Felipe got swarmed, and she removed her protective gear to save him should've indicated she'd be harder to budge than the average Poler. Mids were tough. They had to be. The Razing had burned their nations to ash, so they had no other choice but to stand their ground. Since the billowing sheets had worked wonders on the Svinjan, I tried the same with Lenita. Instead of peeing and fleeing, she sat straight up, pulse throbbing in her neck. Was she terrified? Undeniably. But she didn't succumb. She stared me straight through, as though she could see me – she couldn't – and declared, "You're gonna have to try much harder than that." If I hadn't already respected her before, I did then. More, I regarded her with nearly the same veneration as the Keeper.

Vinícius, Lenita's counterpart from Bizou, the only Mid besides her still remaining with Felipe gone, didn't so much shock me as wholly ignore me. He was fearful, blanket pulled up to his chin, but never acknowledged my presence. I'd have to circle back around to the Mids after devising a more convincing approach.

The most bewildering encounter proved to be Enzo of Raptoria. A Poler, no less. With long inky hair, a stern face, and rigid posture, he could've been one of my kin atop the citadel. Nothing I did stirred him. In fact, my impish pranks only delighted him. Though brave, Lenita was afraid like any human. But this…thing, the way his eyes rippled and gleamed like black waves as they followed me in the dark, the way he twitched, impossibly fast, unnatural, made me – a gargoyle! – shudder. He was *off*. I eventually fled, and his cackling, like a spiteful crow, nipped every step.

CHAPTER FOURTEEN

Voids

Naokah pinched her nose as they pushed through the veranda door. "Divine Daughter."

"Hmm?" Brielle moved rigidly about the shadows, lighting the torches until they cast an ambient, almost cheerful glow. At least compared to the scene they'd left. Kjell, vomiting, writhing on the ground.

"You don't smell that?"

The Poler shrugged. "Musty like any place older than time. Maybe mildew?"

"Not mildew. This is rancid." Like the parcel of corned beef Matri had absentmindedly put in the cupboard instead of the icebox the night Tati left. With the blistering heat in Croi Croga, they'd awoken gagging the next morning. On a tight budget, the Hansen family forewent meat that week. Not that they could've stomached it anyway.

Brielle shrugged again, eyes red-rimmed and distant. The stench was the least of her worries. She didn't even complain when Naokah chose the veranda to get back to their chambers.

"Do you want to see him?"

Brielle's sleeves hung limply by her sides, and it took her a moment to answer. "In the morning." She sniffed, wiping her cheeks, before facing Naokah full-on. "The healer won't let anyone visit tonight. Besides, he should be fine. He's tough to know, to love. Doubt even death could befriend him."

Naokah's pulse stuttered unexpectedly. "Oh, are you courting him—"

Brielle burst out laughing. "No. Never." She pulled out a crystal pin from her coiffure and shook her head. Blonde locks spilled over her shoulders, spritzing the room with orange vanilla, an improvement. "Only friends. Our nations are closely aligned, you know. His father's the largest wing-power producer, and my mother has the most vineyards, so we rely on each other. Our grape pulp feeds his aviaries. His aviaries ensure our vineyards are pollinated. We've known each other since we were young." The Poler turned her back to Naokah, then peeped over her shoulder. "Would you mind?"

"Sure," Naokah chirped after clearing her throat multiple times. She gathered Brielle's hair, so long and silky and utterly foreign in a Mid's hands, and pushed it aside to reach the satin bow, which sat low – beneath the wings of the Poler's shoulder blades that glistened in the torchlight, below the pearly buds of her backbone, to the very base of her spine. Naokah's hands fumbled with the unruly knot. Brielle quivered with repressed laughter until the ribbon surrendered.

"Thanks." Brielle spun around and twisted out of her skirts, standing before Naokah in nothing more than a slip. A slip now transparent from perspiration.

Naokah averted her gaze and sidled back. She'd seen Lenita nude numerous times, but they were sisters. It wasn't proper to see Brielle this way, especially now. Brielle had just witnessed her childhood friend nearly die. She was vulnerable. Naokah's eyes trailed a black fish with luminescent whiskers, long as a cat's, that circled the Poler's pile of skirts. "Has Kjell always been a prick or is that something he grew into?" she asked, not looking up.

Brielle snorted. "Not always. Had an accident as a young boy. Scarred his hand, perhaps his soul. He's had an edge to him ever since. Doesn't help that his father's king of pricks. You think Kjell's an ass? His sire is far worse. Arrogant, loud, domineering. It's a wonder he turned out as well as he has." She moved to the hearth, lit the logs, and sat on a floor pillow. "Anyway, join me? I don't bite, only nibble."

Naokah turned to the wall so as not to gawk at Brielle. She blinked. Motion, from the mural. The woman with butterfly-covered nipples now glared at the hearth. "It's not *your* bite I worry about."

"This place is worse than I expected. But your sister did vanish overnight. Perhaps the murderer...I mean kidnapper...is still here, waiting within these very walls."

Naokah heaved like she'd been gut punched. Lenita wasn't dead. "You're not helping."

"Sorry. Was trying to inspire you to come closer. Did it work?"

"No."

"I have wine."

Naokah let out a nervous laugh. "Shocking."

"I know. Now, will you stop acting strange and keep me company?"

"Strange?"

"Yes. You keep staring at that mural like she's alive."

Naokah wasn't so sure she wasn't. "Haven't you felt like someone is watching you?"

"I'm used to it. Must be my captivatingly good looks."

Naokah's sigh stretched into a yawn. It was no use. The Poler hadn't smelled the stench from earlier, nor had anyone seen the girl from the exterior cliff. The mural, after a quick glimpse, stared blankly across the bedroom as before. Exhaustion was playing foul tricks on her.

"Don't make me finish this bottle alone."

How nice it'd be to bury her dread and relax. Getting to know Brielle better would've been a bonus, but she needed to search for answers tonight when everyone was asleep. When the Praxis picked up, she'd have even less time to solve her sister's disappearance. Yet, if she appeased her new friend, maybe she'd drink her grief away, pass out, and give Naokah ample time to explore.

"Fine." She twisted around, and her breath caught in her throat.

Golden hair flowed over Brielle's shoulders, and flames danced over her cheekbones. She was breathtaking, and she knew it, like she knew Naokah was intrigued. Was grief compelling her to flirt, or an ulterior motive, or maybe, just maybe, Brielle was actually attracted to Naokah too? On wonky knees, she followed Brielle's lead, dropped the remnants of her gown, and sat on the pillow opposite in her slip. She wrapped her arms around herself, exposed and vulnerable to a woman who could've been royalty.

Brielle passed Naokah a goblet of red wine. "To new friends."

She clinked her glass with Brielle's, but as she tried to drink, her hand shook. The Poler smirked. Naokah cursed herself and took a sip. The wine was dry, velvety, like eating a tart plum a few days shy of harvest. "Who do you think poisoned Kjell?"

"Not like he's made loads of friends." Brielle took another gulp. "Maybe Mila."

"Impossible. Not a brutal bone in her body."

"Even the meekest beasts, when cornered, their fangs come out. Best remember that." She held Naokah's gaze then; fire and something just as intense glowed in those mossy depths. Dread.

"That a warning?"

"Not at all, but none of us came here to make friends."

"We don't have to shred other envoys on the way to the top, though."

"Cute." Brielle cocked her head, more locks falling over her arm. Twin violet circles pressed through the thin silk of her slip.

"What's cute?" she asked, trying to look anywhere else.

"That you think we can all be amiable."

"Shouldn't we try to get along? We could be allies. Share in Abelha's wealth."

"With that naïveté, no wonder your sister fell, if all Crogans think along the same lines."

"She didn't fall," Naokah snapped. "She won. Then someone took her."

"Or killed her. Yes. That's a strong possibility." Brielle's pupils were pinpricks. "That's the thing about power. It's typically seized. Before the Razing, there were monarchs who claimed it was their birthright to rule. Those without their bloodline were forced to kneel. This Keepership—" she shook her head, "—they think by competing for the position, that makes it more diplomatic. May the best person win. But those on the outside have no idea who the Keeper tramples along the way. It's no different than the past, in truth."

"But anyone, no matter their blood, if they're determined enough, can win."

"Anyone who doesn't mind playing the politics and pissing on their morals, yes."

Lenita, unscrupulous? Never. "If competing for the Keepership is so dishonorable and moral-shattering, why are you competing?"

"I never said I was honorable." She winked. "Besides, there's much more at play than just a creepy citadel full of bees." She stopped then, lips working like she wanted to say something else, but changed her mind. "Anyway, let's talk about something, I don't know, less dreary?"

"Like?" she said, too defensive. Brielle's words about Crogans had rubbed her wrong. The wine, strong as it was, had done nothing to smooth the irritation. How quickly lust could turn into anger.

"I've offended you. I'm sorry. Were you close with your sister?"

Used to be. Her throat squeezed. "You just said we needed to change the subject. Tell me, how'd you learn how to sew?"

Brielle smiled shyly, swirling her wine. "My uncle. He was a brilliant designer. When I was little, too little to help at the vineyards, he'd let me accompany him while he worked on gowns for the northern balls. He used to let me pick out the trim, the gems, even the fabric."

"Sounds like a wonderful man."

"He raised me. My mother was always gone, running the vineyards, and my father died when I was a baby. I don't remember him."

Absent mothers. A theme, it seemed. "What happened to your uncle?"

Brielle's eyes misted. "He had a huge heart, his greatest strength *and* weakness. He spent the off-season volunteering at Mid refugee camps in southern Vintera. A man masquerading as a refugee accompanied my uncle to his tent for supplies. When he reached into his trunk, the wretch bludgeoned him and robbed him while he bled out."

"I'm sorry." She squeezed Brielle's hand. Although they sat inches from the hearth, it was ice cold, unlike Naokah's outrage. Hadn't Mid refugees suffered enough without scoundrels taking advantage of their displacement and sullying their reputation? "I know it's hardly the same, but...."

"Loss is loss. No one has a monopoly on hardship. Go on." The Poler returned an encouraging squeeze.

"My aunt is gone too. After getting in a spat with my matri, she stormed off and never returned. Lost my mother the same day. She stopped talking. Just waits on the porch, day in, day out, waiting for Tati to come home."

"I think that may be worse than death, the lack of closure."

A faded image of Matri and Tati, she and Lenita holding hands, giggling as the adults sang off key in a cloudcane patch, the sunset spilling over them like rhubarb syrup, pricked Naokah's eyes. Lenita was missing, Tati had chosen to leave, and Matri, deathly silent, was as good as gone. No closure, indeed.

"It's just—" Brielle tucked hair behind her ear, "—some people... we don't know what their presence alone fills, until they're no longer here."

Truly. Lenita's absence had shaken Naokah and, after months apart, she realized a humbling truth: her sister was like the wind – the depth of her aid and importance wasn't fully understood until she was gone. And, just like the world that had taken her for granted, Naokah, too, risked sundering like the Razing. Sorrow was compounded when one had to bear it alone.

"I'm not your aunt, and you're certainly more feminine than my uncle, but I say, we can help fill that void for each other?" Brielle looked more genuine, more open now than Naokah had seen. She scooted closer and turned over Naokah's hand, tracing her nails along the soft skin of her wrist to her elbow. Back and forth, back and forth.

Warm, tingling currents coursed Naokah's arm, eddying in her chest. Her heartbeat growing more sporadic with each iteration. Brielle's sincerity, that rawness, paired with the wine, her sweet, beckoning scent, led Naokah to recklessly lean in, to pause, to close her eyes. But no brush of lips met hers. Only the clatter of someone moving, rising.

Her eyes shot open, cheeks burning, as the Poler grabbed her pile of skirts.

"I'm...I'm...I just. I can't." Brielle swept out of Naokah's room, thunking the lavatory door shut.

Had she completely misread the situation? How would she face Brielle in the morning? She grabbed the half-empty bottle of red, climbed into bed, and slumped against the pillows, though they could've been hard as boulders with how cold and alone she felt. Not bothering with formalities, she yanked out the cork and made friends with the wine, filling her void with something far less appealing than the Poler, and waited for the lights to fade outside, so she could go explore.

CHAPTER FIFTEEN

A Simple Solution

Although I managed to instill fear in most of the envoys, I failed at turning them against one another, so I searched for another course to drive them away and earn the Keeper's trust. My uneasiness hadn't waned since they arrived and, with the telltale marching thundering across the sea floor, my efforts would soon be diverted to handle the upcoming scrim attack. Time wasn't my friend.

The sun's coral lashes blinked over the violet mountains, and the air was thick with dewy promise. Ignoring a disapproving glare from the eldest, I pushed out my glimmer to follow the group as the gardener guided them through the vertical flowerbeds. Far away from the citadel, the isle's border, it took all my concentration to stretch thin as mist and maintain a presence, following Ettori's words. His olive eyes gleamed as he answered their questions. The only thing that rivaled his passion for the chef was his green children.

Despite the darkness lurking within the citadel, and on the rare occasion the fog cleared, Abelha could be enchanting: sky-high terraces, hedge mazes, and lush, flower-frocked hills, all threaded together with silver streams. The group stood before the interior border, which was carpeted with flowers. Foxgloves were the most prominent, cascading down the walls like strings of bells.

"Lovely as they are lethal," Ettori said, "but to humblebees, they're the finest vintage."

The flower pillars were a stark contrast to the exterior – vast droves of brambles and porcupine shrubs. The barbed spines were long as swords and oozed with poison that liquified innards. Even the most dim-witted warrior would've never tried to lay siege to Abelha unless they desired a slow, agonizing death.

One of the Polers, Enzo, I surmised from his onyx locks, leaned close to Lenita. His whispering was too low to decipher, but she elbowed him in the side. He pitched forward, hair rustling, emitting something between a growl and a snicker. Did she sense the Poler's eeriness too? His cackling from the other night still haunted me. Unfazed, Lenita glared at the Poler and moved closer to the gardener, hanging on every word he said. It wasn't hard to tell – she wanted, rather needed, the Keepership more than anyone else. No surprise then, that her competition kept chiding her. I didn't like any of them, especially her, but I respected her.

Something about the small woman in baggy linens resonated with me. Maybe it was her drive, her persistence, her aptitude and good nature, but what pulled me closest, like sutures in a healing wound, was our mutual solitude. That despite our desire to be close to others, to save the people we cared about, we were pushed away, rejected, unwanted. We were alone, but together in that loneliness. Still, I shrugged off my benevolent feelings. I couldn't allow myself to soften for her. She was an envoy and, like all of them, had to go if I wanted to demonstrate my loyalty to the one true Keeper.

The shadow of a bird swooped over the envoys, but as it dove down, no doubt spotting some bees for breakfast, it hit the translucent dome overhead. With such speed, such momentum, the poor creature died on impact, its flesh sizzling, sieving through the mesh like pasta. I gagged, as did the envoys, but then an idea squeezed through with the carcass. The new moon was tomorrow. I couldn't infiltrate the citadel and crush the envoys' throats like I did the scrim, but what if I were to simply let one through? Could the solution be that simple?

I reeled my awareness back from the vertical gardens to the Keeper, who was walking along the nursing wing, serenading the baby bees. The larvae wriggled at her voice, and my eyes welled up. Though my past self must've committed a steep crime to earn her hatred, to be imprisoned inside a grotesque, my current, hole-riddled brain yearned not only for her approval but her touch. I sighed, my glimmer snapping back into my dungeon, and began devising a plan. Hopefully the scrim could finish what I started. The size of a fingernail, what harm could it possibly do beyond that?

CHAPTER SIXTEEN

Razing Close

When the last of the lights and late-night noises dimmed, Naokah pulled on her robe, grabbed a lantern and, ignoring how the mural's eyes followed her, slipped onto the veranda, leaving Brielle's rejection, the savvy's eerie familiarity, and Kjell's poisoning behind in her chambers to deal with later.

It had cooled down outside, relatively – from stifling to tepid – but the fog was thick as ever, blanketing the bee sculptures and strings of lanterns, rendering her own useless. Were it not for the trickle of moonlight seeping through the ivy-choked trellis above, she wouldn't be able to see a foot ahead. Still, bristly shadows played over the mist that clawed at her robe, and Naokah couldn't help but feel like she was in the Scorned Son's afterscape, wading through his Sea of Sorrows, spirits of betrayers trying to drown her. She rubbed her eyes and growled. It would've been so much easier to search for clues inside. But she was safer out here.

Naokah took a right, and damp floorboards squeaked beneath her toes. She'd forgotten her slippers. She shrugged it off. Maybe the discomfort would keep her sharp. From what she gathered on her last stroll around the veranda, the citadel had six sides with four main wings that branched off. The hive halls took up most of the fortress's middle. She crept by the envoys' glass doors, all dark, all asleep. As she stifled a yawn, red flashed at the western end.

She snuffed her lantern and held her breath. Who was up this late? Hushed whispers snarled the fog. High pitched, one was angry. Naokah should've turned back and returned to her chambers. The closer she got to the voices, the more her stomach stirred, but the exchange might've been a clue about Lenita.

"Isn't time," said a woman.

"No choice," rasped another. "Happening again."

"But if we don't—"

Cold fingers dug into her arm, jerking Naokah around.

"What are you doing here?" A shadow eclipsed her. Blue light filtered from above, sharpening the woman's features as she scowled. Hair pulled back in a tight copper bun, she wore a staff uniform, but a braided cord wrapped her shoulder. A sentry.

"Couldn't sleep," Naokah said.

A muscle ticked in the guard's cheek, and she crossed her arms. "So, you trespassed into the Keeper's wing for what? Figured she'd read you a bedtime story?"

"But this is the veranda—"

"Which is part of her wing."

"I didn't know. I was just…looking for the library, wanted to get some studying in before tomorrow's tour."

"And you thought the library would be out here?" The guard narrowed an eye, and Naokah winced. She wasn't a keen liar. "You'll have time to visit the library after orientation. It's best you head back to your chambers."

"Right. Sorry." She padded back the way she came.

"Wait," whispered the sentry.

She froze, not turning. "Yes?"

"It's not a good idea to venture out after dark. You were lucky tonight. I caught you. But next time you might not be."

Naokah spun around, but the sentry was already gone.

★   ★   ★

"Naokah," murmured a silken voice.

Her eyes popped open to nothingness. As her vision adjusted, unfamiliar curves and shadows loomed over her. She blinked a few times. This room was too big, too impersonal, lacking the warm bouquet of baking spices and cloudcane, her siblings' sweaty feet and Patri's muddy boots to be her shanty. She fumbled with her comforter, the velvet purring against her fingers. She swallowed, throat clicking. The citadel.

"Naokah," said a woman beside her. By the mural.

She jolted up. "Who's there?"

Cool air scurried over her exposed arm. She yanked the covers to her chin, forting herself between the headboard and wall of pillows. Mist trickled over the foot of her bed, her knees, floating closer.

"I...said," Naokah chattered, "who's there?" Pulse loud at her temples, she strained to hear.

A cold finger stroked her brow. She whipped back, breath tight in her chest. A translucent woman, butterflies fluttering over her breasts, grinned down. The lady from the mural. Naokah sank into her pillows. The mural's vile smile broadened, stretching into an abyss. A faint buzz trailed. Then more, collective, deafening. Naokah peeped through her pillows and yelped – a cloud of bees swarmed from the woman's jaws.

★   ★   ★

"Get up." Naokah's covers were pulled back, and pale light washed over her face. "You don't want to be late for your first day." Brielle crawled onto the foot of Naokah's bed and started jumping when she didn't move.

Naokah shot her a glare before swiveling to the wall. The mural was back to normal. A nightmare, then. Likely from exhaustion. But the late-night conversation outside had been real. What was *happening again*? Was the Poler's poisoning connected to Lenita's disappearance? A dull pain thudded behind her eyes. And Brielle wasn't helping. The bouncing mattress was going to make her puke.

"Would you cut that out?" Naokah groaned, rubbing her temples.

"Not a morning person?" Brielle asked mid-air. Her chiffon trousers flowed around her like wings.

"Is anyone?"

Brielle grinned but didn't stop.

Naokah grabbed the nearest pillow and launched it, hitting the Poler right in the face. Brielle giggled, unfazed. Annoyingly energetic, but Naokah would take it over the coldness she'd anticipated. If Brielle was upset about Naokah's blunder last night, she didn't show it. Good. She could beat herself up enough for the both of them.

"Is there at least cacao?" she huffed, sitting upright. The barbs of what promised to be a fierce headache warned her to medicate quickly.

"Cacao?" Brielle's nose crinkled. "Oh, right. A Mid thing?"

"A poor thing." Naokah yawned. "Only costs a bushel of cloudcane for a quarter sack of cacao shells."

"Still pretty steep for a by-product Zerşilians used to toss into the gulf."

"Can we delve into world economics and injustices later?"

Brielle sprang off the bed with all the grace of a dancer and pulled the door open. The kitchen staff had left a crystal tray with a kettle and porcelain cups. She brought it bedside. Notes of something roasted and nutty wafted in.

"Real coffee?" Naokah perked up. Tati once brought home a sack of coconut rum roast from southern Zerşil. Naokah had guzzled her cup despite scalding her tongue. It was that good. Her one and only encounter with coffee, drink of the divine. She blushed, recalling the close encounter with the beguiling Dazarin last night. That's what he'd smelled of. And chocolate. Her traitorous mouth watered. She hated herself for being attracted to any of the Polers, falling right into their schemes.

"Almond hazelnut, my favorite. Cream or sugar?" Brielle asked, pretending to be a maid. Naokah tamped down the irritation that this was the closest the Poler had likely ever been to waiting on someone.

Brielle found it funny. Naokah didn't. Any amusement would have to wait until that first sip.

"Black as Kjell's soul," Naokah blurted.

Brielle's face pinched.

Naokah winced. "Sorry, I—"

Brielle passed her the coffee without another word.

Hand jittery, Naokah picked up the delicate cup and took a sip. Sharper and stronger than cacao, like liquid velvet. But lukewarm. It had been sitting there awhile, yet the effects were all the same. Instant energy cropped up from her bones like cloudcane sprouts.

"Any word on his condition?"

Brielle shook her head, hair lustrous in the violet light. "Tried visiting this morning, but the surgery was locked. Suppose they'll update us at orientation."

Naokah gulped the rest of her coffee and pushed off the bed, ankles popping as she hit the floor. Beneath the glass, a scaly black fish, startled by her movement, zipped through a tunnel of algae.

"Sorry." She reached out to place a hand on Brielle's shoulder, then stopped. Last night's humiliation still lingered. "Speaking ill of Kjell, especially when he's in this…condition was insensitive."

"He acts like a jerk, but that's only a mask. He's insecure. It doesn't excuse his behavior, I know. Still, it has me worried. The first night here and poisoned? It could've been any of us."

Naokah bit her tongue. The citadel was strange, the murals and hives chilling, but the murder attempt wasn't random. Either Kjell had irked the wrong person or knew something he shouldn't. Maybe something to do with Lenita. And now, if he recovered, she'd be shortsighted not to befriend him and find out just what that was.

After she pulled on her scamall top and trousers, she headed for the veranda door, then stopped short, breath hitching. Rain poured through the trellis, drenching the floorboards. Naokah slowly twisted back to find a smug Brielle, never a fan of the humid, outdoor passageway, standing by the hallway door.

★   ★   ★

A flash, beneath her. Naokah recoiled, then her eyes adjusted. Just one of the many fish swimming under the corridor floors. The soft lull pulled her attention to the hive wall.

"Sure are jumpy," Brielle said with a snort, tugging her into the next hall. "No more coffee for you."

Naokah smiled weakly. Pale geometric shapes in green, violet, and blue filtered in from the turrets. But before she could enjoy this rare beauty, murmurs chirred from the murals on her left, raising the hair on her arms. She rubbed her eyes. Delusions. All delusions. She needed more sleep.

She sped after Brielle until the murals ebbed; a line of gilded picture frames took their place. Each held a large portrait of a Keeper on the day they swore in, the traditional ruby videira cresting their ears. A small inset showed all at the end of their tenure, passing on the shiny earring to their successor. A mix of women, men, androgynous. All boasted the long hair of Poler nations, eyes glittering with hunger the day they started, shifting to weariness upon retiring.

"They look…miserable." Brielle frowned.

Naokah lifted a shoulder. "It's a tough job." But the Poler was right. Upon handing their position over, they looked as wretched as she felt. She yawned. "Keepers of sorrow, more like."

The last picture held the current Keeper. Red was her color, bringing out her bronzed skin, her fierce eyes. She was lovely. The ruby earpiece looked as if it had always been part of her, like she was born into the Keepership. She didn't have an inset like the others as she hadn't chosen a successor yet. That wasn't the only difference, though. Naokah could've sworn a shadow billowed behind her like a cloak. Perhaps poor lighting. Naokah trailed her fingers along the dusty frames. How curious—

Buzzing, from above. Then a sharp sting to her pinky. Pulse spiking, Naokah collapsed.

Naokah was seven, skipping through the stalks of cloudcane. Lenita chased her. Not paying attention, Naokah grabbed a young blossom and squeezed a bee. It was like a dagger in her palm. Fire spurted through her fingers, her veins. The air vanished like someone stuck a bag over her head. Tilled soil cushioned her fall. Images without shape or form smeared her eyes, fading to black.

"Breathe." A waify figure with cropped hair stood over her. Lenita. She couldn't. The poison, she could feel it—

"You're panicking." Lenita placed a hand on Naokah's chest. "Breathe with me."

She inhaled, following her sister's steady breaths. Slowly, she calmed. Her head still pounded, but the mottled colors sharpened.

"Tears," she blurted.

"What?" asked her older sister.

"Your eyes...are wet," she croaked. "You crying?"

"Don't be silly." Lenita wiped her face. "Got sand in my eyes."

"Naokah. Hello!" Brielle stood over her with wide eyes. "What's wrong?"

"I..." She flipped her hand over. Blood beaded on her pinky. Her eyes sprang back to the wall, and she sputtered a sigh. A nail had pricked her, not a bee.

CHAPTER SEVENTEEN

Regrets

Memories never came to me in full bolts of cloth but rather ripped strips, moth-eaten and useless. Sometimes I hated not knowing who I was, and others, I was grateful. I had a knack for havoc. And after the mistake I'd made tonight, I wish I'd forgotten it too. But I couldn't.

What had I done?

Night hunkered over us, heavy with tension. Hearts in our throats and claws flexed, we waited. Leaves chimed, branches rattled, phantom boots stomped over mud, and the low, yawning hum grew to thunder as the scrim rushed in. And my kin – my noble kin, I'd misjudged them – completed their duties. They didn't deviate from their purpose. But I was hung up on proving myself. Of rescuing the Keeper from the imposters who sought her title. To uncover a past that wasn't worth uncovering. A terrible mistake.

It was just one wee scrim. I'd squashed its clan as they zoomed around me, attempting to squeeze through the ashlar cracks. After scanning the other gargoyles crushing the droning shadows and ascertaining I wasn't under their watch, I let it pass. At first, nothing happened. I relaxed, swatting the others like mosquitoes. The darkness, plush as velvet, settled over the towers, my wings, folding me into bliss.

But then inside, a scream. Shrill, resonating.

Another.

And another.

The haunting cries intensified, vibrating the stone, and then the citadel seemingly belched up a graveyard. A stench that would never fade during my tenure, only fester. Should I force my glimmer inside? Try to capture it? No. I'd give myself away. Besides, more scrim than usual fought tonight. It was already blacker than black, but with their stormy flight, the air thickened, shimmering like hot oil. I tensed, too terrified, too ashamed to face my kin. They couldn't know it was me.

No. They could.

Only your loud, obnoxious thoughts, the elephant-seal had said.

"We have failed," said the eldest, beak dropping.

"How?" I asked, hoping he couldn't smell my guilt.

His milky glimmer shifted inside his feline-crow grotesque, scowl landing on me. "They've never been able to enter the citadel because the passage was hidden. Until now. Someone has forsaken us."

I swallowed a cold lump. More scrim buzzed over the eldest's shoulders, heading for the turrets. He batted them away.

"What now?" I asked.

"We clean up the mess," he said, already resigned. "Or try, anyway."

CHAPTER EIGHTEEN
Without a Second Thought

Rain hissed against the turrets with vengeance, inundating the great hall with hollow pings. After Naokah's bee sting relapse and subsequent meltdown, she'd returned to her chambers before breakfast to scream into her pillows – a purge to avoid future humiliation.

It didn't work.

She used the veranda. Even with her brown cape, she ended up damp. Naokah now shivered, but not from the downpour. The leering eyes from yesterday had returned. She peered around the candelabras sprouting from the table like dead trees. The other envoys spoke in muted tones about Kjell's poisoning over the clatter of flatware. Did they not feel it too?

A cold finger stroked Naokah's cheek. Her breath flickered, and she shut her eyes, exhaling like Lenita had shown her. The woman from the mural was just that – a woman from a mural. Painted, not three-dimensional, not here in the great hall stroking her face, and certainly not showering her in bees. Her pulse slowed, and she opened her eyes.

Only envoys.

Exhaustion was to blame. *Stay keen*, Patri had warned. Tonight, one way or another, she'd force herself to get some sleep.

Clisten and Dazarin sat across from her and engaged in a heated debate. A string of pearls spiraled around Clisten's braid, an inventive creation with wispy fins spiking from the center, a sharktail, and every time he disagreed, it plunked against the table. Dazarin would counter by slamming his inked arm down, his chunky ring clinking against the wood, vibrating the table and startling Mila and Laerte, whose only accessories were blank stares. The Mids had apparently gotten about as much sleep as she did.

She wolfed down her cheese pastry without tasting it. A mistake. She sipped on her coffee, hoping the steaming hazelnut would help break down her greasy breakfast. Luckily, Brielle was more focused on scouting out her competition than talking. The mere thought of carrying on a conversation without grimacing only increased her stomach's gurgling. She'd expected an awkward encounter after her disastrous attempt at a kiss, and especially after her melodramatic performance in the Hall of Keepers, but Brielle was fine. Thank the Divine Daughter. What had Naokah expected after knowing her all of a day? The Poler was an ally, a friend at most. Nothing more.

Brielle winked at her – blurring that final thought.

Naokah absently grazed the grapes on her plate, then stopped. Grapes weren't furry. Nor did they drone. She jumped back, knocking over her chair. The other envoys jolted up too.

"What's wrong?" Brielle tugged Naokah's sleeve, but all she could do was point. The Poler followed her finger, then swiveled back with a concerned frown. "What?"

"You don't see them?" she choked, eyes pinned to her wriggling plate. Hundreds of bees crawled over it.

Brielle shook her head.

"Impossible." Naokah looked to the other envoys, hoping for someone, *anyone*, to acknowledge she wasn't losing it, but was only met with winces. She rubbed her eyes. Brielle was right. There were no bees, only grapes.

"Shall we get the healer?" Brielle asked gently.

"No." Naokah feigned a yawn. "I'm fine. Just need more sleep, clearly."

The rest of breakfast blurred by with envoys sneaking glances at Naokah. She tried to ignore them and sipped on her coffee, wishing it were wine. The bees had seemed so real. Furry and pulsating against her fingertips. At least her stomach's bleating had lessened. A small blessing. Two upsets were enough for the rest of her stay. Too bad Brielle had seen both. No doubt, she was relieved she'd bowed out of a kiss with a madwoman.

Naokah trailed the others, a flurry of pastel chiffons and silks, to orientation. They passed through a door wreathed in trumpet flowers to a dome outside the citadel. With the rain, the conservatory had fogged up, washing the room in a thin, hoary light. White blossoms climbed overhead, spicing the air with nutmeg and home.

She drifted back to her kitchen with Matri, Tati, and Lenita, baking ginger cookies that melted in her mouth like warm butter. One of their favorite pastimes, before the latter two vanished and Matri lost her will to speak. Lenita, true to form, had helped with the first batch and now lazed on a woven chair, dunking a cookie in coconut cream. Naokah just shook her head, but Tati called her out, sprinkling flour in her hair.

"Tati!" Lenita jumped up, spilling cream down her trousers. "Why'd you do that?"

"Baking cookies was your idea. And now that you've had your fill, you're forcing little sister to do all the work?" She tsked and winked at Naokah. Tati often stood up for her.

Lenita shook off the cream, earning a dirty look from Matri. "But she likes baking, right, Nao?"

"When you help." Naokah cocked her chin, leaning against Tati, who laughed.

"See?"

"Fine. I'll give you a hand." Her sister grabbed an egg and tossed it. "Catch."

Naokah did, unfortunately. The egg exploded, oozing through her fingers. Matri snorted, grabbed a cup of sugar, and flung it at Lenita. It pelted her pants, and she gasped before bursting into giggles. Then the room whirled into a tempest of baking supplies. By the time Patri returned, bewildered as he was amused, the cabinets and women alike dripped with eggs and flour.

"Any gingers left for me?" he teased, shells and sugar crackling beneath his boots.

"Hello?" Brielle tugged Naokah down on the bench beside her. "Something wrong, love?"

"No. I'm just...doesn't it seem less eerie here?"

The Poler's eyes, bright as emeralds, rolled over her competition. "Fewer shadows."

"And murals and bees," Naokah said, still in a daze.

"You don't like bees?"

"It's just nice, the quiet. The bees kept me up last night."

"Are you frightened of them?"

Scondra tai. She chose her next words carefully. "No. They're... brilliant, hardworking. I respect them."

"You can respect something and still be terrified of it. Perhaps even respect it *because* you are terrified." Brielle gave her a roguish look. "But that's interesting. An envoy for Keeper, Ruler of the Bees, and you're scared of them?"

"No one rules the bees," said a sharp voice from the front of the conservatory. "Not even their queens."

Both women started. The savvy had arrived, and worse, they'd overheard their discussion. But Samara wasn't upset. They ran a finger over the jasmine climbing the lectern.

"Can anyone tell me what the Keeper's role is?"

"Apparently, it's not ruling," said Dazarin up front, placing his bulging, inked arms behind his head and lounging back like he was at the beach. Did he take anything seriously?

Silence.

Samara tsked, walking between the aisle of envoys, red pants swishing. "Surprising. Such a historic year, hosting the Praxis for Keepership so close to the last cycle, and not a single one of my envoys knows the answer to the most important question that will drive their tenure?"

"The same role you'd serve in your family," said Naokah.

The Polers chuckled, but Samara didn't. Their gaze crept over her like a high tide, patient but persistent. "What role is that, Naokah?"

"You protect them no matter the cost, even sacrifice your life if that's what it takes."

No one laughed this time. The hall stilled, save Brielle fidgeting beside her.

"Precisely." Samara returned to the front, braid thunking their back. As they spun around, the clouds split, and the sun gleamed off their square jaw. "The Keeper will be updated on your progress daily. After reaching senior phase, you'll have the honor of gracing her presence. Not a moment before. The bees are her family. You are not."

"When's senior phase?" asked Clisten.

Samara's face went grim, unimpressed by ignorance. "Anyone?"

"Week seven," said Brielle.

The savvy nodded. "And why does the Praxis run for sixteen weeks?"

"A queen bee is created in sixteen days, but it takes much longer to form a Keeper, the guardian of bees."

"Excellent. Glad someone's prepared."

Brielle beamed, and Naokah returned her smile, even though adrenaline-fueled rivalry charged her veins.

"All right. Before I give you the grand tour and you meet the staff who happen to be *my* family, who you'll treat with nothing less than respect, as they are the worker bees who keep this citadel running, each of you will come up front and give a brief introduction." Groans resounded, and Naokah tensed; public speaking was as nerve-racking as the indoor hives, but the savvy laughed. "I wouldn't complain if I were you. Easiest step of the Praxis."

★   ★   ★

By the time introductions were complete, Naokah viewed the envoys in a warmer light, even the Polers. From wealthy nations, she'd assumed they bought their spots to compete.

That wasn't the case.

Clisten had constructed a line of farrowing houses that filtered the Razing's ash from the air, allowing the lungs of newborn piglets the chance to expand properly before being exposed to the elements. Using her uncle's stitching techniques, Brielle had sewn soft, bubble greenhouses that expanded the vineyards' growing season three extra months. Even Dazarin, the jester she'd yet to take seriously, had developed a hybrid strain of coffee-cacao plants, cacafe, he called them, making Naokah's mouth water. Mila and Laerte had worked together to win their respective bids. Mila was from Bizou, a Mid nation almost wholly ravaged by the Razing, yet still squeaked by on their almonds. Instead of tossing their shells, Mila had begun exporting them to neighboring Okse, Laerte's home known for cattle. The almond hulls provided the perfect amount of fiber for the cows, thus increasing milk production. In turn, Laerte had been exporting the by-product, manure, to Bizou, which nourished the almond trees, thereby burgeoning their harvest too.

You can respect something and still be terrified of it. Perhaps even respect it because you are terrified, Brielle had said about the bees. But perhaps she meant the competition. Naokah's contribution – spraying rosemary mint water on the base of cloudcane stalks to prevent spidermite infestations – no longer felt so grand. Lenita had one-upped her, as always, easily securing her Praxis bid. When a plague of soot locusts swept through southern Croi Croga, devouring the young cloudcane blossoms, it was her sister's idea to build bonfires between the open rows and smoke the voracious pests out. She'd saved sixty-seven farms that day. Naokah had never been prouder. Nor more envious. It was cold and lonely walking in her big sister's shadow, a shadow that, even after her disappearance, persisted.

Thankful that segment was over, Naokah was anxious to meet the staff. They, not the former envoys, were here the night Lenita disappeared. She'd already met Samara, the savvy. With their kind demeanor, they didn't strike her as guilty, but often the least suspicious was the one holding the knife. At least, that's how Patri's stories by the ice pit always ended. She liked the savvy, but they seemed to be hiding something, judging from their behavior at the ball. Naokah hadn't officially met the healer last night, as she was busy saving the northern prick, but she was also last in the line of suspects. Healers swore an oath to protect their patients, not to harm them. Still, she'd get a better reading today when the healer wasn't in a frenzy.

The rain finally stopped, and the clouds thinned. The class rose to follow the savvy, when the pounding of boots echoed from the hallway.

"Captain Avice," Samara welcomed the sentry. "Didn't expect you."

"Nor did I." The woman had a pretty face, high cheekbones, but her features were pulled into a scowl tighter than her bun. Naokah wrung her hands. The same sentry she'd run into last night. "The healer identified what poisoned Kjell. Foxglove."

Whispers shot through the group, and Brielle tottered beside her. Just yesterday, she'd scolded Naokah for trying to touch the cone-shaped flower.

"He'll be fine. If any of you care. The healer caught it early enough, but I find it interesting that on the day you all arrive, one of your pals falls ill to a flower only a fool would eat. So, let me remind you. The Praxis is about finding the best caretaker for the bees. Despite whatever ridiculous rumors you may've heard, it's not a slit-throat, stab-your-friend-in-the-back kind of deal. The only person you must compete against is yourself. And the hives will give us an answer. But, since someone has taken it upon themselves to eliminate the competition, be it known, now the citadel is on high alert. You're all being watched closely. I'll be making rounds this week, questioning each of you. I *will* find the guilty party. And you'll be charged as such." She hmphed, then left the hall as quickly as she'd entered, a smudge of angry red.

None of the envoys were here when Lenita disappeared, so why did the citadel assume it was one of them who poisoned Kjell and not the staff? Naokah tamped down her irritation. The clock above the savvy's head chimed through the silence, each tick pinging Naokah's sternum. Finally, Samara, raising their brows, waved for them to rise.

"Follow me closely," they said, looking over their shoulder. "Don't want you venturing off alone. Good way to get in trouble." Their eyes landed on Naokah and held. She swallowed hard. Had the captain told them about her late-night rendezvous? "We'll start the farthest out, tour the farm and ranch, the vertical gardens and barrier wall, then work our way back and finish in the great hall for our midday meal."

"Had hoped we'd start with the distillery," Brielle whispered. "Could use some strong melgo right about now."

Naokah almost wrapped an arm around her, but not after last night's rejection.

They filed through the flower-thatched door, directly into a sprawling hedge maze. Humidity smacked Naokah like a sticky hand. She let the others go ahead of her while she lagged behind. She preferred being able to see everyone, knowing where they were at all times. Brielle, after noticing Naokah's position, slowed to match her pace.

"It's only morning, and I'm already sweating like a vintner with a dying grape harvest. What possessed them to grow these walls this high? Like a pathway straight to the Razing."

The hedges were thick; only scant gray light filtered through. She glimpsed above Brielle and nearly tripped. The girl from yesterday glided atop the sky-high foliage. Her gauzy dress billowed up around her from a nonexistent breeze. Her eyes, big and bottomless, met Naokah's. Sweat hardened to sleet.

"Do you see her?" Naokah whispered.

"Where?"

"Up."

"I see a hedge. And a crow just suicided into the warded mesh. But no *her*. Unless you mean the bird. And I don't know how you could possibly tell from here that the bird is a girl."

Naokah rubbed her eyes. The girl was still there, but her face had darkened, matching her eyes. When she saw Naokah staring, she snarled, then leapt off the opposite side. Naokah ran to the wall, pulling the waxy leaves apart. No thud of a body. No shadow. Where had she gone?

"What?" Brielle asked, irritated.

"She just jumped off the hedge. It's a good twenty feet high. No way she survived."

Brielle grabbed her arm, tugging her forward. "The savvy told us no wandering. They're going to leave us behind if you don't hurry up."

"Tell me you saw her," Naokah pleaded, peeping back with every step. The shadows rolled over the path behind them like eaters of time, preventing her from returning.

"Would be a lie." She sniffed dismissively. "I'm impressed, though."

Naokah brushed Brielle's hand away, earning a wounded look. "Your grip was too tight," she said, rubbing her forearm. It wasn't. But Naokah couldn't juggle her deteriorating brain *and* a misguided heart. Brielle's touch gave her palpitations. "And what are you impressed about?" she pressed after a few beats of disquieting silence.

Brielle grinned. "Mids sure know how to relax. It's not even noon, and you're already floating on something supreme. Now—" she held out her palm, "—aren't you going to share?"

★   ★   ★

The fields were farther away than Naokah had imagined. In fact, Abelha was much bigger than she'd first given it credit for. It was as if the fog had unclasped its grip on the isle and sketched a bow, trying to redeem its frigid manners. Rolling hills covered in sunset red and purple foxgloves filled her view on each side. A small meandering stream cut through the western half, opening to a sparkling lake with a small island in the center. Unlike the Mid nations that had fallen to the Razing, Abelha was far south, missing its smoldering touch. The sun was still bright, though, despite the veil of thinning fog, and she should've brought a hat to shield her eyes. At least she didn't have Brielle's wavy locks, which now hung limp with sweat.

The Poler sighed every few minutes, and Naokah would've found that funny were it not for that eerie feeling of being watched. It had to be that girl in the white gown. She turned back about as often as Brielle sighed. The girl was never there, but that didn't ease the dread swelling in her belly with the gob of cheese bread. Lenita could've been anywhere. The lake they passed. Buried beneath foxgloves. Drowned at sea. Trapped in that cave of a citadel. The grottos in the south. Naokah was anxious to find her sister, but wasn't overly excited about the possibility, the very real, very evident possibility that Lenita could be more than missing.

What if she were dead? Would knowing what happened to her older sister ease her pain? Her family's? Could give them all closure, perhaps. Lightness fluttered beneath Naokah's rib cage as she pictured herself meeting with world leaders. They shook her hand with respect, with dignity, for she was the new Keeper. Maybe that's what she wanted. Without her sister's shadow, she could finally breathe.

No.

What kind of life could she live without Lenita? Despite their differences – and there were many – her sister had risen up when Matri faltered. Had mentored, raised, and loved her. Lenita was her better half in every way and, if soulmates did exist, Matri had given birth to Naokah's.

The flower mounds gave way to a valley hugged by a wall of mountains. As they got closer, the terrain grew steeper, blocking out the sun, leaving them in a cool shadow, as noted by Brielle cheering up and rolling her shoulders.

"Wow," was all Naokah managed.

"You can say that again." Laerte slowed beside her.

KEEPER OF SORROWS • 97

Naokah supposed any farm kid would've been awed. The mountains formed a large ring, cradling them like a giant's arms. But it wasn't their staggering height that stole her breath. Cultivated terraces rainbowed the mountains, abounding with vegetables and fruit.

"Wish Patri could see this," she said softly.

"Wish mine could too." Laerte crossed his arms. "Would've solved a lot of our problems."

Naokah nodded, eyes still wide on the innovative terraces. Croi Croga didn't have mountains like these. Just flatlands. Farmers had been squabbling over the lack of land since the Razing burned away most of their tiny nation.

A man in clay-stained trousers, long sleeves, and a wide-brimmed hat leaned over one of the middle terraces, plucking weeds around a tomato plant circled by wire mesh.

"That's Mateus, head farmer." Samara hiked up their trousers, pinning them above their calves, and wove around the mature plants, thick with red globes.

The envoys shared confused looks. Mateus wasn't close. Perhaps a quarter-mile up.

"Come on," yelled Samara without looking back. "Mateus is one of the hardest workers in Abelha. The farmer doesn't come to us. We go to him."

Groans commenced, especially from the Polers. Brielle was close behind, complaining. Naokah poured herself into each step, focusing on the damp, spongy soil, the whisper of brushed leaves. The terraces were steep, and her legs ached, but she welcomed the pain. It cleared the must from her lungs, flushing her skin. Fresh air was exactly what she needed.

"Naokah, well done." Samara smiled, then motioned to the farmer. "Meet Mateus."

"Miss," he said, voice husky. His terracotta eyes met hers briefly before returning to weeding.

"I envy your terraces, sir. They would be life-changing back home."

"I know," he said in perfect Midese. "Your home was once mine."

"But—"

"Didn't pick up on my accent?" He winked. "Don't blame yourself. Only comes out when I drink or curse. Moved here a lifetime ago. Had to, after the Razing took our farm."

Naokah's throat tightened. Another Crogan, here with her? Home seemed that much closer.

Gasping and wheezing, below. Samara scanned the approaching group, then stopped, eyes narrowing. "Where's Dazarin?"

Mutters and whispers, swishes of chiffon as the envoys turned, looking for him. Naokah peered over the bustle. No sea god.

"Last I saw him was in the hedge maze," Brielle said.

White flashed behind Naokah's eyes, cold slicking her neck. The girl had been in the maze. Had she taken him? But no one had seen the ghost except her. Besides, Dazarin wasn't small. Would need a squad of sentries to take him down.

Samara shared her unease, clenching their jaw. "Glorious. Anyway—" the savvy bobbed apologetically at the farmer, "—Mateus oversees one thousand seven acres. He, along with our humblebees, is how we survive. We have everything we could ever need only because of his hard work and expertise."

"Hey, look." Brielle pointed at a small creature with a bushy red tail. Its erect ears flicked. It twisted around, pointy face frozen between fight and flight.

"A fox," said Laerte, "I've never seen—"

The air whizzed, and the fox crumpled to the dirt. A white feather stuck in its side, a dart.

"Was that—" Brielle started.

"Necessary?" said Mateus, dropping his gun. "That beast you find so cute is destructive to my crops. Chews the roots right out of the ground. Worse, foxes love to tear apart hives. Can't resist the honey."

"So, you kill them?" Brielle crossed her arms over her chest.

"What else am I to do?" said Mateus evenly. "Can't ask the beast nicely to leave my crops and bees alone. Don't know how you handle things in the north, but here, there's one thing that governs every decision. Above all else, the only lives that matter here are the bees. Any threat, animal or *human*, will be crushed without a second thought."

CHAPTER NINETEEN

Panic

The threat of rain weighed down the air. Thunder growled, rattling the stained glass. The eldest called us to attention. Our bodies were stone, affixed to the towers spearing the night, but when we congregated, our glimmer undulated like an aurora.

"Each gargoyle is charged with their own wing. Find the scrim. Destroy the scrim. There will be no rest until we triumph. Understood?" The eldest's milky eyes pored over us.

"There were multiple screams," said the lamprey-lion. "How do we know there weren't more?"

"We don't. Nor do we know what vessels they could be hiding in." I swallowed hard. "As in, possession?"

The eldest twitched, and their beak flashed in the storm. "Aye, the staff, the envoys, anything sentient. Even the Keeper." Their voice dropped, along with my heart. No! Not her! I'd broken my duty to protect her, to save her. And instead, I unleashed evil into her home?

"We are the watchers of the citadel. Guardians of the night. We know the staff, the Keeper. You'll be able to tell if they're harboring a dark one, but Daughter forbid if any of the envoys were overtaken. They haven't been here long enough to establish behavioral patterns."

"What of the colonies?" asked the capybara-shark.

"I said anything sentient," snapped the eldest. "And if any of the queens were taken, their hives are at risk. A dark-tempered queen means a dark-tempered colony. The whole citadel is in danger."

"We can crush the scrim in their raw form," said the lion-elephant. "But what about when they're attached to a source?"

"I...I can't recall." The eldest grimaced. "It's been centuries since I've had to rip a scrim from a sentient."

Guilt soured my phantom tongue. "What happens to the host's soul?"

"Depends. The strongest fight the parasite, refusing to give in. Either they force the intruder out, or eventually, they hold their ground, and the intruder dissolves."

"And for those too weak?"

The eldest sighed, and their glimmer wavered like a candle on its last breath. "They submit, allowing the parasite to seize their vessel. The longer it stays, the weaker the primary soul becomes until it falls into a deep sleep and dies."

Panic condensed, rolling over the spires like storm clouds.

"But—"

"Enough!" The sky boomed, and icy rain gushed down. I shivered. "We've wasted too much time already. Search everywhere. Leave no corner unchecked. And, whoever slackened on their duties, I will find you. You will answer for your crimes, your destruction," they spat.

The eldest assigned me the south wing, where the envoys and a third of the bee colonies were housed. Did they know I was the traitor? Why else hand me the hardest wing to search?

I nodded a little too enthusiastically and forced my glimmer through the turret into the hallway flanked by murals and hives. Unlike humans, I couldn't simply walk through the corridors. I was soft, melting like sugar in water. Trying to ignore the marching – did it seem louder inside? – I used the walls, the mirrors, the torches to push my scattered awareness through, making my way into the first bedroom. Past the ocean of shadows and mauves, an amber eye blinked in the lavatory. A sconce. Not that I needed light anyway; my vision had adjusted like that of any creature of the night.

Face streaked in sweat, Lenita struggled in her sleep. I couldn't touch her, but I had the urge to wipe the moisture away. She looked vulnerable. A far cry from when she elbowed Enzo or saved Felipe. She was the greatest threat to the Keeper, the reason I let a scrim through in the first place, but I was still drawn to her. A thin line between love and hate, the saying went, and I perpetually straddled it.

I touched her temple, an echo of warm flesh and, consciousness rippling through me, I pushed. Soft, damp, like cornsilk after a good rain, I withheld a cry. I stroked her hair! If I'd only tried harder before, I would've never released havoc. So misguided, so stupid. I touched her cropped hair for vindication. My fingers whisked right through.

Again, I tried.

Nothing.

I pressed my lips together, muting a growl. What had changed? No matter how many times I reached out, my claws glided through her like air. She stopped moving, eyelids no longer fluttering. Perfectly still, how was I to know if she'd been taken? She now seemed at peace. Should I wake her?

Scraping, like knives on slate. Behind her headboard.

I froze. We weren't alone. Silly though it was, I wanted nothing more than to crawl under her blanket and hide from whatever haunted us. I pushed that alarm aside. I was a lost soul. Surely, our visitor wasn't as terrifying as me. I strained my ears, but heard nothing more. Could it have been the scrim, lurking, waiting to pounce? I should have detected its presence as I had outside. Yet, hadn't the eldest said the citadel was warded to prevent attacks? Gargoyles were an auxiliary layer of protection. Maybe they didn't sound like they did outside?

The mattress shifted, the blanket puddling my feet. Big yellow eyes with slitted pupils met mine, gleaming like a viper's. A scream scored my face, launching me into the wall. My motes scattered. Before I faded, a hiss that couldn't have arisen from anything ever alive turned my glimmer into slush.

CHAPTER TWENTY

Strained

The farmer's threat sucked at each step like mud as Naokah descended the steep terraces. The sun glowered through cracks of amassing clouds, and sweat streamed her back, goosebumps nipping her skin. She rubbed her arms, sleeves rustling. A Crogan wouldn't kill another Crogan, surely? Not Lenita. She'd have no sooner harmed a bee than flee from her responsibilities.

When wing-power prices doubled, and Patri was forced to purchase his first colony, the bees circled Lenita's wrists, skittering her cheeks, revering her like she was their queen. Her sister's ease around the very creatures that terrified Naokah had always stung her. Why hadn't the Divine Daughter bestowed her the same gift? Or something as worthy?

Naokah stepped on a soft patch and sank up to her calf, nearly nosediving off the slope were it not for a large hand that grabbed her arm. "Careful. If you fall, who will save me when the Polers decide to glue my trousers to a seat?" Twinkling eyes met hers. Laerte.

"Thanks." She offered an awkward smile as she fought to regain her footing.

He held her steady as she tried to extricate herself. "Was a bit callous, huh?"

"What?"

"The farmer? Killing the beast without pause. Thought perhaps that's what you were thinking about, why you were distracted?" He assisted with one final tug, and she was free. Crisp notes of compost and wet soil came with her.

"Of course," she sneered, and he flinched. "Sorry." She waved at her trousers, now caked with mud. "Ruined these, and it's only the second day."

"I hear once you win, they buy you a fancy new wardrobe. Whatever you want."

"Hah. When *you* win."

"One of us." He winked, copper cheeks glowing under a pocket of sunlight.

They were a little more than halfway down, lush terraces striping their path. Brielle had linked up with Clisten, the fins of his sharktail bouncing with each step as he laughed. The blonde's eyes met hers, twinkling. What was so amusing? She forced her gaze back down to the steep terraces. Laerte had already saved her once. No need for a sequel.

"I can tell Samara likes you."

"They don't like me." Naokah reminded the savvy of Lenita, and everyone loved Lenita. "I think they feel a kinship with any Mid. Probably feel the same about you. Do you know where they're from?"

"Okse, like me."

"See? Probably grew rice before the Keepership snatched them up."

"Squash, actually," an amused voice popped up beside them. They both cringed, but Samara only smirked. "One of the most abundant crops out there, squash. Also the most reliant on bee pollination. I do tend to root for the Mids, though. Growing up near the Razing is a tough life, but it prepares you for almost anything."

"How'd you end up here?" Naokah asked.

"I used to farm in the southwestern part of Okse, where the Weeping Sea and the Sea of Swarms converge."

Laerte winced. "The Scorned Son's Thumb, then?" he said more than asked.

The savvy nodded.

"Sorry, what?" asked Naokah.

"Rain clouds are usually seen as a blessing from the Divine Daughter, and they are, if they dissolve like they're supposed to. But when they don't and, without enough heat to burn them up nor wind to move them along, they're a curse. Will hunker down over acres of land like the Scorned Son's Thumb and, without sunlight, all the vegetation dies."

And she'd thought Croi Croga had it bad with the sweltering heat. "For how long?"

The savvy shrugged. "Let's just say I know a little too well how it feels to eat beetles and moss and whatever I could manage to catch. That aching void? A hunger that never, ever leaves you." An elegant brow lifted. "So yes. My money's on one of you. Don't disappoint me." Samara strode past without another word.

They shared a rueful look and followed the savvy down to the base. Naokah's calves still trembled from the descent as they joined the others. If Samara supported Mids, then they'd wanted Lenita to win. No way they took her. But then, who did?

* * *

Naokah smelled the ranch long before she saw it. Manure and hay streaked the muggy air. Pen after pen of pigs, cattle, and goats lay below the terraces like a patchwork quilt of stink. The clouds banded together, thicker than the hedge mazes, and darkened. With the Scorned Son's Thumb still fresh in her mind, she shivered. Could it happen here too?

Dazarin had yet to return, but no one seemed concerned. Flippant, with more interest in debauchery than actually competing, the rake likely took a tour of the maids' quarters instead.

Small feathery creatures ran about in the closest pen. Red, black, gold, and white, so fluffy one couldn't see their eyes or even their feet.

"Silkies," Laerte answered her squint. "Mild-mannered chickens. Make good pets, but not much meat on their bones. Kept for eggs, mostly." He reached through a gap in the wire and petted a fluffy red one. It crooned beneath his touch.

Squealing sliced through the humidity, and Laerte jerked his hand back. The silkies clucked, running to the far side of the pen. The noise intensified, rattled the roots of Naokah's teeth.

Strung up between two trees was a spotted hog, legs spread. Huge thing. A woman with a messy braid stood next to the squealing boar and pulled out a razor. Naokah averted her eyes. She ate meat like anyone else, but only because she didn't have to see it harvested.

"It's okay," Laerte whispered. "Just castrating him."

Naokah nodded but didn't step any closer. Nor did she look up. The tang of blood stained the air, followed by more wailing, then the rusty spray of iodine. A thud, a bellow, and the pig ran off, grunting his discontent with each wobbly step.

"This is Neves, head tender," said Samara, bowing to a thin, tan woman.

She jerked a nod, eyes shooting to a pen of piglets. The group was interrupting her. "Envoys," she said so softly, they all had to lean in. "Good to have you. Pardon the last patient. A boar that shouldn't have been a boar. Didn't realize we'd missed him."

A man with green glasses stepped out from under a willow, wiping blood on his trousers.

"Perfect. Two for one," said Samara while signing. "Our mercy, Mauricio. He's our first line of defense when we have any behavioral issues with our colonies."

"Nice to meet you," the mercy mouthed, signing.

"If you folks don't know handspeak, it would behoove you to learn." They patted the mercy on the back and only signed, "Everything all right?"

Mauricio gave Samara a strained look, eyed the envoys, then waved for them to accompany him under the weeping willow.

"What did Samara ask?" said Brielle.

"If everything was okay," Naokah answered absently.

"You sign?"

"My brother lost his hearing after…an accident." Another one of Tati's parting gifts.

"He didn't look like he was all right," said Brielle as she peered at the two signing quickly beneath the tree limbs and shadows.

Naokah kicked herself for not lying. Now she couldn't eavesdrop without getting interrupted. But Brielle was right. Dark face drawn, the mercy looked worried. The space beneath Naokah's ribs pinched.

"Any of you care to give a tired tender a hand?" Neves asked.

"I'll do it," Laerte said, getting a smile from Naokah and glares from the rest of the group, including Brielle.

"What?" she asked her friend.

Brielle cocked her chin at Clisten, whose powerful arms folded over his chest. "He's the hog expert."

"So. Laerte raises livestock too. Leave him be."

"When did you two become best mates?"

"Could ask the same about Clisten." Brielle's jaw dropped. Speechless, for once. Naokah smirked. "Why? You jealous?"

"I think you are," Brielle finally said, brushing a damp lock from her face with a sniff.

Naokah took her time to respond. Brielle had pushed her away last night. What had changed? She shifted her gaze. Laerte held a white piglet, back legs spread so Neves could make her incision. "Not that I need to defend my friendship to you, but we have similar backgrounds, is all. And he did prevent me from falling to my death earlier."

Brielle frowned. "What?"

"I wasn't paying attention. I tripped. He caught me."

She grunted, not unlike the unhappy piglet.

"What? Would you rather I'd fallen?"

"No."

"Then what?"

The sun peeped through a break in the dark clouds, gilding Brielle's freckles. "Just would've preferred to be the one doing the saving."

Naokah chuckled.

"What?" Brielle fidgeted with her curls.

"You're cute when you're jealous."

"I'm not jeal—"

"Time to go." Samara appeared. "Now."

Laerte handed the grunting piglet back to Neves, who thanked him and continued her work like nothing had happened.

But something had.

As the group followed Samara, instead of heading east to the vertical gardens and the border wall, they took the central path to the citadel.

"Why are we cutting the tour short?" Brielle asked, either not noticing Samara's mood or not caring.

"Something's come up," they said without turning, only hastening their pace.

Brielle sighed dramatically, but Naokah shot her a warning look. Samara, from the beginning, had maintained an air of ease, even when Kjell was poisoned. The lily fields they passed stuffed the air with perfume that was far too sweet. Naokah's stomach lurched. The savvy was keeping the envoys in the dark. And they weren't the only one.

The Keeper had clearly been arguing with another on the veranda last night. Discussing something 'happening' again. If the captain hadn't intercepted Naokah, she may've been able to glean more details. Kjell retching up poison flashed through her mind. What if Lenita had also been poisoned? But the culprit, instead of just making her sick, had actually succeeded? Bile soured Naokah's tongue at the sheer possibility. Still, she couldn't help but admit, a *live* Lenita would've been harder to hide and easier to find than a dead one. Was the insidious presence she'd felt since arriving the culprit? A staff member? It had to be. But why?

CHAPTER TWENTY-ONE

Cleaved

The pounding of boots woke me. I was on cold glass, watercolors splashing my face. And surrounded by marching. So loud and close I felt like I'd been thrown under a phalanx. Why was it still here? The marching always faded after scrim attacks. Even more perplexing, why was *I* still here? I'd never been able to stay inside the citadel without every speck of my glimmer charged with concentration. I certainly never slept inside, either.

The room was a mess, crumpled sheets hanging from the mattress, pillows strewn about the floor, and Lenita was gone. I hadn't a clue what time it was, but with the sun this high above the turrets, likely she was already at lecture or at her next assay.

I rubbed the crick in my neck – also new; when had I last felt physical pain? – and then a swirl of memories sleeted through me. The bone-scraping hiss, the thumping beneath the bed, the slitted, inhuman eyes freezing my blood, the earsplitting scream.

Lenita saw me last night. The creature had too. But that was impossible. No matter how much I'd wanted the Keeper to see me, my glimmer was invisible. What made gargoyles so lethal was our ability to take the scrim unawares. So, what had changed? Intending to contend with my worries later, I channeled back to my haunt.

Or tried.

The stone smacked me back. I placed a palm to my stinging cheek. What the raze? I focused on the taste of muggy air, my stone curves, now hot beneath the afternoon sun, attempting to return to my tower. The wall wouldn't budge, and I thunked to the floor.

I was trapped.

How could this be? I stood, ankles crackling. What was happening to me? The air that typically skirted around my body like water over stone stayed. My form was – I touched my forearm – soft but firm. Clear as crystal and just as shiny. When I held out my hand, the colors beneath wavered slightly, like a fingerprint smear on glass. I wriggled my clawed toes, clicking the floor. A blur of red darted towards the hallway. A fish. It could see me too?

I paced, the tapping of my feet foreign in my ears. A mirror flashed in the corner, but I ignored it, trying to return to my post. But I couldn't pierce the thick ashlar. My glimmer, usually airy as dust motes, had congealed into this semi-corporeal form. I could no longer dissolve into the stone. What would the eldest do when they learned of my dilemma? Or – my throat squeezed – did they already know, and this was my penance? Stuck inside with the creature I'd loosed?

I tiptoed to the mirror. Its crimson frame glinted as light stirred about me. I cast shadows now. I paused, closing my eyes. Did I really want to see myself? I supposed the day couldn't get any worse. Struggling to drown out the spectral army, brash and present as when I'd awoken, I fluttered my eyelids. I touched my reflection and – sagged.

With no memory of my former body, I'd solidified into the only vessel I knew – the gargoyle. As I twisted from my repulsive reflection, my eyes landed on my wings. Delicate, almost ethereal without their stone constructs. A smile quirked my lips. The sculptor paid special attention to each detail. Exquisite feathers cascaded down my back, nearly touching the ground. I certainly wasn't attractive. That wasn't my creator's intention. Gargoyles were meant to instill fear, to ward off, to kill. But these gleaming wings? Like a rose sprouting in winter, a butterfly amid graves – hauntingly beautiful.

A feather loosed from my past, floating over me. I stood atop a tower overlooking a city. Rows of windows reflected rich oranges and reds, purples and pinks – the sun's farewell. Head back and arms outstretched, I drank in the cool breeze from a flock of blue-footed gulls.

This is how the wind dances.

Who had told me that? A gull landed on my shoulder; its soft plume warmed my neck. I petted its head, and it cooed, nuzzling closer. Was I from Raptoria, land of aviaries? A Poler? The bird's heat dissolved. I'd returned to Abelha.

I placed my hand against the mural, a beautiful woman of antiquity, flowers in her hair, amazed as my fingers glossed the wall like a fine veneer. I'd been given a chance to redeem myself in this form. I would find the scrim, stop the envoys from seizing the Keepership, earn the Keeper's forgiveness, and finally uncover my origin. I had cleaved from my stone prison to…well, another stone prison, but I was one wingbeat closer to freedom.

Now, I would fly.

CHAPTER TWENTY-TWO

Complications

By the time they reached the citadel, Samara could no longer mask their agitation. Nor could the sky. A slab of fury blocked out the light and pelted them in rain. They rushed inside, dripping and squeaking on the glass floor. The savvy dismissed the group. Envoys could do whatever they liked, as long as they followed two rules: no one could enter the west wing, and at precisely the eighteenth hour, everyone was to rally in the great hall. When Brielle asked about the midday meal, Samara waved her off; she could figure it out on her own. Then they almost sprinted down the corridor to the Keeper's wing.

The foyer clock between the stained-glass windows ticked thirteen. Naokah's stomach growled, but her pants oozed, puddling mud around her boots. The veranda was out of the question. Getting drenched was fine, would even help clean her linens, but having to explain herself to Brielle and risk revealing her fear of the bees? Not wise. She'd just have to hurry.

Naokah squeaked towards the south wing, fish scattering beneath each thump.

"Where you headed?" Brielle asked.

She skidded to a halt, pointed to her dirty pants. "Bathe and change."

"Don't take too long. I'll be on the belvedere."

"The what?"

"Place with a commanding view, wraps around the donjon?" Brielle cocked her head as if she'd asked the dumbest question in the world and, at that very moment, Naokah didn't like her much. Was that what she and Clisten had been laughing about earlier? Naokah's Midworld ignorance? "Don't tell me you're scared of heights too?"

Naokah ignored the question. "Why the belvedere?"

"They serve spirits there."

"But it's raining."

"And? Worried I'll melt?" Brielle's eyes glittered when Naokah flushed.

She shook her head and muttered, "Sugar isn't the only thing that melts in the rain."

"What's that?"

"I'll be out for my second shower shortly."

The chatter of envoys faded as she entered the dark corridor. Pulse in her ears, she slinked by the murals. Why did her room have to be flanked by bees?

White flashed at the end of the hall. The healer? Now was her chance to speak with her. Alone. When Naokah passed her room, her legs nearly buckled, unable to reconcile why she'd forgone safety. The healer shrank to a smear. Naokah sped up, sticky trousers flapping. As she passed the Hall of Keepers, her skin tingled. Odd. There wasn't a spike in temperature this morning, but she'd also been too busy panicking over a nail to notice.

After she strode past the oval frames, ignoring the series of Keepers' eyes – why did everything here seem to watch her? – the air warmed. A silhouette entered the last room on the left. She slowed, blotting the sweat from her face, and prepared to knock, but the surgery was open.

"Well, are you going to come in, or aren't you?" rasped a voice from within.

Naokah took a hesitant step inside. Sallow light streamed over her. How could a healer discern how their patients were here? Everyone would look sick.

"How can I help you?" The woman fiddled with a cupboard, silver curls brushing her neckline as she struggled to pull open a jammed drawer.

"Need help?"

"Not as feeble as I look." She administered one final tug, and the drawer flew open; glass vials of purple, red, blue, and clear liquids clinked together. "See?" She turned around, a clear tube in her hand. Her throaty voice didn't seem to go with her eyes, soft blue, warm as the sea. Deep lines trenched around her lips, pulling at her temples. Surely, with all those laugh lines, the woman spent much of her time smiling. Did villains grin liberally? She hoped not.

"What do you need, dearie?" She pulled out a stool, offering it to Naokah, who shook her head. This wouldn't be long. "Please, for my sake?" She waved at the rest of the surgery. "I'm used to my visitors being supine."

Naokah hadn't realized how exhausted she was until she sat. The plush seat gave, and pressure eased off her calves and ankles, vision adjusting to the dim light. The room rounded out, and white cots arced beneath large, stained-glass windows. Shaped into golden hives that dripped with honey and bees, no wonder the room glowed yellow. The queen, three times the size of the others, hovered above the center cot. Naokah counted one, two – seven beds. Seven, as in seven envoys from seven nations vying for the Keepership? Was the healer planning for all of them to end up here? The bed on the farthest side held a man with long dark hair, sunset tips, sleeping soundly. Kjell.

"The beds are just a precaution," the healer said, a smile on her thin lips. "No need to fret."

"Did you need them all for the last Praxis?"

"Not at the same time, no."

"Did *all* the envoys visit you?" Naokah asked.

The trenches above the healer's brows deepened. "Thought you were an envoy, not a guard."

"Sorry. Just curious, is all."

"Because you're Lenita's sister?"

Naokah bit her lip and nodded.

"You don't favor her much," the healer said, not out of judgment, merely clinical observation. "Have that lean, hungry look about you, though. Likely why your sister was so successful."

"What did you think about her?"

"You sure are a curious little thing." The healer smoothed her ivory tunic. "Why do you ask?"

To determine if you took her, Naokah wanted to say outright, but that wasn't the way. Nectar over vinegar. Yet, she wasn't a natural liar. Lenita had taught her, and like most things, her sister was far better at it. If Patri asked where the last cookie had walked off to, even if she hadn't eaten it, Naokah flushed. *You were born guilty, but you must learn how to grow out of it, or you'll never survive,* Lenita had teased.

"I'm just competitive, is all." She met the woman's probing gaze and held it, though every muscle in her neck told her to turn away. "Trying to learn as much as I can, so that I might follow in her footsteps. Croi Croga really needs the Keepership," she said for good measure. It wasn't a lie. Besides, people tended to doubt one less when they pitied them.

"Smart, I'll give you that. Especially since I know the rest of your group is up on the belvedere, drinking. I respect that. Lenita was...different from her competition too." The skin folds at the woman's neck dipped as she swallowed. "I liked her. A great deal. Was my pick from the start. Always had the right mindset. Bees first, people second. Just like our current Keeper. Was an awful shame she went missing." She heaved a sigh, shoulders drooping. "Dumbfounded us all. Was like she simply vanished in the night, melted into the walls or something. Still can't make sense of it." Noticing Naokah's expression, she added, "I'm so terribly sorry for your loss."

Naokah had to clear her throat before she could speak. Lenita had an unparalleled magnetic presence about her. Tati called it her glimmer. Innate, couldn't be learned. Tati never admitted it, but she, like Matri and Patri, had favored Lenita. Naokah even preferred Lenita over herself. But Tati, more than anyone, wholeheartedly cherished her. They shared that same reckless abandon, the same irresistible pull that sucked everyone in. Though they didn't care to notice, Naokah was awake when Tati and Lenita went for their late-night strolls. They'd walk the fields, sharing that old cloudcane pipe, talking about who knows what. Naokah was hurt and envious she'd never been invited, but she convinced herself she wouldn't have enjoyed it. She may've liked the smell of cloudcane smoke, but the pipe always burned her tongue.

"Did she have any enemies, Miss...?"

"Call me Marguerite, dearie. The envoys didn't quite get along. Likely how this poor fellow—" she tilted her head towards the unconscious Kjell, "—ended up here. No doubt, someone saw him as fierce competition and tried to eliminate him." Her brow lifted, metallic in the low light. "But, she was the last one here at the end. The other six envoys had left already."

"She make enemies with any of the staff?"

"I honestly don't know who'd want to harm her. Certainly not the Keeper. Like I told the guards, it made no sense for anyone to want her dead. We needed her. Her disappearance weighs heavy on us all. No body. No closure. I feel most for you, your family, for Croi Croga. To go that far, overcome everything, to merely vanish and die?"

Naokah blinked back the sting behind her eyes. Lenita was *not* dead. Still.... "You don't think it was suicide?"

"No. Perhaps an accident."

"What do you mean?"

A draft sighed behind Marguerite's desk, and she paused, passing Naokah an apologetic glance.

Naokah squinted, surprised. What she'd initially taken for a solid wall was a tunnel to another room. A bronze placard engraved with *Morgue* rested above the arched entrance.

"I've been here since the middle of the last Keeper's tenure, after the healer, far younger than me, mysteriously disappeared too. Fifty-three years, I've served the citadel. And let's just say, there are some rather…strange things, that don't rightly add up."

"Unnatural things?" Like the ghost girl?

"I'm a woman of science, of logic and reason."

"So, that's a no?"

"I didn't say that. You just wouldn't find someone like me admitting aloud that I believed in such…nonsense." The words of disbelief didn't match the healer's eyes, which now not only moved over Naokah's shoulder like she was addressing a presence behind her, but widened with fear.

★   ★   ★

The trip back to her chambers seemed to take longer than when she'd been in pursuit of the healer. Naokah could strike Marguerite off her list. Only someone wholly diabolical could've put on a show of sympathy so convincing. She was another step closer to finding the answer, but it didn't feel that way. Lenita had no enemies that the healer knew of, aside from the envoys who had already been kicked off the isle. And what Marguerite had alluded to, that there were preternatural forces at work, she herself didn't want to admit. Most Crogan farmers, including Patri, were superstitious. Never veering close to the Razing for fear of a crith snatching their soul. Not walking beneath a pollinating flock, for if a bird shat on you, you'd have a decade of failed harvests. Ridiculous. Still, her encounter with the ghost girl had chipped away her disbelief.

The world was full of all kinds of luck, good and bad. A failed harvest was bad luck. Croi Croga and Bizou and Okse getting hit the hardest by the Razing because of their central location? Bad luck. But Lenita vanishing right before taking the Keepership? More than bad luck. Too convenient. Lenita's disappearance was premeditated. Someone didn't want her to swear in. Who had the most to lose by Croi Croga controlling the world market?

When Naokah plodded into her chambers, she peeled her sticky clothes off and threw them into a pile. But as she headed over to the lavatory, a shadow fluttered over the mural. She froze.

"Who's there?"

No answer.

"I said, who's in my chambers? I'll scream if you don't show yourself."

The shadow shrank into a small rectangle but continued to wriggle like a fly caught in a web. Naokah tiptoed to the side of the canopy. Nothing was—

Shuffling, like that of paper. Under the bed. No matter how un-superstitious she was, there was something ominous about what could've been lurking beneath. A fear instilled since childhood. When the farm had a rough year, and they'd had to sell most of their furniture to make ends meet, little Naokah didn't complain about Patri taking her bed frame. No space under a mattress also meant no monster. This illogical fear and perhaps the fact that she was nude kept her from peeping beneath the pleated dust ruffle. Yet, the shuffling continued.

"Get over yourself," she said over her rising pulse. She leaned back, ripped the skirt up—

And relaxed. A book, leather-bound. Caught in the vent. She snagged it and stood. Caked in dust, something dark brown, wine or cacao, was spilled over the first few pages, pasting them together. She slid her fingers beneath the loose side and peeled them apart. Only a corner stuck and tore off, but that didn't matter. It didn't harm the scrawl across the middle of the parchment. The wild scratches that barely passed for letters, she'd known well. Hastily written or not, Lenita had never been the queen of penmanship – the only thing in the world she didn't excel at, but only because she chose not to.

Life's too short to squander, she'd always say, *especially on handwriting.*

Shocked that her older sister kept a journal in the first place, Naokah squinted, trying to discern the scribbled paragraph that looped across the second page. When she finally did, her fingers shook, and the book thumped the floor. The fish beneath darted off. She picked it back up to confirm what she read, but it was the same: *I was wrong. About everything. Divine Daughter, I was wrong. I need help. But who can I trust when even the murals whisper deceit?*

The book fell again, and Naokah flipped over her hands. The rusty powder smudging them wasn't food nor wine. It crumbled like dried blood.

CHAPTER TWENTY-THREE

Transformed

Before, when the scrim would retreat, the army – I assumed they were an army, as they weren't corporeal, but the clank of armor, the pound of boots sure sounded like a legion of warriors – would fade until the next new moon. But now, the phantom marching didn't stop. The scrim and legion were connected somehow. Whoever controlled the scrim controlled the soldiers. And since a scrim was still here on the loose, I'd unwittingly invited the army to stay too.

How reckless I'd been.

I had to find a way to make them go away but couldn't succeed if I lost my wits. To shutter out the marching, I forced my thoughts elsewhere – the fish. They could see me through the floor. Their eyes bulged beneath my dewclaws before storming off in a whirl of fins. If I didn't know I was hideous before, I did now, and yet I was oddly satisfied. Not with being ugly. Surely no one wishes for that.

No, but to be seen. Acknowledged, bad or good. Even with this new form of existence, though, I found myself missing my haunt. Sitting high above the sweeping landscape, drinking in the watercolor sunrises, sunsets. I even missed the cranky eldest. I should've been happy. This is what I'd yearned for since I awakened, to be closer to the Keeper. To be real. Bustling with staff and envoys, bees and fish, sentience surrounded me. So, why did I feel like I'd fallen into a mass grave?

The shadows seemed to breathe, the hallways murmured, and eyes burning with malice followed my every move. The scrim could've been hiding anywhere. If my kin were successful, the air would've felt light instead of dense. I had to locate the beast, and Lenita was my first suspect. Last night, we'd had company.

I seeped into the shading of the mural next to her bed, heat dappling my cheeks as I swam beneath the curve of a hip. Odd taste, humans, having nude women strewn across their walls. Of course, they also had my hideous mug affixed to their donjon. An odd pairing, beauty and beast. I swam through her door, attaching myself to the mural of two women picking foxgloves on a knoll, and followed voices coming from the great hall. From the subtle green light above, it was noon, and the envoys were eating.

Muffled voices from the savvy's quarters stopped me, and I hid behind a damask armchair. Their room, nestled in an eave beside the foyer, was similar to the envoys'. Canopy bed, standing mirror, and a fireplace, but smaller, starker. There were no murals nor window treatments and, although the citadel always exhaled musty air, something within their walls was riper than compost. Somewhat surprising for the person in charge of the citadel's staff and upkeep.

"Did you find the culprit?" asked Captain Avice, arms stiff across her chest.

"Just shattered vases in a few of the envoys' rooms." Sweat beaded the savvy's weary face, and their voice dropped an octave. "One of the envoys said it was a rush of air, like a breeze—"

"Impossible."

"Obviously. But that's what they said. It came from the turrets and billowed off their canopies, scattering their belongings."

"But you said Lenita saw something?"

"She's retracted her statement, likely doesn't want to look foolish, especially after I told her to talk to Marguerite for her night terrors."

"Was it a night terror?"

122 • RACHEL FIKES

"It had to be," said Samara, scratching their wrist. "She says she saw something with eyes like a viper, telling her to submit."

The sentry grimaced. "Will cause widespread panic if that gets out."

"*If*. Like I said, she knew how mad she sounded. Didn't want to dishonor Croi Croga, no matter how superstitious her people tend to be. Would tarnish her chance as Keeper."

"What's your theory?"

The savvy moved their hand from their wrist just long enough to tug it through their braid. A few stray hairs and skin flakes moted their collar, before going back to scratching.

Avice's lips pursed, and I moved to the chair's arm to home in on their peculiar behavior. Why were they so twitchy?

"I don't even know where to start—" scratch, scratch, "—never seen anything like it, but I've also only been in the Keeper's employ for ten years. Certainly not as long as you."

"I will admit, sometimes, late at night, especially during the new moon, I feel as though ...." The guard shook her head. "I sound as crazy as Lenita, but I've felt a growing presence since I arrived. Not as loud or constant as the hives. More sporadic, underlying, like the thudding of an army. Yet thousands of leagues away. Maybe it's just my mind playing tricks on me."

I nearly flopped out of the chair. I wasn't mad. Avice heard the marching too. Samara's face strained, but they didn't say anything. The scrim were linked. Surely the staff was aware of their cyclic attacks?

"Even so," Avice sighed deeply, "whatever it is, be it real or an illusion, has changed the Keeper and not for the better. She hasn't painted in a decade, smokes and drinks all the time, and sometimes I have to call her multiple times before she responds, like she's losing herself to this place." She shook her head. "A few nights ago, she'd have lopped off all her hair had I not intervened. When I asked her why in the Daughter's name she'd do such a thing – she's been growing it since she was a little girl – she said it didn't belong to her."

I glared at the captain. For someone so close to the Keeper, she was entirely unsympathetic. Naturally, the poor woman was acting a bit off. These imposters were here to steal her title, and no one was doing anything about it, save me.

"The sooner the Praxis concludes, the better," the savvy said, scratching their wrist.

I waited, but they switched to damage control, blabbering about sweeping the envoys' accounts under the metaphorical rug, and I grew irritated, proceeding to the great hall. As I meshed into the mural of a plump cherub dancing aboard a ship's prow, a gull taking flight off his hands, a wave of nostalgia hit me.

Brine tickled my cheeks, the sun warmed my back, and weightlessness tugged at my sleeves. I was at sea. Had I been a sailor, a comandante, or steerage? A coral fingernail traced my arm, my collarbone, then the tingle of lips on my earlobe. I arched my back, leaning into the breath steaming my neck.

"Not in front of the crew, darling." I didn't mean it at all.

Their thumb parted my mouth, and they filled it with a spiced rum whisper, "You positively sure?" They traced my lips, unfurling my jaw and, when the tip of their tongue zinged against mine, my knees melted, as did my resolve.

"What wicked games you play," I gasped, surrendering to a kiss that could implode even the most tenacious star.

Glass shattered, yanking me back to the great hall. My throat burned with unshed tears, with unrequited passion. I was cursed, forever handed dried-out paints with canvas too wrinkled to restore.

Pastel light dappled the envoys, only six now. Yet, they didn't sit at the long, ebony table that spanned the hall. Each claimed their own round table, acting like the others didn't exist. On the edges of their seats, eyes distant, fearful. Lenita was the closest. Head downcast, she twitched like the savvy. She hadn't touched her meal other than crumbling her toast. She attempted to sip her coffee, but it spilled down her chin.

I shuffled through last night. The groaning, the scream, the yellow eyes filling her chambers, but I couldn't recall what happened. I'd blacked out too soon. All I knew was, the prideful woman I'd been watching, respecting, scorning, had vanished overnight. The scrim I'd spent every new moon smashing between my claws didn't seem so teeny anymore. The eldest never revealed their origin nor their mission other than, like my destiny to vanquish them, they were created to infiltrate. Whatever it had transformed into, must've been so horrible, so devastating, to render the most confident envoy a nervous wreck. Now, more than ever, did I wish to return to my tower and beg the eldest for answers, but I was stuck. I'd have to fix this mess, *my* mess, on my own.

CHAPTER TWENTY-FOUR

Breadcrumbs

Even the murals whisper deceit. The phrase repeated over and over, relentless as the tub's dripping faucet. Like the ornery handle above, no matter how hard she wrenched, neither the water nor words ceased. Naokah scrubbed the mud from her skin, taking care to look anywhere but up.

With a face like a sea snake and red, membranous wings, the spout was unnerving. Worse, its toothy jaws reminded her of the butterfly woman's yawn. Despite Brielle being drawn to the murals that seemed to wrap every inch of the citadel not already covered in bees, Naokah hadn't particularly liked them. And now, after reading what could've been her sister's last words, she feared them. What if her nightmare was more than exhaustion?

The water went from tepid to ice cold, and Naokah sprang up, shivering. Brown rivulets trickled her knees. Light seeped through the stained-glass turret, splashing the lavatory in a spectrum of shapes. The sun was out, so the storm must've cleared. If she hurried, she could use the veranda.

She was fishing for the stopper's chain, wrinkling her nose at the murky water, when something slimy seized her hand. She shrieked and yanked back. But its hold was firm, tugging her down. She twisted back and forth, currents of brown slapping her calves. Its cruel grip only clamped tighter, dragging her towards the spout.

A bee crawled from the faucet.

Followed by another.

And another.

Droning rumbled from the pipes, the tiles, as a colony of bees surged from the spout. Naokah shut her eyes. This couldn't be real. Only a nightmare. A hallucination. Her hand went numb as icy fingers dug into her wrist and wrenched her into the tempest. Bees prickled her forearms. Buzzed up her neck. Crawled into her ears, her nostrils.

She thrust out a leg, finding purchase on the tub's lip, and wrested with all her might.

It released. She flung back, head cracking against tiles. Shards of pain exploded behind her eyes, and she crumpled into the waves. The gurgle of the stopper lifting was the last thing she heard before Croi Croga, fifteen years back, lapped over her.

Naokah wallowed in a muddy pit. Sharp rocks tore at her fingers and scraped her knees. She tried to climb out. Tried. The walls were too steep, the mud too slick. Still, something cruel stalked the shadows. She had to keep moving. She grabbed a fistful of roots, dug her toes into the damp soil, and started ascending. Smoke burned her eyes, the stink of death plugged her nose, and her throat was raw from screaming. But the worst part of all? Lenita had abandoned her.

"Naokah." A whisper.

Her eyes fluttered. Had Lenita finally come?

"Naokah," said the voice, closer. Warm hands on her shoulders.

She jolted up, mind spinning, and nearly head-butted a wide-eyed Clisten. She was still in the tub, grit that didn't drain biting into her heels. The bees and creature were gone. Her hands shot to her chest and met soft plush. She sagged. He'd had the decency to cover her with a towel.

"Are you all right?" His brow lifted.

Was she? What the razing had that *thing* been? "I...why...how are you here?"

"I heard your screams from my chambers." His long hair, interwoven with braids, gleamed copper and gold in the lavatory's dim light and swished over his shoulder when he bobbed his head.

"Got here fast as I could." He averted his gaze out of respect. He was fully dressed, but Naokah was not.

"Thank you." Any misgivings she'd had about him with Brielle earlier melted away as color rose in his bronzed cheeks.

Eyes still downcast, he stood. "May I...assist you?"

"Please."

She tucked the towel under her arms, and Clisten pulled her up. The room began whirling, and he placed his arm behind her back.

"Shall I escort you to the healer?"

"No." She winced as she grazed the tender lump on the back of her skull. "I'm fine. Just hungry."

"Me too." He paused. "If you don't mind, I'd like to wait until you've changed?"

"Yes," she said quickly, then added, "thank you...again."

He bowed and turned around to face the lavatory so she could change.

She staggered into her chambers, leaning against the wall. Up until now, she'd blamed all the uncanniness on her lack of sleep, her exhaustion. Her mind playing tricks on her. But if that were the case, why did her wrist throb now? Whatever that thing was, it had tried to drown her and would've succeeded were it not for Clisten. The ghost girl, the shadowed stalker, the feigned bee attacks, the murmuring murals? They were linked. Even the healer admitted something was off.

Naokah and Matri had been wrong about Tati.

Horribly wrong.

She wasn't lying about witches. Someone within these creepy walls wasn't just a staff member. They had access to dark, dangerous power and knew Naokah's true purpose for being here. They'd poisoned Kjell, taken her sister and, if she didn't hurry up and figure out who it was, she'd be next.

Naokah sucked in a shaky breath, and scooped up a scamall set, the same faded yellow of dying cloudcane. She wasn't taking any chances. She'd be quick.

"May I ask what caused your...accident?" Clisten asked, back still turned.

Thankfully.

Less chance of detecting her lie. She couldn't reveal the truth. Not after her uproar at the dining table this morning. If rumors of her madness reached the Keeper, she'd get kicked off the isle, and then who'd find Lenita? Naokah slipped on her shirt.

"Haven't slept well. I must've dozed off, had a nightmare."

"A bad one, I take it?"

"The worst." If only it was simple as a nightmare. She pulled up her trousers, cinching the waist. "I'm ready."

Clisten twisted around and gave her an appreciative smile. "You look lovely."

"And you're a liar, but a kind liar. Thank you."

He shook his head and extended his arm. "The belvedere?"

"Sure. If you don't mind taking the veranda?"

★   ★   ★

The clouds were wispy streaks, matching the tendrils of fog snaking the topiaries and bee sculptures. Rain dripped from the trellis, needling Naokah's thin scamall top, but wet foliage and earth sweetened the air, and it had cooled to almost comfortable. She breathed in the roses from above, trying to embrace the calm.

She'd only managed to pry the first few pages of the journal apart and, though she'd have rather stayed and read every word Lenita scrawled, what if that thing returned? She desperately wanted to tell someone, anyone, but who could be trusted at this point? She couldn't risk getting tossed off the isle for being mad. Somehow, someway, Naokah had to muster the intestinal fortitude to face the razing thing, for it was the key to finding Lenita. She would, but later.

Right now, she was headed to exactly where she needed to be. The others would be talking about Samara's strange behavior at the ranch. Maybe they knew what happened. Besides, she'd already ripped a corner off the journal's page and didn't want to chance losing a single clue. Tonight, she'd steal a knife from the great hall to loosen the remaining pages. Why hadn't the journal turned up when they conducted their inquest? More disconcerting, what if they hadn't found the journal because it wasn't there to find? It was stuck in the vent. The girl in white floated through her mind. Had she brought the journal to her, a breadcrumb perhaps? But then, what did she want? Nothing in this world was ever free.

"Care to talk?" Clisten patted her hand on his arm. He was resplendent in his turquoise shirt and fitted vest, gold-embossed leather braces attaching to his navy trousers. She envied his composure, and more, his ease.

"Just tired." She pretended to yawn, and then really yawned. Would she ever be able to wiggle her toes beneath those velvet blankets and sleep? She had to find a way to deal with the butterfly woman, the tub creature. Or there'd be more than exhaustion fuzzing her brain.

He cocked an auburn brow. "Could be. Or maybe you'd feel better if you talked about that nightmare?"

"It's silly."

"It's not silly if it causes you pain." His eyes met hers, big, warm, genuine.

She lifted a noncommittal shoulder. He waited for a response as they wove around a topiary, but she honestly didn't know where to start. One of the sculptures shifted, and Clisten stopped her, throat bobbing. Boards squeaked, and then a crop of red hair emerged from the gray.

Naokah loosed a breath. "Mila. You headed to the belvedere too?"

The thin woman shot a cursory peep at Naokah's companion and jerked a nod.

"Care to accompany us?" Clisten offered his other arm.

Mila chewed her lip. Dark circles burrowed beneath her eyes. Clearly she hadn't gotten any sleep either. Was she seeing things too? A possible ally, then?

"I...." Clisten cleared his throat, cheeks reddening. "I haven't yet apologized for what the Polers did to you at the ball. It was cruel and childish, and I should've stopped them. I was a coward not to, and I'm truly, deeply very sorry."

Mila rubbed the back of her neck, looking first to Naokah, warily moving to Clisten. She answered by accepting his hand. The line of Clisten's shoulders relaxed, and Naokah decided right then and there: she liked him. If Naokah could have mastered an apology like that, pure and sincere, Lenita might have already forgiven her. Maybe she still would.

Clisten attempted small talk with Mila, but she was a woman of few words. The silence between the three stretched on awkwardly, so Naokah answered Clisten's question. If she opened up, perhaps Mila would be inclined to share what had kept her up at night too.

"That nightmare? Stems back to when I was a kid. Crogans can be superstitious, and like most farmers, my patri left a fat border between his cloudcane rows and the Razing. Most adults stay away from the trench for obvious reasons. But kids, to test their bravery, dare one another to see who can get the closest without peeing their pants."

"And you took that dare?" Clisten asked.

"Foolishly, yes. One night, my sister convinced me that since it was the full moon, I'd be safe from getting attacked by a crith. All I had to do was toss a stick into the chasm."

He led them around a column. "What's a crith?"

"A wicked Midworld creature," Mila answered for her, startling them both. "Lurks in the Razing. If you get too close to its home, it'll yank you into its grave and climb out as you." Clisten gave her a bewildered look. "It gets worse. Crith means 'goosebumps' in Midese. Whenever your skin prickles, it means one is near, trying to scratch its way in."

"Even knowing *that,* you still took the dare?"

"I was desperate to impress my big sister," Naokah admitted. "She hated that I followed her around all the time, and I wanted to change that. Maybe even earn her respect. Besides, it's just a spooky legend."

Mila hmphed in disagreement, but Naokah ignored her. "I got within a few feet of the Razing before falling into a pit. My sister left me for her friends, so I spent the entire night alone, trying to crawl out. I succeeded eventually, obviously." She didn't mention the cold fingers that had grabbed her ankles and dragged her into the pit in the first place. She'd once thought it was her imagination. Not so much anymore. "Perhaps that's why I have trust issues."

Clisten chuckled. "You and me both." He nodded at a far alcove where a web of mottled colors wound up through the shadows. Railing. More stained glass, at that. "Might I suggest the lift?" His lips quirked at her bunched brow. "Found it earlier. Follow me."

The trio walked as if headed to the conservatory but took a sharp left before the entrance. A large globe flanked by four sentries met them. The leader nodded and opened the glass door.

Naokah paused. "Not a fan of confined spaces."

"Me neither," chirped Mila.

"Says the two who signed up to be trapped on an isle?"

"*We* didn't have a choice." Mila had found her tongue and wasn't afraid to use it.

He shot them a guilty grin, patiently waiting. Mila sighed but followed. And since Naokah was never one to shy away from competition, she stepped into the lift. The floor rebounded slightly, and so did her stomach.

"It's attached to a pulley system, hence the bouncing. But a strong pulley system, fortified cables," he added, noting her anxious teetering.

As the globe slid up, a halo of light, vines dotted with glowing purple flowers wreathed the shaft. Mila's eyes grew wide with wonder, and Clisten beamed, proud of his discovery. Naokah tingled with airy weightlessness. Was this how birds felt in the sky?

She glanced up at the beautiful Poler. He reminded her of the starlings that used to pollinate their cloudcane. Colorful, carefree. As though he'd boarded the ship to Abelha for a mere adventure, to see what all the fuss was about. Not to compete. Probably how he found this lift in the first place. While the other envoys studied, he explored.

He didn't have to be here. Naokah didn't begrudge him, though. His candor in a place of secrets was a welcome refreshment.

Gears clicked, released. The air thinned, Naokah's ears popped, and more light spilled into the globe. The belvedere was within eyesight now. Yet, her stomach knotted. Clisten twisted, following her gaze. A collage of nude bodies and flowers wrapped the belvedere to the turrets.

"You don't much care for the murals," he stated rather than asked.

"Do you?"

"They certainly aren't the creepiest things here." He paused, and Naokah's breathing hitched. Had he seen something strange too? She wanted to ask, perhaps compare notes, but what if he hadn't? She'd be no closer to solving Lenita's disappearance *and* she'd have risked exposing one of her many weaknesses. Not worth it. Clisten scratched his chin. "Funny. I think the Keeper initially painted the murals to lighten up the place."

"I wouldn't say she succeeded," said Naokah. Maybe if she'd painted flowers or landscapes or something without eyes that constantly followed her.

He nodded.

"Why'd she stop? Run out of space?" Mila cracked.

"From what I've gathered, she stopped right around the time she returned from one of her goodwill missions in Okse ten years back. Whatever happened on that trip must've been bad. Really bad. She hasn't picked up a brush since. Replaced it with a pipe. I've heard Abelha's your biggest customer for cloudcane pulp."

"Think Raptoria has them beat."

"Awww, yes. So that's how those greedy tycoons manage to sleep at night." He smirked, and she grinned right back.

A Poler criticizing another Poler? How surreal. The lift shuddered to a stop. Immediately, Naokah felt eyes on her. She craned her neck to the spired donjon. A gargoyle carved in the likeness of a bull with wings hunched over the stained glass. With the storm gone, the sun out, an oily blanket of humidity clung to her skin. Still, she shivered.

"Thought gargoyles were supposed to face out to guard the citadel from threats?" Mila asked.

"True," Naokah said, "but more often than not, I'd wager it's the outside that needs protection from within."

Brielle and Laerte sat at a bar beneath an overhang of gardenias that shielded them from the sun's glare. Both had a drink, but neither smiled. Dazarin was still missing, surprisingly. She could see the nonchalant sea god skipping the tour, but booze? Never.

"What's wrong?" Naokah asked, pulling out a stool beside Brielle.

"Captain Avice," Laerte and Brielle answered in unison.

"Care to elaborate?"

"She's not stupid," said Brielle, nodding at the eave behind Naokah. "Questioning us when our tongues are loosed."

"About the poisoning?"

Laerte nodded. "Picking on Mids first, shocking. With Mila now."

Mila? But she was just with them. Naokah glimpsed over her shoulder. Indeed. The captain must've grabbed her as soon as they left the lift. Though a little green, Mila seemed calm, a stark contrast to the severe sentry.

"He did ruin her gown," said Brielle.

Naokah shook her head. "Don't think she has it in her. She's too tired to plot. Besides, the poisoning happened right after her dress fiasco. Rather close together for retaliation."

"Then what's your theory?" Brielle folded her arms.

Someone was defensive. "Don't have one. But it's not like Kjell made loads of friends with his rosy personality. Anyone could've done it. Staff included."

Brielle guzzled her drink and clanked down her glass. White wine spritzed the air. She waved at the barkeep for another round. "Why would the staff want him dead? They aren't competing for Keepership."

"No," said Clisten. "But they'd have to put up with him for the next fifty years, or however long he lived to serve. I'd say that gives them just as much motive, if not more. Enemies for a few months during this competition, or a nightmare boss for the rest of your life?"

"Exactly. Same goes for my sister. Her competition had already left the isle. It had to be a member of the staff," Naokah said. "Did she question either of you yet?" Brielle shook her head, but Laerte nodded. "What did she ask?"

"Why?" Laerte grinned. "You worried?"

"A little. She makes me nervous. I wouldn't mind having an idea of her line of questioning. Would've helped Mila. She's innocent but look at her now. Might hurl."

"Captain Avice is intimidating," Laerte agreed. "She just asked where I was, what I was doing, who I was talking to before the prick started blowing chunks. Oh, she also asked if I had any words with him."

"Did you?" asked Brielle.

He laughed bitterly. "Not like he has much to say to a Mid. We are beneath him, literally and figuratively. No wonder the sentry is asking the poor nations first. Upstanding guy, Kjell. Sure hope he recovers." Laerte's words dripped with disdain. Even though Naokah agreed, his hostility didn't do him any favors. It gave him motive.

"Anyone find out what bee flew up Samara's ass, cutting our tour short? I was looking forward to the vertical gardens." Brielle stuck out her lower lip.

"Probably has something to do with Dazarin vanishing after orientation," said Naokah. "Anyone see him yet?"

They shook their heads. Dazarin's disappearance churned her stomach. She wanted to believe the captain wasn't wasting time by questioning envoys, but Marguerite's statement about the preternatural still haunted her. And now, she was all too aware of the bull-shaped gargoyle, glaring down at her as if she were the threat. Was it controlled by some witchcraft-practicing member of the staff too?

"Naokah." Someone tugged on her sleeve. "Hello?"

She blinked. The envoys were studying her.

"The sentry is done with Mila. She called you," said Clisten.

"Oh." Naokah winced and wobbled past Mila, whose face was waxy. The sentry stood with her back to the envoys, eyes surveying the foliage. Fog had settled over the maze, obscuring the lines of green.

"You had some questions for me?"

"Yes." The captain twisted around. "About your poisoned friend."

"He's not my friend. And shouldn't you be more concerned about finding Dazarin? He's been missing since we left for the tour."

"Not that it's any of your business, but I think the two are related." A vein bulged from her forehead as she leaned in, and her sweat soured the air. "Now, tell me about your whereabouts when Kjell was poisoned."

"Where everyone else was, in the great hall. Eating, drinking, talking. Right before he collapsed, I was helping Mila avoid public humiliation after he spilled wine on her."

"You think he did it on purpose?"

"Of course he did. He's an ass. An insecure one at that."

"Sounds like you don't like him."

"Doubt you'll find anyone who does, aside from his Poler pals. I imagine he has more than a few enemies here. Now, someone who hates him enough to kill him? I don't know."

"So, you weren't involved?"

"If history shows anything, Croi Croga doesn't need help earning the Keepership. My sister didn't need to kill anyone to win. I think you should be looking more...internally. Lenita went missing when all the envoys were gone. I wonder if that same person, on your staff, no doubt, is connected to all three situations."

The captain hesitated. "We determined Lenita took off on her own."

Took off on her own? Not Lenita. You'd have to kill her first – she clenched her jaw to swallow her blunder. Her sister was alive. "I can tell by the look on your face even you don't believe that," she said, fury flushing out fear. "Instead of wasting your time interviewing people who weren't here when she disappeared and were with Samara when Dazarin went missing, maybe look at your staff."

Cries rained through the air. Avice blanched.

Naokah twisted around, and adrenaline surged up her neck.

Beneath the adjacent tower, below the window, trailed a bloody rope. A large, striking man with an arm etched in ink hung from the end. Eyes bulging, neck purple, Dazarin was dead.

CHAPTER TWENTY-FIVE

Mist on Ember

Pushing the infuriating army to the deepest trenches of my mind, I followed Lenita back to her chambers. With the sun at her highest, shades of warm honey spilled down the corridors. Spending who knows how many years above the citadel, I'd never fully appreciated the first Keeper's design – her meticulous thus brilliant placement of each stained pane mosaicing the turrets – until I got trapped inside. One would always know what time it was, simply by what hues lit up her halls: follow the spectrum, light to dark, dawn to dusk.

Distracted, I slipped. Lenita whirled around just as I leapt back into a mural. Narrowed eyes burrowed into me. I stiffened, melting into the shadow beneath the painting's elbow. Unconvinced, Lenita bolted down the hallway. Boots pounded, fish darted, and I hastened my strokes, gliding from mural to mural like I'd caught a strong river current. Was this the same woman I'd been watching this past week, or had something evil slipped inside her vessel? If she were possessed, wouldn't she be emboldened, not terrified?

"You know the way," said a gravelly voice from the hive wall. "Now follow it."

Scondra tai! I skidded to a halt. As did Lenita. "Who are you?" Darkness spewed over the corridor, snuffing out the light. "What do you want?" Chest heaving, she scanned the den of squirming shadows. The stench of death coagulated, ripened. She clutched her face and coughed. I choked. Could it be the scrim? "Answer me!" Her voice shook.

A screech rattled the hives, and clouds funneled the hall. We dropped, lying prone on the icy floor as troops of bees swarmed overhead. Shallow breaths fogged the glass. Each inhale grew thicker, fouler. Nausea pounded my stomach, and I squeezed my eyes shut. Lenita's fear was palpable, a trembling kitten by my side. I reached out to comfort her. My fingertips brushed her sleeve, mist on ember, and flames of my past whisked me away.

I slumped over a trench, and smoke burped up around me, stinging my eyes. The Razing. My wrist ached with dangling weight. I stretched, neck cracking, to risk a glimpse over the edge. Smog cradled a small face, eyes like black buttons. Not a doll, a child. Dirty tears tracked her cheeks. She cried a name. My name? I strained to hear over my grunting as I heaved her up. Heavier than she looked, my elbows popped, and sweat itched my spine. I had to save her, this child I didn't recognize, a key to my past. Was she mine?

The Razing birthed her ever so slowly. Wrists, arms, her tiny waist. Her dress was white at one time but now flailed against her legs like a broken sparrow's wing. The twinge behind my shoulders eased as her bare feet anchored the side.

I stood, but she rammed me, almost knocking me back down. How dare she attack me after I saved her? I moved to pry her grubby little hands from my waist, then stopped. Face buried into my shirt, arms circling me tightly, this was a hug. My jaw quivered, and my throat clamped shut. I embraced her back. Though frail, her grip was warm, reassuring, and her heart beat steadily against me. So cozy, so complete, my eyelids grew heavy, but the air softened and brightened like a cloud passing the sun. My arms grew cold, lighter. I bit back a sob. The girl was gone, as was the sinister presence.

Lenita heaved herself up and rushed to her room. I followed, slipping in before she slammed the door. She paced about, hands scrubbing her cropped hair. "I know you're in here," she finally said, eyes like daggers slashing from the mural to the lavatory.

I held my breath. Was she talking to me?

"I've felt your stare since I arrived. I know you're working with whatever beast entered my chambers last night. Those slitted pupils..." she choked. "But you won't win. I fought to get here, sacrificed everything, *everything*." She squared her shoulders. "You saw me fold, but no more. This citadel, the bees, they are my future, Croi Croga's future. I won't buy into your tricks, nor will I give up. I'm here to win." She waited, twitchy, surveying her chambers. Dingy flames sputtered against the walls. Even the torches squirmed from her menace.

My worry about the scrim subsided. She hadn't been overtaken. The creature was still lurking about, likely whatever voice challenged her outside. I would leave her for now and check the others but wouldn't forget her words. She wouldn't back down. Neither would I.

Water ran in the lavatory, and she muttered to herself, trying to instill confidence. But her voice cracked. Humans, they weren't the best liars. I slipped under the door. What she didn't know *would* hurt her.

CHAPTER TWENTY-SIX

Worlds Better

The group disbanded after Dazarin's death. Sentries were dispatched to the chamber from which he'd either been pushed or leapt of his own accord. All they found were a few droplets of blood – he'd slit his calf on exit – and a letter composed by his own hand, a supposed goodbye. After the guards spent the evening in the citadel, questioning everyone, it was written off as self-inflicted. No one believed it. Yet, the one advantage of his death, if one could call it that, was that because all the envoys had been on the belvedere with the captain, apart from Kjell, who was unconscious, they were clear of suspicion.

When they adjourned for supper, Naokah headed for her chambers via the veranda. Murder had a way of suppressing the appetite, and she had Lenita's journal to work apart. She stopped right before her door, hands clenching. The plan had been to steal a knife from the dining hall to separate the pages. She spun around, irritated at her cowardice. If she just learned to deal with her fear of the hive walls, the murals, she'd save so much time. When Naokah encountered Samara outside the main entrance, though, still as tightly wound as everyone else in this wretched citadel, the knot between her shoulders eased. Their presence seemed a source of continuity, reassurance, while all razing broke lose.

"Naokah," they said with a sad smile. "How are you this evening?"

"Could be better. But suppose I can't complain, with poor Dazarin lying in the morgue."

Their eyes dropped to the planks, still damp from the earlier shower.

"Samara, the last round of envoys, were they met with these types of...problems?" Naokah stumbled on the word. What else could she call them?

"Not like these, no. Rare occurrences in nature with swarms and other accidents, but nothing of this magnitude." A muscle feathered their jaw. "Until your sister met her end."

"Disappeared," Naokah said. "Her body was never recovered."

"Right." They absently scratched their wrist.

"What do you think happened?"

"I'm just the savvy. Why would my thoughts matter?"

"The savvy who knows 'everything worth knowing'. Isn't that what you said?" She cocked a brow. "Who better to know the comings and goings of this place than you?"

The sconces flanking the stained-glass door sputtered as if there was a gust. Naokah shrank back. Could a witch be powerful enough to simulate the evanescent wind?

The savvy noticed, frowning as they turned back to her. "All I can say is...within a week of the envoys arriving last Praxis, we were already sending one home for getting swarmed. Had your sister not stepped up to help him, he would've died. And after that, it seemed like most of the envoys just gave up their will to win."

"Not all?"

"Lenita...." They smiled as though remembering a funny exchange, and Naokah's rib cage threatened to sunder. "Was feistier than ever. I knew from the moment I met her, how she interacted with the staff, how the bees swooned beneath her touch, she was the future Keeper. But, it just wasn't meant to be."

She would've made the best Keeper. Naokah knew. Her family knew. Everyone did. "You never answered my question."

"About what happened?" Their voice quavered. From nerves or guilt, she couldn't tell.

"Yes."

"She got along with the staff just fine. I don't think any of my family would've wanted to or could've hurt her. We looked forward to her tenure. The night she disappeared...." Their eyes went distant. "Lots of strange things happened that night. Obviously not coincidences."

"I don't believe in coincidences."

"Me neither."

"What happened?" Naokah pressed, praying the savvy would open up. If she had any trace of doubt on whether or not she was losing her mind, she didn't now. Dazarin, a huge mountain of a man, was dead. If someone could take him out, what did that mean for the rest?

"For one, it was the new moon. The darkest time in the citadel. There was a storm. Not unusual, you've noticed, but it was relentless. A single boom and all our lighting went out. More concerning was the bees' behavior. One of our youngest hives, near the Keeper's chambers, split and swarmed. We didn't realize until the morning."

"Why would a new hive split?"

"Confounded us all. It had plenty of space to expand, and the queen was placed with the hive only days before. They'd accepted her easily. They certainly weren't big enough to split. The staff is trained in beekeeping. We have our assigned job duties, yes, but our first and foremost charge is tending the bees. We know when a hive plans to split, so we take preventative measures to avoid having to rehome them twice. Less stressful."

"So, the swarm was odd?"

"That, and where they swarmed." They hesitated, looking away.

"Where?" Naokah said after a beat, careful not to push too hard. She was getting somewhere, finally, and couldn't afford to bungle it by making Samara suspicious.

Their blue gaze returned, crashing into her with the weight of the ocean. "The next morning, when Lenita didn't show for her gown fitting, I knocked on her door, and it creaked open.

The pillows on her bed were scattered. Blood streaked the floor. And her comforter was covered with the missing colony. She was nowhere to be found."

The hives from inside grew louder. Or was that the pulse in her ears? The dried brown stuff on Lenita's journal…"How much blood?"

"Not enough to establish there'd been a death."

She heaved a sigh. "Am I staying in Lenita's room?"

They squirmed, confirming what she'd assumed upon finding the journal. Still, the sentries would've looked under the bed, in the vents. They would've inspected the entire room. Which meant someone had brought the journal to Naokah.

"Your supper's getting cold." Samara waved at the door. "Would you like me to escort you?" But their question didn't register. When they waved, their sleeve inched up. Claw marks ran down their wrists. Recent, not scabbed over. They saw that she saw and, face dark, pulled their sleeve down.

"What happened? That looks fresh."

They shrugged. "I slipped, grabbed hold of a sconce. Cut back to my elbow."

"Better have Marguerite look at that." Ignoring their proffered hand, Naokah walked as naturally as she could manage to the end of the veranda. The scrapes on Samara's arm didn't come from a sconce. They looked like defensive marks left from someone's nails before he plunged out a tower window.

★   ★   ★

Dinner went by in a rush. Everyone kept to themselves. Even Brielle was quiet, but Naokah didn't mind. She finished a roll with honey butter and nibbled at her peas. She'd requested a steak but didn't touch it. She'd only ordered it so they'd give her a knife, which she discreetly tucked up her sleeve. The last thing she needed was for someone to see her acting strange and cast their suspicion on her.

Suspecting Samara felt wrong, knotted her stomach. How could someone so composed be capable of pushing someone out a window? Dazarin had irritated them, though, with that harem remark. But surely not enough to instigate murder. She didn't want to believe it, but if she wanted to conduct a thorough inquest, she had to set her personal feelings aside. Samara was now at the top of her list. The healer, tender, and mercy likely weren't involved. The farmer had acted off, but only because he was protective of his crops. Since the tour was interrupted, she hadn't met the chef, distiller, or gardener yet, but Kjell was poisoned, so the chef was on her list too. Hopefully Samara would finish the tour tomorrow. *If* the Praxis continued, that is. Before leaving the belvedere, she'd overheard Brielle and Clisten talking about forfeiting, worried they'd be next.

She didn't blame them. If anything, she envied them. People were dropping like flies, and they'd only been here a couple nights. At the rate they were going, they'd be lucky to make it a week. But unlike her rich rivals, for her the stakes were too high to leave. Her only choice was to stay, weather the storm, and solve her sister's disappearance before she was either eliminated via competition or killed, herself. If Lenita wasn't found, Naokah had a whole dying country to worry about.

You'd just love that, a voice much like her sister's mocked. *Playing the hero.*

Worst-case scenario, Naokah argued back. Armed with Lenita's journal, she'd find her.

Naokah slipped into her chambers through the veranda's glass door, laid the blade on her bed, then hustled to the lavatory to wash up. Footsteps sounded in the next room, and she slid to a stop. Brielle had a full plate when she'd left the hall. The veranda was the long way around but even still, there was no way she could have beat Naokah back.

"Brielle?" She rapped on her friend's door, which was tacky with condensation.

No answer.

Sconce flames illuminated the dripping walls. The mirrors were fogged up, and wet footprints smeared the floor. Someone had bathed recently. Half-digested food twisted in her belly as she forced away the sensation of slimy fingers crawling up her arm. What kind of murderer would break in just to bathe? She pushed against Brielle's door, but it wouldn't budge. Naokah frowned. Brielle didn't lock her side. She liked passing between their rooms without having to go around.

"Fine," she whispered, then tiptoed out of the lavatory, across her chambers to grab the knife, and back to the veranda, now latticed in shadows from the trellis. She tried Brielle's glass door, ignoring how still it was outside. It opened easily. The room was empty. But the lavatory door – locked only seconds before – now sat ajar; a tongue of red light flicked over Brielle's floor. Her adrenaline surged, pumping cold sweat under her arms.

"Just what do you think you're doing?" A voice, behind her.

She spun around, lowering her blade. "Brielle."

Wide eyes gleamed in the shadows. "Why do you have a steak knife?"

Naokah twisted away, cheeks heating. "I heard someone in here. Thought it was you at first, but there was no answer. And the lavatory door was locked."

Brielle's nose scrunched. "It's open now."

"I know. Were you in here a moment ago?"

Brielle shook her head.

And then it hit Naokah, a solid punch to the gut. "Scondra tai!" she yelped, sprinting to her chambers. Brielle called after her, but she didn't hear, didn't slow. She lifted her pillow, biting back a cry of rage. She'd been duped – the journal was gone.

★   ★   ★

"What are you doing?" Brielle asked, amused. She placed a tray of tea at the foot of Naokah's bed, hiked her ivory slip up her thighs, and climbed atop the comforter.

"Taking back control." Naokah had pushed her chair against the wall and now balanced on the damask arms, knees shaking as she reached for the drapes. Night had fallen quickly, and the turrets hemorrhaged a sickly hue much like the blood caking Lenita's journal.

She didn't know who she was angrier with, the thief or herself. Easily swindled, she'd lost her only shred of evidence. Her room hadn't been ransacked. How did they know it was there? Whoever stole the journal also left her room smelling like rotten meat, forcing her to breathe through her mouth. At least for Naokah. Brielle, like before, didn't detect anything. Why was this culprit, this…fine, she'd just say it: Why was this *witch* singling Naokah out? Were they trying to drive her mad, so she'd lose her wits and get kicked off the isle of her own accord?

She grabbed a fistful of the stiff fabric and pulled. The curtain rod groaned and creaked, but the drapes whispered against the wall, covering half the mural's face. One fewer pair of eyes following her.

"Pardon my ignorance, but how is covering up the lovely forest nymph taking control?" Brielle picked up the kettle and filled the cups with something bright blue.

Naokah raised a brow. "Is that tea?"

"Yes. Now come here and stop evading my question."

Too tired to argue, Naokah flopped beside her. "Let's just say, I don't find the murals as lovely as you do." *And I'm not the only one.*

Brielle offered her a cup. "Does this have anything to do with what you were cursing about earlier?"

Naokah cradled the tea, its warmth pleasantly seeping through her stiff fingers. "No, already told you, I stubbed my toe."

Her friend hmphed, tossing her braid over her shoulder. She wasn't convinced.

Lying didn't sit well with Naokah. It would've felt good, liberating even, to have someone to confide in, but she couldn't afford to let her guard down. Not that it would make a difference anyway. Brielle had said she found the citadel eerie – one would have to be a gargoyle not to – but hadn't felt the sinister presence nor seen the girl. Admitting anything would only paint Naokah as crazy. No. She'd have to keep the darkness to herself. There was a murderer on the loose connected to Lenita's disappearance, and Naokah had to find a way to carve out some rest. Catching the culprit required a brain that wasn't complete mush.

"At least answer me this." Brielle's eyes glittered over the rim of her cup. "Scondra tai," she said, mimicking Naokah's favorite curse perfectly. "Scondra means Scorned Son. But I can't figure out the latter."

It didn't shock her that Brielle knew Midese. Most Polers mastered enough to trade with the Midworld. But the fact that she wanted to learn more? Naokah would've swelled with pride if the translation weren't so dirty. She sipped on the blue tea and grimaced. "What *is* this?"

"Nope. Answer mine first."

Naokah bit her lip. "Taint."

Brielle spit out her tea. "The Scorned Son's taint?" she said between giggles. "Mids have the best curse words. I'm gonna steal it." Brielle repeated the phrase a few more times, glowing and giggling more with each iteration.

Despite herself, Naokah couldn't help but join in. Laughter warmed up her insides. How long had it been since she had a good belly laugh? Months, surely. Before the fight with Lenita.

"Your turn." Naokah held up her cup. "What's this?"

"Butterfly pee tea. Supposed to help you relax."

"You served me bug urine? What the—"

"Butterfly *pea* tea, like the purple flower?"

"Oh." Naokah's ears burned. "Well…it tastes like Scondra tai."

Brielle broke into another round of giggles. So did Naokah. Hysterical, they laughed until Naokah's sides hurt, until Brielle could only wheeze. It felt good, necessary. The Poler was right. The tea did help her relax.

Brielle wiped her eyes. "It's an acquired taste."

"Doubt I'll ever acquire it." It was like drinking dirt. Naokah set her cup down, sobering. Her break was over. "Did you get a chance to visit Kjell?"

"That's actually where I was headed. Butterfly pea was...*is* his favorite. Was hoping if I brought him some, it might—" she sighed, looking away, "—I don't know, wake him?"

All the money in the world, and Polers drank dirt? Probably ate snails too. "May I accompany you?"

Brielle's brow furrowed. "But you hate him."

"I don't like him especially, no, but I'm not going for him." She maintained eye contact exactly like Lenita taught her. It wasn't a complete lie. She did want to support her friend. But with Samara's scratches on their arms, she needed to ascertain if Dazarin had skin under his nails and, with the morgue beside the surgery, what better way to gain entry than to feign sympathy for the Poler? Asking the healer directly would've been easier but not smarter. The healer was wary of Naokah's questions, and she already had a watcher. She didn't need two.

"All right." Brielle cast her one last skeptical glance, then sprang off the bed and grabbed the tray. "Let's go."

As Naokah pulled on her slippers, she stepped on a soft lump. She stopped and turned over her foot. What looked like a charred piece of parchment crumbled in her hands.

"You coming?" Brielle's voice pinged impatiently from the veranda door.

Brielle had remembered Naokah's preferred route. She would have been touched, if she wasn't already distracted. A large black spot marred the mural's base. Precisely where the curtains had hung before. The drapes hadn't been stuck to the wall. They'd been melted to it.

★ ★ ★

Samara hadn't mentioned a fire. As the savvy, it was highly improbable that anything happened in the citadel without their oversight. Did they purposely omit that fact, or had the fire occurred before Lenita occupied the premises? Naokah scrubbed her hand through her cropped locks as she and Brielle entered the surgery. Maybe it didn't matter at all, and she was wasting time dwelling on it. She tabled it for later.

Long shadows pooled in the surgery, sucking all the warmth out, and the air was heavy with antiseptic and cleaning chemicals, but at least the stench of rot hadn't trailed them here. Brielle set the tray of tea on the candlelit table beside Kjell's cot. Aside from his shallow breathing and the flames flickering over his waxy face, everything was still. Dead still.

Naokah shivered, wrapping her robe tighter as she sat beside Brielle. "The healer isn't here?" she asked, eyes adjusting. The empty arc of beds were wraiths in the sallow light.

Brielle shook her head. "She left the surgery open for me. Had some…Dazarin-related things to take care of."

"Right." An amber half-moon glowed behind the healer's desk. The entrance to the morgue. Great. Not only would Naokah need an excuse to visit below but, once she got there, she'd have to distract Marguerite long enough to get her turned away, so she could check Dazarin's nails. If the Divine Daughter was feeling generous, he'd be easy to access and not shoved in an icy crevice somewhere. But 'if' held a lot of punch for a word so small, and the Daughter hadn't exactly been forthcoming so far.

"Sure you don't want to give the tea another try?"

"Wouldn't dream of depriving you of a single drop."

"Suit yourself." Brielle sipped her tea, fluttering her lashes.

Naokah snorted, then nodded at Kjell. Devoid of any blemish or wrinkle, he couldn't have been more perfect if the Daughter had carved him from alabaster. Except for a thin pink scar beneath his chin, running from ear to ear. Looked like a knife slash. The Poler had a knack for making enemies, apparently. "Asleep, he almost seems peaceful."

Brielle's hand trembled, and her cup clinked in its saucer. "Kjell's got a lot of good in him, it's just sometimes hard to see. Wish you could've known him before his accident. May've even liked him."

Probable as acquiring a taste for that tea, but instead she said, "Tell me about him."

Brielle squeezed his hand. "I'm not going to try to coax sympathy from you, Naokah. I know you've had it hard. Big family tending a poor farm in a nation devastated by the Razing—"

"A wise friend once told me that no one has a monopoly on hardship."

A faint smile quirked Brielle's lips. "Let's just say all the money in the world can't buy you companionship or a family who cares about you a fraction of how much they love their wealth. Being an only child can be lonely. He grew up in a world of old castles and fortresses repurposed as aviaries. His only friends were birds. I hail from a chateau nestled in acres of vineyards. After my uncle passed, my only friends were plants and Kjell when he came to visit. While our parents discussed their favorite p's – production, power, and politics – we'd venture off to enjoy our own: the pigeage chamber beneath the chateau."

"Pigeage?"

"Grape pressing via feet." Brielle's face lit up, radiant with memories. Naokah had been turning over scenarios for excusing herself to the morgue, but the Poler's sincerity halted those thoughts. Brielle had worn a mask from the get-go, putting on a playful show of nonchalance. Her authenticity was fleeting as the sun peeping through a wall of storm clouds. "Wading about the pools of pulp and juice, pretending we were pirates or explorers on the high seas, it was the one time during our childhood we could be children. But that was before...."

"Before his accident?"

She nodded, watery eyes on Kjell. "He had this darling of a starling—" she giggled at herself, "—named Pierre. Accompanied him everywhere. Even brought him to Vintera. One night, Kjell left the window open and, when Pierre fluttered outside to explore, he tried to coax the bird back in, but tripped. He fell hundreds of feet from his tower."

"How'd he survive?"

She turned over the Poler's right hand where a thick scar sliced from his palm to his forefinger. "He managed to catch a wire and crashed through a window on the bottom story. So—" she lifted a shoulder, "—I suppose you could say he survived. Or part of him did. He hasn't been the same since. His fun-loving nature flew away with Pierre that day."

Naokah found herself actually pitying the Poler. Loss had a way of shucking one's soul, leaving behind a cold shell to inhabit. But for how long could you live empty and alone? Matri could hardly be called alive with her glazed-over eyes, her faraway expression. At one time, Naokah had hoped Tati would return and resurrect her mother. Her youngest brother, Marcos, two at the time, had believed that fantasy more than anyone. He'd swum off after her, nearly drowning and losing his hearing in the process. The Hansen family was still recovering in the wake of Tati's departure. Call it naïveté or desperation, but finding Lenita was their last chance at happiness.

"Dearies," said a throaty voice from the front of the surgery. "Didn't know you were still here."

"Sorry, Marguerite," said Brielle. "Got a late start."

The healer yawned, silver bangs glinting in the waning light. "I was just about to lock up. You can visit him at dawn if you like?"

Naokah's gaze flickered between Marguerite and the morgue's amber eye. She'd taken too much time and missed her chance. Brielle grabbed the tray and nodded at her to follow. As they passed the healer's desk, Marguerite set something down with a heavy clink. Bulbous and over a foot tall, it shined like hammered copper.

"Pretty vase," Naokah said.

Marguerite's lips pressed thin, and Brielle whispered a rushed good night before tugging Naokah onto the veranda.

"That's no vase," she answered Naokah's lifted brow. "That's Dazarin's urn. Zerşilians cremate their dead."

*　　*　　*

Naokah padded along the veranda aimlessly. The air was heavy with the promise of rain, and with the new moon only a few nights away, the trellis was dusted in navy, giving the vines a metallic sheen. Though the torches were but hazy orbs, they were still bright enough to guide her way. Everyone had long since gone to bed, and it was quiet, too quiet in truth. No crickets chirred. No frogs croaked. Only the fog, ever-present, was her company.

She was lonely, restless, bitter.

Who would've guessed the remains of the burly sea god could fit in a space so small? Or that he'd be cremated so quickly? A true inspector would've known. Naokah should've raced over to the healer's surgery right after his death was declared self-inflicted. Like everything else in life, she was in way over her head. If she were a better sister, she'd have progressed further. She'd have tried harder. Was she fouling up this inquest on purpose? She rubbed her temples. No one wanted to find Lenita more than she did. She'd die without closure.

And that was it, wasn't it? It had never been about rescuing her sister. Naokah was selfish. The fact was, her pathetic need for forgiveness had been driving her the whole time. Still, someone was knocking off envoys, one by one, and if she didn't get it together, she could be next. The group had been together before heading off on the tour, except Kjell. But one could hardly accuse an amidst person, stuck between the realms of the living and the dead, of murder. On top of that, all the envoys were on the roof when Dazarin took his last breath. They'd all seen him hanging from that window.

"Naokah," a voice whispered behind a far column.

A flutter of white. Naokah started. Was it the girl? She rubbed her eyes. A series of soft footsteps closed in, rounding the side of the veranda. She held her breath. The ghost girl didn't walk, she floated. Naokah backed up against a column. Sharp green eyes pierced the haze.

"Damn it, Brielle. You're on a roll tonight. Trying to take me out before the murderer?"

Her friend grinned and took a step closer, shrouding her in vanilla and orange. "I'd do a much better job." She sliced her finger across her throat, then placed it on Naokah's neck, sliding it down to the hollow of her collarbone, leaving a trail of gooseflesh in its wake.

"Why are you toying with me?"

Brielle looked wounded. "What do you mean?"

"I...I thought there was something between you and me. Hence, I tried to kiss you last night. But you couldn't get away fast enough. Then today on our tour, you were giving me a dirty look when I was with Laerte. I don't know? Maybe you don't like him. But, I thought, perhaps you were jealous. And now, you're in my personal bubble—"

"Why are you here?"

"On the veranda?"

"In Abelha."

Naokah cocked her head, taken aback by Brielle's directness. "To win, just like you," she said, after a beat.

"I don't believe that for a second."

"Don't care. It's true." Mostly. Lenita was her first concern, despite Naokah's self-serving reason for wanting to find her.

"Is it?"

"That, and...to prove myself."

"To whom?" Brielle's tone softened.

"To myself," she blurted, surprised at how truthful she was. "I've lived in my sister's shadow for most of my life. I love her more than anything in this world, but I envy her. Her natural ease, her Daughter-given gifts, her ability to charm a crowd with a smile. As you've noticed, I'm not the most worldly, I'm painfully awkward—"

Brielle stepped forward, cutting her off with a kiss. And though Naokah wanted to fight it, step back and make her suffer, make her feel the same rejection, the same loneliness she felt last night, she couldn't. Her knees weakened, heat tingling up her throat, and she let go, returning the kiss. Soft, warm, like she pictured it would be, but better. Worlds better. Brielle cupped Naokah's jaw, pressing her chest into hers. Heat welled between them. Nipples stiff, aching, she seized

Brielle's wavy hair and pushed her against the adjacent bee sculpture. Brielle parted her lips, searching for Naokah's tongue. Hers, urgent yet soft, with a hint of wine, flicked against Naokah's. She would've collapsed had Brielle not caught her.

"Wait." Brielle craned back. "I wanted to say I'm sorry."

Every cell radiating with longing, Naokah shuddered. "For?"

"For last night," she said, breathless. "I wanted you. I've wanted you since I spotted you on the ship, the way you gazed up at the gulls, eyes full of wonder. I wanted that too. It's just...."

"What?" Naokah said, defensive. "Because I'm a Crogan?"

"Shush." She put a finger to Naokah's lips. "No. Not at all. I just...I was craven, is all. But, no more." Brielle grabbed her wrists and pressed her against the column, hands above her head. Ivy leaves caressed her shoulders, her back, and when Brielle's lips brushed her ear, a bolt of electric heat raced down her neck. Brielle covered her with soft, teasing kisses. Behind her jaw, her collarbone. Her forefinger glided from Naokah's lips, stopping above her heart, then slid between the thin straps of her slip, and it fell to her waist.

Shivering, Naokah forgot about the darkness, the deaths, her sister's disappearance. Stopped caring about her imperfections. Instead, she homed in on this mysterious siren whose green eyes luminesced beneath the torchlight. How her silky hair danced over Naokah's skin as she continued kissing her breasts, then down, down. How heat spread through Naokah's whole, trembling being, rapid as wildfire.

"May I?" Brielle looked up.

Naokah nodded weakly. Brielle traced her waist, smooth hands meeting at her navel, then moved apart, fingers streaming to the slip resting on her hips, and tugged. It fell into a puddle of gray around her shaking ankles. Brielle kissed her abdomen, then moved lower. Chills bloomed along her arms, her legs, and heat flooded the base of her spine. Brielle trailed her hips, the soft skin of her inner thighs with kisses, moving closer. Naokah thought she might burst, waiting in anticipation. Brielle passed her one last fiendish look, biting the bottom of her full lips, before—

Naokah's knees buckled, and she sagged against the column. The ivy cushioned her shoulders, her backside. Pleasure was building, spreading. Time blurred, rippling around her, going faster, slower, stopping. She saw nothing, heard nothing, only felt ecstasy, sweet, searing hot, tremendous as lightning. Later, it could've been minutes or hours, she was too dazed to tell, but when Naokah finally reached her peak, body writhing with uncontrollable, insurmountable pleasure, fireflies glittered around them like magic released.

CHAPTER TWENTY-SEVEN

Becoming

Trying to evade the thud of boots was equivalent to treading water with no end. I was drowning, ever so slowly, so surely, if I didn't find a means to muffle this fray. I'd checked all the envoys. Other than being terrified out of their minds, feigning confidence to continue the Praxis, they didn't seem possessed. Nor did the staff.

Well, most. I hadn't located Avice or the Keeper until now.

It was after dinner, and they didn't show, but murmurs arose from the Keeper's wing. I slinked through the mural, a group of children no more than seven holding hands, dancing around the Razing. The children, wreathed in flowers and necklaces of dried berries and shells, celebrated the first harvest after the Scorned Son stole the wind. It was a mural of hope, of bravado, but I was still uneasy about it.

The little girl I'd saved hadn't left me. Her clammy fingers, her tight grasp, her fluttering, bird-like heartbeat haunted every second of every day. Who was she? I'd overheard the staff whispering about the Razing's unnatural beasts, the damage they could do – collapsing homes, possessing whole villages, poisoning minds with hallucinations that inevitably led brother to slay sister, wife to slay husband. Civil wars of the nastiest caliber. Were the scrim part of that darkness too? No one had ever been able to tell me what the swarm of creatures was doing, what their purpose was, their origin, other than they didn't exist *until* the Razing. They were linked. Abelha, the scrim, the Razing, the spectral army, and maybe just maybe, how I ended up here in the first place.

I tamped those questions down as the hallway turned cold, the humming fading. If only the marching would too. Crimson light snarled the shifting shadows. I was in the Keeper's wing. I slid into the mural of a woman with an outstretched hand, beneath the door, to the hand she reached for on the other side within the Keeper's chambers. I'd told myself long ago, I wouldn't invade her privacy, not wanting to stumble upon her undressing or doing things humans tended to do in the solitude of their chambers.

But this was dire. My moment of weakness had shaken the citadel's defenses, leaving everyone vulnerable to the next scrim attack. The eldest's words grated my ears: *the first scrim paved the way for others to enter.* At least one scrim lurked around this fortress and, if it hadn't transformed into that viper-eyed miscreant as I suspected, then something else entirely also haunted these halls. I'd congealed from scattered motes to a semi-solid, translucent form – think honey left out in the cold – allowing me to not only feel everything more acutely, the texture of murals, the iciness of shadows, the warmth of the sun on stained glass, but also to be seen. An advantage perhaps, apart from the fact that my glimmer could no longer zip back to my spire. But if my alterations were this immense, what could I expect of the scrim? Would they have morphed into a creature too powerful to handle by myself? This fear propelled me to work faster.

I hid in the mural of a queen bee at the head of the bed, curled up in the fat stripe that swept across her swollen abdomen, and waited. The paint here, oil, not acrylic like the rest of the murals, was warm, inviting. It lapped at my eyelids, pulling me into a deep sleep. I should've fought it, for I was in the Keeper's chamber for a reason, yet the brushstrokes cozied up around me like a litter of warm puppies, and I succumbed.

Rum-glazed lips brushed mine. I awoke on a teal blanket; its fringe spread over moss on one side and dipped into a river of red on the other. I jolted up.

"Relax, love." A callused hand reached into the stream of what I'd originally taken for blood and pulled out a bead so dark it neared purple and popped it in my mouth. It burst; tart juice leached moisture from my tongue. A cranberry. They pulled me to my feet. Myriad crimson channels stacked to sky-high peaks above, and vineyards striped the flat valley below. We were in Vintera during cranberry harvest.

I swiveled to my companion. Dark hair fell in waves over their dainty shoulders, winking beneath the sun's dwindling light. Golden hour, artists called it. But when they turned to face me full-on, their features blurred, as if obscured by mist. They grabbed a sketchpad from our blanket and handed it to me. A woman with mischievous, violet eyes stared back.

"Is this—"

My companion dove into the channel of cranberries. Cool water splashed me. I grinned. Forgetting my question, I dropped the sketch and followed. The buoyant berries caressed my skin as I searched for my lover. A splash. A wriggling foot. I grabbed, but the smooth heel slipped from my fingers. I shot to the surface and—

The mural furred around me, welcoming me back. I shivered out of fury, out of frustration. Water still beaded on my skin. Always so close before the memory fluttered away. My previous glimpse, with flocks and tower-top sunsets, I could've sworn I was from Raptoria. But now Vintera was also a possibility? Distinguishing between oil and acrylic, acknowledging golden hour, the sketch…was I an artist too? If so, who was the woman I'd drawn on the sketchpad? Those violet eyes struck a chord. Why couldn't I make out their face?

Scarlet rippled behind the bed canopy. Silk, a nightgown. I breathed easier, glad I hadn't caught the Keeper indecent, and allowed my gaze to sharpen and expand, searching the crevices in the torch's gauzy light. A pressed carmine suit with bronze piping eclipsed the red. Avice. I knew she'd be here. Two birds, one stone. Still, my strange affliction with her, hate for her proximity to the Keeper, for being able to stroke her downy skin, and respect for protecting her, both of which I'd fallen short of, battled within. The only passion right now, though, was via heated argument. They'd had many lately.

"The Keeper is under much stress, has had much to drink—"

"Don't patronize me, Avice," she hissed, spilling wine on her gown. "I know what I saw."

The sentry grabbed a cloth from her chest of drawers. "What's that, a stir of shadows, perhaps from the candle on your nightstand?" She dabbed the wine from the Keeper's dress.

"No. Something that doesn't belong within these walls." She trembled, but from fear or the sentry's touch? Likely both.

"Something...unnatural?"

"I don't know. Whatever it is, it hides in the walls. I've felt it before, yet from afar. It's closer now." The Keeper's eyes narrowed, skittering across the bee mural.

I didn't blink nor breathe. What would she do if she found me?

"Is it...dangerous?"

"That's a loaded question."

"Why?"

"You know perfectly well why. If I say yes, you'll scoot me out, send me off on a barge, far away from my babies. If I say no, you'll say everything has the potential to be. Like a pet lion. It's never a pet. It can claw your throat out if it's having a bad day."

Avice's face strained as she finished cleaning the Keeper's gown. "My charge, above all else, is your safety. If you got hurt, I would never forgive myself."

"Death comes to us all. And I'd rather die here, surrounded by my bees, than elsewhere."

"Fine. You'll stay." The sentry's voice snagged. "For now. But as soon as I feel you're in the slightest bit of danger, you're off on the next bee barge."

The Keeper grabbed her hand and slumped onto the bed. Sheets rustled to the floor, and a fat fish with plum spikes nibbled at the glass there.

"Have you tried painting?" Avice asked softly.

"Tried and failed."

"But it used to bring you peace. It was your favorite pastime before Monsieur Costa encouraged you to take up beekeeping."

The Keeper's eyes were molten amber. "If by taking my paints and brushes and free will away, you mean *encouraged*, then we have a far different understanding of the word."

"It was for the best. For Vintera, for you—"

"I was nine, Avice. Nine. A little girl. For six years I did nothing but eat, sleep, and breathe bees. He stole my childhood."

"And because of your hard work, you made history. The youngest Keeper to ever win the Praxis. Only fifteen. You're a marvel!"

"A marvel." The Keeper snorted into her goblet. "Another word we define differently. I'm an artist who no longer paints, a guardian of bees who will soon have no bees to guard. I'm no marvel."

"Monsieur Costa has never been prouder—"

"What makes you think I give a bee's sting about my father's approval? I do wonder, however, as you came into his employ before mine, who exactly you serve?"

Avice's head dropped, her copper bun shooting into the air, but she didn't answer. Nor did the Keeper. They sat in fuming silence. I'd known the Keeper had painted the murals, perhaps that's why I felt so connected to them and moved about them easily, but the most powerful woman in all Vindstöld had a controlling father? I never would've guessed. The paintings hit differently now. They weren't just expressions of beauty and boldness but defiance. We had something else in common: her life had been stolen from her too.

"I'm sorry. That was unkind. I suppose any scrap of adoration I once had for my father I poured into the bees. I do love them. They are my life. It's just...something's missing, and ever since Okse, whenever I pick up a brush, I feel like an imposter."

"I do wish you'd tell me about that trip." The captain tucked a stray strand behind the Keeper's ear. "I know it couldn't have been easy, all those refugees, the pain and suffering—"

"It was much easier for the volunteers than the displaced."

When Avice withdrew her hand, the Keeper grabbed her wrist, placing her palm on her cheek. I squeezed my eyes shut, but a duet of soft lips pried them back open.

I didn't want to watch. Couldn't bear it. Yet, my head moved on its own, raze-bent on harming me. The sentry was nestled in the Keeper's arm. Their mouths meshed, skin against skin. No beginning, no end. Moans rose between them, bloomed from their bed, over the glass floor. I couldn't breathe. Couldn't break my gaze. The room blurred, the mirror above her armoire fogging up as a lacy slip sighed to the floor, followed by pants. Then I only saw red.

I swam through the murals in a fury towards the mirror. The foggy mirror, made foggy by their sensuality. I had to escape. The glass, usually cool beneath my wings, was tepid, warmed from their steam. The human I wanted most to acknowledge me couldn't see the pain coating me like tar. And now the kissing, the groping, the perspiration trickling down her neck, lit that tar on fire.

A cry of pleasure. I choked, then concentrated; all my cells and nerves and essence exploded in my fists. The mirror shattered and blew through the room, thousands of shards flashing.

The sentry jumped to her feet. The Keeper covered herself, eyes big and beautiful, searching the room. But I'd already slid beneath the door, swimming into the cold palm of the woman in the mural. Safe. As I sped away, a single thought like an agitated bee buzzed around me. I only managed to touch Lenita, her hair, her sleeve, with the utmost concentration. But now, it seemed, I could manipulate the space around me. Actually destroy objects in my presence, from sheer emotion. Terrifying, yes, but also gratifying. I was changing, my powers growing. What was I destined to become?

CHAPTER TWENTY-EIGHT

Rancid

A thump jolted Naokah awake. It was still dark; the candle on her end table had burned to a winking nub. She reached across the bed and, when her thumb grazed a shoulder, a mixture of guilt and relief swept over her. Last night hadn't been a dream. Not only did she get the girl, but the girl had also chosen to stay overnight. A revelation.

With taking care of Matri, the farm, and preparing for the Praxis, Naokah never had a lover. There was no time. Not that she had any business having one now. She'd known Brielle for what, two days? The Poler's remark about the foxgloves still rubbed her wrong, with her friend getting poisoned by the same flower, yet she'd also revealed that her chateau was a lonely place. Her only friends were plants and Kjell. Would she really use one to kill the other? Naokah might've considered that before tonight, but why? Because no one was more gutted over Kjell than Brielle, or because she couldn't have possibly been both a murderer *and* a cosmic explosion in bed?

The lavatory door creaked open and Naokah tensed. Shadows shifted in soft ochre light. Just the torches, but her pulse pounded thick in her neck. A hollow voice, like the night before, crept up her spine, sighing her name. Her gaze flicked to the mural. Still covered. Brielle stirred, eyelashes casting dark fans down her cheeks. Should she wake her? Whatever sinister presence lurked in this citadel, the Poler was apparently immune. When the water gurgled in the lavatory, Naokah pushed her sheets down and slipped out of bed.

One truth she did know for sure: hiding under the covers would solve nothing.

The cold glass squeaked beneath her feet, and goosebumps crawled up her calves. Steam billowed from the thin crack of orange that led to the lavatory. She paused outside, trying to steady her breathing. But the tremors in her fingers leapt to her brain and, before her knees could buckle, she flung open the door.

Steam enveloped her, and she blinked to clear the fog. Water gushed from the sink. She shut it off, canvassing the glossy tub, the misty floor. No tub creature. No killer. No one. She sighed, irritated but relieved she didn't have to face the culprit, then turned to go—

A pile of orange fur lay by the sink. She prodded it. Cold, stiff. Not a scarf. As more steam cleared, small triangle ears appeared. A fox. And from the awkward angle of its pointy head, its neck was broken. Teeth chittering, she backed up and nearly slipped on the damp glass. *Tá tú chugainn* was scrawled on the foggy mirror. There'd be no sleeping tonight. The phrase was Midese for 'You're next.'

★　★　★

Now more than ever did Naokah understand why in most of Patri's mystery tales, the inspector had a partner. The burden of having to balance all the evidence and theories while trying to maintain a clear mind was crushing to the point of debilitating. If she had a partner, then at least someone would've been getting proper sleep and could've distinguished the nightmares from reality. For example, had someone broken into her chambers last night just to warn her? Theoretically, if she was next, couldn't they have just killed her and saved themselves another trip? Unless Brielle's unexpected presence posed too great a risk? The murderer was strong enough to push Dazarin out a window, though. She and Brielle combined didn't add up to his brawn.

Naokah could still feel the wet plush of the fox's fur, its broken neck, how cold and lifeless its little body had been as she'd carried

164 • RACHEL FIKES

it outside and buried it beneath a rose bush. She'd spent the better part of the night scrubbing at the dirt under her nails, sobbing into the muddy sink in utter frustration and exhaustion and helplessness over not just the poor beast, but everyone she'd lost and could still lose.

She'd woken Brielle with her blubbering, but her lover didn't say a word. She simply turned off the sink, wrapped Naokah's wrinkled hands in a towel, and kissed her tears away. The soft brush of Brielle's lips against her damp cheeks, her nails stroking her back, the gentle whispering of, "It'll be all right" – in Midese, no less – as Naokah cried into her warm embrace, *this*, even over the lovemaking, was an intimacy she'd never had before, and would never forget. Brielle's tenderness almost allowed Naokah to open up, to be candid about the threat, but she simply couldn't risk it. She lied, telling Brielle it was only a nightmare.

As of now, the only people who spoke Midese, aside from the obvious Mid envoys, were Samara, Mateus, the Crogan farmer, and the woman who'd been sleeping in Naokah's bed during the event. But most of the Polers had a well-rounded education of Mid languages for trade purposes, and the staff came from all over Vindstöld. She couldn't very well walk around and casually ask everyone if they spoke Midese. The reprobate would just deny it anyway. *Reprobates.* There could be more, working together. Something she hadn't considered before. As for the fox, though, no one had more reason to kill it than Mateus. Like he said, there was nothing he wouldn't do to protect the bees. But Naokah was as much a threat to the hives as Lenita had been. Something wasn't adding up.

Naokah yawned as Samara, chipper despite the circumstances, swished about the conservatory in their pressed uniform, lecturing the remaining envoys about hive mentality – the collective work of bees to ensure the future of their species. Salmon light swam through the tempered glass, gilding the climbing flowers, and infusing the classroom with a rummy glow. But, like Samara's faux cheerfulness this morning, the sun fell short. No matter how keenly it shone, how fervently Samara spoke, the room boasted all the excitement of a wake.

One of the envoys had killed himself – not really, but that's what the sentries concluded – while one still recovered in the surgery. Kjell hadn't poisoned himself, obviously, so there was a murderer on the loose in the citadel. She knew, the envoys and staff knew, but no one was doing anything about it. On top of that and undoubtedly connected, the only tangible piece of the puzzle she'd had of Lenita's disappearance was stolen from her. She never should've let that razing journal out of her sight.

If there was a silver lining in this fortress of gloom, it was that someone had also brought her the journal in the first place. Someone trying to help. And if she could find them, maybe she could pin down the murderer before they killed someone else.

That was a big if, though. Right now, she had three leads: Mateus, Samara, and Brielle. Weak ones, at best. Brielle could've lied about being in her chambers and snuck into Naokah's quarters, stashing the journal in her frilly gown before she was any the wiser. Why, though? She couldn't think of a motive for any of the three, maybe because she was blinded by her fondness for them. Mateus, fluent in Midese and a known fox killer? The fresh scratches on Samara's arm the night of Dazarin's suicide? Brielle, getting in an argument with Kjell during the welcome ball? Brielle had also warned her about foxgloves. Simply knowing didn't make her guilty, though, and Naokah couldn't penalize her for loving plants.

Naokah shifted in her chair, and it creaked, "You're next," as she pulled at her gray trousers. Down to her last set of pants – the others were dirty or dirtier – she'd been forced to squeeze into a pair that would've better suited Lenita's small hips.

This was taking too long.

She had to meet the chef. He was a worthy suspect in terms of poisoning, having access to food, and there was nothing more she wanted right now than to cross Brielle off her list. Her bias and hankering for a toe-curling repeat of last night didn't help, but the lecture this morning was moving at a glacial pace, and her patience was running—

"Naokah? Did you hear me?" Samara stood before her, brow creased.

"Sorry." Her pulse lurched. "What was the question?"

"I said—" Samara forced a smile, "—what sacrifices do the bees make in order to make it through the winter when they're low on rations?"

"Well, drones only exist to perpetuate their colony. But the males are lazy, don't contribute. Eat too much. So, when winter comes along, they get kicked out, exiled essentially, and freeze to death." Had Dazarin been like a drone? Thrown from the tower because his purpose expired? Had he known too much?

"Very good." Samara tapped Naokah's desk, rings clinking, and strolled to their lectern.

Brielle slid from her seat in a flouncy midriff top and matching, almost sheer, pants. Her belly, toned and freckled as her face, glinted with an emerald and gold chain. "Is there a reason we aren't talking about the fact that one of our friends has been murdered, one poisoned?"

"Fretting will do you no good." The savvy sighed. "The citadel is taking care of it. And as of now, the sentries have determined that Dazarin's tragedy was self-inflicted, not murder."

"Self-inflicted," Brielle muttered, giving Naokah a look that could raze a forest. "I'll believe that the day the wind returns and grass starts magically sprouting again."

"By taking care of, do you mean covering it up?" asked Clisten.

Samara held up their hands. "Please—"

"Like last time," Laerte chimed in, crossing his arms over his tunic. "Naokah's sister vanished in the night, and the guards claimed she was too afraid to swear in? Sure. Not to mention, when my predecessor returned, his mind didn't. He's a shadow of what he used to be."

"Mine was the same," said Clisten, flicking an invisible piece of lint off his brocade vest. "We weren't close. But those from his village

KEEPER OF SORROWS • 167

claim he's a ghoul. Only goes out at night and spends his time pacing burial grounds, talking to himself or maybe the ghosts of the dead."

Clouds festered overhead, and Naokah shivered. Maybe Lenita's fate wasn't so horrible after all, at least compared to the others.

"Think that's bad?" Mila said. "Mine came back, beat his husband, murdered his daughter, then killed himself."

Shocked murmurs filled the air. The conservatory, the one place Naokah initially felt at peace, was now dense, suffocating. Even the vines cascading down the walls shuddered.

"What happened to them?" Brielle pressed. "My predecessor didn't kill anyone, but when she returned home, she quit her family vineyard and disappeared."

"And I bet if Dazarin were still alive, and if Kjell were awake, they'd lodge the same complaints," said Naokah. "What happened to the last iteration? Why was there no connection established until we arrived?"

"Exactly. How could you let us come back, knowing this?" Brielle asked.

The remaining envoys jumped to their feet, hands balled.

"Enough," Samara said, still calm, but their eyes pulsed with panic. "We didn't know about the fates of your predecessors. Only Lenita, for she went missing here on our watch."

"Yet you ended the inquest like it was an open-and-shut case. There was no note of self-inflicted death. No reason for her to flee. No body found. Just streaks of blood and a hive that mysteriously split and swarmed her chambers," Naokah spat.

"I share your frustration." Samara squeezed the lectern's edge. "Something is rancid in Abelha, but like I said earlier, fighting over it isn't going to change anything. Let the past stay in the past, shall we?"

"What if the past is coming for us?" said Clisten. "We should leave."

Patience worn thin, Samara scowled. "Most of you are here because you competed against your countryfolk to earn the opportunity and

168 • RACHEL FIKES

honor of safeguarding your nation's future. But, if the pressure's too much for you, and you're either too scared or not here for the right reasons, then leave. I dare you. The guardhogs will gladly escort you out, but I'd recommend against it. Your nations would string you up for treason when they found out you gave up before you even started, leaving them to squabble over how to procure a sustainable way forward."

★   ★   ★

With the other envoys disgruntled, Naokah didn't feel so alone. Terrible things had happened to their predecessors. That didn't warrant rejoicing, but that also meant that they, too, were wary. And if they were wary, maybe she had allies here after all. Despite Patri's warning, *trust no one*, maybe she could open up to someone? Unload this burden that had rubbed her shoulders raw. Maybe. Right now, she needed to keep digging. She was desperate to see the chef in his element, but Samara thought it best that, after the upheaval in the conservatory, they visit the distiller. It was around midday, anyway, so likely the savvy was hoping to get everyone good and buzzed. Drunk people were happy people, in theory.

Since the storm held off, Samara led them via the veranda towards the eastern wing, where arched crimson doors opened to a tunnel beneath a carpet of vines, plump with grapes and strawberries. The air was sweet, calm, and a hush fell over the envoys as they walked through the latticed shade. Two streams skirted the edges, emptying into a pond that cascaded over steep cliffs. A rope ladder, rather tattered and questionable, was anchored to a large, angular rock between the streams. Samara descended first, swinging their long legs over the side with ease.

"You have a lift to the top of the citadel, but not here?" Naokah's stomach flipped as she peered into the void.

Samara stopped. "There are worse things to worry about than falling, and it's only a couple hundred feet. Besides, you're a

Midworlder. You've weathered worse." They waggled a brow and quickly disappeared beneath the shadows.

Their words didn't reassure Naokah. Nor the others. "And what if one isn't a Mid?" yelled Brielle after the savvy. There was no reply, just her shrill echo.

Clisten shrugged and was next to follow. Samara's warning must've made an impression. The others all took turns until it was just Brielle and Naokah left.

"Want to go first? Or would you prefer I go, so I can catch you?" Brielle tried to tease, but her voice pitched high.

"Scared of heights?"

"Nothing scares me, save ruining my day set." She waved at her elegant attire.

Naokah bit back a grin. "Right. Well, I'll go first. Perhaps knot up the bottoms of your pants, so they don't catch?"

Brielle nodded, humor fleeing as she crouched to ready her hems. "Need help?"

"Go, I'm fine," Brielle urged and, when Naokah didn't move, startled her with a kiss.

"If you were trying to persuade me to leave, it didn't work."

Brielle laughed nervously and waved her on. Lips still tingling, Naokah took the top rung, warm from the others before her, and descended. The cavern was dim, narrow, and she shut her eyes, using her hands as guides. The rungs were close together, thankfully. She imagined she was back in the lift with Clisten, how, even though the space was cramped, it was wreathed in happy, purple flowers.

She tried to hold on to that thought, the bonding moment with the kind Poler, but as she neared the bottom, the air thickened, growing dense and sweet. Treacly sweet. Nausea tickled her throat, and she sped up. But no matter how fast she moved, she felt like she was back in that pit in Croi Croga, the inhuman thing with cold fingers coiling her ankles, yanking her down. The dark place she always ended up when confined. She'd trusted her big sister up until then. Would have jumped off a cliff if Lenita said she could fly. That's the power of older siblings. The love, the praise and worship often ended in mistrust, severed by sharp betrayal.

She supposed that's what happened to Tati and Matri. They'd been close when Lenita and Naokah were young, but there'd been a rift a few years before Tati stormed off and never returned, something that made Matri hold back around Tati. Lenita must've known what it was, but whenever Naokah asked, even older, as an adult, Lenita refused to answer.

A slip of her toe. Naokah fell from the rungs. She flailed, clawing in the dark, until she snagged the ladder, rope burning her wrists. She tightened her grip and slowed her pace, one shaky foot beneath the other. But the deeper she delved, the more her belly tightened. Brielle was oddly quiet. Or maybe that was because Naokah couldn't hear over the blood rushing her ears. Her foot reached the base before her brain registered, joggling her. She inhaled notes of honey and fresh water, focusing on the babble of the surrounding streams. The climb hadn't taken as long as she'd thought it would. Her eyes adjusted to the grotto's leaden light. A gold bubble glowed a hundred feet away, and the thud of footsteps and whispers meant the envoys were close. She licked her chapped lips, craving the numbing calm melgo would give her, and knotted her clammy hands.

"Brielle?" she yelled up, tapping her foot. "The melgo's calling. Hurry up."

No answer.

"Brielle?" Only the chortle of water. If she were close, she would've replied with one of her snarky remarks. Should she go after her? Not yet. She'd wait a bit longer.

But *longer* stretched into minutes. Where was she?

Naokah didn't want to go up, down, then up. She cupped her hands around her mouth. "Brielle, if you're not dead, I'm going to kill you."

Still nothing.

"Razing take me." She grabbed the rope just as a hand fell on her shoulder.

"You aren't her sitter," said Samara. "Her loss if she decides not to come. Let's go."

"What if something happened to her?" Brielle had been talking about this part of the tour since they'd gotten here. A vintner, no doubt, would be fascinated with the distilling process. So why wasn't she here? Not a fear of heights. It was against the very motes of her proud soul to admit defeat. Plus, she'd never give up a chance to drink.

Samara grimaced as if they hadn't considered the possibility, then shook their head. "Doubtful. She's tough. Besides, if anyone tried to take her, she'd drive them mad with her whining. They'd return her just as fast."

★   ★   ★

Naokah veered around the thick stalagmites spiking in and around the burbling streams. The cave dripped cool water down her neck, beckoning goosebumps. They ducked into a small, narrower tunnel. Too small. Too narrow. The walls crushed in around her.

"Samara!" she yelped.

"We're almost there." Without turning, the savvy reached behind them and grabbed her hand. "It's okay, Naokah. Inhale slowly. Through your nose. Exhale out your mouth."

The dank walls continued closing in. Flattening her lungs. A series of ancient sketches etched the curved rock corridors. A long, smoking chasm. Small black shadows floated from it. A woman in red spread her arms, sleeves billowing, as though attempting to fly over the black trench. The next juncture had the Razing expanding, the map of the world shrinking. Scary sea creatures with spikes and rows of pointy teeth ripped apart Mid nations.

"Samara," she whispered.

The savvy squeezed. "Time your breaths with my squeezing, okay?"

She winced but listened, and it worked. With each squeeze, she inhaled, exhaled, homing in on the softness of Samara's hands, their smooth fingers. Finally, the walls parted, and the scent of molten honey, fermented fruit swam over her.

"Better?" Samara tilted their head, the torches glinting off their high cheekbones.

Naokah nodded, and so the savvy released her hand, striding to the others around the metal distillery tanks, leaving Naokah feeling... cold, like having her blanket tugged off in the wee hours of the morning. The comfort of their hand, their patience was so much like Lenita, Naokah had to blink away the sting behind her eyes. Oh, what she'd do to find her.

Large holding ponds surrounded them. They'd come off on a catwalk, and each silver canister bubbled with clear, light brown, dark, and deep honied melgo. Steam ensconced them, thicker than thunderclouds and, if these were clouds, then the woman with hair so blonde it neared white was the Divine Daughter in the flesh, smiling down from her mixing post. Her teeth, white as her braid, sparkled beneath the watery light.

"Josmar, our distiller." Samara waved up. "Meet our envoys."

The woman, wearing a cropped tunic the same shade as her mature melgo, leapt from her post up high, gold cuffs clinking. The group gasped, stepping back for fear of getting landed on, just as she perched on a pole and slid down. Samara smiled, pulling up Clisten, who'd almost fallen off the catwalk into a pool of pale melgo. Clisten, eyes still wide, swallowed hard, throat knot bobbing, as he thanked the savvy. Naokah was impressed by Samara's stealth, their strength, their surety of movement and composure. Clisten wasn't small by any means. If any of the other envoys had tried to help, they both would've taken a dive into the bubbling vats. Impressed *and* uneasy. Perhaps they were strong enough to push Dazarin out a window too? Naokah instantly felt guilty, but she couldn't unthink it.

"So," Josmar said with a southwestern lilt, Zerşilian, "these are the envoys, eh?" She scanned the group, full lips twisting as she noted the number. "Couldn't have cut that many already, Samara."

"A couple were under the weather," they said, unperturbed.

When was the last time Josmar came above ground? Surely she knew about her countryman's fate? Or was she just trying to stir the pot, rile up the savvy? If she was, it wasn't working. Samara stood languidly, a vague expression on their face.

"I see. Well, welcome to one of Abelha's biggest enterprises, honied liquor, or melgo, as we call it. And in order to make said melgo, I rely on the skills of the staff and the Keeper. Our own little happy colony. Like hive mentality dictates, the staff's calm and ease of honey collection is determined by the Keeper. Kind queen, kind hive. Evil queen, evil razing hive. Same with the Keeper. Now you know why we're alllllll so friendly." She winked at Samara, who went rigid. "Now, who wants to try my latest batch? Strawberry vanilla tart."

Friction between the two. But why? A chorus of assents chimed around Naokah, envoys pushing into her, around her. Arms and warm breathing and sweat. She moved back to the empty side of the catwalk, her ledge overlooking a canister of spring water, and glimpsed back the way they'd come. Nothing but darkness speared by dripping spikes, up and down. No Brielle.

Naokah had fully expected her to make an entrance. Where was she? The more Naokah thought about it, the more wrong it felt. She should've headed back immediately. If her friend was in trouble, she'd never forgive herself.

She sprinted to the entrance, ignoring Samara calling her back. She tore up the ladder, forgetting about the cramped space, the possibility of death if she missed a rung, cursing herself for ever listening to the savvy. The air lightened, brightened as she surfaced, falling beneath the latticework. Adrenaline fizzing her neck, she wildly scanned the fruit vines, the hazy path.

"Brielle?" she called, then raced to Brielle's room. Her feet thudded on the wooden planks, the veranda's bee sculptures and topiaries and columns all a blur. By the time she reached Brielle's chambers, she was heaving. Her throat stung, her nose ran, and her ankles cried from rope burn. But she didn't care. She didn't even knock. She slammed open the door, nearly shattering the glass panes. The room was the same cluttered mess Brielle had left before heading to breakfast. There was no sign she'd returned. The lump lodged in her throat grew thorns.

It would be hours later, upon searching the entire citadel with the help of Samara – Naokah's fear of the hives and murals utterly forgotten – that she'd learn, like her sister, Brielle had vanished. Only upon returning to the entrance of the distillery, where she'd last seen her lover, did she discover what could've been a clue. A tiny green feather that in no way could've gotten there naturally. Not on an isle where birds didn't exist.

CHAPTER TWENTY-NINE

Too Large

The marching had become unbearable, pressing steadily beneath my chest, my feet. I'd seeped into the streams coursing below the glass, exploring every winding channel, every bioluminescent hollow beneath the citadel, but came up empty. They were here, this spectral army, ever-present as the air. But where? The fish didn't notice, nor, as I slithered up into the great hall, did anyone here. Was this an echo from my past?

If I could trust my frayed memories, I'd had a lover with warm hands, possibly a daughter who I'd pulled from the Razing. I must've liked drawing and traveling, as I'd sailed to many places and even survived a swarm. Or maybe I hadn't? Had the bees ripped me from the mortal plane? I'd either worked in Abelha or in agriculture to have been exposed to such a swarm. Suppose that didn't narrow down much. Every nation relied on agriculture. I growled, biting my claws to avoid slicing the cherub mural I waded in. Too many soft variables.

I moved to hard truths, which wasn't difficult with only two. I couldn't easily touch humans. There was some opaque element I'd tapped into when I'd grazed Lenita but had yet to locate. With enough churning emotions, however, I could manipulate objects around me. I'd need to harness that soon. For, if I wasn't mad, the invisible army was here. And though it made my skin crawl, my gut twist, I had to shelve it because the scrim was my first prey. I couldn't see it, not like outside during a new moon. Within these walls, it must've morphed, become more elusive. We'd both changed, were still evolving, tapping into powers my kin had devoted their lives to protect. I feared if I didn't trap it soon, its strength would surpass mine, and I'd never catch it. I was hunting on borrowed time.

I heard coughing, down the eastern wing. The Hall of Keepers. I swam through the murals, their shaded grays and blacks like a foamy bath. As I drew nearer, the coughing stopped. I thought it was one of the envoys, but the hall was empty.

A flash of white. A girl's shrill scream. Gurgling, the dripping of liquid on glass. I saw nothing. The temperature had dropped, and the mural was no longer warm; the shading frosted my skin, expelling me to the hard floor. I was naked, exposed without the mural's safety. I probed the lurking shadows but still couldn't find anyone. Just muffled breathing. Someone didn't want to be found. Stink curled my nose, and I froze. Behind the hive wall, pinpricks darker than night blinked on and off like twinkling stars. Nothing about them was brilliant, though. Only terrifying.

The portraits of Keepers blurred as the dots trembled and converged into a pulsating shadow. This creature couldn't have been the scrim. It was too large, too angry. Not the bastard I let in. But when its slit pupils met mine, I reconsidered. Those eyes had haunted Lenita's chambers the night I'd loosed one. It snarled, drool dripping from its rotten lips.

I gagged and tried to slip back into the mural, but I'd have had better luck swimming through ice. It crumbled, sharp projections biting my back, pushing me forward. The creature cocked its head, a hideous, unnatural angle as its eyes burned brighter, searing me. I tried to scream, but its hand hardened to steel around my throat, forcing me into the hives.

Bees rocketed out, filling the air with clouds of vengeance. The monster glared and rocked its head back and forth. Bees swarmed off its charred skull like flames, flaring, filling the space around us. I couldn't die from suffocation. I was a lost soul. But its unforgiving hands cinched tighter, and my vision mottled.

"Where is it?" it moaned.

"Where's what?" I couldn't tell up from down, where its icy hand ended, where I began, as it squeezed my throat.

"The one they—"

The beast cut off, shrieking. A swirl of white ghosted by my eyes. The beast spun, dropping me. My knees cracked against the floor.

"Go!" a young girl screamed at the beast.

It roared and fled down the hall like a giant spider, its legs of darkness separating into thousands of humming gnats before dissolving into the walls. More bees clogged the corridors.

"Thank you," I told her, crawling up. "What did it want?"

Her form sharpened, then blurred. She didn't have eyes. Dark, bottomless voids spilled from her sockets. But I wasn't scared. Something about her calmed me. And then it hit me—

"I know you," I said, a moment too late.

She'd departed, slipping into the mural, a tiny green feather dancing in her hair.

CHAPTER THIRTY

Mates

"What a nightmare," Mila slurred, pouring herself into a seat.

If only. Naokah bit her lip. The gaunt-faced woman knocked over her drink, but Naokah grabbed the goblet before it shattered on the floor. Mila gave her a grateful, if not fragile look, then waved at the barkeep for another. Laerte and Clisten shared the same glassy-eyed resignation. They were at the belvedere, waiting an eternity, it seemed, for news about Brielle. The sun had set, painting the citadel a glowering red, and storm clouds bruised the sky. Another night in the citadel, another envoy gone.

Tá tú chugainn, her mirror had read last night. *You're next.* She'd been horribly, horribly wrong. The threat hadn't only been real, but meant for Brielle. This witch must've known what Brielle meant to Naokah. That they'd shared a bed. That taking the only good thing on this whole nightmare of an isle would utterly gut Naokah. And what had she done to prevent it? Absolutely nothing. This was all her fault. Instead of confiding in the woman who'd comforted her when she'd shattered from exhaustion and despair, she'd guarded her fear, lied, and even gone so far as labeling her a suspect. What a misguided, cynical fool Naokah was.

"Think the sentries will uncover anything?" Laerte asked, refilling Naokah's glass with melgo. Since she'd left the distillery in a fury, he'd brought back a sample of what she'd missed. It was a bit sweet, but the scant solace it provided was better than nothing.

"Doubt it," she said. Like before, the guards had made their rounds interviewing the envoys and staff, their expressions grim, defeated. And just like before, after talking to the cantankerous captain, Naokah left the inquisition with a chill. Because she was Brielle's closest friend and suite-mate, she'd been asked a lot of questions. Had Brielle acted odd? Did she have any enemies? Did she ever express wishes to harm herself? All of which chafed Naokah for a couple reasons.

For one, the captain had already implied Lenita and Dazarin took their own lives and she probably would've checked the same box for Kjell were he not poisoned. Even still, if he never woke up, perhaps she'd try to pin self-inflicted death on him too. Now Brielle? It was the captain's default answer when she couldn't explain the mystery herself.

And two, Naokah hadn't known Brielle for even a week and wasn't qualified to determine changes in her character. But she *should* have. Brielle meant far more to her than some random, one-time romp. The very thought of those big, green eyes sparkling with wit, fervor, compassion vised her throat. She had quirks like anyone but wouldn't have taken her own life. Naokah didn't know much, but she did know that. If only she'd ignored Samara and gone back, Brielle would still be here, pouring her next drink.

Naokah sipped her melgo, and sputtered a cough. The distiller amped her alcohol content to match her aesthetic – beautiful but biting. From their brief encounter, Naokah respected Josmar. Perhaps because she reminded her of Tati and Lenita, strong women Naokah could only dream of being like. Yet, there was clear tension between Samara and Josmar. Had the chiding been related to the citadel's death/missing count or a regular work spat? The distiller had been busy entertaining envoys when Brielle vanished, but maybe there was a team, a resistance from within. Some bees, upon sensing a predator, sprayed pheromones to prompt the workers to hide, then ambushed, rapidly vibrating their wings and cooking the intruder alive. Samara had said the staff and bees were family, not to cross them. If the staff was colluding, taking out the envoys, how did that benefit Abelha? The Keeper was retiring. A bit early, having only sworn in thirty years ago. Maybe for the same reason people kept disappearing. Which raised the question…

"Why hasn't the Keeper emerged from her cave?" Naokah asked. What kind of leader could rest with all the bloodshed in her home?

"She doesn't show herself to just anyone. Not until senior phase," Laerte said.

"No one's going to make it to senior phase, the rate we're going." Clisten, having had enough melgo, flung back a glass of cloudcane rum.

With the sun hiding behind the mountain terraces, the mugginess still clung to Naokah. If Brielle were here, she'd have gone off on another tangent about how the wind thief's stones should've been raked over coals. She swallowed hard, wiped sweat from her brow, and lowered her eyelids half-mast – agreeing with her lost friend, wishing she'd been alive when there'd been wind. It had helped with a great many things, pollination, temperature stabilization, but a good, crisp breeze would help dry the humidity pasting her linens to her skin.

"Another?" Laerte asked. Sweat streamed down his back, darkening his tunic.

She nodded. Alcohol seemed the only elixir that could help numb the sharp, unabating pain. Liquid fizzed in Naokah's goblet, cold droplets from the sweating glass biting into her fingers as Samara emerged from the lift. The suave, crisp-collared savvy didn't greet them. Their hair was a mess, a ratty brass knot on top of their head, their eyes distant.

"Samara?" Naokah asked. "Are you…well?"

They strode to the bar between Naokah and Laerte, grabbed Naokah's drink, and guzzled it like water. "Gather 'round."

The four envoys, brows crinkled and sweaty as their linens, circled the savvy. Naokah's gaze slipped to the winged bull atop the donjon. The only gargoyle facing in. A shadow passed over, and its skin writhed. A chill slinked up Naokah's spine, and she looked away.

"Brielle hasn't been found," Samara said. "The sentries don't know what to think. It's a tragedy, what with Kjell still amidst,

Dazarin dead...." They cleared their throat. "And now with Brielle missing, in the middle of the day. Unprecedented times and I'm sorry, though that doesn't bring your friends back. We need to be more wary, more cautious—"

"No shit," Mila said, now lucid. "Something's been wrong since we arrived. Since even *before* we arrived. Abelha had no business inviting us to contend in the Praxis when you couldn't even safeguard the future Keeper."

Grumbles of agreement, and Samara winced. "Please—"

"She's right," Naokah said. "After Kjell was poisoned, Dazarin was murdered, the citadel should've taken greater measures to find the culprit, to keep us all safe. Instead, you questioned us, the envoys, like it's our fault we are getting whacked off. We weren't even here when Lenita disappeared." Her voice grew ragged, anger barbing her words. "One of your *family*, as you call them, is the guilty party. Why not keep the staff locked up until you narrow down who?"

It felt cathartic to vent, to push the blame off on the staff, but as Naokah's pulse began to slow, guilt spiked it again. Too worried about getting kicked off the isle, about confiding in the wrong person, she'd confided in no one. And where had that led her? If she'd told Brielle about the dead fox and the threat, maybe she'd have been more cautious. If Naokah had told Dazarin about the stalker, maybe he'd have laughed at her, but he might've also been more wary. Wasn't she just as culpable as the citadel, if not more?

Samara's face was now red with fury, with frustration. "I'm just as fed up as you are. Abelha has always been a sanctuary, and for these awful events to transpire? It's absolutely shocking. But you've crossed a line accusing my family. Don't do it again."

Yet how easily you implicated the envoys, hypocrite! Naokah wanted to shout. Instead, she folded her arms over her chest and jerked a nod.

Samara's rigid posture warranted no arguing. "All right. Now, listen carefully, please. Report anything that seems off immediately. And from here on out, no one goes anywhere alone. Understood?"

Sighs and grunts, but no one objected.

"And if we wish to leave?" Clisten asked, tugging a hand through his mop of braids.

"I can't keep you. This wasn't what you signed up for. And I'll understand if you wish to leave. But I don't know what your country will think, you leaving early. Could be a great risk."

"Svinja is a rich nation. They'll be fine. Far better than me, if I stay. I'd rather return a coward than die a fool."

"Must be nice," Laerte muttered, eyes meeting Naokah's. Unlike their Poler friend, who could return without reprimand, the others didn't have that luxury.

"So I have Clisten leaving on a barge tonight. Anyone else?" Samara's eyes landed on Mila, expectantly.

"No." A spark of fight lit up Mila's eyes, earning a look of approval from the savvy and Mids.

"Do you want to move in next to me?" Naokah whispered. It felt wrong inviting someone to sleep in Brielle's bed. It wasn't even cold yet. But like Samara said, they had to pair up.

Mila nodded, her jaw working. "Not shocked the Mids are staying."

"Why's that?" asked Laerte, feigning ignorance. He knew the answer.

"What's there to lose when we've lost everything already?"

★ ★ ★

With the savvy's instructions of having a mate, Naokah weighed whether or not to leave her chambers alone to search for clues. After dashing about the citadel in search of Brielle, not only had she learned the corridors and most of the wings, but, so tormented over losing her friend, she'd forgotten all about the hive walls. When the world was intent on crashing down around her, death by bee swarm seemed like nothing. Time was too fleeting to putter about the veranda any longer. Tonight, she'd brave the innermost workings of the citadel and face her greatest foe – her own fear.

During her frantic flight, she'd met Ettori, the chef, and Andre, the burly gardener, in one of the kitchen's pantries. Well, not so much met. More like stumbled upon their steamy embrace beneath the shelves of poppy bread. Samara had called out to Naokah to stop, but she'd already yanked the door open. Naokah ended up retreating to the kitchen island, where sweeping, stained-glass windows domed over her, and hid awkwardly behind a ten-tiered butter cake while they dressed. Though embarrassed about being caught – in truth, she was likely more humiliated – they'd helped her search every inch of the spacious kitchen, their snarky humor mixing smoothly with the sweet, yeasty notes. The lovers couldn't take a single step without touching each other.

She felt a sharp pain in her chest. She missed Brielle. Naokah had finally met all the staff but still felt no closer to finding her sister and friend. Neither the gardener nor the chef gave off any flickers of darkness, and besides, for the couple to premeditate murder, they'd actually have to stop holding each other for more than five seconds. No wonder meals were often served late.

With Brielle gone and the farmer indisposed – she'd have to catch up to him in the early morning before he left for the terraces – Samara remained at the top of the list for Dazarin's death. They pulled late hours and, with almost everyone asleep, they'd be off their guard. She'd follow them. See if they did anything strange. Hopefully, she could catch them unawares and get them to explain what happened with Dazarin. The way they spoke of Lenita, finding her room empty save for blood and bees, the sorrow they'd shown, made Naokah believe they couldn't wholly be responsible for any crime. Still, they could've been taking orders from someone and regretted it later. This was what she'd have to determine tonight.

Only a minor detail was holding her back: Mila. Naokah couldn't leave her alone. She was breaking the rules already by wandering the halls at night. Should she tell Mila her plans? She probably wouldn't volunteer to get involved, but Naokah had seen fight in her eyes tonight. Up to this point, Naokah had been trying to investigate on her own, but where had that gotten her? A lost lover and self-loathing. Would Mila help, though, and if she would, could she be trusted? Her lack of trust had flung her into this mess in the first place.

She helped Mila settle in. Arranging her worn suitcase. Stripping the sheets and fitting the bed with fresh ones. She supposed she could pose the question. What's the worst Mila could say? After sponging clean – she was taking no chances with the tub fiend tonight – and throwing on her camisole top and mismatched bottoms, Naokah rang for some mint tea. When it arrived, she grabbed the tray and knocked on Mila's door.

"Yes?"

"Tea?"

"Isn't it a bit late for tea?"

"It's never too late for tea." Naokah took a note from Brielle's playbook and pushed through the door before Mila could turn her away. "Besides, it's mint. Helps calm the nerves."

Mila snorted softly and nodded at her end table. A small lamp cast shadows over it. Two plum cushions sat beside it. She placed the tray down, poured Mila a cup, then sat on one of the cushions. Mila accepted the cup and saucer but didn't sit. Naokah suppressed the urge to stand back up. Someone towering over her, no matter how harmless, made her uneasey.

"What's the catch?" Mila eyed up the lime-green tea.

Naokah raised her cup in a toast then took a swig. "See? No poison."

Mila bit back a slight smile, then sipped too. "Didn't think there was. No, what I'm asking is why are we having tea at the twenty-first hour? We have an early morning ahead, with the Praxis. I thought you'd want to get some sleep."

Naokah lifted a brow. "Have you been able to sleep since you arrived?"

"True. But still. You want something."

"Cut right to it, don't you?"

"That's how it is in Bizou." Mila shrugged. "Time is a commodity we never have enough of."

Bizou had been sacked by the Razing. Without enough space for even a handful of farmers, the majority were forced to seek employment elsewhere, usually manual labor on Poler plantations or crewing crabbing ships in the east. Hence, Mila's waiflike presence.

"Since I can't sleep, I've been walking the veranda at night."

"Why?"

"Trying to find clues about...." How much should she tell her? "The tragedies that have occurred thus far." She slipped a hand into her pocket, fingers stroking the soft green feather. She'd picked it up before sentries had arrived. Not like they'd have been able to link it to anyone.

"You think wandering about this macabre place at night is the answer?" Mila narrowed an eye.

"Better than rolling about sleeplessly in my bed, hiding, waiting for whatever took them to take me next," Naokah snapped, then regretted it when Mila blanched. So pale, she reminded her of the ghost girl. "Sorry. Just on edge, is all."

"Me too." Mila's hand shook as she set the cup back on its saucer, spilling tea on the gold rim. "Why are you telling me this?"

"With the new rules in place, I didn't feel right leaving you alone, you know, in here."

"Are you asking me to accompany you?"

Naokah flinched at her bluntness. "Err, yes?"

"Why would I want to put myself in more danger?"

"Depends on how you look at it. I'd say it's more dangerous sitting alone in here, with only the shadows and murals keeping you company."

"I don't think it's safe anywhere, to be honest, but I'll take my chances." She padded over to her bed, pulled the ruffled comforter back, and climbed in.

"So, it's a no."

"I'm poor, not crazy. Make sure you lock the lavatory door behind you."

What had she expected? Just because she'd helped Mila, that the woman would feel indebted to her, putting herself in harm's way? She got it. Still, it irritated her. More so, she had to leave her behind. What if she went missing?

"Is your hall door locked?"

"Of course," Mila said, voice muffled in her pillow. "Try not to get yourself killed, eh?"

Naokah locked the door behind her. "You too," she muttered to herself.

She waited until the voices faded, the hallways stilled; only the hum of the hive walls kept her company as she slipped out. But as she padded to the savvy's alcove, the cadence of drums, the pluck of violin strings, stopped her. Music from the Keeper's wing. Her part of the citadel was off-limits, but Naokah was breaking the rules anyway. Besides, the savvy's nook was dark, silent.

She twisted around, opting to take the Hall of Keepers. The moon was a scythe in the sky, and it seeped through the stained glass, smearing the frames in the black purple of pooled blood. The sound picked up, the beating of the drum faster, more chaotic. Her pulse matched, and she sped up, reaching the Keeper's wing in no time. Naokah's breath clouded the air. She should've brought her robe. As she passed the library, the glass above the books cast the shelves in jewel tones, and the nostalgic scent of dust and old pages cloaked her.

When Tati left and Matri lost her wits, Lenita had taken over running the household. Naokah helped. After a long day of weeding and picking cloudcane beneath the sun's glare, the two would have their work cut out for them inside. While the girls were cooking and cleaning, Patri would read from *Foklor de Croi Croga*. Some of the tales were inspiring, of children half Naokah's age setting off on adventures around the world, and some were dark and chilling, foretelling prophecies. Whenever she heard the crinkle of pages, Patri clearing his throat, she worked just a little faster, so she could sit by the living room pit, where smoking ice plumed, and listen to him read – the best part of her day. The farm sustained her, her family, but she worked out of necessity, not passion. Even prepping to win the bid over Lenita hadn't fulfilled her. Something had always been missing, was still missing.

The beating drum pulled Naokah back to the citadel. Now, she peered through stained-glass arches. A woman with a long train moved about the library. The glint of a ruby videira, and Naokah's chest fluttered. The Keeper. A cloud of tiny shadows buzzed around her. She couldn't ascertain where the music was coming from, as there were no musicians, but more shadows peeled off the walls, moving in perfect time to the drums' cadence. The Keeper danced with bees. She shouldn't have been spying, interrupting some intimate moment with the Keeper and her colonies, yet she couldn't turn away. The music ebbed and flowed, hypnotizing her.

A bright light sparked inside the library, and Naokah pulled back, but still didn't turn. The Keeper had a torch, the flames burning white-blue, lighting up her youthful face. Naokah blinked, straining her eyes. How could this woman be in her forties? She didn't look a day over thirty. Which had Naokah even more concerned. She wasn't ill nor old, both reasons for a Keeper to pass on her position. So, why was she stepping down? It made no sense. Not when all this power stemmed from her.

And the bees.

She'd always viewed the bees from afar, respect lined with fear. A necessary evil to continue crop production. But here, as they spiraled around the Keeper, wings iridescent beneath the torchlight, they looked like fairies. The way the Keeper eyed them was how Naokah had eyed Lenita. Pure, unconditional love. What could be so terrible that she'd abandon her post decades before her time?

Bony hands fell on Naokah's shoulders. She spun around and gasped.

Dark eyes, wide with terror, stared back. "What are you doing all the way down here?" Mila seized her arm, pulling her back to the Hall of Keepers.

"Could ask you the same question," Naokah rasped, flicking the woman's cold fingers from her skin. "I told you I was going to search for clues. What are *you* doing here?"

Mila wrapped her arms around herself. "Some...thing is in our suite."

Naokah's stomach pitched. "Not some*one*?"

"Do you know anyone with eyes that glow yellow?" Mila whispered, stopping in the middle of the hall. The sliver of moonlight fell over her face, and not for the first time did she remind Naokah of the ghost girl. "What do we do?"

Had she accidentally left the veranda door open? What beasts lurked about the isle at night? "Find Captain Avice."

"But we aren't supposed to be outside our rooms."

"A beast in our chambers negates that, don't you think? Come on, the captain will know what to do." She hoped.

But Mila didn't follow. She stood in the shadows, rocking back and forth.

"Unless you'd rather go back and have tea with that creature, I'd suggest you follow." Naokah stopped, then swiveled around. "And quickly. Likely, that thing, whatever it is, knows you've left. It could be following us already."

That made her move. That, and a bright, blinding flash, followed by a crash of thunder that shook the citadel. The frames trembled and dust motes floated through the air. Another flash, and the shadow of a horned beast lurked over the murals. It growled, fangs dripping, and twisted its head to the side with a wet thunk, as if it had snapped its own neck. But then it leapt forward.

Naokah grabbed Mila's hand and screamed, "Run!"

CHAPTER THIRTY-ONE

Not a Blur

She saved me, and I didn't even know her name. Nor what the foul creature that tried to strangle me was. Nor how she, by simply yelling at it, scared it away. But those huge, doll-like eyes? I could never forget them. I'd pulled her from the Razing. Had I merely been doing my civic duty or was she something more? Did I have a daughter? I tingled with warmth at the prospect of family, someone to love who'd love me back, but dashed it away just as quick. Now was the time for action. Hope would have to wait.

Above and below, the army never ceased. No matter where I looked, they remained invisible but for their heavy boots on my chest. Grasping for anything that could distract me, be it bad or worse, I searched the shadowy halls for the girl and the beast, fretting over what I'd do if I didn't find them in that order. She'd been able to hold it off for now, but what if it attacked, and she didn't appear? It wanted something, something it thought I had. My gut told me she had the answer. Was it looking for the scrim, or *was* it the scrim, transformed like me? Whatever it was looking for, I couldn't allow it to find it.

It was midnight, the moon a thumbnail in the turrets. With the scrim attack looming, I had a brief window to find the two antipodes, light and dark, before the fray. My actions had paved a path for the scrim to enter the citadel, and if they turned into similar fiends, I'd have more to handle than just shifty envoys. The Keeper's life was in danger. Avice, resentment towards her aside, was a good sentry, an unremitting shadow of the bee guardian, but even she was no match for the beast. If there was any chance of retrieving my identity, the Keeper had to survive. Illogical as it was, my fondness for her had only grown. Maybe one day we could be friends.

Chants and yells rang from the fitness arena. I swam through murals, past the library, great hall, and conservatory to an oblong room that uncoiled into the hedge maze like a serpent's tail. Banners of flowers depicting sigils of Vindstöld's seven nations unfurled from the top of the arena's skylights down to the glossy floor, now covered in tumbling mats. Abelha's banner was easy to pick out: yellow dahlias were groomed together, creating a queen bee wreathed by her workers. The rest of the panel was filled with dahlias so burgundy they neared black. Banners with symbols of cloudcane, birds, grapes, and cattle snagged me, and I tried to dive deeper into my endless well of memories, but a bellow from the arena diverted me.

Samara had the envoys conducting combatives. As usual, Lenita stood out. She was smaller than the rest, a good foot shorter, but toppled one after another, throwing them over her shoulder. Samara nodded, grinning with each envoy she bested. They favored her. Crogans had endurance, working on cloudcane farms day in, day out. If the Keeper were to walk in right now, she'd have told the others to concede. I would have too. More impressive, Lenita wasn't smug when she won. She fought like a dancer, limbs feathering out, full of grace.

Not that the future Keeper needed to train for combat. They'd spend more time coaxing bees than punching enemies. This segment of the Praxis was symbolic. There were often multiple queen bees born at the same time. They had to fight to the death to ensure their code passed to the next generation. A little primitive, but had I not spent my existence killing creatures I knew nothing about? Hivemind was real, compelling, and I'd often wondered whether it was the eldest or the Keeper who controlled me? Why did I know so much about the citadel and the bees? Had I been a staff member here, or did my knowledge of Abelha offset my past because I, a gargoyle, was part of the citadel? With the end near, the marching in my chest, should the citadel fall, I'd go with her.

I homed in on the envoys, their set jaws and sweaty skin, the crinkle of their linens as they grappled, searching for anything out of the ordinary, anything inhuman. Lenita fought the envoy from Raptoria. I'd unwittingly squirmed behind his sigil, a hydrangea bird, wings outstretched into a sunset, but shifted, taking cover in the wine banner of Vintera instead. I'd yet to shake off those shrewd eyes, that cackling. Had I encountered Enzo after I loosed the scrim, I would've sworn he was possessed. Tall and lean, he moved like a praying mantis. But Lenita was faster and bladed a leg beneath him. He tripped. She reached down to help him. He punched her in the throat instead. She coughed, collapsing to her knees. The other envoys, having fallen to her, cheered him on. Samara's arms were tight over their chest.

"Keep it clean," Samara told Enzo when, while Lenita wheezed, face purple, he thrust her down. The urge to return the favor itched my heel. As he threw an arm around Lenita's neck, pulling her onto her back, a memory throttled me with the same force.

I was on a ship. It seized to a halt; the gulls behind the sails flew away, abandoning me. Us. The whole crew. I cursed, furious my costly investment had vanished. I'd ventured up to the Weeping Sea, the wedge of glassy water separating Vintera and Raptoria. I didn't remember what I was doing here, perhaps picking up goods from the north, but this particular sea, despite its teal color, was sinister. I was confused, wary, and, even more frightening – lost. Soupy fog encapsulated my ship. I couldn't see a foot in front of me. With no wind, no flock, I was stuck here. Where was my lover with the obscure face? Something splashed the hull, then the bow. The fog darkened. A cacophony of screeches. A flock, a massacre. Mine?

"Tyrant!" a woman yelled.

Something hard whacked my head, pain stabbed behind my eyes, and I face-planted into the deck. Darkness gushed over me.

Screaming jerked me back to the fitness arena. Lenita had one black eye, the other swollen shut, but that hadn't stopped her.

She'd pinned Enzo, punching his face bloody. The envoys huddled around, crying for her to get off. His nose made a wet, crunching sound, and he bellowed. Samara tried to pull Lenita off, but she fought with such strength. Blow after blow, she moved so quickly, she was a blur.

No, not a blur.

As she lifted her right arm, something beyond her linens, a veil, flapped outside her skin like wings. More sheer fluttered over her legs, her back. And when Samara pulled her off Enzo, the presence in Lenita fizzled, evaporating like mist in the sun. Before it disappeared, it twisted my way. Shadows oozed from *her* sockets. The ghost girl. No wonder I couldn't find her. She'd been inside Lenita. She pummeled that envoy for what, taking a cheap shot? Now I wasn't so keen on seeking her. If she could possess vessels, forcing them to do terrible things, was she any better than the viper-eyed beast or me?

What if she was worse?

⋆　　⋆　　⋆

After the tussle, I followed the girl to the gardens. She pranced atop the hedge wall, floating faster than I could stride. No clouds in sight, the sun perched high in the powdery blue sky, and the air effervesced with honeysuckle. A disgrace. The weather was flippant as she was. With doom's legions so near, the horizon should've been devastated, trembling, weeping. Not throwing on a sparkly gown, spritzing on cheap perfume, and pretending we were attending the ball of the century.

"Why'd you do it?" I asked, averting my gaze. The girl's dark sockets sucked the heat from my marrow.

"He deserved it," she finally answered with a shrug.

"For a tactless jab? Lenita can hold her own."

"For now, yes." The girl blew at a butterfly that promptly fluttered away. "But darkness falls this night."

"It falls every night." Her cryptic answers irritated me.

"The envoys will come for her. For revenge. She won't be able to stop them."

"Why?"

She sighed. "Could be jealousy, greed, corruption. I don't know why, just when."

"And you can't help her?"

"It's your turn."

"Mine?" I'd devoted my time to taking the envoys down, and now she wanted me to help?

"You ask too many questions."

"Sorry," I said. Her cold stare stole my breath. "What will happen to her?"

"Nothing, if you save her."

"Why would I want to do that?"

She plucked a white blossom and sat. Her small body glowed from within like a cloud crowning the sun. "Because she's important to someone you care about."

"You know who I am?"

She tittered. "I do."

Divine Daughter! Finally. "Who?" I pressed.

She laughed, mirthless, and I growled. I could've pried more from the eldest gargoyle.

Are you mine? I wanted to ask, but I was afraid. If she was my daughter, was it not my fault she had this brutal side? "At least tell me where you came from?"

"Don't you remember?" She blew on the honeysuckle blossom, and pollen danced between us. "I came here with you."

I sneezed, and she vanished. So razing close. I was tied to the ghost girl *and* the envoy I'd planned on eliminating. No wonder I felt attached to Lenita. But now what? The ghost disappeared before I could ask about the beast. Flustered, I rushed back inside—

The foliage sucked me in. I fought, flicking the waxy leaves, but the sun's warm hands intervened, tugging down my eyelids. I couldn't remember the last time I slept, probably before I loosed the scrim, but there wasn't time.

Deep within the maze of my nightmares, a swarm of bees and the viper-eyed beast chased me. Sweat poured down my back, my legs. I slipped. Fell into the mouth of a mural. The mural gaped, then collapsed. The floor split between my feet. I jumped to one side, hitting the ground with a painful thunk. Smoke billowed from the expanding trench. Pressure yanked my arms, pulling me into the Razing. My lover with the hazy face hung from one hand, the girl who may've been my daughter, the other. Both pleaded with me to save them, but my joints popped, fingers slipping. I'd have to choose.

I can't, I sobbed. *Please don't make me.*

The girl with big round eyes nodded the saddest nod I'd ever seen, then released.

I shot up, drenched in sweat. The sun had sunk below the mountains, spilling orange, purple, and pink across the horizon. But I felt no peace. Had I killed my own daughter? I rubbed my aching skull. I was acquiring all the weaknesses of humans without any of the benefits.

A shadow swooped overhead. A small green bird flew above the dome. The warded mesh glimmered beneath its shadow, its *nosediving* shadow.

I waved frantically. "Stop—"

The bird exploded, a ball of feathers and flames.

Didn't they have mates? Couldn't they have warned each other this isle was merciless? I shook my head. A needless death. A feather no bigger than my thumb tickled my chest. Tipped in emerald, its violet center speckled gold. I traced the soft fibers. The girl had worn a similar one the night she saved me. I had to find her.

But first, Lenita.

I swam back inside. The shadows slipped over me like a heavy cloak. I'd started out wanting to get rid of Lenita, of all of them. They threatened the Keeper's tenure. But now the Crogan could be the key to my existence.

I slipped by the great hall and, though the food had been served, steak and potatoes sat on porcelain platters, and goblets of wine spanned damask tablecloths, no one was there, save the staff. The chef was in a heated argument with his lover. Probably over the food sitting out, getting cold. Every second I didn't find Lenita was a second closer to her death. Panic thinned my blood, and I swam through the halls, then stopped.

Distant voices. I slammed open the door leading to the distillery outside. Hollow screams burbled up from the grotto.

I flew beneath the lattice of vines, over the cliff. If I had skin, I'd have burned it off, so fast did I slide down the rope ladder. Navy shadows lapped over me. Treacly murmurs of honey and cloves and berries thickened to jam on my tongue. I gasped for air, chasing the voices. As I ran down the catwalk, metal clinking beneath my claws, I found them.

A huddle of linens and pastel silks, screams and sobs. Enzo, with a bandaged face, had Lenita by the back of the collar and another Poler held down her shoulders, submerging her head in a cooling melgo tank. She flailed about, amber liquid frothing. One of the other envoys, the scrawny one, was the sobbing I'd heard. He yelled and begged, tearing at the others to let Lenita go, but they pushed him away, threatening to drown him if he didn't shut up.

Lenita's body slackened; the bubbles grew smaller. Her arms no longer moved. Something within me snapped, and everything went red. I sprang forward, claws and fangs out.

"Cravens!" I snarled.

They whipped around, releasing Lenita. She fell into the vat. I careened by the envoys, their eyes wide. I forced all my fury into my claws, imagining how they would feel sinking into Enzo's skin, and slashed him across the throat. He dropped like a rock into a boiling vat.

An envoy shrieked and tried to save him. I squeezed by her, pushing her in with him, and laughed like a loon. My guffaws thundered the cave. Each echo chimed in my ears as the other envoys scrambled away. Lenita had sunk beneath the melgo; ivory linens clouded up above her. I dove in and grabbed, but my hand slid right through.

"No!" I wailed, bubbles engulfing me. Melgo, sweet and thick, plugged my mouth. I grabbed. Nothing. How did I slash that bastard's throat, push his friend in, yet now I couldn't even manage to hold on to this drowning girl, a task far simpler?

No more bubbles left her mouth, and she sank lower.

There had to be a way. I thought back to the Keeper's chambers, that night I'd seen her and the captain kissing. The anger I'd felt; it was uncontrollable. I'd blown out her mirror. Pain was power.

Instead of feeling sorry for Lenita, I threw my rage at her. Angry that I was in this blasted citadel and still didn't know who I was, where I was from, what my purpose was, and why I felt the asinine need to save the woman I'd planned on killing. I retracted my claws and seized her arm. Impact, soft and spongy. I pulled her up and flung her over the side. But she was cold and still, limp as a fish. I jumped out and dragged her to the catwalk. *Hit her chest*, said a voice within. I was wary but had no alternative. I slammed my fist down. Stone against bone.

Once.

Twice.

Thrice.

She coughed up amber foam and, though my throat tensed, I relaxed. Her breathing steadied, violet eyes flickering on me.

"It's you," she said, smiling faintly, then passed out.

A strange sensation swelled within, stinging my eyes. I saved her, and she remembered me. I'd finally been seen, and now, for the first time since waking, I glowed with pride.

CHAPTER THIRTY-TWO

Mad

"It's gaining on us!" Mila glanced over her shoulder.

"Conserve your air," gasped Naokah.

They tore through the dark hallway, glass thudding under their feet. She ignored the leering murals, the humming hives, the fact that the horned gargoyle from the donjon had somehow jumped off its perch and was now inside, chasing them. The corridor would end soon. She'd have to make a decision, but the closer she got to the conservatory's frosted door, the more panic stifled her thinking. Her sleepless nights had caught up to her, weighing her down.

"Where can we go?" Mila gleamed with sweat.

Naokah groaned, irritated she'd done all the problem-solving so far. Mila was a keen, scrappy survivor. Why couldn't she pitch in? Was the gargoyle leashed to the grounds like the crith tethered to the Razing? If they left the citadel, would its strength fade? Her mouth dried. Her gut writhed. The rancid stink from her room had returned and ripened.

As her lungs fought for air, her eyes played tricks, fuzzing the shadows into more beasts.

No.

Goosebumps tracked her damp skin. Not tricks. She skidded to a halt, panting, filling the dark corridor with cloudy breaths.

"Where are we?" Mila huddled beside her, teeth chattering.

"Don't know." Naokah wrapped an arm around her shoulders and pulled her in tight, away from the...the.... "Please, Mila," she whispered, rubbing her eyes. "Tell me I'm not mad. Tell me you—"

"I see them too."

A sea of rotten hands flailed about in the murals. Painted with such skill, their long, spiraled nails seemed to claw from the walls. Beneath, grotesques with slacken jaws and oozing teeth drowned in black waves. They were contortions, mockeries of the human form, and couldn't have possibly come from the Keeper. Her depictions, albeit often erotic, were poetic, hopeful. Whoever created these was demented.

"Sea of Sorrows," Mila whispered, and Naokah nodded, shivering.

Because the Divine Daughter considered betrayal the worst offense, upon death, anyone committing it would descend to the Scorned Son's afterscape, sentenced to drown for eternity in the Sea of Sorrows. These murals, filled with regret and agony, were so real, too real, as if the artist themself had endured it.

Something warm splatted Naokah's neck. She jumped, swiping her skin. Her hand came back red.

Mila shrieked, "Don't look up—"

Too late.

Hanging upside down from the turret was a lean figure in carmine, their long brassy braid dangling like a fraying rope.

"Samara!" Naokah cried, and Mila threw her a puzzled look.

The savvy twisted their neck in an unnatural angle, and it popped with a wet crunch, not unlike the horned gargoyle's, and their vacant gaze landed on the women. A ghoulish sneer that didn't belong to Samara stretched across their face, and then a voice, ancient and diabolical, said, "You were warned not to wander." They cackled and clawed repeatedly at their wrist, dribbling hot blood over Naokah and Mila. Naokah gagged.

She grabbed Mila, not caring where she was going as long as it wasn't here, and bolted into the shadows. Pushing until her legs cramped, pushing until her chest might explode, until finally, the hives greeted them. Never in all her life had Naokah been so grateful to be surrounded by bees. But they still weren't safe. Not yet.

She changed course, pulling Mila towards the doors where a teardrop of moonlight leaked through the gazebo.

"The hedge maze?" Mila squealed as they dashed into the darkness.

"Unless you have a better idea?"

Mila shut up, trailing close behind, and Naokah was grateful, catching her breath. As they sprinted deeper into the maze, the towering walls of green, now black in the dead of night, wound around them like a resting snake. Naokah wiped the sting of sweat from her eyes. Crisp dew and notes of crushed foliage settled her stomach and wreathed her with an aching for home, for Lenita.

Did the gargoyle take her sister? Possess her? Death, in this case, seemed a better fate. Was poor Samara doomed too? Guilt squeezed Naokah. Instead of staying to help, she'd fled. If Lenita were here, she'd have stayed and fought. She did. And that's why she was missing. Naokah shuffled through Patri's tales but couldn't recall anything about gargoyles coming to life.

A column of smoke rose in their path, solidifying. Mila took a step back, and Naokah grabbed her hand.

"You're safe, at least for now," the amorphous figure said, voice crackling like fall leaves. It didn't seem to match the girl emerging from the fog. Her eyeless sockets bled shadows, and Mila gasped. Naokah gripped her hand tighter. The girl was now solid and tilted her head at that odd, bird-like angle she'd first shown Naokah on the cliffs. Adrenaline flared, but Naokah held her ground. The gargoyle and the Samara puppet were scarier.

"What was that thing in there?" Naokah asked.

"Which thing?" The girl's filmy face bore no expression.

"The gargoyle. I recognize it from the donjon."

"That's not what I saw." Mila wrapped her arms over her robe. "It was a huge, scaly shadow, eyes slit like a serpent."

"But you did see Samara hanging from the turret?" Naokah pressed. "Their body, I mean. That thing wasn't the savvy."

200 • RACHEL FIKES

"No." Mila's brows furrowed. "With long black hair, sunset tips? That was Kjell."

"Different visions but the same monster," said the ghost. "It curates your greatest fears and twists them into personalized nightmares."

Naokah shivered. The moment she'd stepped foot in Abelha, she'd felt eyes on her, had even cringed beneath the gargoyle's stare. "And you are positive that…thing wasn't Samara?"

"Nor Kjell?" Mila murmured, grimacing at the blood drenching them both.

The ghost nodded, and a heavy weight rolled off Naokah's shoulders. Despite her cowardice, the savvy was fine.

"Then what is it?" Mila asked.

"You're familiar with the Scorned Son's afterscape, I take it?"

"Who isn't?" Mila sassed, surprising both Naokah and the ghost. She had pluck after all. "It's where the Divine Daughter banished her little brother for stealing the wind. Where we'd end up should we ever betray our family." What they seemingly just escaped from.

"And where precisely is it?"

An uneasy look passed between Naokah and Mila.

"Millions of leagues away?" Mila asked.

"So some say." The girl tossed her hair over her shoulder, and it oozed like melting icicles down her arms. "But what if I told you it's not so far? What if the entrance to the Scorned Son's afterscape is actually quite near?"

"As in, *here*?"

The ghost nodded, guttering like a dying candle.

Mila shook her head. "But why would the Divine Daughter want her brother in Abelha?"

"Keep your friends close and your enemies closer." Naokah swallowed a scratchy lump. "So, this thing is the Scorned Son's spawn?"

"The Divine Daughter certainly didn't create it. Anything nasty could've only come from him. He lacked imagination, creativity, so his world is a shadow of ours, a warped echo. The Razing is but a bitter taste of what he can do and, if it doesn't claim Vindstöld first, he will."

The night was still, but they were stiller. "How?" Naokah asked.

"If the beast finishes what it started."

"What does *that* mean?" Mila rubbed her neck.

"Someone intervened last Praxis and ended it." The ghost twitched, losing shape. "Or so we thought."

Lenita. It had to be Lenita!

But before Naokah could ask, Mila pressed, "Can we stop it?"

"I'm counting on it," the ghost whispered, then melted into vapor.

★   ★   ★

Something warm and wet nudged Naokah's cheek. She stirred, waking Mila. Too afraid to return last night, they'd stayed up late, washing off the blood in the maze's giant fountain. And while the sculpture within the pool was odd – a cherub riding a shark – a comforting presence lingered, as if Lenita had not only been here, but sought refuge here too.

It was still early. Trimmed hedges and dew spiced the thick air, and the sun had barely crested the mountain terraces, spilling orange beams across the valley. It should've been a promising start to the day, but the conversation the night prior stacked her gut with bricks of dread. Naokah had been on the wrong trail the entire time. The staff hadn't kidnapped her sister. Something unnatural had. Advocate was Lenita's middle name, and if the world needed saving, she would've stepped up no matter the cost.

The gargoyle must have taken Lenita, driven the prior envoys mad, and picked Naokah's classmates off, one by one. She and Mila had been lucky last night, escaping outside. Still, why the poisoning, the hanging, the kidnapping? Awfully human-like crimes. She rubbed her temples. She missed the days when dying via bee swarm was her biggest worry. A sharp grunt resounded off the fountain. She grabbed Mila, and they stumbled up. The stone was cold beneath her toes.

"See anything?" she asked, squinting through the fog.

"No," Mila whispered, shivering beside her.

Another grunt. Closer. Clacking against rock.

"There!" Mila gasped, pointing at the base of the fountain.

A hefty animal with spiked hair stalked closer. Naokah and Mila backed up to the fountain's edge. Mist licked Naokah's neck.

"What is it?"

"Don't know." Hands shaking, Naokah frantically searched the vast quartz fountain for something hard, a weapon. Mist clung to what looked like a rake in the cherub's fist. A trident? It sheened metallic in the watery light. The beast grunted, ears erect as it climbed the levels of stone towards them. Mila whimpered.

"Shush. It'll be okay." Naokah jumped into the fountain. Icy water seeped into her nightclothes, rising up to her chest as she waded to the sculpture. The water was a deep navy, and she tried not to think about how the pebbles beneath her toes were coated in slime, how it was too dark to ascertain what was in the fountain with her. Something smooth zipped by her ankle, and she yelped. Like the citadel's aquarium floors, there were fish in the fountain. Nothing else. Surely, she'd just frightened one.

"Naokah." Mila backed up. Her thin shadow stretched over the water. "It's getting closer."

"Hang on." Naokah charged the cherub, grabbed its cold trident, and yanked. Slick with mist, her fingers lost their grip. She cursed.

"Naokah!"

"I'm trying," she spat, finally wrenching the metal rod from the sculpture's hand. Its arm, wreathed in moss, came off with it, plopping into the water.

"Naokah!" Mila had climbed into the water, wading to her.

A chest-high creature now stood on the highest ledge. Its long nose cast an angular shadow over them, like a horn or spike. It grunted, throwing its hairy face to the side. Beady eyes pierced the veil. Naokah sighed, dropping the rod into the water.

"What are you doing?" Mila asked. "Kill it."

"No need." Her pulse slowed, steady as the water spurting from the shark's jaws.

"Why?"

"Don't you recognize it?" Naokah stepped closer. "From the outer gates?"

Mila shook her head, backing up even more.

"It's a guardhog."

"What's it doing here?"

"Good question."

Despite the sunrise, the temperature had dropped. Naokah's breath fogged the air. The guardhog with its bulging legs, muscular groove down its back, and long, curved tusks didn't look friendly. But it jerked its head to an alcove behind them.

"Think it wants us to follow." Naokah offered her hand, and Mila took it.

As they sloshed out of the fountain, water rushing down their legs, steam billowed up around them. Only then did Naokah miss the fountain. Within, her skin had gone numb. Now, the air razored her damp nightclothes. A chill ran through her, chattering her jaws.

The guardhog, once it established they were following, took off at a trot.

"Didn't know pigs could run," Mila said, speeding up.

"Abelha's full of surprises." Last night was hazy and, had Mila not been there, she would've sworn it was a nightmare.

A puff of white materialized on her left, but when she spun, it dissolved into a ray of light. The ghost girl? Mila had seen it too, evident by her jerky movement, but didn't say anything. The guardhog squeezed through a small, arched doorway that both women had to duck to enter. It gave way to sweeping beds of dark purple foxgloves and crimson roses where forager bees hummed softly, buzzing from flower to flower. Naokah's throat constricted, her skin tingled, but she crushed her fear into fists. She'd weathered worse.

A stone bench covered in ivy rose from the center of the garden. A small pond sat before it, lily pads skimming the surface. Flowers perfumed the air, sweet and delicate, and with the sun now streaming over the hedges, caressing her cheeks, her mood lifted. She almost allowed herself to relax, the stiffness in her thighs thawing, until Mila screamed. Both the pig and Naokah flinched.

A statue of a praying woman knelt over the pond. Tears of blood trickled down her stone cheeks and, below her clasped hands, floated a man with lovely sharktail braids – Clisten.

CHAPTER THIRTY-THREE

Happiness, a Drug

The two envoys I dumped into the melgo canisters survived, unfortunately. They deserved far worse than the burns covering their skin. Lenita refused to name them, but the envoy who'd tried to intervene did. Even so, for some reason, despite the prodding of the sentries, she wouldn't press for punishment. They were simply sent home, as were all parties involved. That left only Lenita and the envoy from Bizou for the finale.

I'd been visiting Lenita in the surgery, down the long, dim stretch of corridor from her chambers. If she knew I'd been coming, she hadn't let on. I hid in a mural of swans holding up a young girl, saving her from the smoky claws of the Razing. It was the best vantage to watch over Lenita, adjacent to the crown of cots that sat beneath the stained-glass alcove, but not necessarily for me. I often teared up; the brushstrokes stung my eyes and crumbled to ash in my mouth.

Unlike most memories that fizzled as soon as they'd formed, the one of my possible daughter freeing herself from my grasp and plunging into a plume of smoke stayed, solidifying into a jagged rock that scraped the soft nodes of my mind. Out of all the memories, *this* was the one that latched on? It taunted me, haunted me, even worse than the marching. The specter's resemblance to the girl from my nightmare was too uncanny to be a coincidence. I'd searched the citadel a hundred times over, but whatever business she'd had the night I saved Lenita must've detained her. Every search ended in despair. Surely, no harm had come to her? She'd easily put the viper-eyed beast in its place, so nothing should've been able to touch her. If she wanted to be found, she'd appear. Until then, I'd focus on Lenita, the key to my past.

Despite my shortcomings and the hastily ticking clock, I allowed myself a brief interval of joy for the one task I hadn't mangled – saving Lenita. Happiness was a drug. Addictive, consuming. One sip and I wanted more. No, *needed*. Lenita knew me. I wasn't some lonely slab of stone. I was real. Alive. Sunny and floating. Was this how it felt to be a hero? Not once did this ray of ecstasy ever touch me on my haunt. Squashing scrim was a cold, empty chore. Never fulfilling. No matter how evil they supposedly were, I always felt like the villain. Could this, then, maintaining this doer-of-good-deeds countenance, atone for my former unscrupulous decisions? Maybe even squash the spectral army that only seemed to bother me?

The afternoon sun smiled through the surgery, splashing Lenita in warm butterscotch. Propped up against her pillow, she wrote furiously in a worn leather journal. I didn't attempt to read her scrawl. For all her strengths, penmanship wasn't one of them. She'd regained her healthy, coppery glow, and the ember in her eyes, which the envoys had tried to douse, had reignited.

Though I'd gone over multiple scenarios on how to strike up a conversation, they'd all fallen short, nor did I want to hinder her recovery. After such a traumatizing ordeal, the last thing she needed was to see my ugly mug. Upon returning to the realm of the living that night, she may've only considered me a fleeting delusion. I, more than anyone, could attest. Whatever happened to me – that choking darkness, a thousand stings piercing my body, waking up here, frozen inside a gargoyle – had sundered my brain. I suppose I should've been grateful. If one memory, no matter how disturbing, chose to stick, maybe the others would eventually return too.

"With that scrawl, I think you missed your calling in healing," Marguerite teased. The healer's pale eyes flicked in my direction. I held my breath until her gaze returned to her patient.

Lenita flashed her a guilty grin. "A shame. But I prefer bees to humans."

"Can't say I blame you." The healer pulled out a tufted stool, silver curls bouncing, and sat beside her. "Looks like you're feeling better."

"Much." She set down her journal. "Am I free to return to the Praxis yet?"

The healer smiled as she probed Lenita's neck. "How very Crogan of you."

"How many Crogans have you met?"

"Enough to develop a theory that you're all incredibly stubborn and somewhat mad."

"I'll take that as a compliment."

"You should." The healer winked. "In fact, I daresay, you remind me of someone."

Lenita's eyes gleamed. "Are you about to say all Crogans look the same too?"

"Not at all." The healer laughed, cheeks rosy. "I spent some time working in refugee camps in Okse and Vintera. Met many displaced Bizouns and Crogans. All colorful characters, but one in particular, a privateer from your homeland, had eyes like amethysts, much like yours. Never seen that hue, and I've traveled all over Vindstöld. But more than that, she had a...presence about her, a draw. It was magnetic."

Lenita went rigid, as did I. Tart juice smeared my tongue, and Vintera's cranberry channels surrounded me. I'd been there, at some point in time, with my lover. A picnic. They'd shown me a sketch. A woman with dark hair, bright violet eyes. Had I known this Crogan too? Was that how we were connected?

"How long ago was this?"

"Goodness, it was during the Mid Refugee Crisis, so about—"

"Ten years back."

"You know your history."

"I lived it."

Marguerite placed a shriveled hand on Lenita's. "I've offended you, dearie."

"No need to apologize. Just the truth. Even after a decade, I've yet to believe...to understand or forgive—" she shook her head, "—this woman you met, do you recall her name?"

The old healer stared at the stained-glass bees as though they could refresh her memory. "Jordana. Surname started with an H. Hmmm. Helm? Hastings?"

"Hansen."

"Yes, that's it. She kin?"

"Was." Lenita trembled; with anger or sadness, I wasn't quite sure. With the words that followed, though, it took reining in every tendril of my glimmer not to reveal myself and hold her tight. "She was my world, my *everything*, the very reason I even made it here. She was my aunt until she walked out and abandoned my family. Now, she's deader than the wind to me."

CHAPTER THIRTY-FOUR

Split Hive

Naokah never had a chance to really know Dazarin, so his murder, although gruesome, was bearable. Clisten, however, had been kind when she needed kindness, thoughtful and even vulnerable to ease her discomfort. He'd been a gentleman, a good man, and the fact that his own guardhog found him, nudging his waterlogged face with its snout, trying to wake him, breaking into mournful squealing when he didn't rise, nearly split her in two. That, and though she'd known carrion bees existed, actually seeing them at work – harvesting the spongy flesh from the back of his neck and arms – had proven too much. She'd hardly made it to the neighboring rose bush before heaving up melgo and mint tea from the night before. Why would the gargoyle kill Clisten when he'd already planned to leave? She vowed with every fiber of her being to avenge him. His death would not be in vain.

With Brielle missing, Clisten and Dazarin dead, and Kjell unconscious, that left Naokah, Mila, and Laerte. All Mids. There hadn't even been a test yet. Now, they sat in the conservatory, the sunrise splashing the globe in bold pinks and rich oranges. Its beauty did nothing to cheer the group. Even the flowers now reeked overwhelmingly sweet, like fruit gone bad. The sentries had determined Clisten had drowned. There were no bruises, no struggle wounds, nor skin beneath his fingernails. It was as though he'd woken up in the middle of the night for a stroll, took a wrong turn, and decided to take a nap in the pond. It wasn't deep, and with his height, he could've easily crawled out. So, what really happened? Murder, obviously, like all the others. Who was next?

Samara strode to the front of the conservatory. Naokah shuddered, blinking to unsee their broken neck, their feral eyes. They weren't hanging from a turret nor clawing their wrists. The savvy was fine. Tired, but fine. Clearly, the gargoyle had played on her suspicion of Samara being culpable for Dazarin's death.

Laerte sat beside Naokah, squirming. When the savvy arrived, he straightened, yawning into his hand. It seemed no one had gotten any rest. The only person who did would never wake up. Poor Clisten. Samara rubbed their temples. Tufts of hair stuck out like tail feathers. They paced back and forth, brow furrowed, fraying Naokah's already raw nerve endings.

Naokah asked, "Any news on Clisten's death?"

They shook their head. "No, not surprising, though. Marguerite did find a small green feather lodged in his throat. Whatever that means, your guess is as good as mine."

The coincidence settled in Naokah's belly about as well as a fish tossed onto land. Another green feather? There'd been one where Brielle disappeared too. Last night, downright distraught, Naokah had almost revealed everything to Mila. Daughter, how good it would feel to share all the horrors she'd bottled up. And still, she'd held back. Worried about maintaining her position in the Praxis, she'd waited too long. Now, if she were to confess, would she be accused of withholding valuable information that could've prevented two deaths and a kidnapping? At best, she'd get kicked off the isle. At worst? Locked up for obstructing justice – or more. She could be condemned as the actual murderer. Distrust was the rope she'd hung herself with. She had no choice now but to suffer in silence.

"Did they at least figure out how a guardhog got through the exterior wall and ended up in the hedge maze?" Naokah asked. They'd been lucky it was a nice pig.

"The main gate was left open." Samara's eyes constricted into blue slits. "Who knows how many birds got in. Or other creatures. We'll have to comb the whole isle."

"That's not even the worst of it," said a voice with a metallic click, as though she didn't speak often.

Everyone turned to the conservatory's entrance, where a tide of red drowned out the light. Dark hair piled atop her head, lips crimson as her gown, and with a spiked ruby videira, it was the Keeper. No one moved.

"Thought we didn't have the pleasure of meeting her until senior phase," whispered Laerte.

But the Keeper heard, arching her brow. "Unprecedented times." She rolled her shoulders. She was radiant, more like a celestial being, than human. And unlike the rest of the citadel, it looked as if she'd gotten enough sleep for everyone. Now, more than ever, Naokah wanted to ask, why? Why end her Keepership so soon?

"As you've noticed," the Keeper said, "not all is well in the citadel. We had minor...hiccups during our last Praxis." Lenita going missing and the rest of her class returning mad didn't seem minor. "I had hoped things would go differently this time. And now, on top of the deaths and missing persons and attempted death, something even more alarming has occurred. I need your help to fix it."

What was worse than murder?

"My compass hive, a very powerful, important colony, has split without cause."

Naokah's breath snagged in her throat. On the night before Lenita's induction, Samara said the same thing happened. A hive split before their time and ended up in her sister's room. The next day, she was gone.

Laerte's chin dropped. "Madam Keeper, I'm sorry if this comes off as obtuse, but what does that have to do with us?"

"Since one of you will be the new Keeper, it concerns all of you, your future. A hive splits when it gets too large. But we monitor our colonies, our queens, closely, ensuring that when it is time for them to split, they have adequate space. Yet, this hive was nowhere near ready for such drastic actions. And worse, we cannot find them. Which means they've left the citadel and have swarmed somewhere on the isle." The Keeper's hands knotted, her long, gauzy train dusting the glass as she circled the hall. "We'll be changing the stakes, slightly."

"As in, whoever manages to live through the night wins?" Laerte joked.

No one laughed.

The Keeper stiffened. "With only three of you left...*awake*, today's Praxis will consist of one goal. Whoever achieves this goal wins. Simple as that."

Hah. Nothing was simple here.

"What's the test?" Mila asked, legs bouncing with nervous energy. Everyone was on edge.

"Each of you will be given a day's supply of food and water, and you'll be sent on your separate ways to comb the isle for my lost colony. Whoever finds the compass hive and retrieves it will be the victor."

"Easy enough." Laerte popped his knuckles.

Naokah frowned. What did this hive have to do with the deaths and disappearances, the gargoyle and ghost girl? Was the Keeper clueless about the fray inside her home? Had she gone mad or was she just callous, cold as stone?

"The compass hive isn't large by any means. Once you locate the queen, you'll place her in a protective clip that the savvy will give you, along with your pack of supplies."

"What's the catch?" asked Naokah. She'd been tricked enough as a naïve little sister. When something seemed easy, there was always a catch. And most of the time, the cloudcane wasn't worth the squeeze.

Samara said ever so calmly, "The colony will follow the queen, so if you're holding her—"

"They will swarm you." Laerte paled. "You want us to trek miles upon miles across this isle, over mountain terraces, around lakes and rivers, covered in an entire colony of bees?"

Naokah's hands went clammy, and she balled them.

The Keeper bit her lower lip as she looked the envoys over. "Tonight's also the new moon."

"And?" pressed Mila, face white as Laerte's.

The Keeper took her time answering, and Naokah's nerves were already on end. She, the woman terrified of bees, was supposed to have an entire hive swarming her body? What if they were all the way across the isle by now, in the grottos in the south? The idea of having to walk miles in the hot sun, covered in creatures that could kill her, did not inspire confidence. And what of the Scorned Son's spawn? Was it out there too? Just waiting for the envoys to separate, so it could kill them off, one by one? Splitting up was a death sentence.

"The new moon is the most dangerous night on this isle." The Keeper's eyes probed Naokah, and she swallowed hard. "One doesn't step foot outside the citadel until the sun rises the next day. So, your trek will have to be fast. For if you don't return before night falls… you won't return at all."

★   ★   ★

When Mila and Laerte took a left out of the conservatory and headed for their chambers to pack, Naokah turned right and followed the telltale red train to the west wing. She felt compelled to speak to the Keeper before she left. Why? She wasn't sure. Perhaps to confront the woman whose ill leadership allowed her sister to disappear in the first place. There were words that needed to be said. It was a risk. But she was about to head off on a death quest anyway.

The Keeper passed the library, her chambers, and various nondescript rooms before reaching an arched door at the back of the wing. Gilt branches framed each side and reached across, meshing into intricate scrolling in the middle. As the last of her train faded behind the wood, Naokah tiptoed in. Bright light blinded her momentarily, and then as her eyes adjusted, giant clusters of pink fanned her peripheral vision. She blinked, trying to clear her view, when the stench hit her. Eyes tearing, she lurched over and coughed into her hand.

"First time encountering flowering pigwood, I take it?"

Naokah staggered up. Gleaming amber eyes met hers. "Pigwood?"

The Keeper's sleeves were crimson waterfalls as she motioned left and right. Stout trees laden with fluffy pink blossoms and bees lined the spacious room. Ferns in gold pots hung from the sea-glass ceiling, and a thin, gemstone path cut through the center to a dais holding a large chair festooned in red ivy. She'd followed the Keeper to the induction room.

"To answer your question, though the trees smell like death, the bees love 'em, and that's all that matters here. Now answer mine." She steepled her copper hands beneath her chin. "Why aren't you packing?"

The sheer magnitude of the place, vibrant and pungent, coupled with the fact that she was now alone with the most powerful woman in the world, had sucked her brain dry.

"Just wanted to tell you…that you have nothing to fret over," she rapid-fired, knees trembling. "The Mids won't let you down." She bowed and turned to get the raze out of there.

"Wait!" the Keeper's voice chimed, and Naokah reluctantly twisted around. "You're my Crogan envoy, is that right?"

She lowered her chin. "Yes, Madam Keeper."

"Your predecessor was a remarkable woman. Would've made a fine Keeper. You have big shoes to fill."

Chest tight, she only nodded. *Tell me something I don't know.*

"Before you leave, perhaps you can help me with something. I was in the Midworld when you were just a young girl, a decade ago? It was a short trip, from what I can remember. Time has a way of muddling memories together, especially here, so I'm not quite sure, but I did spend some time with some truly marvelous Crogan farmers during my stay."

The Keeper had visited some camps during the Mid Refugee Crisis. She may've been the first Poler who'd volunteered and didn't rub it in Naokah's face — *Oh, look at me. I helped your displaced people. May I have a pat on the back for being a decent human being?* — and for that, Naokah was grateful, and her dread waned, if only a fraction.

"There was a term," the Keeper continued, "your countryfolk kept using to describe the painful longing, the sundering melancholy they felt for their homes taken by the Razing. A Midese word that has no translation. I can't for the life of me—"

"Caillte," Naokah said over the lump in her throat. Tati's mantra. Her reason for exploring new worlds. Witnessing Croi Croga crumble into the Razing had been too much for her to bear. "The name comes from the Crogan legend of Saudra and Adena. Their parents refused to grant them permission to marry, for they wanted grandchildren to carry on their family name. The young lovers planned to marry in secret and run away, but the night of the ceremony, Adena's brother learned of their plan and tried to stop them. Just as the women sealed their union with a kiss, he broke Saudra's neck."

The Keeper's brows meshed as though recalling something, so Naokah paused.

"No, go on, please."

"Heartbroken, Adena begged the Divine Daughter to bring her dead bride back, but Saudra had already crossed over into her eternal afterscape. Because they'd been married, though only for a second, and united, the Divine Daughter extracted all the late wife's memories, her essence, and poured them into Adena's soul, so that until they'd be reunited, she wouldn't have to walk the world alone."

Jaw tight, the Keeper was silent for a moment. Why had Naokah felt the need to share the story? With her pending departure, she was clearly overcome with caillte for her bees, and Naokah had only compounded that pain.

"Thank you. You may go now," the Keeper said softly.

Naokah didn't have to be told twice and strode, almost bolted, to the arched door. As she grabbed the cold metal handle, the Keeper called, "Be careful out there, Naokah. Wouldn't want anyone burdened with caillte for you."

CHAPTER THIRTY-FIVE

Extra Royal Jelly

After the distillery incident, the citadel had been emptied. Only two envoys remained: Lenita and Vinícius. He and she, tall and short, stood abreast in the Hall of Foxgloves, their smoke cloaks glimmering from the sconces studding the relief of flowers behind them. It was the day of the finale, and the night would welcome the new moon. The other assays were nixed due to the lack of envoys. They faced a domineering wall that wriggled and hummed with hundreds of colonies and millions of bees.

I'd melted into a carved foxglove, adjacent to where they would compete. Both envoys seemed calm, eager, but I was nowhere near restful. I'd failed to prove my worth to the Keeper and earn her trust. Not that it mattered in the grand scheme of things. Lenita, were I ever to grab the gumption to ask, was coupled to my past. But I ached with hollowness, with desperation for closure. I still needed the Keeper's approval.

Samara stood before the two envoys with an open book and a silver pocket watch. If a stranger were to stumble upon this scene, they'd likely infer the savvy was an officiant marrying bee enthusiasts in their smoke cloaks.

"The Keeper passes on her sincerest apologies for not being able to attend the finale," Samara said, their gaze wavering like the air in my chest. The most momentous examination of the Praxis, naming a new Keeper, and she wasn't here? "She's a little under the weather this evening but has confirmed she'll see you at breakfast to congratulate her successor. Now, as you both know, placing a new queen with a colony can be tricky. If the worker bees don't accept her, they'll ball up around her, stinging her to death."

Lenita passed Vinícius a grin. "That a warning?"

"No. But perhaps it should be. Whoever is named Keeper tonight, if you end up being an obnoxious little twit, I wouldn't put it past the staff to dispose of you." Samara waggled an elegant brow. "Unlike our new queens, who are introduced to their hives via a protective clip, you won't have any armor." They were teasing, obviously, but the threat hung as thickly in the air as the citadel's stench: Keepers were disposable. Bees didn't operate under a monarchy but a matriarchy, and the Keepership wasn't much different.

"Vinícius, I'll have Marguerite walk you to the end of the corridor. Lenita will stay here with me. On my count, you'll have five minutes to locate as many queens as possible. A test of your ability to read the colonies, homing in on their behavior. To see if you can truly handle the privilege and burden of safekeeping the world's most important life-bringers, our future. Any questions?"

Both envoys shook their heads.

"All right, Vinícius follow Marguerite," Samara said, nodding at the approaching healer in her ivory tunic.

"Best of luck, mate." Lenita offered her hand, and Vinícius accepted it with a firm shake.

"May the best Mid win." He winked, then followed Marguerite to the end of the hall, hazy green from the afternoon sun pouring through the turrets.

I hoped Lenita would prove victorious. My initial dislike towards her had long faded. I now only harbored respect. Trying to take out the envoys had been a foolish whim, a mistake. If the Keeper really wished to leave twenty years premature, I had to honor her decision, hasty as it seemed. Still, that didn't prevent me from wanting to know why. I bore incredible guilt on my weary shoulders, fearing my past, reckless self was responsible for her short tenure. If I'd been wrong enough to release a scrim, to allow my daughter to die, what else was I capable of?

"Time!" Samara barked, and Lenita sprang for the ladder.

The savvy had barely climbed to the top of theirs when Lenita held up a hand to signal she'd found her first queen. They leaned in, nodded, making a mark in their book. Lenita dropped a few rungs to the hive beneath, and her hand went up. Another mark. She moved in quick precision, one hive after another, one queen after another. After identifying the bottom hive's queen, she gently slid the ladder a few yards over and repeated the same sequence.

Her process was hypnotizing. Like a future queen bee fed extra royal jelly to ensure her fate, so was Lenita. She was born to be Keeper. I should have never tried to erase her existence. My throat tightened in awe, in weepy pride for this woman who'd overcome all odds to get here.

I blinked back phantom tears, glimpsing in Vinícius's direction. Poor fellow never had a chance. When Samara called time, Lenita was on her seventy-seventh queen. Vinícius had just found his third.

CHAPTER THIRTY-SIX

One Dilemma at a Time

Outfitted in scamall trousers, a thin tunic, and a ratty pair of ankle boots, Naokah grabbed her pack and paused, glaring at the smoke cloak crumpled on her bed, its sheer fabric only evident as it winked beneath the stained glass. Samara brought it by earlier, and it was exceedingly difficult not to shout a slew of Midese curses at them. A cloak that protected her from bees was here the whole razing time? All those long, out of the way excursions on the veranda had eaten up valuable moments when she could've been searching for leads. What might've changed, who could she have saved with the cloak? The anger was misplaced, though. Fear had guided every single bad choice she'd made since arriving, and now she had to make up for it. Besides, as Samara had explained, the cloak *could* protect her from a sting here and there, but it hadn't helped the envoy who'd been swarmed. Lenita, not the enchanted cloak, had saved him.

The cloak, though a nice gesture, would prove useless today. Having to trek somewhere upwards of thirty miles over difficult terrain in the bleating sun was already asking for heatstroke. And with cobwebby fabric that had the breathability of a sail and reeked of smoke? She'd be dead before she found the swarm. She was facing her greatest fear head-on, armorless, with misgivings that rattled her core. Misgivings were for people with options, though, and she had none. Naokah gave her room, pale violet in the morning light, one final look.

"Wish me luck, Lenita," she said, voice cracking, her conversation with the Keeper like a rising tide. Caillte represented painful longing and nostalgia but also, though often repressed – irrevocable loss. In her mind's eye, her sister was alive. Death wasn't an option. But this week had shown her how fleeting life was. She'd embraced Brielle just a couple nights before, only to have her ripped away. Naokah needed to prepare herself for the worst because, if she'd learned nothing else in her twenty years, it was that life didn't have a translation for mercy.

A guppy the shade of overripe cloudcane swam in the meandering stream beneath her, and she smiled weakly, pulling her door shut with a thud. The fish, at least, she'd grown accustomed to. Would the same prove true for the bees? Mila was waiting in the hallway, wearing a similar outfit, save a big, floppy hat, its strap tied in a bow beneath her pale chin.

"Ready?" Mila asked.

"As much as I'll ever be," Naokah said, and they strode to the foyer, where they'd meet Samara for supplies. The air seemed denser today, the shadows clinging to her like cooling tar, slowing her down, holding her back, as if the citadel didn't want her to leave. She pocketed her dread as they entered the foyer. Samara awaited them, face grim. As they stood beneath the flickering chandeliers, Laerte plodded in, eyes hard with flinty resolve.

"Here are your provisions. Food. Water. Some melgo, for your victory lap home," said Samara. A brown sack flew through the air, and Naokah caught it. She pulled off her pack and tucked it inside. Notes of roasted lamb, cheese pastries, and chocolate cranberries wafted through the bag, upsetting her stomach. Nausea had been percolating since her visit with the Keeper.

"Gather round." Samara raised their arms and pulled open a large map. The three envoys squashed in close. "This is us." The savvy pointed at a red triangle at the northernmost part of the isle.

Laerte sucked his teeth as they pored over the rolling terrain. "Lots of ground to cover."

"It is," Samara said. "Which means you'd better get going…if you plan to return at all. Any questions?" They pulled out three smaller, rolled-up maps fastened with rosewood string, and handed one to each envoy.

"Yes," said Mila, ginger brows furrowed on the mountain terraces that sprouted along the map's center. A trek a pampered Poler would've undoubtedly struggled with. "Are we allowed to help one another?"

Samara's face softened. "You can, sure. But whoever enters the citadel, bees covering their skin, is the true victor. There will be no room for debate."

Envoys before had spent all their energy undermining one another in an attempt to win. They hadn't been hunted down by a wicked creature, though. They could help each other, but before returning, a decision would have to be made. With the Polers out of the mix and Laerte's promise to administer aid to the other Mid nations, Naokah's competitive streak had faded. Any of them would make a good Keeper. Besides, she was more focused on finding her sister and Brielle. Ridiculous, she knew. Not likely. But she needed something to cling on to, no matter how dim. Today could be her last. She preferred to spend it hopeful.

"These packs," Naokah said, shifting hers onto the ground. "Weapons included?"

"Surprised you didn't steal a blade from the kitchen," Samara teased, and Naokah squirmed. Their eyes met, and something beyond mirth flickered in the savvy's stare. They knew about her botched attempt at reading Lenita's journal. "Yes, there's a wrapped dagger in your sack. Though it's not nature you'll need to watch out for."

Tense silence followed, reminding everyone of the stakes. Yes, per the Keeper, finding the split hive was of the utmost priority. But, supposing one of them was actually successful and retrieved said hive, they had to make it back in one piece before nightfall. Either the murderer was out there waiting or would be in the citadel waiting. Neither possibility was heartwarming.

She swallowed hard, riffling through her pack. The other envoys followed her lead, tugging the blades out of their sacks and attaching them to their shoulder straps for ease of access.

What if this was all a setup? After all, what better way to take out the envoys than have them dispersed, alone, around the isle? The killer could pick them off, one by one. The citadel hadn't proven to be a sanctuary by any means, yet whoever the culprit was, human or beast, had had to work around the bustle of the staff.

She eyed Samara, whose jaw strained, yanking on the thread of Naokah's ever-unraveling sanity. When she had attempted climbing back up the ladder from the distillery, Samara had been the one to shuffle her along, claiming Brielle could handle herself. All the while, someone else could've swooped in and taken her.

Still, the question remained. Why? Samara knew the bees, perhaps even better than the Keeper. Why hadn't they competed for the Keepership? Maybe, after two iterations of the Praxis going incredibly wrong, the first group returning home out of their razing minds, the second, not returning home at all, Samara would step up and take the reins? Surely the Keeper wasn't in on it too? Yet, why was she leaving early? What did they know that the rest of the world didn't? Was the gargoyle the master puppeteer and everyone here on strings? Naokah tugged her pack on. First, she'd find the bees, then her sister, then Brielle. Next, she'd find the culprit. One dilemma at a time.

Naokah's gaze shifted back to her map. A large span of grottos sat at its southernmost tip, and something about the location, its proximity to the end of the isle, closeness to the sea, sprouted cold sweat on her palms. Daughter forbid she find them there. What a horrible trek back, covered in bees, climbing up and down. The room began spinning, shadows and unintelligible whispers meshing with the hives.

A cold hand grabbed her arm. "You all right?" the savvy said, not making eye contact.

"Yes, thanks, Samara." She stared at their canted face, waiting for their gaze to move upwards. It didn't. Despite the warm morning, they wore their usual uniform, but a longer, ruffly sleeve billowed from beneath the red, concealing their scratched arm.

What else are you hiding? she wanted to ask but refrained. Not the time.

"Everyone, we think it best you know," Samara folded their arms over their chest, "a bit more news must touch your ears before you head off."

Groans filled the foyer. A fish moved beneath Mila, giving her a start before it zipped down the eastern hall. Naokah placed a hand on her bony shoulder.

"Kjell is no longer in the healer's quarters."

"Great," Laerte said, meaning anything but great. "He's now competing too?"

"You misunderstood me," Samara said, shaking their head. "He was still amidst when Marguerite checked on him this morning. He didn't just wake up and walk out."

"Unbelievable." Naokah let out a derisive laugh. "Someone took him."

★ ★ ★

The envoys clambered out of the citadel and through the hedge maze. Though it was early, the sun shone brightly through the clouds and foliage, dappling their shadowed path in feathery, canary patches. Honeysuckle glazed the already heavy air, riling Naokah's belly.

What kind of monster kidnapped someone unconscious? Kjell may've been a prick, but he was Brielle's prick. They both deserved better. Unease crept up Naokah's neck, and she spun around. A slender shadow stood at the panel of arched windows beneath the donjon. Her gaze then climbed to the creepy, bull-faced gargoyle that stared in the wrong direction, its eyes on the Keeper's silhouette.

Logic told her to run. Head for the gate that led to the port. Jump on the closest ship, even if it was a bee barge, and get out of there. This place was getting more sinister by the minute. But she had to stay the course. Or all this, her long hours of training, her sacrifices, missing her family, would be for nothing. She had to find out what happened to Lenita, to Brielle and Clisten, the rest, even if it killed her.

They passed by the shark fountain where she and Mila had somehow fallen asleep together, seemingly safe out of the confines of the citadel. It was only last night, but it felt like eons ago. Fatigue was manipulative – stretching time.

"Should we band together?" Laerte asked when they reached the south gate.

"As much as I want to, I think the best way for us to find the hive is splitting up. There's just too much ground to cover if we don't," said Naokah halfheartedly. She didn't want to be alone right now. Not with Kjell's disappearance too.

"You're right," Mila said, shaking her head. "Well, good luck."

"Be careful," Naokah said, sounding foolish. Why wouldn't they be? The other two nodded, then were on their separate ways, and she was alone. She pulled out her map, hands trembling as she unrolled it, trying to steady her mind, solidify her plan. She'd walk along the stream that emptied into a great lake, then proceed along the fjord until she reached the southernmost part, the grottos. Should she get lost, she could always head westward and hit the large spiky wall that surrounded the isle, then head north to the citadel.

She walked through ankle-high brambles heavy with dew, soaking her shoes, until she hit the stream. It wasn't too wide, but it was thick with moss, stirring with fish, frogs, and who knew what else. She wouldn't wade through it unless she had no other choice. Flat boulders ran along the side she was on; groves of jabuticabas lined the other. Big black berries coated the bark of the unusual trees' trunks and branches like thousands of eyes, watching her every move. Naokah ignored their stares and moved like a hunter, senses piqued, waiting for the hum of the hive, the wriggle of translucent wings under the sun.

Within a few minutes, the weight of the pack and trekking over the uneven rocks, combined with the heat, had already summoned sweat that stung her back and chafed her thighs. Mila's big floppy hat didn't seem so silly now. It was only morning; the temperature would get worse before it got better, and without cover, her face, ears, and neck would soon burn. The jabuticabas across the way, though menacing, also promised shade. The stream she'd just told herself she wouldn't dare cross, save an emergency, now gurgled for her to pass. Not to mention, hives *could* swarm to boulders, but the groves were more plausible.

The stream narrowed in a couple hundred feet. A stone spear carpeted in lichen pierced the width. If she could hold herself steady without slipping, she could jump to the other side.

Naokah tightened the pack, ensuring the blade was secure on her shoulder. She stuck out her boot, testing the midsection of the stone sliver with a bit of pressure. Solid. Holding her arms out on both sides for balance – she'd seen her sister do the same on the raised cloudcane beds – she took her first step.

The rock shifted, but minutely, so she took another step. Her boot slipped on the lichen, and the awkward weight of the pack threw her off balance. She corrected herself, took another quick step, and stabilized. She waited a moment, knees trembling and, though she told herself not to look down, her brain disobeyed. The sun reflected off the dark green water, swinging a blade of blinding white into her eyes. She squinted. She'd made it to the center of the stream. Only ten feet left. She could do this. The water was green, clearish. A straight shot down to a school of minnows. Their scales flashed silver beneath the ripples of currents. Minnows were harmless. Minnows she could deal with.

She took a secure step, then halted.

Something black, coiled, shifted next to her. Her gaze locked on the dark, slithering beast, and she continued. Therein was her mistake. For, if she'd had her eyes on the placement of her foot instead of the creature beside her, she wouldn't have missed her next step.

CHAPTER THIRTY-SEVEN

The Wrong Woman

Upon Samara announcing the winner of the Praxis and thus the new Keeper, Vinícius took a knee and bowed before Lenita. Before he could rise, she, violet eyes gleaming, grabbed his hand and heaved him up, pulling him into a tight hug. Stiff at first, he finally relaxed and, chuckling, reciprocated, his large tan arms nearly concealing her small frame.

"Don't worry," she whispered, lips brushing his cheek, for she was too short to reach his ear, "this is a win for *us*. The Mids now have one less thing to fear. I give you my word. Our future will rival the stars."

"I'll hold you to that, Madam Keeper." He released her, kissed her forehead, and strode off.

I myself bowed to Lenita within the foxglove relief and, feeling inspired, left to find the soon-to-be-retired Keeper. I had burning questions for the Crogan, too, but since time had run out on my cowardice, I had to approach the former before she departed forever. With the scrim attack tonight, the army marking time beneath my sternum, surely the Keeper had answers that could absolve my foolish mistake. At least, that's what I told myself. In truth, I yearned for her acceptance almost as much as my identity. Couldn't I have both?

She was making her early afternoon rounds when I found her, talking to the many hives that lined the towering corridors. She didn't appear under the weather like the savvy had claimed, at least not physically. She carried a glass of melgo, and as she approached each colony, she bowed before their queen and prayed to the Divine Daughter.

"*Le do thoil oh le do thoil. Cosain mo theaghlach, mo theach, ár dtodhchaí.*" It was lovely, lyrical, and most definitely Midese. *Please, oh, please. Protect my family, my home, our future.* Odd. Vinterans spoke Poli, the international language of trade. I suppose she learned Midese for business, but wouldn't one usually revert to their first tongue for prayer?

Either way, the bees didn't care. They swayed to her words, their purring amplifying, crawling over her hands. A sad smile flickered, and she crooned like she was holding a baby. Hundreds of thousands of stinging babies.

In the beginning, I'd falsely assumed that, as head of the citadel, the Keeper would've tasked these rounds to Avice or Samara. Since I'd been inside, though, it was only she who strolled up and down, day after day, night after night, slippers padding softly against the glass floors. Her evening dress, red, always red, drifting aimlessly yet with purpose at the same time.

Like the queen of each hive, whose sole job was to pop out offspring, working tirelessly, the Keeper endeavored to take care of her bees in the same indefatigable manner. Her title struck me as merely that, a title. She rarely ordered any of her staff about and I wondered if, like the queen bee, should she cross some unseen line, would her staff, like the worker bees, toss her out? Was that why she was so guarded? Even with Avice, her lover, she kept up a boundary as thick as a wall. No wonder, while she tended her bees, I was most enamored. With the bees, she didn't wear a mask. She was raw and maternal and distinctively sincere.

Heavy sadness rolled off her and fed into the mounting tension of the hallways, the icing of my chest. As she pressed her lips into a tight line between each hive, trying to keep the tears at bay, it dawned on me: she was saying goodbye. I hated to interrupt her now, but I didn't have a choice—

A glass shattered, followed by a gasp, then liquid gushed over the floor.

I steeled myself as a new memory took hold. I stood atop a narrow rock overlooking a deep fjord. Glimpsing down, hands bound behind me, my stomach plummeted at the steep drop. A figure wearing a ratty Midworld cloak and a grotesque mask approached me. I scrambled back, tripped over my ripped trousers, and fell to my knees.

"One last chance to confess." The masked fiend yanked me up with an elegant, manicured hand. Their unusual ring, a six-sided emerald with gold filigree, glinted in the dwindling light. I'd seen that before, hadn't I?

"Confess what?" I said, voice ragged. It hurt to speak.

"Who have you been working with?"

"I don't know what you're talking about." I told the truth.

"Someone has been contracting with the north, intercepting our bee barges for profit."

"And I'm supposed to know who?"

"You do. Now tell me. No lies."

"I can't tell you something I've no clue about," I spat, blood oozing down my chin. "You have the wrong woman."

"Have it your way." The masked figure punched me in the chest, their ring puncturing my sternum, knocking me over the edge.

Air whizzed by, reminding me of starling flocks and tales of when the wind lived. I'd sailed around the world, tasted delicacies, stood in awe of all the wonders, the different, melodic languages and cultures. I had lived. My last thought was that of my blurry-faced lover; I hoped they were alive and well. If only I could've told them goodbye. I hit the water, harder than stone, and fuzzed into downy black.

I came to on the floors of the citadel. In the now. The torches had waned, the hallways had darkened, and the Keeper was gone. Then I remembered – the gasp, the shattered glass, the spilled melgo. I dashed into the mural and sped to the Keeper's chambers. Razing take me if she wasn't all right.

CHAPTER THIRTY-EIGHT

Worse than a Snake

Naokah flailed, stirring up the riverbed, muddying the water to a bruised green. She couldn't see a thing. Nor did her feet touch the bottom. Slickness coiled around her leg. She screamed and sank, gulping a mouthful of water. She kicked hard, the creature let go, and she soared to the surface. In a few wild strokes, she reached the other side, then crawled out of the murky mess.

Tugging off her pack, she tossed it aside and collapsed, swilling air and sunlight, coughing up shreds of moss. Something in her cleavage wriggled. She squealed, yanking off her blouse. A small silver fish plopped out and, manic, she laughed, cupped the minnow, and returned it to the churning stream. As she leaned back, a speck of metal glinted on the banks. She followed the winking, paying close attention to the river in case the snake or whatever that thing was came after her.

Twisted around a knot of sticks was a necklace. A bit rusted. Only streaks of gold shined through. She picked up the tangled debris and began working the necklace loose. A locket in the shape of a ship's sail dangled from the bottom. As she worked it free, an old memory tremored her hand.

Tati returning home after a long voyage to tell Naokah's mother she'd be leaving only the next day for more 'privateering'. Her mother, irritated, asking how she could love her family when she was always gone. Tati, pulling out her locket and proudly showing Matri the miniature. One side was *The Unsinkable Clara*, her beloved ship, which, according to Tati, was better family than most. And the other....

Naokah popped the rusty locket open. A faded painting of Tati and Matri, Lenita and Naokah, cropped black cuts and all violet eyes save hers, sitting atop a bale of cloudcane, filled the other half. She clenched the locket, peering back at the stream. The sediment had started to settle. The long serpentine creature was no snake nor monster, but a rotted sleeve covering an arm. An arm attached to a skeleton. She would've preferred a snake.

With a heart of sinking lead, Naokah waded back in, held her breath, then dove, gently retrieving the remains of Tati. Throat aching, her eyes burned, and sobs punched her chest as she placed her aunt down on the bank. A cold wave of guilt crashed into her. How did Tati end up here of all places? With Abelha's repute as of late, it was highly doubtful she died of natural causes. What then, had been her end? Naokah pulled out her dagger and dug a hole. Tati deserved a proper burial, but this was the best she could do.

She spent most of the morning digging and sobbing, then placed her aunt to rest.

"For years, we yearned for closure, Tati. I was so angry with you. We all were, especially Lenita. How could an argument sever a family? After you left, Matri never spoke again. She waited, day in, day out, hoping you'd return. Patri said part of her died when you left. And now—" she choked; more hot tears streamed her cheeks, "—I was wrong. *We* were wrong. Please forgive us for blaming you. I hope you didn't suffer, that your death was at least quick, painless. Tati, in that next place, wherever you are, I pray that it has wind. Good, strong wind that fills *The Unsinkable Clara*'s sails and takes you any place you'd like to go. I also pray that, should Lenita also be gone, she's been reunited with you." She patted the mound of soft soil, Tati's grave, and slid the rusted necklace into her pocket. Naokah was no forensic expert and had proven a pathetic inspector so far. But she would stake her life, her sister, even her whole razing family, that this was no accident. Someone had killed Tati.

★　　★　　★

After rinsing her blade and scrubbing her mud-clogged nails in the stream, Naokah slipped her pack on and proceeded. She walked under the jabuticabas, the cool shade a reprieve on her swollen face. She couldn't stop crying. If she could've just cleared her head, swallowed her grief, this part of her trek would've been tranquil with the flower-frocked hills, the trickling of the spring. But nature's beauty was overshadowed by anxiety, fear, compounding panic, the closer she got to the grottos. Not only was there a killer on the loose, but maybe that same monster had killed Tati too. And for what? Tati would never hurt a soul. She was a wanderer, a woman of the ocean, a free spirit. She loved her family deeply but loved the freedom the seas gave her more. Naokah had always envied Lenita for taking after her. Bold, resilient, unapologetic when it came to following her heart. Naokah yearned for that liberty but had never broken free from the prison of her mind.

She reached a juncture where a patch of dark pink foxgloves leaned into her path. A few bees languidly swept from bell to bell. As she got closer, a plant heavy with blooms sank lower than the rest. She peeped inside the top bell, and grinned.

Two humblebees, fuzzy hair coated in pollen, slept in the flower's center. They curled up head to toe, holding each other's legs. A well broke loose inside her. She was back on the farm, maybe five or six, sharing a cot with Lenita. Naokah had a terrible cough, and her mother warned her older sister that it wasn't safe to sleep near her. But Lenita, stubborn that she was, told Matri that Naokah needed her older sister to get better faster. They slept much like those humblebees, head to feet, so that Naokah couldn't cough on her sister's face. For as long as she lived, she'd never forget Lenita's warm hands curled around her frozen feet. Her whispers that no one could divide sisters if they stuck together.

Years later, when Naokah had brought the memory up, Lenita had laughed it off. *Just didn't want to sleep on the ground*, she'd said, eyes averted. Her older sister wasn't one to show emotions, especially ones that made her appear weak. But Naokah knew, though her older sister feigned being tough, she had her soft edges too.

Naokah smiled wistfully, taking one last look at the humblebees, before pressing on, a little faster now. She had a mystery to solve and, Daughter willing, a colony to find, a Keepership to claim.

CHAPTER THIRTY-NINE

Rings Don't Lie

"I saw it, Avice. It's there, hiding in the hives," the Keeper uttered, exasperated, pulling the ruby pins out of her hair and tossing them on the dresser. They clinked against the wood. One fell to the ground, and the captain picked it up and placed it down gently with the others.

"Madam Keeper—"

"Don't speak to me in that tone."

"What tone?"

"Like you're humoring me. I'm not a child."

"That wasn't my intention." The sentry walked over to the Keeper, who now sat on the rug beside her bed, picking at her nails. "May I?"

The Keeper waved her hand, and the sentry sat beside her. Her vanity mirror had yet to be replaced from my last tempest. Slivers of glass dangled from the frame, reflecting the flickering torches, swinging spectrums across the chambers. Brilliant but, like the sun singing through icicles at the mouth of a grotto, only brilliant due to the bold contrast. Had my former, shattered life seemed bright, redeemable, because like the glass shards, my mind was draped in pervading darkness? With pieces falling back into place quickly these days, what if I reassembled into the mosaic of a monster? I must've done something truly appalling to get tossed off a cliff. Still, I maintained my innocence, even if ignorance was my sole alibi. Good or bad, I had to learn the truth.

"I believe that *you believe* what you saw." Avice grabbed the Keeper's hand.

She wrenched from the sentry's grip, who frowned.

"Don't you see? Something has gone awry. Ever since the last new moon, I felt like there was...no, I've *known* there was an evil presence within these walls. Something got past the guardhogs, the gargoyles, the wards, and it's been hiding behind the hives. Stirring up my queens. Those viper eyes, Avice. I'm telling you, whatever it is, it's trying to break through."

"Through what?" I gasped over the army charging my bloodstream, my eardrums, momentarily forgetting my hiding place, the creased palm of the mural's extended hand.

Both women recoiled, eyes darting my way. I stayed still. So stirred, if I moved, they'd spot me and run. I'd never get my answers.

"So you at least heard that," the Keeper said, smug.

Avice didn't have to respond. She grimaced, holding back, as if suppressing the truth was what the Keeper needed. She was wrong. And it was my turn to be smug. Even I knew that, more than anything, the greatest insult to her was questioning her sanity. Her head sentry and lover should've known better.

"Your face speaks the truth, even if you don't, Avice." The Keeper's voice shook. "Is there a reason for your blatant dishonesty? You hiding something? You know I can't take any more lies. I'm too—"

"Please, Madam Keeper. It's not like that. I just know—" the sentry tried to hold her hand, but the Keeper pulled it from her grasp, "—you've been under considerable stress as of late. What, with the new moon incident, the envoy getting swarmed, two of the Polers nearly turning to pottage in the distillery. Pray, when was the last time you actually got any sleep?"

"Oh, so I'm not mad, just delusional, is that it?" She plucked at a bag of cloudcane pulp and started stuffing her pipe.

"Madam Keeper—"

"Get out."

"But—"

"Go!" She slapped her bed frame. "I'd sooner be alone than with someone who's questioning my mental state." More mirror slivers clinked to the floor, exposing the wall behind the frame. It wasn't bare. Wanton, hair-entwined hands, full lips kissing…was that a half-finished mural behind the frame? Why was it hidden?

The sentry tried to take her hand once more, but stopped, curling her fingers into a fist. "As you wish. I'll be outside your room, should you need anything."

The Keeper didn't respond. She'd torn a cuticle, and a few droplets of blood trickled to the floor. The sentry gave her one last pleading look, then grabbed the door. A ring, an emerald with fine gold filigree, caught the torchlight and flashed in my eyes when she turned the knob.

I went cold. Those long slender fingers, that unusual ring. I'd seen them before. In fact, they'd been the last thing I'd seen before getting thrown off a cliff to my death. The Keeper's right-hand woman, Avice, had been my executioner.

CHAPTER FORTY

Too Far South

A shriek echoed over the rolling terrain, and Naokah halted. It came from the shoreline, near the western grottos. Another scream. The hair on her neck needled. Mila. Before she could eye up the distance – sprinting half a mile was not only ludicrous but far too ambitious – Naokah was in a mad dash. She tore through the brambles, wet boots and spongy socks squelching with each step. Her pulse hammered her eardrums and sweat mixed with river water drenched her back. The groves thinned, the elevation dropped, and the stream shot over a sheer cliff, falling into a teal lake that stretched east to west.

"Scondra tai!" she shouted, then clamped a hand over her mouth as the curse echoed back. Ankles trembling, she sucked in sweltering air, surveying possible routes.

If she were as daring and crazy as Tati or Lenita, she'd grab the canoe anchored to the stone by her foot and try her fate with the falls. But it would be hard to help her friend if she lay crumpled beneath the roaring waves, dead. Instead – like a beacon, gleaming from the forest – a narrow footpath unfurled from the fall's western side.

She wiped the sweat from her brow, tightened the straps of her pack – they'd loosened on her run – and descended. Slowly, meticulously. The ground was hard, but a thin layer of sand and dust coated it. A recipe for a quick slip and snapped neck if she wasn't careful. Luckily, the path was also filled with large, angular stones. With their rough texture, she was able to guide her boots, finding anchor points along the way. Her thighs quivered, and her calves seized as she maintained her slow descent. The trail was incredibly steep.

By the time Naokah reached the base of the cliff, the falls hissing beside her, the sun had begun her journey westward. The lake, now a jade bolt of silk, dominated her view, unraveling and shimmering beneath the afternoon light. The air was hot and thick but fresh, smudged with moss and damp soil. Though she was surrounded by nature and wildlife, everything was quiet. Eerily quiet. She hadn't expected birdsong, not with the warded mesh encasing the isle, but at the very least the chirr of insects or scurry of squirrels or some other sign of life.

You must return before nightfall, or you won't return at all, the Keeper had said. It was that warning and the promise of closure for the women she cared for most, Lenita, Tati, Brielle, and now Mila, that cinched Naokah's ribs as she pressed on, pushing through the towering sunflowers thronging the lake. She didn't want to move too fast, for her heartbeat, her breathing could mask what she needed to hear – Mila's scream and the humming of bees. The grotto loomed over the far side, the base of the isle, beckoning her. That's where she'd find Mila, maybe even the bees. How else could her voice have echoed so far if she weren't trapped in a monstrous hollow of rock?

A heavy splash startled Naokah. And then a plop. Now, unable to see the lake's surface as she was surrounded by sunflowers, she wove towards the bank. The stalks, unlike the velvety cloudcane back home, were sticky, covered in prickles, and made her fingers itch. As the giant flowers thinned, she peeped through the bordering plants.

A series of black spikes jutted out of the water, followed by spaded fins. The scales were thin, crumbling like they were deteriorating or burnt. The creature thrust its bulky head out like a ship's prow, eyes thick with milky cataracts. Naokah's pulse hitched. Its skin matched the lake's dark green in the receding afternoon light. The perfect camouflage. The size of a shark, its mouth dripped with decaying, spiky teeth. When its lower jaw unhinged, it emitted a familiar shriek. Mila hadn't screamed. This strange lake beast had, likely trying to dupe her for a meal. Naokah shuddered, blinking away what might've happened if she'd taken the canoe. Steam puffed into the air from its blowhole before it dove beneath.

This, whatever it was, didn't belong here. It had taken the dame o' war three days and nights to cross the Razing's churning black-green waters, and for three days and nights, the passengers and crew had had to endure the torturous moaning and thunking and scraping of the mutant sea creatures against the vessel's hull. Sweat pricked her armpits. Abelha was too far south for the Razing's spawn. And in a freshwater lake? How had it swum down here?

Naokah didn't stay to find out. She sprinted, sunflowers hitting her limbs, pack knocking her neck. She ignored the itching of the stalks, the piercing screams, knowing quite well that she was making so much noise that if the hive were near, she wouldn't have been able to hear.

★   ★   ★

The sun was crowning the mountains when Naokah, drenched in sweat and covered in chills, adrenaline waning, finally reached the grottos. Grimacing at the confined space, she squeezed through the opening, a tunnel dripping with stale rain. Her eyes slowly adjusted, and the damp walls expanded to a lovely surprise. Above, glowworms in bright blues and lime greens cascaded over the dripping rock. Left and right sprouted bioluminescent fungi. Their fat fleshed-out heads, big as stepping stones, cast an ethereal glow over the rocks. A small stream carved out the bottom of the grotto, murmuring a hollow homily. She held her breath, dreading the telltale droning that would bring her the Keepership. She spun, scanning this lustrous new world. This was it. Call it intuition or divination or maybe even desperation, but an insistent pull at the base of Naokah's gut swore that this was—

Nothing.

The hive wasn't here. But it had to be. Why else had the cave called to her? She deflated. Had she honestly expected her tracking to be any better than her inspector skills?

Chittering above, from a dripping overhang. Had she disturbed bats? Surely there wouldn't be any in Abelha, not when birds weren't permitted. The creatures were nocturnal, though, and wouldn't harm the bees, which were active in the day. She sniffed. There was no acrid stink, no indication of guano. Still, she stepped back. She didn't have any intention of riling whatever it was—

A stone beneath her boot gave way. The ground shuddered, dust clouding the air. She leapt over the stream, landing hard on the coarse floor. The walls fissured. Jagged rocks broke loose, splashing into the stream. The golden eye behind her, the entrance, blinked. Then stayed shut. Darkness seeped over her. The glowworms and mushrooms became more vivid. They were now her only source of light.

Forget about the bees, she had to find a new way out. And fast. Before it all caved in. She dashed to the closest wall, hand tracing the cracks for a weakness, perhaps another tunnel she couldn't see in the gloom. The floor rumbled, and her knees joggled. Sweat dripped down her spine. What had drawn her to the grottos in the first place? Images of Samara's wicked puppet, the menacing mural, the dead fox flashed through her. Had the gargoyle lured her here?

Thunder, below her elbow. She recoiled. A stream of light shot up the wall. And then more cracks. A multitude. Heart thudding her ears, she pressed back, back. Until she could retreat no more. A resounding groan, and then a huge slab crashed to the floor. Dusty light engulfed her as another hollow revealed itself. The trembling waned, muffled by spraying water.

Naokah's eyes adjusted, and the knots in her shoulders eased. A gap beneath the far wall showcased the Sea of Swarms, waves nibbling at the sandy shore beneath the border. As she approached, the cavern rounded out to mossy walls, and the quakes halted. Whirring pulled her gaze to a large, lopsided partition that wriggled.

Naokah, thrilled as she was terrified, clumsily set down her pack, and pulled out the clip that would transport the queen back to the citadel. She'd known what awaited her this entire trek across the isle. That, if luck was in her favor, or if she had no luck, depending on the way one looked at it, she'd encounter the hive. She'd tried to push her thoughts elsewhere, running through the fields with Lenita or kissing Brielle on the veranda, but as she tiptoed to the colony, it was like facing Death in the flesh.

Her skin tingled, an echo of her sting before. Naokah inched closer, the mural of stingers circling her, and dread weighed down her legs. She recalled the pollen-dusted humblebee pair she'd found in the foxglove hours before. They could be kindly creatures like some humans, but like humans, they'd do anything to protect their kin, their queen.

She cradled the clip in her sweaty palm and searched the undulating wall for the queen. She would be larger, longer than the rest. The attendant bees by her side. Once Naokah found Her Highness, she'd gently scoop her up, wait for the pheromones to transfer, and then wait, still, thoughtless as possible, for the colony to follow.

There—

In the middle, attendants preening her, Naokah spotted her destiny. Long, elegant, covered in velvety black and yellow, she certainly had the bearing of royalty. Naokah sucked in a deep breath, stepped forward—

"Naokah." A voice she thought she'd never hear again stopped her on wobbly knees.

Eyes burning with confusion – surely this was a delusion – she pivoted around, minding the space between her and the hive. Chandeliers of blue-green glowworms had the woman's freckles glimmering like stars. The clip fell from Naokah's hand, clacked against the hollow, and she sprang forward, pulling Brielle into a tight hug.

CHAPTER FORTY-ONE

Seen

I'd been able to channel rage to toss Lenita's would-be assassins into their boiling baths. Rage to shatter the Keeper's mirror. And, though I'd found it hard before, every time I'd tried to communicate with the Keeper, my adoration or lust or whatever power she held over me had impeded me from tapping into my volcanic ire. Learning Avice had tossed me over a cliff, ripping me from my human vessel, however, had cleared the ash clogging my spout. Now, I had no problem erupting. And erupt I did. With swords clanging in my ears, muddy, bloodstained boots thunking up my spine, I propelled myself from the mural's mouth and landed in the middle of the Keeper's chambers, claws clicking like knives on glass.

The Keeper jumped back, amber eyes darting over the slivers of light dappling her room. She'd heard me but couldn't see me.

"W…wh…why?" I growled, voice dull from disuse. I'd been able to communicate with the ghost girl, my kin, even the scrim-turned-monster via my thoughts. But, since she couldn't see me—

"Show yourself," the Keeper pressed, scanning her chambers. Her arched windows, daubed in dusk and fogged up, sat ajar, and long shadows cast by the canopy, the liquor cabinet, striped the floor like a dungeon cell.

"Regrettably, I believe this is all I have to offer," I said, stepping forward. I didn't have a reflection in her end table's mirror. I looked more like water on the verge of freezing. But where I walked, the glass fogged up.

She exhaled forcefully, rolling her shoulders back. She'd found me. And with each clink forward, her jaw dropped lower. "What are you?"

"I was hoping you could tell me." I stopped a few feet away so as not to strain my neck.

"A crith?"

I snorted. "I hope not. Can't you tell by looking at me?"

The tan skin between her brows wrinkled as she studied me. After a moment, she shook her head. I sighed, glimpsing at the mirror. I had no shape. I closed my eyes; my mind returned to the stoop where I'd spent most of my second life, atop the citadel's donjon. Remembering my form. My bullish face, small horns, claws. My long tail.

A gasp. "The…you…gargoyle." The Keeper leaned back, folding her hands under her chin. "How?"

I'd spent most of my existence trying hopelessly, desperately, for her to see me. But now that she did? I was furious. "Again," I said with pained patience, "I don't know. The last thing I recall is your captain tossing me over some cliff. That's it."

"Avice?"

"The one and only. Unless you have some other striking, stone-faced sentry you like to kiss in your chambers?"

Her cheeks flushed to the red of her nightgown, making her even more beautiful, if that was possible. I hated that I noticed. I wasn't here to dote on her.

"You've been spying on me?"

"I try to avoid…intimate moments." I met her eyes, so she knew I wasn't lying. "Don't know what I am. Could be a demon. But I have standards. It used to get pretty lonely, high atop my tower, and you aren't boring, by any means." It was my turn to blush and turn away, tail between my legs.

"I see," she said, straightening.

Was she no longer afraid? Emotions tore through me. Did I want her to be frightened? But what was that saying, about attracting more bees with cloudcane than vinegar or something of the sort? "Something happened during the new moon, and I woke up here, inside the citadel," I offered, hoping she didn't ask for further details.

"Your kind has been charged with protecting the citadel for centuries. What was different this night?"

Should I tell her she had a jealously deluded gargoyle on her hands? That, instead of watching their post, they decided to let a scrim in, just because they wanted revenge? Would she believe me? Hate me? I'd been misguided in my pursuit. Ignorant, really. I didn't know any better. She couldn't loathe me for simply wanting to protect her? I studied her, fear and angst shrinking my will. But I had to be honest. After all, was I not expecting the same from her?

"I let a scrim through," I said, feigning defiance, but really, I was ashamed.

"You what?" Her nostrils flared and, still, even in her anger, she radiated grace.

"I thought one of the foreigners was trying to steal your title. Since you're relinquishing your position almost twenty years early, and I just didn't, no…still don't understand. I've seen you with the bees. They matter to you, above all else. You're cold to everyone, even your lover, but not to them." 'Lover' tasted like moldy cheese and not the fine kind. "So, why would you leave other than by force or trickery? I wasn't capable of harming humans, at least, not at that time, and I'd yet to find a way to channel my emotions into making an impact. So, I figured one little scrim could do the dirty work for me."

"One. Little. Scrim." She bit off each word. "You have no idea what you've done. The chain of events you've unleashed. You naïve little—"

"If your next word is a curse, I strongly advise against it. Remember, I've had a hard time reining in my emotions. And anger, well—" I nodded at the shattered mirror, "—you see what I can do. Unbridled, I don't know how to control it. I could harm you or those you care about." My statement was from fear, a warning, but her eyes flashed; she'd taken it as a threat.

"You've already caused enough harm." Midese curses spewed as she paced about the chambers. Her slippers slapped against the glass, and the fish beneath skittered off into the hall. "Now I must clean up your mess."

"Let me help."

"Like you've helped already?"

"Don't let fury cloud your judgment. I know you've seen the viper-eyed beast, as have I. It's tied to the scrim I let in. My kin, after it happened, searched the citadel high and low, hoping to catch it, but they weren't fruitful," I yammered, nerves speeding up my delivery, "and whatever I did trapped me inside. I can't return to my haunt until I've been absolved."

Each of my admissions pelted her like sharp stones. She grabbed her crimson robe, a torch, and headed for the door. "You coming, or do you need a personal invitation?"

"Where?"

She whirled around, velvet robe swishing. "The library. You didn't just let in one scrim. You've lit a beacon for *all* wayward spirits to enter. We must find a way to seal the wards, and quickly. You should've come to me sooner."

I lowered my head. She was right. Yet.... "Why would they want to enter a glorified apiary?"

"You really don't know much, do you?" she snapped over her shoulder.

"I wouldn't be ignorant if you educated me," I said, sprinting to catch up with her long strides. My claws clacked over the glass. The bees teemed, acknowledging our presence.

She opened the gilded door and ushered me in. The fruit salad tree – pioneered by Abelha's own farmers to save space on the small isle – welcomed me. Grafted limbs heavy with pomegranate, avocado, mango, and lychee stretched outside an ambient dome. The Keeper pulled out a fat red tome with worn leather binding and slammed it down before me. Dust motes scattered in the dim light. I sneezed.

"The citadel holds the key to the other side," she finally said, flopping into a tufted chair.

"Other side? As in—"

"The Scorned Son's afterscape, where traitors go to die."

CHAPTER FORTY-TWO

Battle Cry

"You're...you're really alive!" Naokah gasped into Brielle's ear. Relief gushed from every pore, but her friend, the woman she'd made love to on the veranda, who'd held her and kissed away her tears, stiffened in her arms. Naokah pushed back, assessing her, ice riming her ribs. "How exactly are you alive, unscathed?"

Brielle wouldn't look her in the eyes. Aside from having her lover's physical appearance, the long blonde locks, the starburst freckles, the person before her had none of her mannerisms. Her confidence, her tenacity, her fearlessness and downright bluntness. No. This woman? Naokah didn't recognize her at all.

"Brielle? What happened?"

Brielle's gaze lifted from the floor. The glowworms covered her in a sickly blue. Mauve lips twitching, she seemed to be looking for the right words, but couldn't find them. Finally, pulling a hand through her curls, she began pacing in circles, boots dragging over the damp stone, compounding Naokah's anxiety. The churning behind her grew louder. The bees sensed her agitation too. Would they strike? Samara had said bees *could* pick up on emotions and respond accordingly. The last thing she needed was a grotto full of provoked bees. She had to calm Brielle.

"I...we were worried about you," Naokah said.

No answer, just pacing, muttering.

"Brielle. You can tell me anything. I'm here. Just talk to me."

That made her stop. Her head floated up like she was part ghost, an agitated one at that. "If I'd known you before...all of this—" she spread out her hands in sweeping motions, then pulled them back into a tight fist, "—I wouldn't have followed through with it, I promise." Brielle took a hesitant step towards Naokah, then stopped, chin dropping.

"What are you talking about?" Naokah placed a finger beneath Brielle's trembling chin and lifted her face level to hers. Red, puffy eyes stared back.

Brielle grabbed her hand. "You have to know, I liked you more than anyone I've ever known. Truly."

"Liked?" Past tense. Naokah felt like she'd dove into a lake of ice. "Brielle, you're scaring me. Please. Just tell me what happened. I won't be mad."

Brielle squeezed Naokah's hand so hard, she feared her bones might snap. "You can't possibly know that."

"Oh, she'll definitely be mad, but that's the way of it, no?" A shadow slipped out behind Brielle, hair a black curtain with sunset tips. "All is fair in love and war. Though technically, she didn't say she *loved* you, just *liked* you so very much." Kjell nodded at Brielle, handing her something that glinted in the dim light. A dagger. "Honor is all yours."

Naokah stumbled as she backed up, the pieces all snapping together now. The tiny green feathers from Brielle's disappearance and Clisten's throat? A hummingbird's. The comandante confiscated Kjell's earrings that first day, but like hair, feathers stuck to clothes too.

"It was you, this whole time," Naokah whispered, recalling their heated argument at the ball, Brielle's love for both flowers and the Raptor. "You had Brielle poison you, so you could pretend to be amidst and murder your competition with no one the wiser." Diabolically brilliant. She'd never suspected him, nor that betrayal could hurt so much.

A muscle twitched in Kjell's sculpted cheek, but otherwise, he acted like she wasn't there. "Kill her," he told Brielle. Her former lover clutched the blade but didn't move.

Had the bees grown louder, or was it Naokah's rising panic, her spurting adrenaline? Anger had long been her arch enemy. Uncontrolled, her mind went blank, as did her logic, and she'd made costly mistakes like the argument she'd picked with her sister. Maybe she could rile Brielle and Kjell up, turn them against each other. At least it might give her time to get her own dagger from her pack, now a bulge in the shadows behind Kjell.

"So, your father's the mastermind behind all this, is he? Raptoria's already one of the most powerful nations in all Vindstöld. Yet, he wasn't happy. Needed more? So you, poor little neglected rich boy, volunteered to do his bidding. But you fell short. Knew you couldn't win the Keepership the honest way and, so desperate for your father's approval, you started killing off your competition. How pathetic—"

"Will you shut the raze up!" Kjell yelled, his voice bouncing off the dripping rock walls. Then he turned to his accomplice and said softly, "We're running out of time, love. If you can't do it, fine. Give me the dagger." He reached out, but she took another step back.

Waves purred beneath the grotto, their reflections splintering the shadows over his shoulders. His eyes darkened, flickering like a crow's, like the ghost girl's, like something that wasn't entirely human. A cold droplet fell from the stone lip above and needled Naokah's spine.

"That's a nasty scar you have there." She nodded at the ring around his neck. "Gift from a loving father?" She inched forward, and the pack brushed her boot. "I suppose it takes a bastard to raise one."

His face contorted into the monster she'd already deemed him to be and, as he whirled around to grab her, she crouched down, snagged the dagger from her pack, and shot back up, slicing his forearm. Blood sprayed over the rock, sheening black in the faltering light.

"Witch," he growled, holding his wounded arm, and lurched forward.

Brielle stood frozen beside her, wide eyes pinging between them, giving Naokah an opening. She grabbed Brielle by the hair, and her blade dropped. Naokah kicked it into the sea and held her own, still dripping with Kjell's blood, to Brielle's neck. "Another step and she gets a necklace to match yours," Naokah spat.

"You wouldn't dare. You love her." But doubt crossed his face.

"She used me. So, no. I do *not* love her. If anything, I loathe her and killing her would give me the utmost satisfaction." She pulled the dagger up closer, demonstrating she wasn't bluffing. Brielle trembled in her grip, and Naokah suppressed a wince. Despite what Brielle had done, she had no intention of killing her. Kjell had something on Brielle. The way she flinched in his presence? She felt beholden to him. Maybe Naokah could use that as leverage. She backed up to the rock shelf where the sea murmured from a slash of light. The bees seethed over her rioting pulse. "So, what was your plan, to kill everyone off, and then…who was going to take the Keepership?"

Kjell glared at his sliced arm. Blood poured liberally now, forming a puddle around his once pristine boots.

"Talk," Naokah said. "Or I'll kill her right now."

"Brielle doesn't want to be Keeper. I'll rule, with her by my side. Her only job will be producing heirs. Because once I take over, the Keepership and Praxis will cease to exist. My flesh and blood will rule as kings from here on out."

Brielle tensed in Naokah's arms. "I don't think your baby baker shares your dream," Naokah said.

"We all have to make sacrifices. That's what family does. She'll get used to it."

"Stop speaking for me," Brielle hissed, unmoving. The blade was a whisper from her pale skin. "The plan was for you to rule the north, lord of birds, and I would rule the south."

"Did your mother tell you that?" He started to move.

"Stop, not another step," Naokah said, "or she's done, I swear my life on it."

"This wasn't the plan." Brielle trembled against Naokah, but from the betrayal or sadness? She couldn't be sure. Either way, her plan was working.

Nose twitching, Kjell looked as though he wanted to shout, but he stopped. A lethal calm dropped over him, smoothing his features. "Dearest, can we not discuss this later?"

"We can discuss this now," Brielle said firmly.

An elbow jabbed Naokah in the gut, and she doubled over, gasping for air. The blade clattered to the ground. Brielle sprang forward, grabbing the knife, but instead of wheeling around for Naokah, launched at her future husband. Tears fogged Naokah's view as she gasped for air. She'd done it.

"You miserable liar." Brielle swung the blade at Kjell and missed.

"I didn't lie." He ducked, holding his arm. "Can't we talk about this after she's gone?"

"No. We'll talk about it now. I'm supposed to rule the bees, not you."

"Honey," he said. "There will be no ruler of the bees."

"Why?" Brielle's voice echoed off the cave walls. The bees stirred, amplifying.

"Because wing-power is the future. But we've been running out of land to build our aviaries. Too much of the north is covered in ice. There's a reason why the birds of times past used to fly south for the winter. It's warmer. We can build here. Think how many aviaries we could have. With the netting above, our work has already been partially completed."

"But, what about the bees? We need them."

Though he was clearly trying to soothe her, he couldn't help but smirk. "Yes, birds love humblebees. Full of protein. The birds will grow faster. We'll be able to ship off more for pollination, for ship sails. We'll control the north and the south."

"At the expense of the bees? Have you not learned anything from before? The birds cannot possibly pollinate everything. What about the small farms?"

"Raze the small farms. We don't need them. Besides, once we raise enough birds, bees will be a pollinator of the past."

"Naokah was right," Brielle said. "You are pathetic." She jabbed the knife forward but slipped on Kjell's puddle of blood and crashed to the ground.

"Thanks, dearest." He pulled the knife from her grip and spun for Naokah.

Clutching her throbbing belly, she stood with effort and backed into the damp wall. The sea's waves purled below her feet, the brine searing her nose. She was trapped.

"Kjell, please," she said, hands up in surrender.

"Funny. You look so very much like your sister when she pleaded for her life."

Air whooshed from Naokah, and the cavern spun. "What? Wait. But how?"

"Tell her Enzo sends his best regards." He sneered, then stabbed.

Something heavy slammed into her and threw her to the side. She hit the stone hard, knees cracking.

"No!" Kjell screamed. "Razing take me!"

She stumbled up. Brielle lay crumpled before him, blood oozing from her chest. A sob broke loose from Naokah, and she knelt beside her friend, her lover, her betrayer. Lenita was gone. And now Brielle too? Warmth pooled her knees. She didn't have to look down to know it was Brielle's lifeblood. She grabbed her hand, ignoring Kjell's weeping. *He* did this. "Why?" she asked, hot tears gushing down her cheeks. "Why'd you save me?"

"Had...to make amends," Brielle said, blood foaming her lips. The same tender lips Naokah had kissed, melted into, only nights before. "Was wrong. Save..." her voice faded, the green dimming in her once, brilliant eyes, "...the bees." She gasped, eyelids shuttering. Her grip slackened, along with the dam holding Naokah's fury.

"*You.*" Kjell was a blur leaning over Brielle's still form as Naokah wobbled up. "You did this. All of this. Killed everyone, even your betrothed, for power?"

"Well," Kjell gathered himself, wiping any evidence of humanity away, gaze steeling, "I suppose her death would be in vain if I don't finish the job."

He leapt forward, bloody dagger poised at her. She pitied him. He looked like a little boy, covered in blood, trying his best to make his patri proud, and failing. Her sympathy faded, though. No one's life was easy; everyone had monsters they battled, darkness they possessed. He'd taken away the women she'd cared for most, and now she'd claim his life without a second thought.

Samara had said bees picked up on emotions, reflected them. That was Naokah's motivation as she ran straight for the colony, Kjell only a few steps behind. She spun around just as he stabbed at her and missed. His blade plunged into a large gathering, a big writhing knot. He yanked and tugged, trying to remove the blade, spurting curses left and right that echoed off the leaking walls. She'd only guessed the queen's proximity. Kjell's knife, thank the Divine Daughter, didn't pierce her but came close. Close enough for the bees to take up arms and fight back. One after another, they landed on Kjell, stinging him until not a speck of his flesh showed. He was a shrieking, sputtering swarm.

Panic burned in Naokah's chest and, without taking her eyes off the stinging mess of what was left of Kjell, she inhaled calm, exhaled peace, perfuming the air with the same tenderness she'd felt for Lenita, Brielle, Tati, her family. The awe she'd experienced spotting the two humblebees holding each other in the foxglove, realizing they weren't much different from her and her sister. Perhaps the bees sensed her good will. But whatever the reason, once Kjell crumpled to the ground, covered in raised welts, the bees returned to their queen. The atonal hum softened to that of a well-tuned choir. Naokah could've sworn the bees weren't just buzzing but belting out a battle cry, celebrating their victory and glorifying their queen.

CHAPTER FORTY-THREE

Penance

"Will you stop that?" I hissed at Avice as she paced about the library. The Keeper had forgiven her, far too quickly, in my humble opinion. But with impending disaster, all hands on deck, I suppose. I already had a brigade of warriors clobbering my mind without her adding to the din. The chandelier above the reading nook trembled, the strings of crystal foxgloves tinging with each thud. Just as bad as the Keeper. What was with humans walking aimlessly?

Through the scaling, fog-laced windows, coral smudged the peaks in the west, and mist veiled the valley. Night was approaching, as was our deadline. We had about two hours to get our affairs in order, to strengthen the wards before the scrim struck and all razing broke loose.

The captain slowed, frowning. "Walking helps me think." She couldn't see me for some reason, and I was glad.

"Well, it makes me nauseous," I said, right as she passed. She jumped, and I sneered.

"Will you both just shut up and sit down?" The Keeper glared at us both before returning to her tome. With each page she flipped, musty paper and dried glue perfumed the space.

"Can someone at least tell me why the world's largest bee sanctuary is actually a key to the Scorned Son's afterscape?" I asked.

The Keeper nodded at the sentry before returning to her pages.

"You mean the world's *only* bee sanctuary." Avice plopped beside her charge, and dust motes swirled the air. I sniffled, taking my seat across from them. "Unable to recover the wind her brother stole, the Divine Daughter created bees to perpetuate our future. She honored Abelha with the esteemed position of guarding these life-bringers, but it came at a price. Power is never free."

"And is always tested, apparently," I added, pointing at the Keeper's book. "Does that thing tell us what the scrim are?"

"The Scorned Son's last spiteful attempt at humor before his sister exiled him," Avice huffed. "The scrim, as you call them, are actually the twisted shadows of the very populace we're charged with safeguarding here."

"Like bee wraiths?" I'd used that comparison before. Had I always inadvertently known?

"Unlike their friendly counterparts, who thrive in spectrums of color, they can only travel when it's full dark, and instead of nectar, they garner dread."

I shivered. "Not to make honey, either, I reckon?"

The sentry let out a scornful laugh, and a large vein pulsed across her pasty forehead.

"So, when one wins the Praxis, they inherit both a blessing and a curse?"

"Essentially."

How hard would it have been for the eldest to explain all this to me? I never would've made such an error. Unless, they hadn't known. I didn't until infiltrating these walls. "Is that why you're leaving twenty years early? Too much for you?"

The Keeper's eyes flicked up from her book and hardened. "That's none of your business. Now, if you'll excuse me." She flipped to the next page, where a woman caressed a globe of Vindstöld bulging from her belly – the Divine Daughter's birth of the world. "I'm trying to find the chapter where a gargoyle charged with protecting the citadel actually destroys it."

Avice chortled, despite twitching like a squirrel who'd just lost its nut. Her discomfort remedied mine. I rolled my claws over the table's thick veneer, debating. Now, with the current crisis, it wasn't exactly the perfect time to ask about what I'd done to deserve an early grave, but the Keeper had that handled, for now, and my executioner was here. When would I get another chance to ask if tonight ended badly?

"Stop that," the Keeper snapped.

"Sorry," I said, chastened. I'd mindlessly been clacking my claws on the table.

But she didn't look up from her book. We sat in silence after that. The only sounds, the rustling of pages, the exaggerated sigh of the Keeper as she shuffled through them, not finding what she needed. Perhaps it was the tension vising the air, but I couldn't hold back any longer.

"Don't you recognize me?" I asked Avice. The Keeper's lips squinched, but she kept reading.

"Hard to recognize what I can't see."

"Let me refresh your memory. I remember that ring on your right hand, clear as the emerald in it, better than my former life. Was the last thing I saw before getting pushed off a cliff."

She blanched, turning to the Keeper as if to ask how to proceed.

"Don't look at her. You're the one who accused me without evidence, then continued to pelt me with vague questions before killing me. Whatever happened to a fair trial?"

"The bees reign supreme in Abelha. We don't need a trial to protect their well-being."

"Well-being? How did I threaten the bees? I have no memory of Abelha until I woke as a gargoyle. Pray tell, what did I do that was so horrific, I deserved to die in cold blood?"

The Keeper stopped reading, then. She settled to the back of her chair, eyes on the sentry. "Avice? Answer, please."

The captain laced her fingers together; her emerald ring caught the light and flared in my eyes. I shielded my face before I realized she'd done it on purpose. We were discussing my murder, and she wanted to play games? I growled, deep, guttural, and she flinched. Though she couldn't see me, I grinned. The Keeper did, however, and gave me a stern look.

The captain rose, strolled over to the fruit salad tree, and snagged a plump pomegranate. She rolled it around in her hand, savoring wasting my time.

"Well?" I asked.

The lines around her lips crinkled. "Jordana Hansen, the infamous pirate comandante of *The Unsinkable Clara*."

"I'm sorry? Pirate? I seriously doubt—"

"Not just a pirate." A shadow played over Avice's severe features. "But a witch."

"That's absurd! I think I'd remem—"

"You said you have no memories of your past? A blessing, truly. Let me fill you in. We had an eye on you for some time. Every port you stopped at, you and your crew would pay for your goods with counterfeit coins, always changing the form and grade of each nation's currency so they couldn't track you down. I think the reports say that during your stretch as a *privateer,* you ripped off more than half a million merchants."

Coins engraved with birds, fish, grapes began jingling in the back of my mind. A pirate? Never. I was not Jordana Hansen, nor was my ship *The Unsinkable Clara*. Neither name struck a chord. They would, wouldn't they? Like the lyrics of a cherished song.

"You're wrong. I'd never hurt anyone." But from someone who couldn't remember much, my claim was as reliable as the counterfeit coins.

"Not humans. But you made an error in crossing the Weeping Sea a decade back. You see, someone had been ripping off our bee barges. We suspected a northern sympathizer. They were diverting our routes to agrarian continents, sending the bees to Raptoria. Since you ran your operations when the fog in that region was the thickest, clever girl—" she waggled a ginger brow that I would've loved to rip off, "—we hadn't been able to nail down who was involved."

"What would be the purpose of sending a bee barge to the aviary nation? They're the only continent that doesn't require— oh. They were feeding the bees to the birds?"

Avice's eyes were daggers as she nodded. The Keeper's face pinched.

"Impossible," I said. "Raptoria employed a Midworld witch to enchant the birds, so they wouldn't feed on bees long ago."

"Exactly. It would take a witch to break another's spell."

"And you think *I* was conducting this foul business?"

"We don't think, we know. We set up a trap. Sent a barge out during a full moon so we could catch you making port in Raptoria."

I shook my head. "Why don't I have any memory of sending bees to slaughter?"

"Perhaps because it's so vile—" She slammed the pomegranate on the table, missing my hand by only a hair. Juicy red seeds erupted from the cracked skin. "—like your other, many ghastly crimes, your brain repressed them so you could sleep at night."

"I've never harmed anyone. And I didn't pillage ports. I must've… just…. I don't know, tricked them. My gut tells me you killed the wrong woman."

"Well, your gut can't prove otherwise." The sentry shrugged. I wanted to claw that smug grin right off her face. She was wronger than wrong.

"So, fine. You caught the supposed thief who killed your precious bees, but why is my spirit still here?"

"It's your sentence, don't you see? For what you've done."

"But how?" I glanced at the Keeper. She was no longer reading. She stared over my shoulder, brows meshed, confused. I spun around, but nothing was there, save the fruit salad tree, its long, spindly branches casting shadows across the floor.

"That cliff I pushed you off is no ordinary cliff. It's a gift from the Divine Daughter and named Penance for good reason. It lies in the far west of Abelha, and whosoever is pushed off falls through a timewell that strips you of your vessel. By the time your corpse hits the stream below, your soul has already been released and sentenced according to your crime. As a pirate, the timewell deemed you worthy to inhabit a gargoyle, our guardians and protectors of the citadel. Since you spent your life killing our bees, you'll spend your eternity making amends and protecting them."

The room was spinning now, crashing into me like spiteful waves. Tears burned my eyes, but I had to ask, "Every morning, you dress like a Midworlder and jump into a paddleboat that takes you off the isle. Have you been—" my voice cracked, "—torturing my crew?"

Avice threw the Keeper a panicky look. "That doesn't concern you or your crew."

"Then where are they?"

"Their penance is similar to yours, though less clean." She tossed a handful of pomegranate arils in her mouth, crunching loudly as I waited. I hoped she would choke. She was enjoying this far too much. "When they aren't guarding the outer wall, tearing apart any intruders, they spend most of their time on cloven hooves, rolling about in mud."

My nostrils flared, and I actively had to focus on inhaling, exhaling, for fear of ripping her face off. "They're inside hogs?"

"Guardhogs. Very loyal. They'll do whatever they must to protect the bees they spent their former lives harming. Worthy atonement, don't you think?"

CHAPTER FORTY-FOUR

Caillte

By the time the swell of bees had calmed to gentle currents and returned to their queen, light was dwindling. The small gap at the bottom of the grotto radiated blood orange. Though it pained Naokah to leave Brielle behind, once she and the bees were safely nestled within the walls of the citadel, she could ensure the sentries were dispatched the next morning. Luckily, the grotto was cool and damp versus the heat outside. Her body would keep.

As Naokah picked up the queen clip, walking past the bump-riddled corpse of Kjell, she felt like she was walking back towards the edge of a cliff. If the colony chose to attack, she'd be dead as fast as the Raptor. She channeled her inner Lenita, her adventurous Tati, for both would've walked in, heads high, without batting an eye. The queen moved languidly along the walls, her attendant bees close beside her like ladies-in-waiting. Her wings reflected the cerulean light from the glowworms above, emanating beauty, and more, power. A creator of worlds. Naokah focused on that facet as she placed, with great care, the clear clip around the queen, then moved her to her chest, cradling her like a baby.

"Your Majesty," she whispered. "I ensure your safety. Would you mind ensuring mine?"

And then the first attendant bee flew to Naokah's palm, nuzzling the clip. And the next. Their tiny feet tickled against her skin. She breathed slowly, thinking only of things that brought her joy. The food fight in the shanty's kitchen, Lenita's hands squeezing her feet as she fought a cold, Brielle's first kiss. The waves of bees lapped over her, warming her shoulders like a cloak of sunlight. They covered her cropped hair, her neck, her arms, until the entire colony had concealed her, save her face. Maybe they sensed she needed clear vision to bring them home.

After carefully climbing from the seafront gap, over some precarious cliffs, she began her long trek back to the citadel. At first, her steps were rigid; she was afraid that at any moment, a bee would spook and sting. But as the watercolor sunset infused her with reassurance, with tingling hope, it dawned on Naokah: the cold, unremitting shadow cast by her sister was gone. Lenita hadn't placed her in the darkness; she'd put herself there. Envy and doubt had kept her prisoner, yet it had always been her choice to gather the courage to step into the light. She was stronger, braver than she'd given herself credit for. She'd just proven it.

Her throat thickened. If only she'd realized this *before*, when Lenita was still alive. If only she'd had more time to press Kjell about what he'd done with her sister's body, so that she might give her a proper burial. How had he done it? He wasn't even here when Lenita disappeared. Maybe his predecessor? Who the razing was Enzo?

The bees squirmed, sensing her agitation. So, she tabled her questions for later.

And with that, passing by fields of sunflowers, she joined the bees' rhythmic thrum, humming a lullaby. One that Matri used to sing, about a woman named Estrela. With a broken heart after losing her family, Estrela yearned only for a dazzling death. A flock of starlings heard her cry, lifting her high up into the sky, where she caught a ride on a falling star and soon joined her loved ones in oblivion. A little dark for a lullaby, but Matri, even before Tati's exit, had suffered from bouts of melancholy.

Maybe Naokah was swept up in the moment, but the bees seemed to sway to her words, rippling softly against her skin. No, not swaying. They'd noticed her flushed skin, her perspiration and, just as they maintained an apt temperature for their hive, they'd begun fanning her, helping her cool down. If only Brielle could see her now, swept away in a bee breeze. Her new, magical family. Despite all the death, all the tragedy, for the first time since she'd stepped foot onto the isle, she didn't feel so alone. Her fear dissolved with the synchrony of their wings, glittering like gems beneath the fading light. Confidence swelling, she trekked back up the cliff, past the waterfall, and followed the river by the jabuticabas.

She'd unfairly judged the Keeper, thinking her callous for treasuring her hives over all else, but Naokah had also misjudged the bees. They would not harm her. They knew, somehow they knew, that her intentions were good and had adopted her into their colony. Tears pricked her eyes as the violet mountain terraces faded into foothills, the rich, yolky sun melting into the peaks.

She'd wasted so much time dwelling on how Abelha had failed to meet her expectations instead of appreciating the isle for what she was – the beating heart that kept the whole world alive. She wasn't perfect by any means, darkness lurked beneath, but did that detract from her worth? If anything, it made her even more admirable.

After the wind was stolen and Vindstöld hung precariously from the precipice of existence, it was Abelha who seized her weary hand and raised her up, nurturing the sole bee population for centuries, ensuring millions upon millions of humans and animals and plants thrived, all the while battling an enemy within. Abelha was a survivor, a warrior and mother, and Naokah, now more than ever, finally understood: like the isle, she too, had been fighting her own demons of jealousy and rivalry, of self-loathing and guilt, and continued grappling with them every day. Still, she, a woman with a debilitating bee phobia, had volunteered to stay on an isle brimming with them to save her sister. The act of a coward? Never. She was a good person, a better person than she'd given herself credit for, and was stronger not despite but *because* of her flaws, perfectly imperfect as Abelha.

The citadel no longer leered at her like a monster, but rather, her striking towers, wreathed in crimson ivy, seemed to wave, and her conservatory, sitting above the hedge maze like a diamond, smiled radiantly, welcoming her home. She'd solved part of the mystery, and now she'd find out what the gargoyle wanted, what darkness lay beneath its stone curves. The answer was near.

As Naokah moved closer, the sun disappeared, and navy blanketed the maze, dousing the flames of color left in the sky. *Return before darkness, or you'll never return at all.* She entered the hedges, which lumbered over her like disapproving parents, warning her to move faster. She told her pulse to slow, so as not to stir the bees, but marching, deep and thunderous, sounded behind her. She shifted around, but there was no army. A cloud of darkness droned at the bottom of the valley. As it crept closer, it separated into small whizzing shadows the size of bees. Swarmed like them too. The lowest level of the hedge maze darkened to pitch black, and she sped up. The bees writhing over her began moving faster too.

"It's all right." She tried to continue Matri's lullaby, but her mouth had gone dry. Within steps of the conservatory entrance, the ghost girl appeared beside her, eyes like sad voids. She bowed and opened the glass door, allowing Naokah inside.

"Take care," the girl whispered, then faded into the shadows.

Dusk bled through the glass panels, and the chandeliers where Samara had lectured flickered before winking out. Naokah shivered, unnerved by the stillness, and the bees shivered with her, tingling her skin. Where was everyone?

"Come," said a voice of lead crystal. Red stirred the shadows behind the lectern. The Keeper. "Follow me quickly, before the colony gets feisty."

Naokah didn't hesitate. She'd already witnessed the bees' anger and had no intention of seeing it again. With the new moon, the corridor was darker than usual. Torches hissed as they walked past. Thunder boomed through the donjon, irritating the colony, and accelerating the Keeper's pace until they reached a vacant hive at the end of the west wing. The Keeper held out her hand, palm up, and Naokah placed the clip with the queen in her hand.

"You're home, dearest," the Keeper crooned, then opened the clip. The queen crawled to her haunt. "Follow, my darlings," she added unnecessarily. The bees had already begun shifting to the hive, the attendants wreathing the queen.

They poured off in great streams, lessening the friction that had been covering Naokah's skin. Yet something dwindled within. Something she hadn't predicted, couldn't explain. Ice took the place of the bees' warm comfort, and Naokah felt naked, vulnerable.

Not until the last bees launched off her skin did the Keeper turn to her. "Not what you expected?" she said, amber eyes knowing.

"I...." She laughed at the absurdity of it. "Can't believe I'm saying this aloud, as I've never been more terrified, but after carrying them across Abelha, they became part of me, and now...." Her throat welled up and, startled, she peered up at the Keeper, who put a hand on her shoulder.

"Caillte would fit here, I believe."

Naokah nodded, throat tight. The deep, aching emptiness she'd felt so long for Tati, for Lenita, paled in comparison to the trench the bees had razed down her sternum.

"The feeling never fades. It only grows stronger with time. A good thing, though. Exquisite pain, I call it." The Keeper headed towards the library, heels clacking, a tide of crimson chiffon.

"What do you mean?" Naokah asked after catching up.

"They call to you like they call to me and the generations of those before us. It means you're the right one to take my place. Now, hurry." Sleeves fluttering, she ushered Naokah into the library and closed the door. More thunder followed, along with the heavy, thumping of – was that an army approaching? The Keeper nodded at Avice. "The bees are in place."

The sentry strode to the large fruit salad tree that sprung up from the library's center. The dome above, without the sunlight, bled red. She looked up the tree, spotted a prickly lychee, twisted it, and let it drop back into place. The tree juddered as if struck by lightning: the colorful fruit shivered, and heavy cracking resounded all around them. Whispers crawled up from the shelves' shadows, and Naokah's pulse lurched before her eyes adjusted. Why was all the staff here—

Legions of fat tomes rattled, peppering the dense air with dust motes, then the floor beneath hollowed, and the shelves sank, disappearing beneath the glass. Naokah glanced at the Keeper, who offered a reassuring if not smug smile. As the shelves dropped below their feet, sinking into the abyss, spritzing the library in musty paper, leather, and dust, a new scent took their place – that of pollen, honey, wax. A wall of hives on a track detached from its central spot within the citadel and slid, creating a curtain wall around them. Some of the staff, the distiller, the gardener looked stunned, but as for Naokah, the emptiness she'd felt upon leaving the bees melted away. The Keeper, after noticing her relaxed posture, offered a genuine smile and even winked at Naokah before turning to the rest of the group.

"Welcome to the bunker. Our home for the next twelve hours, should we last through the night."

CHAPTER FORTY-FIVE

Amends

The captain paced. Her crisp uniform swished with each step. The marching was a lullaby in comparison. Though she irritated me, I held my tongue. I'd passed enough words with her. I asked for the truth, and she gave it to me. Her version anyway.

It was a lot to process. The fact that I was a pirate. The fact that my crew was now stuck inside the guardhogs outside our gates. That, if we really were the pirate crew they said we were, I wasn't only responsible for the deaths of millions of bees but my crew as well. Why couldn't I remember any of this? Had my mind erased anything that would remind me of all the sorrow I'd caused, or if I really was a witch, had I cast a spell to forget?

Jordana Hansen, Jordana Hansen, Jordana Hansen. The more I turned my supposed name over in my mind, the more familiar it became, but I'd also repeated it hundreds of times, hoping something would shake loose, and I'd magically recall it all. I'd naïvely hoped that once my past was revealed, all my shattered, displaced memories would miraculously unite into one image like the striking, stained-glass windows in the turrets above. Instead, this revelation only pounded those shards into dust. I felt more lost than ever, and worse, I ached with disappointment, with bitter loss for a life that wasn't worth remembering. This just couldn't be.

The pomegranate arils beside me oozed the bright red of arterial blood, and my stomach lurched. Even if I wasn't a pirate, I was still responsible for the current disaster. I had to find a way to send the scrim back to the razing they came from first. Then, clear my name.

The glass dome above the fruit salad tree had darkened. Time's voracious jaws were snapping shut. We had an hour at best before the attack. The hollows beneath the Keeper's eyes lengthened, spilling down her cheeks as she leaned closer to her current page, reminding me of the ghost girl. Could she have been part of my crew? No, too young, and she would've been a guardhog if that were the case. Where did she fit into all of this? Maybe Lenita would know?

"I may've found something," the Keeper said.

The sentry rushed over. "What's it say?"

"Yes, about that." The Keeper chewed her lip. "Some of this Poli is a bit...complex for me."

Avice jerked her head to the side, eyes wide. "But that's your first tongue—"

"I know razing well it is," she snapped, rubbing her temples. "At least, most days. But this Poli is...dated, and I don't read it on the regular. No one does unless they're a scholar. Now, are you going to stand there and condescend or help me out?" She nudged the book towards the sentry, who stood stiffer than a gargoyle.

"I'm no scholar either, Madam Keeper." She flushed.

"Perhaps you'd prefer Midese," I said, earning a jaw drop from the Keeper and a scowl from the sentry. "What?"

I shrugged. "I overheard you praying in the Midworld tongue this afternoon."

Avice crossed her arms. "Just what are you implying?"

I climbed over the table to the book's edge. The Poli was clear as the mountain terraces on a sunny day, and for someone from the rich Poler nation of Vintera like the Keeper, where babies were sent to school nearly as soon as they vacated their mothers' wombs, this should've been elementary for her too. "My kin—" I cocked my head up to the spires, "—didn't know much about the scrim. They did, however, say they were capable of possession."

"I think I would know if I were possessed." But the Keeper didn't sound so sure. Her frightened eyes leapt to the captain for support.

Avice placed a hand on her shoulder and glared at me. "Shut your mouth, before I shut it for you."

"You'd have to find me first." I glared right back. "Since you're both in denial, I, a humble pirate witch, can easily read Poli. Let's see if the text reveals any juicy nuggets on how to prove possess—"

The sentry yanked the book from my hands. "You're wasting our time."

"Unless you both forgot, the scrim are almost upon us. If one's inside of her—"

"It's not!"

"How do you know?"

"I've already checked!" Avice shouted, spittle flying, startling me and the Keeper, who now regarded her like the world's most poisonous snake. "Your mishap loosed a scrim last new moon, which means the Keeper, *were* she possessed, would've started acting...off then. But—" she passed her charge an apologetic wince, "—you haven't been yourself since you returned from that goodwill mission in the Midworld. That was ten years ago, Madam Keeper. Something terrible must've happened, and whatever it was, changed you. You no longer paint, a hobby that predated your passion for the bees. The whole citadel is covered in your murals, for razing sake. And well, the last ones you attempted were...dark, horrific, so unlike you. That, and you smoke like a fiend, you revert to Midese more often than not, especially during your night terrors, and sometimes I worry you've forgotten who you are."

The Keeper's chin trembled, but she sat rigid, staring straight through me like I wasn't there.

"Every morning, when I'm not meeting with our spies embedded in the north or setting up operations to capture treacherous creatures like yourself—" she glowered at me, "—I've been seeking answers. I've spoken to high priests, the best healers from every nation, I've even consulted with Midworld witches. The Keeper is *not* possessed, she's traumatized, and this place with its whispering shadows and lingering secrets only worsens her pain. That's why she's leaving before the end of her tenure, for if she doesn't leave now, she'll never leave at all."

My chin dropped. "I...I didn't know. I'm sorry—"

"Save your apology for someone who isn't running out of time." The sentry pushed the book into my hands. I looked up, startled. "Yes, I can see you now. And if you care about the Keeper as much as you claim to, *fix this*. You made this mess. Now get us the raze out of it."

★   ★   ★

"Sorry, I'm paraphrasing here," I said, squinting at the scrawled Poli. The Keeper and Avice shared a look of impatience. "But letting the scrim through the wards lit up the path to the Scorned Son's afterscape like an army of vengeful fireflies from, well, the Scorned Son's afterscape. His beasts now have an illuminated map on how to climb out, into our world."

The marching that had stayed with me since my mistake, growing louder as the new moon approached, was that them? The Scorned Son's legions? The torches around the library flickered, their flames now a menacing blue. A fresco of the Divine Daughter with a spear cornering the Scorned Son on a cliff's edge, a cliff that looked far too much like the one I'd been pushed off, gleamed in the low light. I shuddered.

"So, how do we encourage it to wink out?" the sentry asked. Sweat stains spread beneath her arms, and her typical slick bun was now a fray of auburn at her temples. She looked how I felt – a razing mess.

I glanced at the Divine Daughter's faded words. Lying was an option. It's not like either the Keeper or Avice could read the archaic Poli. Why could I, a pirate, read it and they couldn't? The question still bobbed like a cork in my mind, but that was neither here nor there. My time for self-discovery had passed. If I didn't admit the truth, not only would the citadel go up in flames, but Abelha and

Vindstöld could fall to the Scorned Son too. I sighed. I might as well be reading my death sentence. "The lights of the passageway will gutter out once a dark entity crosses its threshold and surrenders their life to the Scorned Son. Like draws to like."

"But we don't have time to find the scrim. The legions will be here any minute." Avice's hard eyes ricocheted between me and the Keeper, who hadn't said anything since her sentry's admission of why she was giving up her title. She sat stiff, her ruffled shoulders pinned to the back of her chair, her copper face frozen with sorrow. I pitied her. I knew how it felt to lose your mind. I still hadn't found mine.

"I know. That's not what I was suggesting."

Both women turned to me, brows raised.

"I still believe I'm innocent. I'm no mass bee murderer, but I have no proof. The only thing I do know is that I, out of anger, revenge, stupidity, whatever you want to call it, made a grave error." I tensed, afraid of my next words. "I cannot live…well, this isn't living, I can't *exist* like this, neither alive nor dead, watching the world fall because of me. I must atone for my sins. It is I who will forfeit my life to the passageway and close it."

"And what about the scrim that haunts the citadel now?" asked Avice.

"My kin will dispose of it eventually. It's their duty, after all. What's important is that the beacon fades before the Scorned Son's undead army can crawl into our plane."

Avice looked relieved, but not the Keeper. "Are you sure?"

"My life has been meaningless since I awoke in a gargoyle. If I truly lived such a life of treachery, I deserve my place in the Scorned Son's afterscape. It's not like there are numerous traitors around here who can volunteer in my stead. Besides, I want to…make my life mean something." My throat caught, regret clawing my chest. "So all of this wasn't for nothing. Perhaps, I'd even be deemed worthy in your eyes, Madam Keeper."

She nodded, but sadness and some other underlying emotion I couldn't place haunted her stare. "You've volunteered to sacrifice your life for the future of our world. I'd say that makes you more than worthy not just in my eyes, but for all generations to come."

★   ★   ★

The hedge walls swayed in our path as if pushed by a phantom breeze while we strode to the maze's center. It was full dark outside, not a star in sight, and the air was thick with cloying flowers. Each step towards my end was heavier than the last. I'd volunteered to dive into a place built to torture traitors for eternity. Deem it wishful thinking, but I still believed I wasn't guilty of the crimes they accused me of, and when I did pass over into the shadowy afterscape, that innocence would absolve me, and the Divine Daughter would send me to my own eternal paradise. Maybe I'd even come to realize my past and finally have closure? Yet as we drew closer, that fantasy crumbled like ash. The Divine Daughter hadn't intervened before when Avice chucked me off a cliff. Why would she now?

The Keeper, cloaked in the compass colony, was unfazed by the brambles that kept clawing at our feet. I suppose the thousands of bees wriggling over her proved distraction enough.

"I still don't know why we needed to bring this hive, if you already know the way," Avice said, keeping a more than adequate distance from the Keeper. Her face glowed red-orange from her torch.

"I don't know the way. The book says the channel to the Sea of Sorrows is through the hedge maze," I answered. "Only this hive, and their ancestors before, know the dance that will lead us there."

"A dance?" Avice said, skeptical. "To the Scorned Son's afterscape?"

"Unless you know of another way bees give directions?" I sneered.

As we neared the fountain of a cherub riding a shark, the soft murmur of the colony swelled to thunder. Eyes wide, we stopped.

"Now what?" asked Avice.

Some unseen force guided me like a river current, and I dropped the tome onto a pile of brambles and climbed atop. Avice cursed, but I ignored her. Ancient words of a forgotten language poured from me, smooth as warm honey. The ground quaked, and the hedge wall shuddered, then split, the rest of the maze following suit, rifting and reconnecting into a long, serpentine passageway that floated above the slab of fog.

The Keeper clasped her hands, curtsied to the bees, raised one bare foot to the inside of her thigh, and began twirling in a pirouette. The bees coalesced and swirled around her, their wings a tempest of glittering tulle. Avice and I stood in awe. When the Keeper and bees picked up their tempo, water, bright and luminescent, bloomed from the hedges, and filled the floating, seemingly endless passageway. Any fear or dread I'd carried before dissolved and, as the Keeper leapt high into the air, legs stretched into a breathtaking jeté, beads of water separated from the main channel and suspended above like stars in a constellation, a constellation guiding me home.

I bowed to the Keeper, to my executioner and, chin high, approached the glowing stream. It called to me in a soft, sweet tone, and peace tugged at me. Who'd have thought this would send me to my end? It was beautiful, and I, enamored, forgot about my past, my lack of closure, my adoration for the Keeper. My fate awaited. Who was I to deny it?

"I knew it was here, somewhere," snarled a voice like the fabric of time ripping.

I spun around. The viper-eyed scrim slithered from its mount, the cherub's gaping mouth. It towered over the Keeper and Avice, stretching, sucking the light from her torch, sullying the air with ripe carrion. The Keeper halted and the bees keened, the dark night rippling. The passageway gurgled behind me, and I twisted back. The water was draining.

"Keep dancing!" I yelled, then charged the scrim. It swatted me like a fly, and I sailed back towards the evaporating channel, colliding with something hard and trembling. Big amethyst eyes met mine. "Lenita?"

Those round eyes grew wider, but she nodded.

"The Keeper must finish the dance," I said, winded. "The future of Vindstöld depends on it."

A curt nod, and the thin, tawny girl, nightshift clinging to her knees, charged the scrim as Avice was flung into the fountain. Her head cracked on the quartz, blood dripping from her ear. But the Keeper recommenced dancing, and the shimmering droplets began forming once again. I felt guilty, abandoning them, but Lenita was strong. I'd seen her fight that vicious Enzo. Surely, she could hold off the scrim long enough for the currents to pull me in. I didn't look back as I dove into the water. Warm waves purred around me, and I felt myself drifting apart, moving on.

The scuffle of the scrim, the captain and Lenita, faded to distant echoes, and the bees' humming softened as the water swept me away. At the end of the stream glowed what looked like a giant beehive. Within were more hives, hundreds of thousands, the glittering particles dancing in different directions. As though – oh, Daughter.

Ice replaced the comfort I'd felt, and I gasped, mouth filling with crystal ether. This wasn't a single passageway. It was a hive of thousands, all crooning their lullabies, calling for me to enter. But which was the Scorned Son's afterscape?

I swam above the current to yell for help, to ask guidance from the Keeper, when a heavy weight slammed into me. Frightened eyes met mine and before I could say *Lenita*, the nearest passage seized us both, and we plummeted into a waterfall, into jagged rocks, into blinding light. The thundering, collective buzz of a colony followed, and then all went white.

CHAPTER FORTY-SIX

Clarity

The library bunker was stuffed to the brim. Damask floor pillows fluffed the perimeter, and a corner table held heaping piles of cheese, fruit, and smoked meat. All untouched. No one had an appetite with the thunder outside, the droning within. The vat of melgo, however, was a huge hit. Most of the staff had already gone back for seconds and thirds, their formerly crisp uniforms now wrinkled with sweat as they clumped between the shelves, whispers and eyes darting through the weak light. Naokah could've used a strong drink too, but she had much to say, much to ask, and she didn't want to fumble any of it.

She veered around the fruit salad tree, nodding at Marguerite, who attended a cut on Mauricio's hand. The mercy caught her gaze, his pupils magnifying behind his green-rimmed glasses, and he offered a thin smile as she passed. Her lips curved into more of a grimace than a grin, as she neared the Keeper and head sentry, who were sitting on a bed of fringed pillows under an eave. The iron chandelier above flared, throwing dark shards over the library, shadows far too similar to the creatures she'd barely escaped only moments before.

"Madam Keeper," Naokah said, clearing the apprehension in her throat. Had she not just crossed an isle wearing a lethal bee cloak? This was nothing. "Excuse me if this is too bold, but it seems you've been preparing for this for some time."

"You're right. You are too bold." Avice leaned forward, uniform pulling at her shoulders, pallid skin pulling at her temples.

The Keeper, upon placing a manicured hand on the captain's, glimpsed over her goblet. "Safety measures were placed after the last… mishap."

Naokah crossed her arms, trying to contain the heat boiling her veins. "I'd call it more than a mishap."

The Keeper looked like she'd just sipped vinegar instead of melgo, long lashes fanning her cheeks as she searched for words. Likely she didn't know the extent of how dark and twisted the maze went.

"You might want a refill." Naokah raised a brow at the Keeper's half-empty goblet. "I learned a lot on my little jaunt across the isle." She told them about Kjell's duplicity, the very real and unfortunate possibility that, since Laerte and Mila hadn't returned, he'd killed them too, and his sick motivation behind it all, turning Abelha into an aviary and destroying the bee population altogether. She left out Brielle's part in it, though. She'd intervened at the end, saving Naokah, and she wouldn't sully her name by admitting her forced involvement.

Gasps assailed the hazy library, trailed by fraught silence. The Keeper's hand quaked, melgo sloshing in her goblet, and Avice shook her head. Still, neither offered anything. Something large and heavy clanged overhead, riling the room. The Keeper flushed the shade of her gown. Another clang, outside the arched window overlooking the hedge maze, but night had already pooled over them, quick as ink.

"Kjell is responsible for the unexplained deaths and claims to have killed my sister." Naokah's voice wavered. "But he wasn't here when she went missing. He mentioned an Enzo?"

"Enzo was his predecessor," said Samara, frowning. "He was kicked off the isle for *attempting* to drown your sister in a melgo vat. He failed."

Marguerite gasped, and all eyes shifted to her. "I should've put two and two together."

"What do you mean?" asked Naokah.

"I treated Enzo for severe burns to his face and a knife wound across his neck before he left." The healer pinched the bridge of her nose, cursing under her breath before looking back up. "Kjell had gone through some extensive aesthetic treatments and—"

"Had a scar running ear to ear," Naokah said. His makeup, his waxy, too-perfect face. "He disguised himself and returned to compete."

The Keeper exchanged a loaded look with her sentry, then nodded, but Avice answered.

"But Enzo/Kjell didn't kill Lenita. Those darting shadows outside? The scrim is what we call them. A final *raze you* from the Scorned Son before the Divine Daughter banished him from Vindstöld. Abelha's not only charged with guarding the world's bees but the Scorned Son's afterscape. Last Praxis, our wards were breached, and when we managed to close this passageway, or so we thought, your sister sacrificed herself for the greater good. She died a hero."

Tears pooled in Naokah's eyes. She'd suspected her death. Even if Kjell hadn't been the culprit, she'd felt that absence. But hearing it aloud, the confirmation, ripped her heart out. What she'd give to see Lenita one last time. To thank her for raising her, to apologize for being cruel. And now she never could. She clenched her jaw, fury chasing away sorrow. "And you never thought to release that bit of information, so, I don't know, her family could grieve?"

Avice stared down at her lap, knotting her hands. "It would've caused worldwide panic if the other nations knew—"

"You labeled her a coward, running away from her responsibility."

The sentry blenched when Naokah said 'coward', but still didn't make eye contact. "We didn't have a choice. Lenita would understand. She—"

"Don't you *dare* speak for my sister," Naokah snarled, and Avice finally looked up. So did the Keeper. Eyes wide and mouths agape, the staff mirrored her shock. Everyone save Samara, who shrugged as though agreeing Naokah's anger was valid, then took a sip of their melgo. "Are the scrim also responsible for this?" She yanked the locket out of her pocket and shoved it into the Keeper's face.

"I…what is this?" She looked genuinely confused.

Naokah opened the rusty hinge, *The Unsinkable Clara* splaying on one side, her family on the other. Still, the Keeper shook her head, but she caught Avice's guilt trudging across her drawn face.

"Ask your captain," Naokah said.

"Avice?"

"The woman in the locket was a pirate," Avice said, flipping her hands over as if stating a well-known fact. "We apprehended her for diverting our bee barges to salvagers in the north."

"You're lying." But Naokah's words came out a whisper. She'd always wondered how Tati had come across such unique goods, some so incredibly random, it made no sense for her to buy them at port. They were personal. Tati had argued the best trades were done with someone who loved their material goods, that their love for that memento carried over and stayed attached to the object for good luck. "My tati was an honest privateer."

"Don't be naïve." A cruel laugh escaped the captain, but it was cut short by more clanging on a nearby tower. The bees keened, heightening the tension. "As you're all too aware, inflicting harm on Abelha and her bee population is a grave offense. In fact, there is no crime greater. Those caught in this illegal trade, their ships are burned and the crew and captain, repurposed, if you will."

"Repurposed?" Adrenaline-fueled fury coursed through Naokah. She couldn't stop trembling. The Keeper took another drink, stiffly eyeing her sentry, but didn't answer. What was her role in this? Had she even known? "If I'm to swear in as the new Keeper, am I not to know of the skeletons on this isle? I found my tati unceremoniously dumped in the western river. You owe me an answer."

"I owe you nothing," Avice sneered. "Your aunt was a pirate. She did unspeakable things. Unforgivable things. Whether you believe that or not doesn't change the fact that she was a villain, an enemy to Abelha, and was executed."

A headache sprouted at the base of Naokah's skull. She rubbed her neck, attempting to unclench her teeth, but it was hard. She'd won the

Praxis, was expected to be sworn in, and still, the citadel kept secrets? She scanned the agitated group. No one would look her in the eyes. Her rage was on the verge of bubbling over, and the rest of the room felt it, growing deathly quiet, save the bees. They fumed with her. She felt their power growing, their venom throbbing.

"What did you do with her—"

The dome above the fruit salad tree exploded, flinging shards of glass across the library, dousing the room with muggy night air. The torches flickered, snuffing out. The hum of bees and something else, something ominous and ancient, intensified to deafening. An elbow collided with her temple and blinding light shot behind her eyes. As screams ricocheted off the hives and the library erupted in chaos, Naokah fought to stay sharp, but a heavy wave of pain crashed into her, sweeping her away.

★   ★   ★

Naokah awoke to scuffles, groans. The room, thick and stifling, seemed to have been yanked up and rolled over. Stomach twisted in knots, she spat out blood and crawled over the cold floor, debris and dust biting her palms and knees. A single torch beside the fruit salad tree cast halos over the crumpled Keeper and Avice, the latter running shaking fingers through the Keeper's long hair, pleading for her to wake. But she didn't move.

"Is she all right?" asked Samara.

Naokah couldn't actually see the savvy, the rest of the room hazy with dust motes and clutter, but she recognized their firm voice.

"Her chest is rising," Avice said.

A shuffle of steps and the healer came into view, kneeling by the Keeper. Her silvery-white hair glowed. Figures sat bunched up against the shelves; a few were sprawled beneath the windows. Still, unnaturally still. Even the bees were quiet, as if mourning.

"She'll be fine," the healer said finally, and a collective sigh echoed. "Suffered a heavy blow to the back of her head. We must wake her. With her brain swelling, it's dangerous to let her sleep."

The captain whimpered, shaking the Keeper's shoulder. Gently at first. But when she didn't move, with increased vigor. Finally, a groan trickled from her, and the sentry's shoulders fell like she was breathing for the first time since the lights snuffed out.

The Keeper's eyes popped open. "You," she groaned and jolted up, steadying her head with her hand. "Get away from me."

Avice squinted, scanning the group. "Who—"

"You!" The Keeper pointed a shaky finger at the sentry. "She trusted you, and you betrayed her."

The sentry slid the healer a perplexed look. "Why don't you lie back down? You hit your head and—"

"I'm perfectly fine," the Keeper said, wincing as she backed farther away from Avice. Her eyes shot wildly around the room's wreckage, making her look more like a trapped animal than the world's most powerful leader. "What am I doing here with that traitor?" Avice opened her mouth to respond, but the Keeper cut her off with a wave of her hand. "Not you." She turned to the healer and raised an expectant brow. "Marguerite, right? I remember you from camp."

The healer's brow creased. "What's the last thing you remember, Madam Keeper?"

"Keeper?" Her lips pursed, and she cocked her head to the side, now looking more puzzled than ever. "That disgrace for a captain over there conspiring behind my wife's back and coercing one of my best mates into turning on me so that I'd sail *The Clara* right into a trap."

"*The Unsinkable Clara*?" Naokah's chest caved in. She knelt by the figure who, only moments before, she'd thought was the Keeper and dropped the necklace into her hand. "Do you recognize this?"

She popped the locket open and gasped. "Where did you get this?"

"Found it today near my tati's…grave."

Earnest amber eyes met hers, growing bigger, misty. "Are you…?"

"Naokah," her voice quavered, "an older, hopefully wiser version than the last time you saw me."

"What in the Daughter's name is going on?" Avice threw Naokah a bewildered look.

"I don't know how it's possible, but...." Naokah squeezed the woman's hand. "Meet Comandante Jordana Hansen, my aunt, who you executed for piracy."

Blood drained from Avice's already pale face, and then her eyes flashed with fear, with malice. "If you're not the Keeper, *witch*, then where the razing is she?"

CHAPTER FORTY-SEVEN

Found but Lost

No one tells you this, but dying is unraveling. Alive, you're a spool of tightly wound thread and, although your mind fades and frays from time's kiss, each new day, new experience, you wrap another loop, another shade, expanding that spindly knob that once was you, before you lived. Death wrenches you from that mortal rack and tosses you off a cliff with no end, and all your memories and mistakes and sorrows rapidly fly away from your dwindling spool. You flail through vast emptiness, molting everything until you're a mere shell, a hollow cylinder, leaving you just as naked and alone as the day you took your first breath. Past loves, though, the heartbreaks and gut-wrenching losses? Those tend to snag, and you rebound, if you're lucky.

The thread that yanked me back was purple, the rich hue of royalty, of deep sunsets and fiery amethysts – just like my wife's eyes. They peep over my easel, twinkling. I snort and tell Jordana to sit still. She pouts, my brush drops and – the spool unwinds, her warm lips are on mine, tasting of cloudcane and sweet wine. A new thread tugs, glimmering white. Hand in hand, we're married, now spinning, dancing aboard her ship. Her singing – truly dreadful – has me roaring with belly-aching laughter. Aurea, our darling daughter I saved from the Razing, joins in. Doe-eyes glittering, she giggles, showering us in rose petals.

The spool jerks, and I'm on my knees in a vineyard. Sobbing, everything's wrong. I squeeze my hands together, repeat my wife's name seven times. Magic rips my soul from my body, plunging me into...the thread bleeds red. I'm back on *The Clara*, but she's gone. A betrayal, an iron to the back of my head, blood stings my tongue. I'm branded a traitor, in... Jordana's body? How am I inside my wife's body? Thrown from the cliff, my life unravels, thread by thread, and as Jordana's body dies, it comes to me, oh razing, it comes to me...I am Gabriella França Costa, the seven hundred, seventy-seventh Keeper and Guardian of Bees. And my beloved Jordana is trapped inside my body.

I gasped, waking on a beach. Rosy pink sand glinted around me. Something soft tickled my shoulder, and I recoiled. Long, black strands danced over my shoulder. I reached up, like cornsilk beneath my fingers. I had hair. Which meant—

I stretched out my trembling hands. Long fingers, smooth brown skin with glossy nails. I was me. But where? Gentle turquoise waves purred at the beach, then receded just as smoothly, leaving behind pearly shells, some whole, some broken, like my memories before getting pulled through the passageway. A gull squawked overhead. But that was the extent of the noise. No crunching of boots nor rattle of chain mail. Finally, the blasted army was gone! I craned back and inhaled a deep briny breath, shivering from the warm, coarse granules against my skin, hot blood throbbing my neck, the whisper of hair on my earlobe. My soul had found its way home, and my whole body, flesh and bone, tingled with ecstasy. To be human, what a blessing.

"It's really you," yelled a young woman.

I twisted to my side, and Lenita ran along the shoreline, her thin nightdress whipping with each step. The Crogan envoy, but she was more than that, wasn't she? I stood as she reached me.

"Madam Keeper," she gasped, out of breath, and bowed.

"My friends call me Bee." I smiled.

"Bee," Lenita said shyly. "How are you...how can this be?"

"You mean, how did I get trapped inside a gargoyle?"

Lenita nodded.

"That's a rather long story, and like most, it starts with love and ends in betrayal." I choked on the last word. "Before I could remember anything, Lenita, I was drawn to you back at the citadel. I thought it was your tenacity, your scrappiness, your sheer will to win, but it's something more, something much closer. A decade back, I met a fiery Crogan privateer on a goodwill mission to the Midworld. I painted a miniature of her sister, her nieces for her locket. You've grown into a lady since then, but your eyes haven't changed. You're the spitting image of Comandante Jordana Hansen, a woman charming as she is stubborn, who'd later become my wife, which means you're *my* niece too."

Lenita clenched her jaw. "Tati…left us for you?"

I took her small, coppery face in my hand. "No. Never." I sighed, wishing I had my wife's cloudcane pipe to explain the rest. I sat on a small dune and patted the sand beside me. She hesitated briefly, but relented. "I didn't always want to be the Keeper, you know. I was an artist, a painter, but my father had other plans. Suppose that's what we bonded over, your tati and me, both fulfilling duties that were thrust upon us. My charge of keeping the bees, guarding the Scorned Son's afterscape, and her quest to find a cure for the Razing, a spell or charm to stop, maybe reverse it." I laughed, shaking my head. "She'd been using the guise of a notorious pirate. Said it helped persuade the unhelpful into being helpful, but it caused more trouble than it prevented."

"She was a witch?" Lenita picked up half an oyster shell, its mother-of-pearl lining gleaming in the morning sun, and tossed it into the ripples of vivid blue. "She never told me."

"For good reason. It caused the rift with your matri. Jordana had planned on returning to Croi Croga to make amends, but my father got to her first, bastard that he was, luring her with a bogus artifact that could stave off the Razing. I was in Vintera when I learned of his trap and recited the protection spell she'd taught me, hoping it would bring her back, but it went wrong. I ended up on her ship, got my head bashed in, and then was tossed off Cliff Penance by Captain Avice. My own sentry didn't even recognize me."

Lenita scrubbed her hands through her cropped locks. "Because you switched bodies. So, the Keeper, your body, back at the citadel is actually—"

"Your aunt." No wonder I'd been fawning over her since I awoke, *my* wife inside of *my* body? Surreal. "Avice was worried about her/me. She'd taken up smoking, stopped painting, tried to cut her hair, and could no longer read ancient Poli." I laughed in disbelief. Now I also understood why the murals were so receptive, why I knew so much about bees, the Keeper – me. "The body-swapping accounts for a lot, but what about my memories? I wasn't able to recall any of this until I fell through that passage – definitely not the Scorned Son's, it's too cheery here – and the reason the Keeper/Jordana is giving up her tenure? She's losing her mind."

"You were both displaced from your bodies. It would make sense your memories left you too," Lenita offered, brow furrowed. "Or—" her lips stretched into a big grin, "—maybe that, on top of *caillte*."

Jordana had told me this tale our wedding night. "Caillte." My eyes stung. Since I was killed in my wife's body, my memories were transferred to her, but I was still alive, a spirit inside a gargoyle. That would've muddled things a tad. I scanned the effervescing horizon. The ocean went on and on, as did the cloudless sky, fresh and clear of the Razing's smoke and stink. A marvel I never thought I'd behold.

"You're right," Lenita said, "this isn't the Scorned Son's afterscape. Where are we?"

"Not a clue."

"We should try to find a way back."

"We should," I agreed. "Tomorrow." This was the first time in a decade I'd worn flesh instead of stone. I planned to take full advantage of it. Today, I wanted to soak in the sun, to taste the brine, to feel the—

Lenita's short curls fluttered around her scalp like butterflies, just as my long black locks pirouetted my shoulders. Heart racing, I turned to her. Her violet eyes widened, tears dewing her cheeks. My eyes misted too.

"Is that...." She started but choked.

"The *wind*." Though I hadn't been around before the Scorned Son's thievery, my gargoyle vessel had. Remnants of its memories, whatever spirit had possessed it before me, had melded with mine. I threw back my head, treasuring the breeze's cool, wispy fingers as they curled through my hair, skittering my lashes. Her touch was nearly as magical as Jordana learning my curves for the first time.

"This isn't Vindstöld," my niece said, "but it feels familiar. Like it's welcoming us back."

"Perhaps we should explore first. Determine if this world's viable before returning. Should our efforts be fruitful, maybe we, along with the rest of Vindstöld, could call this home."

"Maybe." Lenita leaned against my shoulder, skin against skin – not stone! – and I buzzed with hope.

CHAPTER FORTY-EIGHT

Into the Fray

The pounding outside had stopped, and the night air was a soaked cloak, settling heavy in the library. No one spoke.

"Where is the true Keeper?" Avice repeated, breaking the stunned silence. "The woman I've pledged my life to. The woman I've sacrificed everything for and would die for," her voice keened as she frantically scanned the library, "where is she?"

Scratching — from the library's corner. A figure huddled in the haze, then began drubbing their head against the stained glass like a broken marionette. Over and over, they thumped. Shadows writhed over their uniform, now blue-black in the low light. Heavy and slow, the cadence chilled the blood pounding Naokah's neck.

"The Keeper," a voice rasped from everywhere and nowhere, "could be in my afterscape with Lenita." The staff member in the corner spun around, braid swinging. The eerie stare of a nocturnal beast raked Naokah's skin. "That, or a thousand other worlds. Take your pick."

On instinct, Captain Avice threw a protective hand over Tati, then huffed, backing away. The air, thick with dust and terror, now reeked of rotting meat. The rest of the staff shuddered, inching back until they nearly touched the hive walls.

"Samara?" Naokah asked. No. This wasn't real. Like before, the gargoyle was feigning—

"I prefer Scorned Son." The Samara puppet grinned.

"As in…" Naokah's stomach flipped. "The Divine Daughter's brother?"

"I would say the one and only, but I recently learned we are legion." He jerked an unnatural shrug. "Hence the other worlds."

Naokah wasn't sure what to process first. The fact that there were more than two Divine Siblings, that the Scorned Son was here in the flesh – inside Samara's no less, that Tati now inhabited the Keeper's body, or that Lenita and the true Keeper were in some other world, hopefully *not* the Scorned Son's afterscape.

Hope is for the weak, an ancient voice scratched against the soft nodes of her brain. Naokah glimpsed around. No one heard it but – *Ask your lover, Brielle*, it cackled.

What did you do with her?

Nothing. She did it to herself. A traitor, she's exactly where she belongs, drowning in the Sea of Sorrows for eternity.

Naokah felt like the wind had been knocked out of her, and she struggled to stay upright.

Oh, a shame. Thought you'd be happy? the Scorned Son taunted.

Whirring amplified. The bees detected the Scorned Son's presence like Kjell's fury. Should she rile him up, adding fuel to the hives' agitation? But what could they possibly do to a fallen god? They'd only kill the savvy and the rest of the library's occupants, herself included.

The Scorned Son's eyes slitted like a viper's. *Smarter than you look.*

Get the raze out of my mind! her brain shouted, sprouting an instant headache.

"What…how…?" Avice schooled her face to its distinctive tight stance, but her voice pitched. "Why are you here?"

The Scorned Son cracked his – Samara's – hands, and the entire room shrank back. "Easier shown than explained." He slashed the air, and the arched windows spanning the western wall shattered, one after another. Stained glass sprayed the library, a fray of shards and bloody sleet, before swirling into a series of blurry images. A woman with glowing, celestial hair and eyes like fire tossed a man – her brother, from his looks – off a cliff. His soul detached as his body hit the water, shooting across the horizon like a falling star, to the citadel, into the one gargoyle, face like a bull, who leered inward. The stone vessel slurped up his soul. And though his glimmering limbs kicked and punched and shrieked, he stayed locked inside the grotesque. He sank and withered, eyes dripping with despair, with sorrow, trapped for eons. Until another soul, brighter than the sun and akin to the Keeper, slammed into the bull gargoyle and freed the ancient spirit of the Scorned Son.

The Scorned Son dropped Samara's stolen hand, and the glass showered down. Naokah shielded her eyes as shards bit into her neck and hands.

"Suppose I have you to thank for my freedom." The Scorned Son turned to Avice, who cringed. "Had you not betrayed the Keeper and her lovely witch of a wife—" he nodded at Tati, "—I'd still be locked away in that ghastly prison."

Tati was a witch *and* had married the Keeper? Naokah had so many questions. Brielle's words from the first day reverberated through her. *The wretch should've been chained to this very isle, where he could forever slog through his own filth.* Her friend had been right. The Divine Daughter hadn't exiled her brother. She'd imprisoned him inside a gargoyle. But her aunt had been missing for only the last ten years....

"You've been free a decade, and yet you've failed to find your afterscape?" Naokah said, eyes locking with Tati, who gave a conspiratorial bob. "I'm surprised you don't want to go home. Or perhaps you're not as powerful as you claim to be?"

"As I said, there are thousands of passages—"

"Impotence, then. Can't find the hole, is it? Common problem. Why I prefer women—"

"Enough!" Eyes flashing, the Scorned Son snarled and, before Naokah could duck, grabbed her, slamming her against the cold floor. The room slanted, shifting as his fingernails grew into claws and burrowed into her neck. Her lungs deflated, eyes shuttering—

Until a wail. A heavy thud, then the buzzing of a swarm. His grip slipped, and she crawled on all fours, slinking beside the hive walls. Samara collapsed on their back and coughed. Dark, oily smoke billowed from their mouth. The swarm peppered the Scorned Son's released spirit, and he bawled and shook; the torch near the fruit salad tree brightened to blinding then sputtered out.

"To the hedge maze," Tati whispered. "The passageway to his afterscape must be snuffed out before his army breaks through." She closed her eyes, chanting something in an archaic tongue, and the colony closest to the door peeled from their comb and cloaked her. "The compass hive will show us the way," she answered Naokah's furrowed brow.

Had Kjell known of this hive's importance, spraying pheromones to have them split? Or was he just one of the Scorned Son's puppets? Naokah assessed the staff, all lying on their bellies, eyes wide as the bees swarmed the flickering form of the fallen god. She'd have to figure that out later. She cupped her hands around her mouth. "Follow me."

Her eyes halted on Samara, the real Samara, and she forced down a cold knot. She'd risked the savvy's life, all their lives, to distract the Scorned Son. Naokah wasn't even the Keeper yet, and her virtues were already bending – like Brielle had warned. She tabled her morality and offered a curt salute to the bees before crawling beneath the swarm, heading for the door. The Scorned Son's entrance had cracked it, and she pushed it ajar, holding it open as the rest of the staff snuck out after her.

The corridors were cool, slick beneath her hands and knees, and fish darted beneath. When the last person made it through, Naokah peeped back inside. The Scorned Son was shrieking, enraging the bees even more. All the colonies had dismounted, attacking him. Her chest swelled with pride. The bees were life enders, but also life bringers. They'd just saved them all. She snicked the door shut.

"What's the plan?" Avice whispered, warily helping Tati to her feet.

A nest of shadows broke loose from the turret above, circling like bats. The Scorned Son's henchmen. The scrim. Were these the same beasts she'd encountered in the grottos?

"Hedge maze." Naokah sprang to her feet. "Now!"

The shadows twitched and dove, their wings gleaming red from the stained glass, and the staff stampeded through the west wing. Their feet thudded the floor, booming like thunder. A cry, lone and shrill, pierced the air. A door slammed open, and the thrum of angry bees, of a fallen god raze-bent on vengeance, followed. And still, chests heaving, throats burning, they ran.

★   ★   ★

The maze was dark and damp, a slumbering lamprey coiled around gulfs of fog. When they reached the fountain, water gushing black as midnight, something uncanny, preternatural, like a ghost's fingers tingled Naokah's spine. Her body knew before her mind – she was tracing her sister's final steps. The staff huddled around, and Naokah's gaze slid to the savvy.

"Samara," she whispered, knotting her fingers.

Their cobalt eyes were unfocused as they moved to her. "Yes." They nodded in typical savvy fashion. "At your service, always and forever, future Madam Keeper."

"Those claw marks on your wrist, they aren't from a sconce, are they?"

They shook their head, jaw clenched. "They're from me."

"You?"

They leaned in, their breath steaming her ear. "Yes, I tried to claw out of my body. But the Scorned Son wouldn't let me."

She cringed, but then it struck her. "It was you who brought me Lenita's journal?"

"I...he also took it away."

She squeezed their shoulder, now covered in dust. "We'll fix this. I promise."

Thunder ripped through the slate sky, and a tempest of howls answered. Ozone, sharp and fresh, sparked Naokah's tongue. Lightning struck the donjon, and the towers draped in red ivy ignited, bright as midday. Brigades of shadows mushroom-clouded from the turrets, but glowing spirits leapt from their stone haunts and fought the Scorned Son's henchmen. The gargoyles battled to protect them.

"We don't have much time." Tati's icy fingers wrapped around her wrist. "But it must be you who performs the navigational dance."

Before Naokah could protest, the bees, one by one, began trickling over her linens. "I don't know the steps."

"No need. They will lead you."

The colony crawled over her arms, her legs, skirting her hips like a gossamer ballgown. As the last of the bees covered her skin, the hollow beneath her ribs warmed, and hope and purpose clasped the broken chains of her soul, making her whole again. The ground quaked beneath her, and the hedges split and reformed into a floating river with no end. So bright, so blue, the water effervesced as though all the stars in all the worlds had melted, filling this passageway anew. Naokah's limbs moved on their own, mimicking the graceful arcs of the bees. Her steps were light, springy and, when she leapt into the air, the darkness winging her shoulders, she could've sworn she was flying.

Countless constellations of beehives arose at the far end of the stream, blinking, pulsating with power that lifted the hair along Naokah's arms. Beads of water separated above the coursing river, chiming like cathedral bells, calling her home. Lenita was in one of those worlds and, if the Scorned Son was telling the truth, Brielle was trapped in the Sea of Sorrows. The droplets beckoned her, tugging her forward. She had to find them.

"No," Tati said, pressing a firm hand against her chest. "I've seen his mind, his plan for retribution. The Scorned Son will stop at nothing to rip open his passageway, letting the horrors of his afterscape bleed into our world. We must send him back and shut it forever." She turned to the staff, eyes blazing. "Protect the future Keeper no matter what—"

A wave of nauseating power knocked everyone to their knees. Brambles clawed Naokah's skin, and the passageway started fading, draining.

"Don't stop!" Tati yelled, dragging herself off the fountain's ledge. Blood slicked her neck.

Naokah staggered and almost fell, but Samara towed her up. Once the bees resumed, as did she, the savvy broke off to fight the Scorned Son with the others. Naokah gasped, filling her lungs with dank air, then let the bees guide her. They flowed like soft waves, their rhythmic current carrying her to weightless peace.

Without flesh, the Scorned Son's spirit churned and burned, tentacles of reeking ash lashing out like whips. When his claws sliced the dense air, spilling the gardener's blood, the chef pushed back, boxing him square in the jaw. The Scorned Son backhanded Andre, and he plunked into the fountain's black water. Then he swiped, connecting with Avice, slicing open her arm. More blood splashed the mud and brambles. Marguerite rushed to staunch the wound. After flinging the mercy and savvy against the fountain, the Scorned Son came for Naokah.

She sprang back. But not fast enough. He clawed her cheek, almost snagging her left eye. Her face throbbed like she'd stuck it in fire, and blood trickled her eyelids, dripping rusty and hot in her mouth. The hedge was a mottled mauve, and the passageway gurgled and drained. As Marguerite reached out to help Naokah, a flaming tentacle whipped her into the hedge with a thunderous crack. She didn't rise after that.

"There's a half-finished mural in my chambers, and behind it, there's a trap door, holding something you'll need," Tati gasped beside her. "I'm proud of you, Naokah. Always have been. You're just as worthy and remarkable as *all* the Hansen women. Never forget that."

That felt like a goodbye. "Tati, what are you—"

Tati clasped her copper hands together and began chanting in that archaic tongue again. The Scorned Son lurched forward, flickering. The river moaned, pleading, but he fought it, grasping the lip of the fountain. His tentacles wept brackish ink, and he howled like a snared beast. As he fought, Tati wavered back and forth by the river's edge, nostrils flaring, never stopping chanting. She pulled off her ruby videira, thrust it into Naokah's shaking hand, and without another word, leapt into the water of the passageway. Arms wide, she grabbed the Scorned Son's tentacles, yanking him under the choppy surface. The swarm of scrim from the towers bellowed, channeled into a funnel cloud, and surged after their dark lord. Avice, arm soaked in blood, face ghostly pale, staggered to the riverbed.

"No, wait! What are you doing—" Naokah started.

"I must atone and find the Keeper." She proffered the saddest salute the world had likely ever seen and jumped, vanishing beneath the blue.

The passageway boomed. Walls of water geysered the night air. The hive constellations winked out, the river evaporated, and the hedges marched back into place, as if the passage had never existed. Naokah stumbled to her knees, and the colony stilled into a soft, sheening cloak floating on an illusory breeze. A few bees buzzed about, landing atop her ear, her shoulder, beading down her chest like a necklace.

"They've already accepted their new Keeper," Samara said, smiling, blood oozing from a gash in their forehead. "Long may you keep."

CHAPTER FORTY-NINE

Persuasion

A moon cycle later

"You positively sure *this* is where you want to meet them?" Samara frowned at the murals of grotesques with unseemly fingernails cascading the floor. Tati's rendition of the Sea of Sorrows. Terrifying when Naokah and the late Mila had gotten lost here a month ago. But now—

"There's no place more perfect, in truth." Naokah's grin likely bordered on feral.

Samara cocked their head, folding their arms over their uniform. "You and your tati have…interesting taste."

"Suppose the citadel's rubbing off on me," she teased. "Go ahead and send them in."

The savvy shook their head, braid thunking – there'd be no use in arguing – and left, returning a moment later with two older, grimmer versions of Kjell and Brielle. The late envoys' parents had written and 'demanded' Naokah's audience before the ceremony this evening. Typical Poler audacity.

"Madame, Monsieur." Naokah bowed, black skirts whispering over her slippers. "Welcome to the citadel."

Brielle's mother had foregone mourning her daughter, standing tall and proud in her loud pink and gold appliqué gown. Her pagoda sleeves trimmed in lace ruffles swept in front of her as she covered her mouth; her green eyes doubled in size.

"Enchanting murals, don't you think?" Naokah asked with tempered patience, then turned to Kjell's father, whose stare rippled like a raven's. His hair, dark as his countenance, rolled in long waves over his green-black suit. Peacock feathers, very apt for the tycoon, spiked from his collar and sleeves.

The Madame twisted her painted lips. "They are... certainly something."

"But we aren't here to discuss art, are we?" Naokah pressed. "I've a busy day ahead, as you very well know, so please speak."

"Fine." The Monsieur looked down his sharp nose. "We demand reparations for the loss of our son and daughter."

"Reparations?" Naokah laughed. But neither parent stirred. They were serious. "For what?"

"Kjell was to take over my wing-power enterprise and Brielle was to be his wife. Our nations are at a loss—"

"Oh yes," Naokah snapped, shooting them a look that could slaughter an army. "You both seem terribly broken up over it."

"But—"

Naokah silenced Brielle's mother with a wave. "Reparations," she repeated, still in shock. Where did she even begin? "You, Monsieur, have a lot of nerve coming to Abelha demanding we pay you for your son's undoing. I have irrefutable proof that during the last Praxis he tried to drown my sister in a melgo vat and would've succeeded had someone—" the Keeper/gargoyle, "—not intervened. And even after getting kicked off the isle, he concealed himself and returned as a runner-up, with the intent to kill off his competition. And he did. Kjell or Enzo or whatever you call your spawn and Brielle murdered envoys from Okse, Bizou, Zerşil, and Svinja. And they almost killed me."

The Monsieur scowled, and the Madame tilted her chin in the air, aloof. But Naokah wasn't finished.

"Kjell may've tried to hide behind all his rouge and powder and waxy skin grafts, but I saw behind his mask. Pain and desperation and darkness lay beneath, and it's all thanks to you, Monsieur. Your greed, your exorbitant prices on wing-power that starved thousands of Midworld farmers, that drove them into poverty, forcing them from their homes into nations that wanted nothing to do with them? And even after that, all the wealth in the world, and you still weren't happy. You neglected your son, so much so, that he murdered for your approval, and would've continued to do so, had he not been stopped. You turned him into a monster, and for that, you only have yourself to blame. So yes, I agree with you. Reparations will be paid, Monsieur. But by you and the Madame. Not Abelha."

"And just how do you plan on making us?" Kjell's father stepped closer, towering over Naokah and dousing her in acrid cologne, but she didn't falter. She'd trekked the isle in a cloak of bees and fought a fallen god. He, a mere mortal, was nothing.

"Only Abelha knows of your treacherous plot. I've kept the other nations in the dark, for now. But should you displease me, I won't hesitate to let them know who's responsible for killing their envoys. Vintera and Raptoria may be powerful, but to withstand a war against the rest of the world? Your fortunes only exist because of the rich merchants who buy your services and goods at a premium. What would happen if they pulled their support?"

The Madame clenched her jaw, cracking her icy composure. Lucky for her, Naokah had controlled herself. Smacking the nonchalance right off her pretentious face would've been an epic way to kick off her Keepership.

"I believe we're through here." The Monsieur grabbed for Brielle's mother.

"We are," Naokah agreed as they turned to leave. "But please take heed—" she waved at the hideous murals to her left and right, "—I keep more than just bees here. Don't cross me." Then nodded at her translucent accomplice, her informant and cousin, whose big doe-eyes glittered with mischief as she ran her spectral hands down the Polers' spines.

They shrieked and stormed from the corridor, feet thundering over glass. Naokah and Aurea waited for them to disappear around the corner before guffawing. When the laughter finally ceased, she gave the ghost a wistful smile. Aurea, daughter of the former Keeper and Tati, had been used as a pawn by Captain Avice to force Tati's first mate to betray her, leading *The Clara* into a trap. But Aurea was killed anyway. The sentry, more than anyone, deserved to drown in the Sea of Sorrows.

"What?" asked Aurea, tossing a wispy lock behind her shoulder.

"I won't rest, you know? Not until I find a way to reunite you with your mothers."

Her cousin's hand, soft as a starling's wing, squeezed hers. "I haven't passed over to my eternal afterscape because you still need me. My mothers would agree. Besides," she winked, no doubt recalling their latest prank, "I'm having too much fun to leave."

★   ★   ★

On that very first night Naokah stepped foot in Abelha, Samara had said every Keeper contributed something to the citadel during their tenure. When the sentries retrieved Brielle's body, they also found Laerte and Mila nearby – stabbed to death by the same blade that killed Brielle. Both had defensive wounds, Kjell's sunset locks in their fists. In true Mid fashion, they hadn't left the world without a fight. Since Naokah had failed to protect them in this life, she intended to safeguard their next. With all the lives lost for and over the isle, bees included, a memorial garden seemed the perfect addition. She'd worked alongside Ettori, healed nicely now, to dig flowerbeds and carve out a meandering stream that cradled the hedge maze twists. Rows of rainbow tulips and hyacinths, lavender and honeysuckle caressed the sparkling water, and bushy orange trees, laden with sweet white blooms, cast shade over the path to the ivy-thatched gazebo where Naokah now sat. There were no graves for Tati, Gabriella, or Lenita, only marigold mounds, blooming promises that she would bring them back safely from wherever they were.

But first, she'd need help.

Naokah rose as Patri guided Matri to her seat beneath the gazebo. She wore a chartreuse headscarf today that shimmered in the soft afternoon light. Hope fluttered through Naokah, even if Patri had been the one to pick it out. Aurea had convinced Naokah that the black mourning attire she'd worn the past month wasn't befitting for her swearing-in ceremony. And with some prodding, she'd finally relented. Brielle would've agreed. Gabriella Costa's color had been red. But the night Naokah's lover had made her a train of chartreuse curtains, warm and gold and brilliant against her tan skin, there'd never been any other choice.

"Where's Marcos?" Naokah asked Patri, as he sat beside his wife.

A faint smile touched his lips as he pointed his chin. Her little brother in his faded blue tunic followed after Mauricio, who excitedly signed about the bees buzzing around the bleeding heart flowers around the veranda. A hard knot formed in her throat. Marcos had found a friend.

"Matri," Naokah whispered, trying to get her mother's cloudy eyes to focus. She set down the fat leather tome Tati had left behind in her chambers, behind her mirror, behind her crude, half-finished mural in a secret vault. She wasn't sure when Tati had placed it in there. She'd only regained her memories after her accident in the library bunker, but Naokah hadn't wasted time wondering. The book wasn't just a book. It was sacred and special. Even still, Matri didn't move. So, Naokah told her mother and Patri everything, about her discoveries, her failures and victories, how Lenita had sacrificed herself for the greater good, how Tati had been happy and in love, that she would've come back to Croi Croga to make amends had the prior Keeper's father not tricked her. Tears spilled down Patri's wizened cheeks, but Matri remained unfazed, a statue. Naokah worried her chest might sunder.

She pressed her mother's stiff hand on the tome. Just like when Naokah had touched the old parchment, crackling sparked the air. Ancient magic tingled around the trio. Intoxicating power, sweeter than honey and stronger than tilled earth, raw and primal and consuming, whirled around them like the stolen wind. The magic coursed over Naokah's hands and up her arms, spreading over her skin, warm and inviting and impossible to deny. Matri's eyes beamed, shining like polished amethysts, like the mother she'd had before Tati's disappearance, like the witch she'd always been but denied.

"For years you blamed yourself for Tati's departure. You thought your fight was irreconcilable. You were wrong," Naokah said. "Your sister would've come back if she could. But she, like the wind, was stolen from us. And now, with the Razing expanding—" she shuddered, blinking away the ashy creature she'd found in the southernmost lake, "—we must ensure her life's work wasn't in vain. If I've learned anything from my short tenure with the bees, it is that power is in numbers. We will send out a beacon to other Midworld witches, and we will find another, more habitable world where we can evacuate all Vindstöld. Will you help me?" She placed her hand, palm up, atop the spellbook, trembling, waiting.

Matri's jaw hardened before smacking her hand into Naokah's, who stifled a wince. So strong. "Yes," her matri said, in a voice that could grow flowers and sprout springs. "I will help. But with one condition."

"Which is?" Naokah asked.

"That upon this expedition, we find our sisters too."

Naokah's heart ballooned, and Patri, twitching in his navy tunic, looked like he was about to jump up and fly. She'd join him. "Of course, Matri. That was the plan."

Unassisted, Matri, the woman Naokah had waited for to speak and sing and *live* for over ten years, stood and pulled both Naokah and Patri into a tight hug. "Good, now let's get you sworn in."

★ ★ ★

Before heading to the ceremony, Naokah excused herself to stop by the fountain. The quartz glittered in the afternoon light, and she sat on the lip, running her fingers through the cool water. Where Lenita had spent her final moments. Maybe that's why out of all Abelha, she felt her presence strongest here.

"I never thanked you for everything that you did when we were kids," Naokah said to the rippling water. "Matri was gone, sedated by pain. But you didn't think twice, stepping up, raising me and Marcos. Never once complained. Daughter knows I was a handful." She shook her head, smirking at a memory of Lenita chasing after Naokah and her little brother with a broom. Annoyed she'd made them clean their room, they'd switched out her sugar bowl, giggling as Lenita took a heaping bite of salty porridge. "I'm so sorry about what I said that final day. I was angry and bitter, ridiculously jealous. You were always just...so good at everything—" she swallowed hard, "—suppose I wanted something of my own. I've come to realize, though, it was always me holding myself back, not you. You only wanted the best for me, yet I was too blinded by envy and self-pity to see. I don't know if you can even hear me, but I promise on my life, I won't give up until I find you. I love you, big sister." Tears spilled down her cheeks. "Miss you more than the world misses the wind." She grazed the water one last time and sighed, crawling to her feet. If only she had Lenita's blessing—

The water congealed around her hand, pulling her down. Her breath caught in her throat as a silhouette with amethyst eyes stared up from the waves.

"I already forgave you," the water gurgled. "Forgive yourself."

Naokah's chin trembled, and more tears streamed. "I'll try."

"Go swear in. You've earned it." The shadow shifted into what could've been a smile. "And Nao?"

"Yes?"

"Care for a little wager?"

If she had any doubt about the vision before, she didn't now. Typical Lenita, always up for a challenge. Naokah wiped her eyes and sniffled. "Terms?"

"Bet the Keepership that I find you first."

She chuckled, rivalry igniting. "You've got yourself a deal."

CHAPTER FIFTY

Keeper of Sorrows

Stop fidgeting, Naokah could hear Brielle say as she sucked in a steady breath, cocked her chin, and settled in the plush seat. Easier said than done. She felt like a hive had split and swarmed to her belly. A river of chartreuse taffeta cascaded her wobbly knees and spilled over her feet, puddling below the dais. The overhanging pigwoods, fluffy with pink blossoms, rustled as all of Vindstöld's leaders took their seats on each side of the aisle. Matri and Patri, with her younger brother, sat in the reserved section up front. Marcos wrinkled his nose, no doubt from the fishy pigwoods, and signed his displeasure to Mauricio.

The mercy's lips curved into a big grin, and he signed back, "You'll get used to it, eventually."

Her little brother shook his head, and Naokah snorted. She'd reacted much the same when she'd followed the Keeper/Tati into this room for the first time. So foul, she'd never thought she'd acclimate either, yet here she was, suppressing a grin as her dignified guests attempted and failed nonchalance, their puckered lips giving them away.

A hand squeezed her shoulder. "You ready?"

She nodded at Samara, healed and glowing in their pressed uniform. "Can't wait to get this hoopla over with," she whispered to the savvy, who smiled.

"I know, I know. Much work to do, and no time to do it," they agreed before calling the room to attention. They started the ceremony and began speaking about the honor and privilege of serving as the bees' guardian, but Naokah's mind drifted elsewhere.

Along with caring for the bees, past Keepers had vowed to keep the Scorned Son's afterscape protected, hidden in plain sight. So tonight, Naokah would not only become Keeper of the Bees but of the Sea of Sorrows, and the multitude of other passages she'd soon explore.

"The Seven Hundred and Seventy-Eighth Keeper and Guardian of the Bees, Naokah Elida Hansen," Samara declared proudly, placing the induction videira – rubies replaced with white fire opals to complement her gown – on her ear before she rose to applause.

As she descended the stairs, the savvy fluffed her train, and she swallowed a hard lump, thinking of Brielle and the chartreuse curtains she'd worn to the welcome ball. For the past month, Naokah had woken restless in the middle of the night, her lover's phantom fingers and soft kisses caressing her clammy skin. She'd climb out of bed and sit at her vanity, carved with bees and foxgloves. Brielle's dainty hand would emerge from the other side of the mirror, pressing against the foggy glass, begging for absolution. Though Naokah had long forgiven her, Brielle was imprisoned in the Scorned Son's Sea of Sorrows. She pledged, no matter what, even if it took the rest of her mortal life, that on top of finding a new world and bringing her sister and aunts home, she, too, would find a way to break into that shadowy afterscape, and free her lost love.

Naokah strode down the aisle, and the forager bees from the overhanging pigwoods hummed with resounding reverie and fluttered from their pink blossoms, collecting on her dazzling train. Kjell's father squirmed when she walked by, and she didn't hide her amusement at his discomfort. Nor from Brielle's mother's haughty glare.

Upon exiting the ceremonial room, she veered down the Hall of Keepers. The hallways were brighter, friendlier, and the murals no longer intimidated Naokah. Her cousin had told her that Gabriella had painted them out of protest against her father, and many were even inspired by Tati herself, like the half-finished one hiding the spellbook. So, in a way, she was surrounded by reflections of her family. The citadel was home, quirks and all, and she would honor it. More, she'd honor herself. No longer did she lurk in her sister's shadow nor dwell on her flaws, of which she had plenty. After all, Naokah wasn't made of stone.

AUTHOR'S NOTE

Like Naokah, I had a debilitating fear of bees before writing this book. I prefer drafting outside, surrounded by fresh air and my plants, but if a bee started circling? I'd grab my laptop, dash inside, and send a frantic message to the two beekeepers I know, my agent Naomi and my big sister Rebekah. "Why is this bee stalking me?" Tickled, they'd respond with, "Well, you probably smell like a flower. Leave it *bee*."

But I have pride. Come on, I used to be a soldier. I didn't want to be afraid of the very creature responsible for pollinating every third bite of food we take. I had to face my fear, and so I did over the span of a summer in my sister's overgrown vegetable garden, clearing out a forest of careless weeds taller than corn stalks – that also wriggled with thousands of her honeybees.

At first, I could barely move, barely breathe. I was sure I'd get stung and my throat would swell and *where the hell did Bekah keep her epi pen*? But as the days passed by, I started talking to the bees, asking about their day, where their travels had taken them, and they surprised me with an answer. There's a collective hum that a large gathering of bees emits, and it's nothing short of magical. This resonance is calming, like listening to your favorite song on repeat while sinking chin-deep into a warm bubble bath. Finally, after years of battling dark, intrusive thoughts, of never being able to mute all the damaging, ultra-critical self-talk, my mind stilled.

I'd found peace. And I'm not the only one. Bees don't just keep our world going around, but they're also healing. Their resonance can help folks with anxiety and PTSD. So, if you're looking for a way to thank the bees or if you have a friend or loved one who's struggling after returning from war, I encourage you to check out Hives for Heroes. This wonderful nonprofit is dedicated to conservation, sustainability, and helping soldiers transition into the civilian sector via their national network of beekeepers. Please check them out at hivesforheroes.org.

ACKNOWLEDGMENTS

When you're no wunderkind, yet still decide you want to be a novelist at age twelve, you amass quite the collection of shelved manuscripts, rejections, liquor/therapy bills, and judgy winces from people who tell you that perhaps it's high time you find a real job. But if you're lucky, you also amass a tremendous group of humans who, instead of King-Leonidas-kicking you into a well for having to tolerate allllllllllllll your self-absorption, self-pitying, reclusive ways, pull you back up. The 'found family' trope is my favorite for this reason. The folks below happen to be mine:

The unstoppable Naomi Davis, my dream literary agent. I still pinch myself that you represent me, that you believed in me through even the rockiest of times when I'd stopped believing in myself. Stephen King speaks of an ideal reader for whom authors should write their books. For me, that person is, and will always be, you. I love you.

BookEnds Literary Agency's Jessica Faust and James McGowan for your hilariously transparent advice that gave me life while I was querying, and for leading me to Naomi.

Don D'Auria, I couldn't have asked for a better editor. So creative and kind and patient. I know you probably scoffed when one of my characters tried to hiss without any sibilants for the umpteenth time. Perhaps even considered dangling my manuscript (like I tend to do with modifiers) out the window. But, clearing your throat, you gave me another chance. Thanks for bringing a feral writer home to Flame Tree Press, whereupon the kindly publisher Nick Wells agreed to adopt me, fleas and all. I owe you both a cask or ten of whisky.

My Flame Tree Press family, eagle eye Michael Valsted, for calling me out on all my convoluted prose and redundancies; lovely Amanda Crook for her proofreading; Josie Karani and Gillian Whitaker, for creating such a gorgeous book; and Sarah Miniaci, Olivia Jackson, Leah Ratcliffe, and Jordi

Nolla for getting my debut out into the right hands. Y'all have made my greatest dream, one I've worked towards for a quarter century, FINALLY come true. A million thanks still fall short. Thank you, thank you, thank you!

Essa Hansen, Naokah took your last name because she wouldn't be here without you. Thank you for squeezing KOS in for one last invaluable pass before it went on sub. I've grown so much under your guidance and moral support, your ridiculously gorgeous writing and well-timed booze. Your blurb – the first ever! – made me weepy. I'd be lost without you, dear friend!

Gabriela Romero Lacruz, I don't think I'll ever stop fangirling over the fact that 1) you're my crazy talented writer friend and 2) you're my crazy talented artist friend. Your map and illustrations for KOS are absolutely stunning, and I love them and you so much!

Jen Haberski, I've lost track of how many life debts I owe you. You saved me from getting my ass kicked in basic training, took me in when I fled to New York and had no place to go, and over the years, whenever I've started slipping, sinking back into that dark abyss, you've always helped me regain my footing. You are fiercely loyal, and your faith in me, my writing, has never wavered. Thank you for being you!

C.E. Vandiver, thanks for fighting off the wee buggies to give me a full sensory report on Spanish moss and for always finding time to read my drivel. I live for our long, aimless banter on crafting, drinking, and other random crap. I owe my sanity, albeit flimsy, to you.

Sunyi Dean and Scott Drakeford, I'm so glad y'all started the *Publishing Rodeo Podcast*. It came at a crucial time in my life, and it's opened my eyes to the good, the bad, and the bloody ugly of the publishing industry, heh. I salute your bravery, your candidness, and your mission of lifting up fellow authors.

Chelsea Mueller and Melissa Caruso, every writer needs a C.M./M.C. duo in their life. With the sheer amount of industry knowledge between you two sages, they'd never be adrift.

Rebekah Faubion and Lindsay Cummings, thank you for guiding me through my first chaotic fantasy draft and helping me snag my dream agent.

Scarlett Woodruff and Rachael Woerner Marshall, thanks for celebrating my book deal via a comical gathering on Zoom. We met in basic training over fifteen years ago and, though we live very different lives, far apart, you are the kind of friends who, when we do finally reunite, pick up right where we left off. I'm constantly in awe of you both.

Kritika H. Rao, H.M. Long, Sara M. Harvey, Sue Lynn Tan, Nadia Afifi, Prashanth Srivatsa, Tlotlo Tsamaase, and Valo Wing, it's such an honor to be part of an author fellowship brimming with kindness and endless support. Because of you all, I never feel alone.

Erika Thompson of Texas Beeworks, your mesmerizing videos not only helped Naokah (and me) overcome our fear of bees, but now we wholeheartedly cherish them too! You inspired the mysterious Keeper. Thank you for being the perfect muse and saving the bees.

Teachers Denise Stehling, Tiffany Hartmann, and Caroline Weber, who planted the first seeds that grew into my dream. I wouldn't be a writer if not for your warm encouragement.

Librarian of the Year, Mr. James Grote, for finding all the books featuring pigs and never once begrudging formative Rachel for it.

Bill Botard and the late Scott Fields, for nurturing my love of agriculture through the leadership opportunities via 4-H and FFA. You gave me a voice when I didn't think I had one. Mr. Fields, I miss your silly jokes every day.

John Martinez, one of my fondest memories to this very day, was being your drum major. Your passion for music is unmatched and has never left me. Music is magic, and I can't imagine writing without it.

Patrick Gribbin, for telling me all the stories from your childhood in Ireland, making those long bus rides to school seem shorter. I fell in love with your beautiful homeland, her folklore and sparkly legends, before I'd even met her, because of you.

The scores upon scores of amazing EF Education First students who've listened to me prattle for the last decade about getting published. Special thanks to a few who've yet to flee: Gabriella "Bee" Balista, Aline França, Lenita Marochi, Christoph Schwab, Mauricio Borges, Andreas Steinert, Rodrigo Alcantara, Daniela Lazzarini, Clara Fagundes, Larissa Arruda, Ludmila Pesotski, Mikiko Sato, Tayrine Batista, Helen Zhou Chen, Diogo Ramos, Viktória Villaça Rocha De Oliveira Placides, Vinícius Barbosa, and Edima Barbosa.

306 • RACHEL FIKES

Early betas and dear friends who, despite how crappy my first fantasy draft was, encouraged me to write on: Karissa Sullivan, Marissa Pentz, Chelsi Bierschwale, Shana Lea Riviello, Michael Cameron Davis, Arin Spann, Jill Hannemann Minshew, Lisa Rigby Ballard, and Bonnie Richardson.

Army family who's always had my back: Brigadier General Hope Rampy, Pierre Fuentes, Joshua Mendoza, Eric Frances, Caroline Williams, Damita Stollings, Debe Clark, Danny Scott, Ian McBride, Bryce Land, Bertie Bolingbroke, Antonio Sanchez, Marcus Collier, Zachary Heath, Liam Engle, and all the soldiers, NCOs, and officers from the former "Spartans" 4BSTB, 4BCT, 1CD. Our time in Iraq and Afghanistan shaped me into a better, more grateful human.

VS Angels, who welcomed me with open arms, helping me heal after I returned from the Middle East: Heidi Bachor, Lori Altobello-Barbini, JeriLynn Ost, Sharon Collins-Strong, Chelsea Vierstra, Chiharu Guido, Corine Drumm, Erum Ovalles, Heather Williams, Bri Barresi, Jess Staiger, Meg Scanlon, and Samantha Khan.

My NY fam, for educating me on proper Italian cuisine (eggplant should always be an option on pizza), keeping my Texas license plate to warn New Yorkers that a Texan has *no* business driving in the snow, and why it's never a good idea to take your trash out at night unless you plan on hosting a black bear soirée: Kevin Haberski, Chloey DeCicco, D.J. Koeppen, the whole Schneider Family (yes, even you, Christopher), "Sarge" Drescher, and Ashley Agar.

Steadfast friends I don't deserve but still put up with me, despite my hermitage: Wade Vetiver, Lauren Almanza, Heather Hahn, Sandra Jacoby, Charlie Grice, Maria Batten, Davey Edwards, Virginia Maurer, Mrs. Earth Maadhuri Sharma, Mrs. India Earth Paris Keswani, Ms. Universe Yolanda Koelhof, and Ms. West Virginia Kristin Delligatti. Kristin, please thank Momma Wilson for always asking about my writing. I hope I finally made her proud.

The brilliant magicians Steven Grant and Sandra Mata, for this lovely author photo. If only I always looked like this instead of the fully unhinged Jack Torrance from *The Shining*.

The ever-patient Kyle Howie, for introducing me to Murtagh Fitzgibbons Fraser aka Murty, my great highland bagpipe. You've both helped me through some dark times.

All the wonderful staff and lab rats at PPD Austin, whose generosity made the writing of this book and others possible: Maggie Harper, Nayel Ahmed, Wendy Castro, Michelle Jubinal, Royce Vasquez, Dani Porra, Dan Burns, Dot Cruz, and Dusty Horne.

The ever-inspiring Austin crew, who know how to work hard and party harder: Mark Valenzuela, Mel Borgan, Keivan "BDS" Imani, Jane Sohn, and Steve Latham. You all are just fantastic humans, and I'm so touched to be part of your group.

Don Boyle, Jacqueline Flynn, and Dr. Garcia, for helping me continue to fight off the minotaur that often wreaks havoc in that mushy labyrinth beneath my skull.

Grandpa Joe, for all your war stories, compassion, and gardening tips.

Aunt Gerry, you were the first to read this teeny opening chapter and, though fate kept you from reading the rest, I hope that, as you do crafts with Booger and Leif above (Grandpa undoubtedly beside you in his chair, smoking his pipe, sipping his gin), you both smile.

Aunt Sandy, I'm pretty sure you've read everything I've ever written, and I know that wasn't easy. Especially the early stuff. Hot garbage! Thank you for always encouraging me.

Aunt Sharon, I've always been in awe with the love you've given to everyone in our family, especially your sisters. The unbreakable bond between you three helped me craft Naokah's tati.

My siblings, blood and bonus, for putting up with all my idiosyncrasies over the years, and not disowning me: Rebekah and Dusty Cathey, Buddy and Chelsea Fikes, Matthew and Kenzie Fikes, Sarah Fikes, and all your adorable kiddos.

Mom and Pops, for the late nights washing squash under a precarious shed during thunderstorms while distracting us with scary movies, buying me every Stephen King book you could find on eBay, and for raising me on a farm. I attribute my love of agriculture, horror, and a lifetime of anxiety to you.

Saint Margaret, you always end up in my books, your name changing to adapt to each world I've built. How fitting, then, that my debut features you as a doctor. Thank you for loving me unconditionally. Truly. I could murder someone, and you'd pat me on the back and say, "I'm so proud."

The bees, I'm sorry for being terrified of you, for mixing you up with your cantankerous cousins. Luckily, I had beekeepers Erika Thompson, Naomi Davis, Rebekah Cathey, and Adam Felton, to set me straight. I hope this book highlights how important you are to the future of our world. I humbly bend the knee.

Matty Ronald Bowen, ahhh mate. Where to start? I believe our souls were best mates in another life, and I'm so glad we found each other again. Thank you for always having Bruno's back, for being there for him when I was a garbage human and failed, and for bringing SO much joy into our lives. Thanks in advance for officiating our handfast. I love you!

Ellie, before I met you, I didn't think I had a speck of maternal instinct in me. I put off meeting you because I was absolutely terrified. I should've known, though, that you'd be a ball of sunshine just like your father. So kind and thoughtful, brilliant and brave. It's my utmost honor to be part of your life. Also, thanks for calling me your bonus mom, on account of 'stepmother' having too many evil fairytale vibes. I love you so damn much it hurts, kiddo. You are the bee's knees! Never stop being you.

Bruno, I met you when I was a shell of a human. I'd only gone out that night because the VA said I might have lung disease. I think at some point, snockered beyond all reason, I told you not to get too attached: I was dying. (I know, I know. So dramatic.) But get attached, you did. As I hid away in my hobbit hole, writing and pouring my soul into getting published, you waited by patiently. For two years! Never once begrudging me, only offering support. Finally, I pulled my head out of my ass and came to my senses, and I'm so glad I did. Thank you for waiting for me. You are truly the best person I've ever known. In writing, I used to stick to romantic subplots, never veering beyond that because I'd have felt like a fraud. Too many failed relationships and heartbreaks holding me back. But now, with you? I finally know what love is. And wow, is it liberating! You are the sun to my void, the vanquisher of all my demons, and if there is a god in this infinitely bizarre universe, I'd bet everything I have, it's you. I love you, Darling.

And finally, you, dearest reader. Thank you for giving a debut writer a chance. If you liked *Keeper of Sorrows*, excellent! Let's be friends. If you hated it, excellent! Please don't tag me in your disappointed review.

ABOUT THE AUTHOR

Growing up, Rachel Fikes wanted to be Sir William Wallace, James Horner, or Stephen King. Unfortunately, the U.S. Army doesn't issue claymore swords, and she's painfully tone deaf so that left writing – a campaign that would wage on for a quarter century, leaving Rachel bruised, bloody, and downright defeated. She's been a soldier, maid, door-to-door bookseller, Fikes Family Farm field hand – thanks Pops! – leasing agent, baker, journalist, pageant queen/director, wiper of butt sweat (tanning salon), seller of overpriced lingerie at Victoria's Secret, and dejected Wal-Mart cashier. Eventually, with skin thicker than chain mail, a shield of resolve, and the reckless, indefatigable hope of a warrior poet, Rachel finally fought her way into publishing. After quite the adventure, Rachel takes refuge in her hobbit hole in Austin, Texas, squirrelling away all the coffee, whisky, and plants she can get her paws on, and teaching ESL to the most amazing students in the world.

Connect with her on IG @rachel_fikes or rachelfikes.com.

FLAME TREE PRESS
FICTION WITHOUT FRONTIERS
Award-Winning Authors & Original Voices

Flame Tree Press is the trade fiction imprint of Flame Tree Publishing, focusing on excellent writing in horror and the supernatural, crime and mystery, science fiction and fantasy. Our aim is to explore beyond the boundaries of the everyday, with tales from both award-winning authors and original voices.

•

You may also enjoy:
The Sentient by Nadia Afifi
The Emergent by Nadia Afifi
The Transcendent by Nadia Afifi
Junction by Daniel M. Bensen
Interchange by Daniel M. Bensen
Second Lives by P.D. Cacek
Second Chances by P.D. Cacek
The Widening Gyre by Michael R. Johnston
The Blood-Dimmed Tide by Michael R. Johnston
What Rough Beast by Michael R. Johnston
The Sky Woman by J.D. Moyer
The Guardian by J.D. Moyer
The Last Crucible by J.D. Moyer
One Eye Opened in That Other Place by Christi Nogle
Brittle by Beth Overmyer
Tempered Glass by Beth Overmyer
The Goblets Immortal by Beth Overmyer
Holes in the Veil by Beth Overmyer
Death's Key by Beth Overmyer
A Killing Fire by Faye Snowden
A Killing Rain by Faye Snowden
A Sword of Bronze and Ashes by Anna Smith Spark
Fearless by Allen Stroud
Resilient by Allen Stroud
Idolatry by Aditya Sudarshan
Screams from the Void by Anne Tibbets
The Roamers by Francesco Verso

•

Join our mailing list for free short stories, new release details, news about our authors and special promotions:

flametreepress.com